OTHER BOOKS BY
KAY LYNN MANGUM

The Secret Journal of Brett Colton
A Love like Lilly

WHEN THE Bough Breaks

A NOVEL

KAY LYNN MANGUM

DESERET BOOK

SALT LAKE CITY, UTAH

This is a work of fiction. Characters and events in this book are products of the author's imagination or are represented fictitiously.

Library of Congress Cataloging-in-Publication Data

Mangum, Kay Lynn.
  When the bough breaks / Kay Lynn Mangum.
    p. cm.
  Summary: Fifteen-year-old Rachel uses poetry and her Mormon faith to cope with grief over the loss of her father, the horrors of her brother's alcoholism, resentment of her new stepfather, and the awkwardness of having an attractive schoolmate as her stepbrother.
  ISBN 978-1-59038-748-1 (pbk.)
  [1. Grief—Fiction. 2. Alcoholism—Fiction. 3. Stepfamilies—Fiction.
4. Poetry—Fiction. 5. High schools—Fiction. 6. Schools—Fiction. 7. Mormons—
Fiction. 8. Christian life—Fiction. 9. Self-esteem—Fiction.]
  I. Title.
  PZ7.M31266535Whe 2007
  [Fic]—dc22   2007021162

Printed in the United States of America
Publishers Printing, Salt Lake City, UT

10   9   8   7   6   5   4   3   2   1

To my parents
H. Ben and Janet M. Mangum

And in memory of
Josephine Townsend
who taught me how to write
and to believe I could

ACKNOWLEDGMENTS

Thanks to everyone at Deseret Book, especially Chris Schoebinger; my editor, Suzanne Brady; and Sheryl Dickert for the beautiful cover design. And of course, much thanks to my good friend and an amazing writer, Cheryl Lynn Navas, for reading and editing my manuscript, and for not only pushing me to keep writing, but helping me to brainstorm plot lines, dialogue, and future novel ideas!

Thanks to everyone in my family for your support and enthusiasm and your willingness to read and edit my manuscripts, but especially a big thanks to my brother Darrell Mangum, whose hysterical e-mails helped to provide much of Ryan's dialogue in this book. I wouldn't be sane without your e-mails!

Gigantic thanks as well to Officer Mark in Minneapolis, Minnesota, and Officer Susan Simonson-Mullis of the Anderson City Police Department in South Carolina for your help with my many law enforcement questions. Your detailed responses were invaluable. I appreciate your patience with me and for taking the time to work with me on this novel.

And finally, a huge, huge thanks to Dave Hoerman and Michelle Hoerman, without whose help I never could have written this novel. Thank you so much for your willingness to share your experiences, and for your honesty on the subject matter of this novel, and for directing me to a lot of great, important information on the subject that was also invaluable. I appreciate your help more than you'll ever know.

CHAPTER ONE

Okay, Rachel. It's your turn now. Truth or Dare."

It was Friday night and Leap Day, February 29. Teresa, my best friend since we were eleven years old, and I were sitting cross-legged facing each other on her queen-sized bed, hanging out together as we usually did on Friday nights. We were halfway through ninth grade at Central Junior High, and once the summer was over, we'd be heading for Central High as sophomores. I was scared to death to start high school, but at the same time, part of me could hardly wait.

"Well, Truth is dumb, because you know everything about me!" Not only that, Teresa looked like me, too. We both had big brown eyes and long, naturally curly hair, but where hers was more of a dark blonde, mine was a bright yellow blonde. Blondest blonde. And I was a true blonde, too—not a fake, dye-job, bleached blonde.

"Okay, then I guess it's Dare?"

I shrugged. "I guess so!"

Teresa grinned back at me. "Then I dare you . . . to prank call Jason West!"

I couldn't stop myself from gasping. "Jason West?" I'd had a huge crush on Jason since sixth grade, and Teresa knew it. *He* didn't, though, and that's the way I wanted it to stay. "I can't call Jason West!"

Teresa only laughed. "Why not?"

"Duh—everyone's phones have caller ID. He'll see the number!"

Teresa stretched behind her back towards her nightstand before lightly tossing something at me. "Then you'll have to use this!"

I stared at the tiny pink cell phone that had landed in my lap. "Since when did you get a cell phone?"

"I didn't. It's my cousin Cindy's. My aunt and uncle and their kids were here last weekend, and she left it behind on accident."

"I can't waste her minutes on a prank call!"

Teresa grinned evilly. "Yes, you can, and it serves her right. She bored me all weekend bragging about how she has a cell phone now. And then she left it here anyway! What a ding-dong."

I giggled, but my heart wouldn't stop pounding. "He'll still see a number on his phone!"

"So what? He'll only see Cindy's number. Besides—if he calls back, he'll get her voicemail. Just say you're her. She'll never know." Teresa snatched the phone from my lap and thrust it an inch from my face. "Come on. You picked Dare, so you have to do it!"

I jumped back a bit. "Okay, okay—you don't have to shove it up my nose!" We both giggled while I flipped the cell phone's lid up and stared at the shiny blue number pad. "I don't even know what to say—"

"How about something like this: 'Jason? Is that you, Jason? Your voice sounds so sexy on the phone.'" Teresa said her lines in the most seductive voice she could muster without giggling too much. I couldn't help laughing. "See? It's easy. Now it's your turn!"

"I don't even know how to use this thing!"

"Just punch in the number and hit Send. Here—I'll do it for you."

Before I knew what was happening, Teresa had snatched the phone back and pressed in the numbers. I was fighting to stop giggling nervously, my mind racing to think of something to say for my prank call to Jason West.

"It's ringing!" Teresa handed me the phone, and while I held it to my ear, we both giggled harder. Ring number one. My heart kept pounding. Ring number two. It was pounding faster—

"Hello?" A woman's voice. Probably Mrs. West.

I gripped the cell phone tightly to my ear. "Hi—is Jason there?"

"Your voice is shaking," Teresa whispered. I grabbed a pillow and threw it at her.

"Just a moment, please." I heard a dull clunk as Jason's mom put the phone down.

"What are you going to say?" Teresa was bouncing up and down excitedly. I quickly covered the cell phone with my hand.

"Shut up, will you? He'll be on—"

"Hello?"

Jason West! My eyes nearly popped out of my skull.

"Jason?"

"Yeah. Who's—"

My heart was beating at an incredible rate, but somehow, I managed to speak. "Oh, *Jason*, you have no idea how long I've been trying to get a hold of you! Have you been waiting for me very long?"

"Waiting? For what?" Jason sounded so confused I nearly burst into a fit of nervous giggles.

"Well, my car's got a flat tire, and—"

"Angela? Is that you?"

"Angela? Who's Angela?" I made my voice sound confused as well.

"Wait a second. Who's this?"

"Jason, I can't believe you! It's me, Cindy!"

Silence reigned for a long second. "I don't know any Cindy."

"Isn't this 5-5-5-7-7-0-3?"

"No, this is 5-5-5-7-7-0-2."

I made myself laugh. "Oh! Oh, I'm so sorry! I guess I dialed the wrong number. My boyfriend's name is Jason, too. Kind of ironic, huh?"

"Yeah, I guess so."

"I feel so stupid! I'm sorry for bothering you—this is totally embarrassing!"

"It's okay, really." I could tell he really *did* think it was okay. He didn't sound annoyed at all. Almost amused, actually.

"Well, thank you for putting up with me. You sound really nice."

"Well, so do you."

I smiled into the tiny receiver. "Have a nice evening."

"You, too."

As soon as I hit the End button, Teresa released her tight hold on her mouth and screamed. I screamed, too, and we both laughed until we fell off the bed.

"Your voice—how did you change it to be so—so *sexy?*" Teresa gasped.

"I don't know—I just did!" I gasped back between laughs.

"You should think about acting instead of being a writer!"

That brought my laughing to a screeching halt. "What? Don't you think I can write?"

Teresa rolled her eyes and threw a pillow at me. "Of course you can write, but wow—you were amazing!"

I wasn't sure I was amazing, but I was definitely amazed I'd been brave enough to call and talk to Jason West, easily the hottest guy at Central Junior High and sure to be the hottest guy at Central High, too.

Teresa stood up and frowned as I struggled to get up, too. "By the way, who's Angela?"

I shrugged and sat back down on her bed. "I don't know. Jason thought at first I was someone named Angela."

Teresa considered this for a moment before lifting an eyebrow. "I wonder if he meant Angela Barnett!"

Angela Barnett? She was a year ahead of us, blonde and too beautiful, on the high school drill team, and chased by way too many boys. But with all of that going for her, she wasn't exactly the nicest girl in the school. Too popular and snobby for her own good.

"I don't know. Why do you think he meant her?"

Teresa shrugged and sat down by me. "I've seen her VW Bug at his house a few times. Just makes sense to me."

I wrinkled my nose. "Jason with Angela Barnett? Ick. She's snooty *and* snotty. He can do better."

Teresa nodded. "Yeah, *he* can. She can't, though."

I had to agree with Teresa on that one. There wasn't anyone better than Jason West. I'd known that since sixth grade. Great looks, super personality, smart, nice, and good LDS, too. I sighed and lay back on Teresa's bed. "He'd be the perfect boyfriend!"

Teresa grinned. "Unfortunately, every other girl thinks so, too!"

I sighed loudly again while Teresa jumped off the bed. "Come on, Rachel. Forget about Jason. I'm starving. Let's order a pizza and watch a movie."

Teresa stuck into the DVD player in the family room an old 1980s Bill Murray comedy that one of her older brothers assured us was a classic, and we laughed and ate ourselves sick. It wasn't until the movie was over, and we'd made ice cream sundaes with chocolate fudge and gummy bears and eaten ourselves sick again that I squinted at the clock on the DVD player.

"It's almost midnight—my brother Ryan should've picked me up by now!"

Teresa ran for her cousin's cell phone and threw it at me again. "Here—call home."

I pressed the phone to my ear before shaking my head. "The line's busy."

"I'll see if someone here can give you a ride."

Luckily for me, Teresa had a million older brothers and sisters. Peggy, two years older than Teresa, was still up and grudgingly agreed to take me home. Teresa rode along, and because Peggy didn't want to listen to us giggle and "act stupid," she blasted the radio for the three miles from Teresa's house to mine.

"Hey—wasn't that the turn to my house?" I yelled over the radio's deafening roar.

"Yep—it sure was!" Teresa screeched back.

"Where are we going?" I screamed back.

Teresa laughed at my apparent stupidity. "We're making the rounds first, dope!"

"The rounds?"

"Yeah—I want to go by Brian's house! And Mike's house!" Teresa piped up as loudly as she could.

"What about Bill?" Peggy yelled, rolling her eyes.

I couldn't believe Peggy was being so cool, because she knew Teresa was in love with way too many guys at our school. I giggled alongside Teresa as we slowly drove past each guy's house, hoping to catch a glimpse of any of them, until a few quick, casual turns down familiar roads had me sitting up stiff and straight.

"Where are we going?"

Peggy laughed and looked at me in the rearview mirror. "Like you don't know!"

Panic set in as I realized where we were headed. "Don't go by Jason's house—*please!* Just take me home!"

Now Teresa was laughing at me, too. "Ah, come on, Rachel! Aren't you curious to know who goes over to Jason's on a Friday night?"

I fell back to slouch in my seat at what I saw once we slowly drove by Jason's house. Angela Barnett's unmistakable baby blue Volkswagen Bug was in his driveway.

———

Minutes later, Peggy stomped on the brakes and hit the radio On/Off button. "Holy cow, Rachel—what's going on at your house tonight? Another wild party of Ryan's?"

Teresa and I had been so busy giggling in the backseat over my chat with the great Jason West that I hadn't even noticed Peggy had turned down my street. I turned to look out the window and was nearly blinded by the blue and red lights.

Teresa whistled low. "Wow—there's a cop at your house!"

I stared out the window at that completely out-of-place police car in front of my house and couldn't breathe. Then panic kicked in, and I was frantically climbing over Teresa to get out of the car and into my house.

I couldn't move once I stepped through the doorway. There were two police officers in the house. Two. One of the officers was sitting by Mom, who was crumpled on the couch, her face in her hands, crying hysterically. And Ryan, my seventeen-year-old brother—he was sitting in a recliner near her, his eyes bloodshot, staring vacantly ahead of him. His hands were shaking. I could see that, even though he had a hand flat on each of his knees.

"What—what's going on?" Somehow that whispered out of my lungs. "What? . . ."

Ryan looked up at me dully with dark, bloodshot eyes, though there weren't any tears on his face. "Dad was in a car accident."

I couldn't move, I couldn't breathe—I couldn't hear what the other police officer standing beside me was trying to say. "What do you mean— 'Dad was in a car accident'?"

Ryan just kept staring through me. "Just what I said. He went to pick you up. Some"—Ryan used a considerably foul word here—"driving on the wrong side of the road, going too fast, hit him head on. He was on his way to pick *you* up from your stupid friend's house!"

The room was starting to spin funny. Mom was calling to me to come sit down by her, reaching her arms out to me while she continued to sob.

"But he's okay, right? I mean, he's going to be okay. He has to be!" The panic was rising in my throat, strangling my words, and now I was shaking, too.

Ryan looked away while Mom kept begging me to sit down by her. And then the police officer standing by me said the worst thing in the entire world. Something no one should have to hear about their dad. Ever. Not from a stranger, and not now—not when I wasn't even sixteen yet. It wasn't time—it was too soon—too soon—

"I'm sorry, honey. There was nothing anyone could have done. Your father was killed instantly . . ."

There was a chair near the door, and I dissolved into it, silent screams echoing inside my head.

At that exact moment, I realized that the world had truly ended. I'd always wondered what that moment would be like, and now I knew. I could see Mom and Ryan, but Dad—Dad, whose presence filled every inch of any room he entered—Dad, who was big and loud, full of life and always fun, always wild and crazy, warm and outgoing, and spontaneous—Dad, who loved to take us camping and exploring, who loved to joke and sing and even sang in the church choir—he wasn't anywhere.

I knew without a doubt, even during that horrible, first moment, that there was no way any of us would ever be able to overcome this night. Or any of it—this horrible *It* that had now invaded my life, and Ryan's, and Mom's. And Robert's, too—my oldest brother, who'd moved out and married a couple of years ago.

"Robert?" I whispered.

Ryan answered flatly. "We called him. He's flying home tonight."

I sat there and felt my heart pounding as nausea gripped my stomach, forcing me to bend forward while I held my head in both hands.

I will never get over this. How could I when I had no idea, even, how I was ever going to be able to get out of this chair and stand up again?

This was a fact that sat heavily on me now, a fact I knew would never leave me.

CHAPTER TWO

N o—*No!*"
I jumped and struggled to sit up in bed. I could still see the blinding blue and red lights flashing behind my eyes, twirling in circles, over and over and over, blinding me through the living room picture window.

"A dream. Just a dream," I whispered dully, but instead of fading out of my brain like dreams are supposed to do, that Leap Day night took more solid shape and pressed itself firmly in place in my consciousness, as it had every single morning ever since. I sat quietly, hugging the covers to my chin, and knew that horrible *It* was true. If it hadn't been, I would've smelled pancakes cooking, and I would've heard whistling and cheerful teasing and laughing coming from the kitchen. Dad always made us pancakes for breakfast on Saturday, and he and Mom would laugh and joke and be silly all morning long. But ever since—no one had even thought about making pancakes. Or whistling or teasing. And laughing? I wasn't sure I remembered how to anymore.

I lay back down and pulled the covers over my head. Even though I had my eyes shut tight, I could see the days that followed. It had all happened too fast—too sudden, too unexpected. I'd helplessly grappled to understand anything, and yet life had suddenly become crazy, confusing, and traumatic. The funeral had to be planned. An actual funeral. Luckily Robert and my sister-in-law, Wendy, were able to take over with most of the details. I still didn't remember much about those first few blurry, unreal days. I could only hold onto the thought that I was sure there must've been some mistake. It couldn't have been my dad. Not my dad, who was the safest driver around. He'd practically invented the "defensive driver" theory. No one could make me believe it was true as long as I hadn't seen him.

But then, on the day of the funeral, when I couldn't put it off any longer and I finally had to confront the huge, dark oak box surrounded by all kinds and sizes of flowers in gigantic vases and arrangements, I knew it was final.

I thought I'd held in crying for so long that I wouldn't cry that day, but seeing my dad—I couldn't stop myself. I cried throughout the entire funeral. Mom and Wendy cried, too. And Robert, my oldest brother— even he cried. But Ryan didn't cry. Not even one tear. He just sat on the front bench by Robert in the chapel of our ward house, his eyes still bloodshot but empty of tears.

It was strange, watching them together. Both of them were big, brown-eyed, dark-haired guys who looked so much like Dad, and yet that was where all similarities between the two ended. As bizarre as it was to watch one brother cry and one brother stare vacantly into space, what shook me most was that moment before the casket was closed, standing alone in front of it after Robert and Wendy had quietly moved away. I'd been staring hard at Dad's unmoving face, knowing beyond a doubt that although his body was right in front of me, he wasn't there anymore. And then I'd heard someone step up beside me, and without looking over, I knew it was Ryan.

"I . . . I can't believe this," I'd whispered. "Can you?" I'd turned to look at Ryan, tears already beginning to run down my cheeks.

Ryan was staring vacantly ahead, dry-eyed, his hands shoved deep into his dress pants pockets, his dark blue tie already crooked under his chin.

"I feel nothing."

And then he'd turned and walked out of the room, leaving me alone.

After the funeral and the grave dedication, he didn't even come back

10

to the church for lunch to talk with all of Dad's brothers and sisters and our cousins and grandparents and ward members and friends but instead left me and the rest of our family to make up excuses for his absence.

Those first two weeks after the funeral, Mom made a pretense of holding it together. At least while we had extra family in the house and friends and ward members coming by constantly. There were plenty of cards and flowers and Relief Society sisters and neighbors and casseroles parading into our home for a while, but after a few weeks of that—nothing. Basically nothing, anyway. Oh, Mom's visiting teachers and our home teachers and lots of ward members, including the bishopric and Relief Society presidency, continued to check in with us a lot, but Mom was good at pretending everything was limping along all right with our family and refused any help from anyone. She put up a great front at church and for everyone else, but none of them saw the way she really was. Not like I did.

I wished Mom at least had a few close friends she could trust to talk to about how she was really doing—how all of us were doing—but Dad had been her best friend. She'd never felt the urge to continue close bonding with women friends once she and Dad had married, and she didn't want to start now. So, beyond the brief phone calls and visits from ward members that Mom made sure remained as brief as possible, everyone else went back to their own normal lives, while I had to deal with the broken remains of what was left of mine.

Before the funeral I'd been numb, wrapped in a shroud of disbelief, but after the funeral, harsh reality began to set in. I could hear Ryan's accusing voice in my head, over and over—"He was on his way to pick *you* up from your stupid friend's house!" And then I couldn't stop myself from shaking hard all over.

Worst of all was having to go back to school again. I could feel everyone looking at me, staring at me like I was a freak. Like there was some mark on my forehead that let everyone know that *It* had happened. The only person who wasn't weird around me was Teresa. I didn't know what I would've done without her, especially at school. I couldn't talk about it.

Any of it. Not with anyone. Not my mom, not Robert, and definitely not Ryan. And not Teresa. But she was okay with that and just stayed being my friend.

For a while, I thought for sure I was going crazy. One day walking home from school with Teresa, I saw a man crossing the street in front of us.

"Dad?" I'd whispered.

" . . . oh, and then after—What did you say?" Poor Teresa. She had no choice but to just stand there while I actually ran across the street to see if maybe, just maybe—but of course, it wasn't Dad. I'd never felt so stupid in my life.

If I had to walk home alone, I got really good at diving behind trees and bushes if I saw anyone I knew, especially if it was people from our ward walking towards me on the sidewalk or coming out of their houses to jump into their cars. I couldn't stand the thought of one more person coming up to me and saying, "Oh, sweetie—how are you doing? And how is your mom doing?" School couldn't let out for the summer fast enough for me.

I could feel my body starting to shake, so I threw off my covers and made myself stand up and move around the room, rubbing my arms. I squinted at the clock by my bed. Ten-thirty. Still rubbing my arms up and down, I stared at the calendar hanging above my alarm clock. Saturday, July 1. Four months now.

I turned my back on the calendar and made myself focus on the rest of my bedroom until my eyes locked onto an old Mormonad that hung above my desk. The one of a vase filled with red roses and a single daisy smiling away boldly in the center of all of those gorgeous red petals. "Be Your Own Kind of Beautiful" was printed in large, bold letters at the top of the poster. That was me: a daisy, usually surrounded by a lot of rose-type of people. But I didn't consider it to be a bad thing. Daises are strong flowers. Honest flowers. They stand out in a crowd in their own way. Even among roses.

It was hard not to feel like a daisy when I looked in the mirror alongside the Mormonad on my wall. Although I didn't look much like anyone in my family, being the only blonde, I liked that I looked like my best friend. The only thing I didn't like was that Teresa was definitely skinnier than I was. She was probably a size two, if that. I considered myself to be fat, but Mom always told me I was voluptuous and had more of a Marilyn Monroe type of figure, which she said wasn't the same as being just plain fat. But even so, that was just Mom's opinion. And moms were supposed to say nice things like that to chubby daughters. I turned to the side and sucked in my stomach as hard as I could before turning to grip the doorknob to my bedroom door and force myself through the open doorway.

The house was so quiet that I could hear my bare feet moving down the hallway. Mom's bedroom door was closed. I tiptoed up to it and pressed my ear against the solid, dark wood until I could just make out a sigh, then a sniffle, followed by the rustling of a sheet as Mom shifted in bed.

"Still with us," I whispered softly.

Ryan's door was also closed, and after listening at his door, I cautiously, slowly, turned the doorknob and peeked inside.

Even though I knew Ryan's room would be the picture of chaos, I still felt my breath suck in and my heart jump at the mess. *Dad would never have let him get away with this.* Clothes were thrown all over the floor; CDs were strewn about the desk and bookshelves instead of in their cases; and fast food and candy wrappers, empty pop cans, magazines, and crumpled paper took up every free inch of space left in the room. But most important, even though the lump under the bed covers could've been anything, I could see Ryan's dark, tousled hair on his pillow. I breathed a sigh of relief.

"Made it home," I said out loud.

I carefully closed the door before grabbing a trash bag from the kitchen and then sneaked back into Ryan's room. I wrinkled my nose at the strong, familiar stench in the room before snatching up the garbage everywhere and shoving it into the trash bag. I carefully put all the CDs back in their cases, and lastly gathered up the dirty clothes all over the floor. Ryan didn't move a muscle, not even when I accidentally knocked a thick phone book off his desk onto the floor.

Next door to Ryan's room was the bathroom that we had to share. I attacked it next and scrubbed it down from top to bottom. I opened the mirrored medicine cabinet to make room for some new makeup items of mine and stared at the bottles of eye drops, boxes of cough drops, and several small bottles of different flavors of mouthwashes, one of which was brand new, on Ryan's side of the cabinet.

I closed the cabinet, leaving my makeup by the sink and stared at the toilet. The toilet tank, to be exact.

You have to do it—you know you have to—

I pushed myself from the sink, and after moving the box of tissue on top of the tank, I carefully removed the lid of the toilet tank before peering inside.

I sighed. Three bottles this time.

I knew I should pour them out in the sink—just get rid of it all—but instead, I carefully replaced the lid and the box of tissues.

A minute later, I was back in Ryan's room with my garbage bag, only this time I knelt down by the bed, flipped up Ryan's comforter, and made myself look underneath.

Easily a dozen—maybe two dozen—empty, mostly squashed beer cans littered the floor along with empty glass beer bottles. I snatched as many as I could reach and shoved them into the garbage bag.

I quietly closed Ryan's door for the last time. In the kitchen I poured myself a bowl of cold cereal and milk. I carried the bowl, munching spoonfuls along the way, until my feet brought me to the open door of my dad's study. I didn't walk in. None of us did, even though it needed dusting and vacuuming badly.

There was Dad's desk, his chair still shoved back as if he'd just gotten up and would be back soon to work at his computer. Books were still open by the keyboard, with lined pages of notes on top of the books in Dad's cryptic handwriting. The small, real Tiffany desk lamp by his computer had stayed on until the bulb died two months ago. My eyes moved slowly from object to object: The old cuckoo clock that had belonged to Dad's grandma. Family photos in frames everywhere. Dad's stereo. The old sofa with its matching pillows tossed on the floor. And the two crumpled pieces of paper that lay near the garbage can. The garbage can had a mini basketball hoop attached above it—a Christmas gift from Ryan two years ago. Dad had loved it.

I sighed and turned away from the study. I set my nearly empty bowl in the sink before attacking the mounds of laundry that hadn't been touched all week. After separating the colors from the whites and throwing a load into the washer, I softly knocked on Mom's bedroom door again and hearing her mumbled "what?" I called back through the door.

"Mom? Do you want some breakfast?"

"Mmmm—what time is it?"

"Eleven-thirty." I knew what Mom was going to say, and she knew it, too, but it'd become a routine for us both now.

I heard Mom groan and turn over in bed again. "Thanks, sweetie, but I'm not feeling well. I'll fix myself something later."

"Can I get you anything?"

"No, no. I'm fine. I just need to sleep."

I turned away from the door and headed for the shower. Once I was inside with the hot water turned on full blast, beating down on me mercilessly, I let myself cry as hard as I had the day of Dad's funeral.

———•———

The city cemetery was only a few blocks from my house. That fact had creeped me out for years, but now, I was glad it was so close. I liked being able to walk over whenever I wanted to see my dad, even though I knew I wouldn't actually be seeing him. I was in the habit of walking over on Saturday afternoons, and so once the laundry was done and I'd made sure Mom ate something, I picked up my blue notebook and a pen and walked over to the cemetery.

Dad's stone was near a huge old oak tree. It was one of those raised

15

stones that had our family name, *Fletcher* at the top, with my dad's name, *Robert,* underneath on the left, and my mom's name, *Elaine,* on the right. I wondered if it bothered Mom at all, seeing her name carved on a tombstone. I wasn't sure I'd like to have such finality in front of my face just yet.

A picture of a Latter-day Saint temple was between my mom's and dad's names with "Families Are Forever" etched underneath. The back of the stone read, "Our Children," followed by Robert's, then Ryan's, and then my name. I stared at the stone for a long moment before settling down cross-legged beside it to open my notebook and watch words glide from my pen onto paper.

> *Quietly,*
> *she rocks herself.*
> *Words whisper*
> *echoing to her*
> *brain's ceiling*
> *slamming stubbornly*
> *against the wall*
> *of her mouth.*
> *Her soul has fallen,*
> *smashed into mirror pieces*
> *staring up at her from filthy gutters*
> *sorrowfully.*
> *She has gathered the pieces,*
> *cradles them inside her breast,*
> *quivering*
> *soothing their rips*
> *weaving them together*
> *with shaking fingers.*
> *Her mouth is a closed door.*
> *The pieces can't take any more.*

I glanced up from my scribbling and gazed wearily at the headstone again before lying flat on my back to stare up at the cloudless sky.

"Where are you going, Rachel?"

I'd stuffed my Snoopy backpack with my favorite doll, my fastest running sneakers, and as many cookies as I could. And I'd almost made it out the door— almost—

I'd looked up—way up—at him and said defiantly, "I'm running away!"

"Running away?" Dad had scrunched down to be at eye level with me. I was sure I was in trouble, but Dad had only grinned. "Can I come, too?"

I'd laughed back and nodded, and with that, Dad left his study, swung me up on his shoulders, and we'd spent the afternoon playing at the park. I could still see his hair, ruffled lazily by the wind, as he pushed me in the swings and caught me in his big, strong arms at the end of the slides.

"That was one of the best days of my life, Dad," I whispered.

I told Dad everything that had happened last week and how Mom was still having a hard time. I didn't tell him about Ryan, though. I couldn't. How could I when Mom and I never talked about it? Ever?

"I'm still writing, Dad. I'm going to take creative writing at Central High. You always said I had a talent for poetry. Maybe I'll finally be able to write some decent stuff." I scribbled a few more lines in my notebook before glancing at my watch. "I've got to go, Dad. I'll see you next Saturday, okay?" I rocked forward on my knees and brushed bits of grass away from the stone before kissing my fingertips and lightly running them across Dad's name.

"I miss you, Dad."

I would've gone over to Teresa's that night for a while, but she was out of town on vacation with her family. Instead, I spent the rest of the day cleaning the house and convincing Mom we needed more groceries. Then I ended up going with her to get the week's shopping done. We tried to watch a movie together later, but Mom left in the middle of it.

"I'm tired, honey. It's been a long day. Sweet dreams, okay?"

I wish, Mom.

As usual, Ryan had taken off for who-knew-where for the evening, and as usual, I snuggled down on the couch in the living room with the

TV on softly, waiting. It didn't take long before I could hear Mom crying, followed by the sound of her crying out Dad's name in her sleep. I fell asleep myself as soon as the crying from Mom's room stopped, and I saw Dad's face bright and smiling before me.

"Where are you going, Rachel?"

"I'm running away!"

"Running away? Can I come, too?"

I was sliding down, down, waiting for Dad's strong arms to catch me, but instead, it was a stranger's arms that caught me, falling—a stranger in a blue uniform, with red and blue flashing lights bouncing off his shiny gold badge, grabbing my shoulders, and Ryan's voice, screaming—"He was on his way to pick *you* up from your stupid friend's house!"

And then the slam of a door, and I was jerked wide awake, my heart pounding, and my body shaking hard.

CHAPTER THREE

W ell, hey—what're you watchin'?"
Ryan's voice was loud as he staggered into the living room, his body jerking funny against his footsteps as if his upper body and his legs couldn't get in sync with each other.

"Be quiet—Mom's asleep!"

Ryan ignored me and continued his strange, staggered steps, stumbling across the carpet until he had his face pressed against the TV screen.

"So what're you watchin'? Some movie?"

"You're drunk. Again!"

Ryan didn't turn around. "Am not. Where's Mom?"

"I just said she's asleep. Be quiet—I'm right here, not ten blocks down the street!"

Ryan said something back, but his speech was so slurred I couldn't tell what he'd said. It didn't matter, because it wouldn't have made sense anyway.

"Okay, it's time for you to go to bed." I stood up and tried to pull Ryan away from the TV, but he pushed me away.

"I's not tired—"

"'You's not'?" I mocked. "Well, I am, so let's go." I tried again, but this time Ryan pushed me hard enough to knock me over as he lost the last remaining thread of his balance and fell over, too.

"Oh, man, that hurt!" Ryan started giggling and wouldn't stop laughing no matter what I did to try and stop him. Moments later, though, he was moaning about needing the bathroom, and somehow dragged himself to his knees and crawled down the hall. I heard the toilet flush after a few seconds, and when I heard him moaning louder, I hurried down the hall to see Ryan kneeling in front of the toilet seat, his head hanging over the bowl.

"Sorry—I missed."

And once again, he had. The evidence was all over the floor. Before I had to smell that for long, I ran for the paper towels and cleaned everything up as fast as I could, nearly throwing up myself.

Ryan looked up from the toilet bowl with red, bloodshot eyes. "What're you doin'?"

"What does it look like? Cleaning up so Mom doesn't find out."

Ryan laughed bitterly. "Or so she can keep on pretending."

I finished cleaning up the mess before watching Ryan moan with his head in the toilet bowl for a minute, his hair matted with sweat on his forehead.

"Well, you must've had quite a night. Where were you?"

Ryan didn't look up. "Go away!"

"Can't. Not until you're in bed."

Ryan was silent for a second. "Go away, you stupid idiot!"

I went back to the couch and waited for an hour until he'd lurched himself out of the bathroom and thrown himself face down on his bed. I yanked off his shoes and wrenched his now-stained shirt off him. After I threw it into the washing machine, I went back into Ryan's room. He turned his head to glare at me while I glared back.

"You're welcome. Again."

"I'm really hoping you didn't just say that. I never asked for help!"

"You need help!"

"You're boring. I'm livin' large!"

I laughed bitterly. "Living large? The only thing large here is the amount of puke and its smell! I wouldn't call this living."

He laughed dully and turned onto his back so he could squint at me. "Better than a sharp stick in the eye!"

I shook my head back at him. "*You* need a sharp stick!"

Ryan buried his face in his pillow. "Oh, go ahead—Blah blah blah this, and blah blah blah that. Who cares."

"Who cares? *You* should! I can't believe your coach lets you stay on the football team." And I couldn't, either. Ryan had been on the team his sophomore and junior year and somehow made it onto the varsity team. How he made it to early-morning clinics and practices this summer I'd never know, but somehow he got himself there enough of the time to stay on the team.

Ryan tried to throw a pillow at me and missed me by a mile. "Maybe I don't wanna! Maybe I don't wanna feel nothin.' Feeling nothin's better. Nothin' matters—feels great—everything just floats way, way, away—"

I shook my head at his ramblings. "Do you really think getting drunk makes stuff that bothers you go away?"

"Doesn't work with everything. You're still here." Ryan laughed and wouldn't stop laughing, so I left him there in his jeans and socks, lying on his stomach. I almost had the door closed when I heard him mumbling again and stood still to catch his words.

"I'm seventeen. One seven, one seven, one seven . . . If I live to be an old, old, old, old man, it'll be forever before I see Dad again. If I ever do."

I walked slowly into my own room and quietly closed my bedroom door before glancing at the clock. Four A.M. I crumpled to my knees. Church was at 9:00. Less than four hours and everyone had to be up and moving. I sighed and buried my head on my arms as I knelt by my bed, and as usual, prayed as fervently to God as I could, begging Him to help Ryan, help my mom, and help all of us to do more than just survive. I'd been reading my scriptures faithfully every day and promised again that I'd do better—that I'd read twice a day and that I'd go to church without fail every Sunday and actually pay attention the whole time. And that I'd go to all the Young Women's activities and all the service activities. And that I'd never skip seminary once the school year started again and that I'd keep fasting for Ryan. I prayed—begged—again that God would take away all of our family's problems. Especially Ryan's.

I crawled into bed and set my alarm for 7:30 in the morning.

CHAPTER FOUR

I looked forward to Sundays, mostly because it was the one day of the week Mom would rise early to get herself all cleaned up and looking nice. It was almost too bad that Mom didn't have to join the working world after Dad died, but Dad had been successful in his business. On top of that, he'd left behind a great life insurance policy, so Mom didn't have to go to work at all. I'd hoped she would anyway, just to get out of the house and around people, but she wouldn't. So Sunday was the only day of the week I could count on her getting up and about.

I could also count on her to push Ryan and me out of our beds, since she was determined the three of us needed to go to church together. Sometimes she could get Ryan to go, and other times he'd claim he'd had "bad Chinese" the night before. And Mom always seemed to believe him.

I was sitting on a bar stool in the kitchen munching scrambled egg on toast sandwiches with Mom when Ryan stumbled down the hall. Ryan scowled at both of us before slumping onto a bar stool near me, elbows on the kitchen counter, holding his head in his hands.

"Morning, Ry-Guy. How about an egg sandwich?"

Mom was smiling cheerfully, but Ryan looked like he was going to throw up after watching me squeeze ketchup onto my egg sandwich.

"No thanks. I just want water. And some aspirin."

I watched Ryan's hands shake as he tried to wrench the small aspirin bottle open that Mom handed to him before he cursed and threw the bottle onto the kitchen counter.

"Here—I'll open it." I grabbed the bottle and twisted off the Ryan-proof lid before handing him two aspirins.

Ryan washed down both aspirins with three huge gulps of water before slamming the cup down on the kitchen counter, cursing as he squinted at the sun streaming in through the kitchen window. "GOOD GRIEF—do we have to live in a fishbowl? Close the stinking blinds!"

Mom looked at Ryan worriedly while I stared straight ahead, munching more bites out of my sandwich.

"What's the matter, Ry-Guy? Not feeling well again?"

Ryan only glared back at Mom's concern. "I've got a massive headache, my stomach's sick, I need to sleep, and you're too loud!"

Mom shook her head and poured herself some juice. "Sounds like the flu. You shouldn't have stayed out so late. Who were you with?"

Ryan scowled and looked away. "Some friends."

"Paul and Brian?"

"No. You don't know them."

"I haven't seen Paul and Brian come over in a long time. In fact, I only see them on Sundays at church. Aren't you getting along these days?"

Ryan shrugged irritably and glared at Mom again. "I have other friends besides them!"

Mom tried to volley more questions at him, but Ryan angrily announced the interrogation was over and stood up, only to sway dizzily on his feet before gripping the countertop and dropping back heavily onto the bar stool.

"Ryan, are you okay? Sit back down, honey!"

I wanted to scream "Open your eyes!" at the look of confusion on Mom's face, but Ryan ignored her next series of questions and a second later lurched back down the hall to the bathroom. I'd finished my egg sandwich and followed Ryan down the hall, pausing outside the bathroom door in time to hear the clunk of the toilet tank lid being moved and the snick of a bottle cap coming off. I sighed and moved past the bathroom to my own room to find a dress to wear.

"Ready for church, kids?"

Ryan was still irritable, but he wasn't shaking anymore by the time Mom drove us to church. I watched him stick two pieces of gum in his mouth before he turned his usual bloodshot glare on me.

"What are you staring at, stupid?"

I quickly turned away to look out the side window. "Nothing."

We barely made it to church on time, as usual. Sacrament meeting was our last meeting, and as usual, I left Sunday School early to save a bench for us in the back of the chapel. I wanted to sink through the floor when the older couple Ryan had to crawl over looked him up and down with facefuls of disapproval—almost disgust—as if he were a large, dead cockroach. The two wrinkled their noses, and after sniffing and coughing and whispering together, stood up and moved to a different bench.

It wasn't the first time something like this had happened at church and likely wouldn't be the last, but it felt like a knife in my chest every time it happened. Mom pretended not to notice anything while Ryan hunched over with his elbows on his knees. And then I'd wonder why I let myself look forward to Sunday at all.

During the sacrament, I prayed that God would help Ryan and hoped again that maybe this time help would really come.

After church, the bishop's wife, Sister Carter, smiled and cornered me in the hall on my way to the car.

"Rachel, how are you?" Her smile actually looked both sincere and concerned.

I did my best to give her a huge smile back. "I'm good, Sister Carter. You?"

"I'm well, thank you. How's your mother?"

"She's fine."

"And . . . Ryan. How is he?"

I could tell by the look on her face that she knew—she knew, and I wanted to burst out laughing at the irony. People in the ward who hardly knew us could see, but my own mom couldn't.

I pretended to be confused at her question. "He's good, too, of course. He's fine. Just fine. We're all fine."

"You're sure? Because if there's anything I can do—or anything the bishop can do, or your home teachers—"

"No, there's nothing. We're fine. Really. Thanks, though." Before Sister Carter could say anything else, I hurried down the hall away from her with as cheerful a smile as I could muster and added a wave for effect.

After church, Ryan slumped in the backseat and stared out the side window while Mom drove us home. The second we pulled into the garage, Ryan did the infamous traffic pattern that he always performed whenever he was able to actually walk instead of stumble into the house. First, he headed straight for our bathroom before stomping into his bedroom, firmly shutting the door behind him. Within minutes, he jerked open the door to head for the garage before reentering the house minutes later. I soberly watched the procession from the kitchen while Mom busied herself trying to put together a Sunday dinner.

"Leave something in the car?" I said dryly.

I'd found alcohol stashed in some strange places in the house, including a bottle wedged behind the hot water heater, and wondered how many hiding places Ryan actually had. Before I could torture him some more, Mom turned around and smiled curiously at him. "What did you forget, Ryan?"

But Ryan wouldn't look at Mom and just mumbled something incoherently while he yanked the tie from around his neck.

"Let me know when dinner's ready." And he was back to his bedroom, shutting the door firmly behind him.

As usual, Ryan was a true joy during dinner. He picked at his food and drank water like a fish and kept telling me I was too loud.

"I thought Sister Benson's talk on endurance was inspiring today. Didn't you?" Mom tried.

Ryan snorted. "*Inspiring?* Is that the polite word for *boring* now?"

Mom lightly poked Ryan. "Boring? How can you say that?"

"Her whiny voice was annoying. I wish I'd had a phone book to hit her over the head with!"

Mom actually chuckled while I stared incredulously at both of them before speaking. "She made a lot of good points and quoted some good scripture verses, if you'd cared to listen. Like when she talked about the importance of not just enduring, but enduring well—"

Ryan guffawed angrily. "Enduring well? Like she knows the first thing about enduring! The most she's ever had to 'endure' is a testimony meeting that goes painfully into overtime. I get so sick of people babbling at the pulpit about stuff they don't know anything about!"

Mom shrugged and dug her fork back into her salad. "Well, I thought her talk was good. And so was her husband's on the power of prayer. Didn't you at least like his talk?"

Ryan snorted. "Everyone thinks praying is the answer to everything. I hate those Sunday School answers: pray, go to church, read your scriptures. It's just what churchgoers do to hide from their problems and keep from dealing with their miserable lives. I'm sick of hearing about it!"

I wasn't surprised at all by Ryan's moment of venting. I was too used to it as part of our family's post-church routine. It didn't matter what I said to try and smooth over his practically blasphemous rantings, because I could never get through to him. It was like living with someone in a plastic bubble: I could see him, but I couldn't touch him.

Ryan pushed away from the table and stomped off, back into his bedroom. But by evening, he came back to join Mom and me in the living room in front of the TV, slumping onto the couch near Mom, his eyes bloodshot, mumbling about needing some cash. I watched Mom hand it over while telling him that he needed to go out and find a job.

"If Ryan's not going to get a job, then it's only fair that he should have to do more stuff around the house!"

Ryan barely glanced at me. "You need the exercise more than I do."

"Shut up!"

"In fact, you could stand to run around the block a few times!"

"Mom!" I pleaded with Mom for help, but all she did was tell Ryan to be quiet. That was it. And Ryan only sneered at me before snatching the money from Mom and heading back into his bedroom.

CHAPTER FIVE

Be Your Own Kind of Beautiful.

I could see the rose petals and the words out of the corner of my eye while I struggled to get my hair to be some kind of not so ugly. I gave up and strangled it all into a messy bun at the back of my head before glancing at the calendar. July 3. I'd been so tired all day Sunday that I'd slept in until noon the next day. One peek into Ryan's room and I breathed out a sigh to see him flopped face down on his bed, his covers kicked to the carpet.

I peeked into Mom's room next. She, too, was still asleep. A dark green, oversized photo album was barely hanging on to the edge of the bed. I knew one good kick from Mom would send the book flying, so I tiptoed in and rescued it before softly closing the door behind me.

I curled up on the couch in the living room and couldn't help smiling when I opened the book. The first photo inside was of Dad making an evil face at the camera, pretending to shove an unsuspecting Ryan into the Erie Canal in Palmyra, New York.

"July. Last July," I whispered. I'd been trying to remember what we'd done for the Fourth of July last year, and now I remembered. We'd gone to New York to visit Grandma and Grandpa, Dad's parents, in LeRoy, New York. Robert and Wendy had flown to New York to be with us. And since we'd been there for more than a week, we'd taken in the Hill Cumorah pageant and a tour of Palmyra. I grinned at the picture of me sweltering in the heat and humidity in my bright, neon pink Jell-O T-shirt, complete with a picture of the original Jell-O box design on it. Utahns might have been well known for their use of green Jell-O, but Jell-O had been invented and originally made in LeRoy, New York. Dad had always been proud of that fact.

We all liked the Hill Cumorah pageant. A lot. It was impossible not to with the music, special effects, and the huge stages all over the mountainside. But best of everything in the area, Dad loved the Jell-O museum and the old Jell-O factory in LeRoy where the stuff had originally been made for years. I laughed out loud at the picture of all six of us grinning and chomping Zweigle's red hot dogs with the skins on in our Jell-O T-shirts at the Oatka festival parade with Grandma and Grandpa: Dad was in purple, I was in pink, Mom was in yellow, Robert was in red, Wendy was in orange, and Ryan was hamming it up for the camera in green.

After touring the building where the Book of Mormon was first published, we'd visited the famous Four Corners area of churches in Palmyra, on the corners of Main and Canandaigua Streets in Palmyra: the Presbyterian, Methodist, Baptist, and Episcopal churches. I smiled at a picture of Dad and me clinging to the bell tower rope in one of the churches. Dad's eyes were filled with amazement, and his mouth was wide open, laughing.

"Come on, Rachel—ring that bell!"

"Dad—no!"

The tour guide had smiled encouragingly. "It's okay. Go for it!"

"Here, baby, I'll help you." Dad had wrapped his arms around me to grab the rope above my hands.

And then, music—clear and strong and amazing. Dad had laughed, awed at the power of the bells, his arms tight around me.

"Good job, baby girl!"

I smiled and turned the page, but my smile faded sadly at the next picture—one of Ryan and Dad together, arms around each other's shoulders, smiling broadly for the camera. There were lots of pictures like that in our family albums, pictures of Ryan and Dad grinning and laughing together. I'd forgotten Ryan had Dad's smile. The fact forced me to close the book firmly, brushing tears off my face.

CHAPTER SIX

July Fourth started early. Way too early for me, complete with plenty of fireworks from the moment the day began.

I'd fallen asleep on the couch the night before, waiting for Ryan, but instead of the usual slam of the front door, it was the phone ringing shrilly that woke me up.

I jumped and squinted at the clock in the living room. Seven A.M.! I groaned and listened to the phone ring again before it was stopped in mid-ring. From down the hall, I could hear Mom's muffled, half asleep voice saying "Hello?" I felt blood rush into my heart, making it beat too hard and fast. Ryan wasn't home.

I prayed silently that he was home—that I just hadn't heard him come in—as my feet flew down the hall. I threw his bedroom door open, but I knew—I knew what I was going to see. Or what I wasn't going to see.

Ryan's bedroom was a messy shambles, as usual, and although the blankets on his bed were in a jumbled mass on his bed, there was clearly no Ryan in it. I gripped the door handle, trembling, as I strained to hear as much of Mom's phone conversation as I could until my ears burned and rang.

"Mr. Fletcher isn't here . . . there's just me." Silence. "What? I don't believe it!" Silence again while my heart beat faster. "Please, I—I'm hardly even awake. Maybe we should meet and talk about this later." Silence again, followed by the click of the phone being set down.

I pushed Mom's door open. "What happened to Ryan?"

Mom looked at me with baffled, confused eyes. "I—I don't know. Isn't he home?"

"No, he's not home! He never came home last night! Who were you talking to?"

"I—I don't know."

I stared at Mom. "You don't know?"

"Yes. No. I mean, I've never met him."

"Who was it?"

Mom frowned and rubbed her temples with both hands. "A Mr. Ackerman. His son was at a party last night. Apparently he and Ryan were in a fight, and his son was hurt. I don't know—he said he's coming over to talk more about it. I don't know what else he said. He was incredibly angry."

"When is he coming?"

Mom glanced at the clock by her bed. "He'll be here in an hour. I'd best make myself presentable."

Mom had just swung her legs over the side of the bed when the front door slammed shut.

"Ryan!"

Mom rushed down the hall with me trailing her. Ryan was standing in the middle of the living room running his hands through his hair. The smell of cigarettes and the stench of stale, cheap beer were so thick all around him I would've believed it if he said he'd been marinating himself in a mixture of both all night. He turned to look at us with bloodshot eyes, but before he could open his mouth to say anything, Mom and I both shrieked.

There was dried blood on Ryan's hand and smears of blood on the front of his T-shirt.

"Ryan—what—what happened?"

Ryan didn't even look at us. "Nothing."

Mom raced to him and grabbed his hand. "Your knuckles are all cut—and bruised! Are you okay? What in the world happened?"

Ryan grunted angrily and yanked his hand out of Mom's grasp. "Stop it—don't! I'm fine. Fine!"

Mom stepped back and stared at Ryan. Just stared. Nothing more.

"Where have you been?" Mom whispered.

Ryan sneered at her. "With Paul and Brian, obviously."

"Ryan, what were you doing last night?"

I could only stare in disbelief at Mom and do my best not to scream, *What do you think?*

Ryan tried to move past Mom, but he tripped on the lamp table, and when he did, a small glass bottle fell out of his front pocket and rolled silently to Mom's feet. Mom stared in horror at the tiny bottle as if it were a dead mouse before slowly reaching down to pick it up.

A mini bottle of vodka. Right in front of her face and in her hands, falling right out of Ryan's pocket. I could only stand and wait, wondering what Mom would do, and say, and think.

Finally, finally!

But Mom unbelievably looked at Ryan with confused eyes. "Where did you get this?"

"It's not mine. Someone gave it to me."

"Someone gave it to you? Who?"

Ryan scowled and shrugged. "Dunno. Some guy last night. Asked me to hold it for him. I forgot I still had it."

Mom was silent while I waited. "Oh."

I kept waiting for Mom to do something, say something, say anything, but she didn't. Instead, Ryan shoved past her, mumbling, "I don't feel so good. I'm goin' to bed."

Mom watched him walk away before turning and following him down the hall into her own room, gripping the mini bottle in her hand.

———•———

True to his threat, one hour later the doorbell rang, followed by loud, firm knocking.

"That must be Mr. Ackerman. Will you please answer the door, Rachel?"

The man at the front door didn't look much older than Mom. For some reason, that surprised me. He was tall and slender with light brown hair cut incredibly short. It was his eyes, though, that gripped me. Angry eyes. I could tell he was doing his best to keep from bursting like a flood, and that made me want to shut and lock the door in his face.

"Are you Mr. Ackerman?"

"Yes, I am."

"Please come in." I motioned for him to sit down once he was inside, but he didn't. "I'll just go get my mom," I mumbled before running like a scared rabbit out of the room.

Mom, of course, wasn't ready yet, so I was forced to go back into the living room and try to make polite conversation with a man who was clearly looking for a knock-down, drag-out fight. He'd sat down by the time I returned, but he stood up when I reentered the room.

"My mom will be here in a minute."

He nodded irritably and then paced a bit before sitting stiffly on the couch. He was wearing jeans, a nice polo shirt and sneakers, but his clothes looked too new. There wasn't even a scuff of dirt on the sneakers. Anybody else would've looked relaxed and comfortable in such clothes, but Mr. Ackerman looked as uncomfortable as if his clothes were a hundred years old.

I had no idea what to say, so I sat on the edge of one of the recliners, nervously bouncing my legs with my arms folded tight, praying Mom would get herself into the living room presto-pronto. Mr. Ackerman didn't speak, either. Just sat stiffly on the couch with an angry, I'm-trying-my-best-to-stay-under-control look on his face.

I breathed a sigh of relief when Mom finally entered the room. Mr. Ackerman stood up when she entered, and when I looked at his face, although he still looked ready to do some serious damage, something had slightly, ever so slightly, changed. I knew my mom was pretty, and I could tell that fact was registering in Mr. Ackerman's mind, even though he was ready to erupt volcano-style.

Mom smiled brightly and extended her hand. "Hello, Mr. Ackerman. I'm Elaine Fletcher."

Mr. Ackerman curtly nodded and gave Mom's hand a quick shake.

"Is your husband going to be joining us?"

"No. As I explained on the phone, there's just me." Mom turned to me and smiled, but her lips were trembling. "Rachel, please go check on Ryan."

I left the room, but I stayed in the hall, just out of sight. I watched while Mom asked Mr. Ackerman to please sit back down, and within seconds, the real fireworks began.

Mr. Ackerman's voice was loud and angry. "My son Dallin was at a party last night, a party your son Ryan crashed. Your son was clearly intoxicated and felt the urge to antagonize Dallin, resulting in your son punching Dallin in the eye. Dallin was in so much pain I had to rush him to the emergency room, and after being x-rayed, the doctor confirmed that your son had broken Dallin's left cheek bone and two of the bones by his left eye. He's going to need surgery now. I hope you're prepared to pay for the plastic surgeon's work, because if you refuse, I'm an attorney and you'll find yourself paying not only the doctor's fees but my legal fees as well!"

Mom stared at Mr. Ackerman, horrified. "Ryan—Ryan doesn't drink!"

Mr. Ackerman was silent while I held my breath. This time when he spoke, his voice was lower and almost calm, as if he actually felt sorry for Mom. "Mrs. Fletcher, I've spoken not only with my son but with several of his friends who were also at the party. They all confirmed that your son had indeed been drinking last night. And that he was clearly drunk when he arrived. And they all agreed to sign sworn statements to that fact, if necessary."

"I—I don't believe you. I don't believe it! I talked to Ryan when he came home. He was fine, and he didn't mention anything about hitting anyone!"

Mr. Ackerman just stared at Mom. "I have witnesses who all saw Ryan strike my son."

"Maybe—maybe your son hit my son first. There *was* blood on his shirt when he came home."

Mr. Ackerman shook his head almost sadly. "I was told your son was bothering Dallin for no reason and that he cut his hand on a broken bottle after hitting my son. He must have wiped his hand on his shirt."

"I—I can't believe this."

Mr. Ackerman was silent and looked at Mom carefully. "Perhaps I ought to talk to your husband. I don't want to have to file a complaint with the court, but my son will require surgery. Surgery that will most likely be expensive, especially if there's any nerve damage to his eye. Is there a number you can give me where I can reach your husband?"

I held my breath, waiting for Mom to have to say the words she hated saying more than any others. I could see her lips tremble as she collapsed into the recliner behind her. Then she forced the distasteful words out of her mouth in a whisper: "My husband passed away." I could hear the defeat still coupled with disbelief in Mom's weak whisper. "I'll take care of your son's medical bills. Please just forward them to me. I apologize for Ryan's behavior last night, and I hope your son is going to be all right."

Mr. Ackerman's eyes widened before he sat down on the couch by the recliner and leaned towards Mom. "I'm so sorry about your husband—I didn't realize that when we spoke earlier. I'm truly sorry."

Mom offered him the customary nod she gave to people whom she believed had no idea what she was going through and tried to smile. "I see you didn't bring your wife with you?"

Mr. Ackerman stared at her again, but the stare was different now. "My wife passed away a long time ago."

Mom's eyes widened. "Really? I'm so sorry. So sorry—"

I stiffened and gripped the doorknob of the hall closet. Something had changed. In the course of those strange, few seconds of discovery, something had changed. I could feel the blood draining from my face, while at the same moment, I could see shock and wonder on Mom's and

34

Mr. Ackerman's faces. I could hear that same shock and wonder in their voices. Mr. Ackerman's tone was no longer angry, and Mom—she sounded almost relieved.

I couldn't stand to hear or see anymore. I turned my back on both of them and walked into my room and shut the door behind me before leaning against it heavily. Fifteen minutes later, I heard the front door close, followed by Mom softly knocking and calling to me through my bedroom door. I opened the door and stared at Mom's face. She looked different. Something in her eyes was different.

"What happened?"

"Oh, don't worry, Rachel. Everything's fine."

"Fine? Maybe for Mr. Ackerman. We have to pay for his son's surgery!"

Mom actually smiled. "Eavesdropping, Rachel? Well, don't worry about it. We're going to work everything out."

"What do you mean?"

Mom shrugged and tried to sound casual. "I invited Mr. Ackerman and his son over for dinner on Friday night."

I gasped loudly. "You did *what?*"

Mom shrugged and bit her lip. "Well, I thought it would be a nice gesture on our part. A way to apologize for everything . . ."

I didn't hear anything else Mom said, because the look on her face and the way her eyes almost sparkled forced me to concentrate on not bursting into tears.

CHAPTER SEVEN

Hours later when Ryan finally emerged from his room, grumpy and headachy and wanting only water and aspirins, Mom shocked all three of us by cornering Ryan and making him sit down at the kitchen table. Ryan irritably dropped into a chair while I sat on a bar stool, watching.

"What do you want? And make it snappy. I'm not feeling so good."

Mom frowned and twisted a kitchen towel in her hands. "Did you hurt a boy last night?"

Ryan glared at her. "What? No—I didn't touch anyone. Why?"

"Do you know a boy named Dallin Ackerman?"

Ryan shrugged. "I know of him. He goes to Central, but he's a year behind me. Why?"

"His father was here earlier. He said you hit Dallin last night and broke his cheek bone and some of the bones around his eye. He's going to need surgery now."

"I don't remember hitting anyone," Ryan said flatly.

"Well, apparently you did." Mom was about to say more but stopped with her mouth slightly open. "Ryan, what's the matter? Are you all right?"

"What are you talking about?" Even though Ryan was sitting, he was swaying back and forth in his chair. "I told you my stomach hurts!" I could see Ryan shaking a little as he swayed sickly back and forth, looking like he might throw up any second.

"Ryan, were you . . . drinking last night?"

Ryan stared almost hatefully at Mom. "What?"

"Mr. Ackerman said he'd spoken with his son and others who were at a party last night. They said you were there, too, and that you'd been drinking."

"And you believed some guy who wasn't even there? And a bunch of scared idiots who want to blame me for his kid getting punched?"

"You came home with blood on your shirt, and your hand was cut up and bruised—"

"And so of course that must've been because I hit someone?"

"I don't think you would've hurt anyone if you'd been sober!"

"I *was* sober!"

"Mr. Ackerman said you called his son a—" Mom hesitantly said a string of a few strangely placed profanities and playground language that made no sense and actually sounded funny. Especially from Mom.

Ryan scowled at her, still swaying slightly. "Everyone says stuff like that. It doesn't mean I was drunk. You're out of it."

Mom sat down in a chair by Ryan and looked at him worriedly. "Ryan, I think you may have a . . . a problem."

"A 'problem'?"

"With . . . drinking. Alcohol . . ."

Ryan gasped in outrage. "Mom, I don't drink! I can't believe you don't believe me! You believe some stranger trying to blame his kid's problems onto someone else, but not me, your own son!"

"It's not that I don't believe you—it's just . . ."

"I don't have a problem, Mom. *You* obviously have a problem trusting your own son!" Ryan struggled to stand up from the chair. "I'm outta here—"

Mom jumped up from her chair and blocked Ryan's path, even going so far as to put her hands on his arms. "Ryan, please—I'm sorry, okay? I'm sorry. We'll drop it, okay? Please, don't leave!"

I jumped off the stool then myself, making sure it smacked loudly against the kitchen counter before running into my room to slam the door.

CHAPTER EIGHT

True to her word, Mom didn't bring up the Problem to Ryan again. But then Friday night arrived, and Mom had to explain to Ryan why Mr. Ackerman and his son Dallin were coming over for dinner.

Ryan flew into a rage over the idea of the two of them breaking bread with us, as well as being told he had to stay and play nice at the table with everyone *and* apologize to the Ackermans for breaking Dallin's face.

"I'm not going to stay here. There's no way I'm going to stay here tonight!"

Ryan could've left. He was tall and big, and Mom wasn't. She couldn't have kept him from leaving. I stared at myself in the mirror in my room, listening to Ryan rant and rave at Mom while she pleaded and finally threatened to make him stay.

"I'll have that car of yours towed to the junkyard unless you stay here tonight and have dinner with everyone and act like a decent, polite human being!"

I could see my Mormonad poster as I tried to make my hair do something—anything—that wouldn't scare a small child.

Be Your Own Kind of Beautiful.

And then the doorbell rang, making me jump, followed by Mr. Ackerman's voice and what must have been Dallin saying hello to Mom.

"Rachel, everyone's here! Come say hello!"

I sighed and walked down the hall.

Mr. Ackerman was wearing nice pants and a button-down shirt, and Mom—I gasped when I saw her. She was wearing a dress I'd only seen her wear when she went out to dinner with Dad. I had to bite my lip to keep myself from saying anything.

Dallin was tall like his dad, only not as skinny. He was as blond as I was and wore jeans and a nice shirt and sneakers. My heart started pounding, but not because Dallin was handsome, which he was, even with his swollen, black-and-blue eye. Ryan had entered the room right behind me, and I just knew fists would start flying and Dallin would pay Ryan back for the damage done to his face.

Amazingly, nothing violent happened between the two at all.

Ryan grunted, "Hey, Ackerman."

And Dallin nodded carefully back. "Hey, Fletch."

And that was really it.

Awkward introductions were made all around, and when Dallin was introduced to me, he smiled and shook my hand. It seemed like such a strange thing to do, but his hand was warm, and he didn't squeeze hard.

I looked at Dallin's face with a stiff smile pasted on my lips, and when our eyes met, there was something about his curious, surprised look that made me feel as if I was looking into a mirror. I froze as I realized what I was seeing. *You know what* It's *like, don't you?* I'd felt marked since *It* had happened, and something about the way Dallin was looking at me—I knew he could see that mark, and the only reason it was recognizable and clear to him was because he had that same mark. He'd gone through *It*, too. He, too, had seen the end of the world and looked over its edge into nothingness.

I blushed and quickly let go of Dallin's hand and stuck both of my hands into my back jeans pockets. I did my best to shake every deep thought out of my head and resolved to look at Dallin as little as possible for the rest of the evening. After all, I wasn't likely to see him up close and personal like this ever again. Tonight was a one-shot deal only.

"Well, dinner is ready, so let's move into the dining room!"

We hadn't had dinner in our actual dining room in forever. Not since *It* had happened, and walking in there to see food and our nice china on a fancy linen tablecloth was a shock.

Mr. Ackerman smiled at Mom. "It smells wonderful, Mrs. Fletcher."

Mom blushed and smiled back. "It's nothing, really. Just salmon and some salads. I didn't even ask if you like seafood. Do you?"

"I love seafood!"

Mr. Ackerman pulled out a chair for Mom, and before I knew what was happening, Dallin did the same for me.

"Oh—um, thanks," I mumbled.

Dallin smiled and nodded before moving to sit across from me. Only Ryan stood and stared narrowly at everyone before finally slumping into the chair beside me.

"Thank you both for coming to dinner. I—we—just feel terrible about what happened. I know Ryan feels terrible, don't you, Ryan?"

Ryan glared at Mom before mumbling something that sounded a little like "sorry."

"How is your eye feeling, Dallin? It's so swollen. Does it hurt badly?"

Dallin smiled and lightly touched his eye with one hand. "Not too bad. I'm taking pain pills for it until my surgery on Monday."

"Your doctor is waiting that long?"

"He wants to see more swelling go down first."

"Oh. Of course." Mom turned from Dallin and smiled at Mr. Ackerman. "And, as we discussed before, please forward all of the medical bills to me—"

"Oh, I think it's going to be all right, Mrs. Fletcher. I checked with my medical insurance, and I think all of Dallin's surgery is going to be covered just fine. So there's no need to worry about anything."

"But I have to do something . . ."

"You already have. You kindly invited my son and me for dinner with you and your family tonight."

I wanted to eat, but the salmon didn't taste right. Not at all the way it should have tasted. Not even the salads tasted the way they had the last time we'd had salmon in the dining room. After seeing how Mom's eyes were sparkling and Mr. Ackerman was smiling too much and how often both of them kept glancing at each other, I couldn't gag down another bite of the cardboard-tasting salmon.

Ryan kept himself slumped over his plate and forced a few bites down, but after staring hatefully at Mom, who was totally oblivious to his glares while she babbled with Mr. Ackerman about raising teenagers, Ryan shoved his chair back and stood up.

"Sorry. I'm not feeling so good. I need to go lie down. Sorry again about your eye, Ackerman." Before Mom or anyone could answer him, Ryan stomped out of the room and down the hall into his bedroom.

"Ryan?" Mom watched Ryan leave with a deer-in-the-headlights, panicked look on her face, but then Mr. Ackerman said something to her in a whisper, and Mom did something I hadn't heard her do in four months: She laughed. Mr. Ackerman laughed, too, clearly pleased with his heroic feat. Dallin grinned and looked at me and lightly shrugged when I didn't return the smile.

It took less than nothing after that for Mr. Ackerman to keep smiles on Mom's face. Although it was good—really good—to see Mom smile and laugh, it was hard, too. Harder than I'd ever imagined it would be.

"I hope you'll stay for chocolate cake and ice cream!"

Mr. Ackerman was more than happy to stay for dessert. Dallin not only ate a piece of Mom's cake but happily accepted seconds and thanked Mom with a huge smile. He clearly didn't mind hanging around longer, either.

I watched Dallin eat bite after bite until he looked up and caught me. Before I could look away, he smiled at me again, his black-and-blue eye squinting shut from the effort.

"Good cake!"

I wanted to scream, "Can't you see?" and wondered if having one eye out of commission blinded a person completely.

CHAPTER NINE

Mom showed up at the hospital and stayed with Mr. Ackerman the day of Dallin's surgery, and she had a basket of fried chicken ready to take over to the Ackermans' house when Dallin was released.

I folded my arms after inspecting the red-and-white cardboard basket. "Fast food?"

Mom shrugged. "It's Dallin's favorite."

"How do you know?"

"Joseph told me. Joe, I mean."

I stared at Mom, who refused to meet my eyes. "'Joe?' What happened to 'Mr. Ackerman'?"

Mom forced a laugh and waved me away from her. "Oh, it's silly for us not to use our first names! We're both adults, and Joe's only a couple of years older than I am."

Mom included another chocolate cake in her care package, and a day later, Mr. Ackerman showed up to return the cake pan and take Mom out for ice cream. The day after that, our garbage disposal mysteriously malfunctioned, so Mr. Ackerman of course went with Mom to buy a new one and then followed her into our house and removed the broken one and replaced it with the new one. I could've sworn he purposely made it take twice as long as it should have. But Mom didn't mind and fixed him lasagna for his trouble. And he thanked her by taking her out to dinner the next night.

After that, a day didn't go by that Mom didn't spend at least part of it with Mr. Ackerman, even if it was just talking on the phone. Ryan made himself scarce more and more often, apparently intent on ignoring the situation. Fletcher Tradition at its finest. I tried to keep myself calm and not worry too much. Mom was lonely, that was all. Mr. Ackerman wasn't Dad. He wasn't at all like Dad, and Mom would see that soon enough once the novelty of hanging out with "Joe" wore off. Besides, Mr. Ackerman wasn't half as good-looking as Dad, and he wasn't funny like Dad, either. Sometimes he tried to be, but mostly he was serious. Too serious. And Mom liked funny. I almost felt sorry for Mr. Ackerman. He couldn't see that Mom was in love with Dad and would never feel the same way about him.

By August, though, Mom was still going strong with her "friendship" with Mr. Ackerman, and then I really did start to worry. They'd been hanging out together practically every day for six weeks now and didn't show any signs of slowing down. They'd become so into each other that I was truly amazed Mom remembered to make me a cake and say "happy birthday" to me when the day arrived.

"Really, Rachel—I'm hurt! How could you think I'd forget your birthday?"

"You're busy a lot now."

Mom only laughed and kissed the top of my head and asked if I'd like her to take me to the DMV to try for my driver's license.

Besides being able to get my driver's license without much trouble, my sixteenth birthday that August came and went without much fanfare. Teresa gave me a dark blue, zip-up hoodie and some music CDs for my birthday and then stayed overnight. We watched all three of the extended versions of the *Lord of the Rings* trilogy and ate plenty of pizza and birthday cake. Ryan had thankfully stayed away all night. He'd been doing that more and more often the past few weeks: sleeping over who-knew-where rather than stumbling home at two in the morning. It'd been a nice break for me, but as much as I enjoyed not having to clean up after him and put him to bed at night, I worried about him more when he didn't come home until the next morning or afternoon—always sober but always horribly hung over.

CHAPTER TEN

O n the first day of my sophomore year at Central High, Ryan was supposed to give me a ride in his car and pick up Teresa along the way. He didn't want to, of course, and spent the night before complaining about having to give us a ride. Then he purposely slept in and dragged his feet getting ready. I hurried down the hall to check on Ryan's progress for the tenth time that morning and about died to see him leaning over the bathroom sink, still in his sweatpants and no shirt, socks, or shoes.

"Ryan—hurry! You've got early-morning seminary, too, and it starts in fifteen minutes!"

Ryan turned his head to squint at me. "What makes you think I'm going to seminary?"

My mouth fell open at that. "Well—because—because you signed up for it, too!"

"Doesn't mean I'm going to go, though, does it?"

"But—but you're supposed to give me a ride!"

"Yeah, well, life's full of disappointments. Get used to it!" And with that, Ryan kicked the bathroom door shut in my face.

Since I was ready to have a nervous breakdown over the idea of being late on my first day of high school and Mom was sick of listening to Ryan and me yell at each other, Mom ended up giving me and Teresa a ride in her car. We both had early-morning seminary, but unfortunately we didn't have the same teacher.

"Good luck in there!" Teresa waved and grinned at me before disappearing into one of the classrooms in the seminary building while I checked my schedule one more time to make sure I was at the right room.

Book of Mormon. Brother Clawson. Room 101.

Please, please let this year be better than last year. Please don't let anyone ask about my family—about It. Please let me be normal like everyone else this year.

I took a big, deep breath and walked into the room, picked a desk, and started my first year at Central High.

I was one of the first to arrive, since I was nerdy enough to want to be a little early. Brother Clawson hadn't even entered the room yet. I had my backpack with me, so after picking a desk in the back by the windows, I opened it and took out my blue writing notebook.

So what
If it bounces
Like a tennis ball
Back into my mouth,
Past my larynx
Until I gag
And vomit every force-fed hamburger
I ever ate in the past
Fifteen years.
My feet
Are tired of being rooted to the dirt,
A home for worms
And dandelions—
Yellow and ugly.
It is time.
It is time
For weeds to be ripped up
Leaving deadly half-fingers of root behind
Never to be thumb-screwed
By Them again.

The silent screams are over.
All songs must be heard
Even if the singer
Coughs,
Spits blood,
Maybe apologizes and faints
When it's over.

"Wow. Interesting poem!"

I jumped and nearly smacked heads with a man in a white shirt and a tie reading over my shoulder.

"Um, yeah," I mumbled as I slammed the notebook shut and shoved it into my backpack.

The man smiled and stuck his hand out to me. "I'm Brother Clawson. And you are?"

"Obviously way too early."

Brother Clawson laughed and shook my hand anyway. "Well, that's okay. See—you're not the only one here early." He waved his arm toward a half dozen other students now in the room and seated at desks before smiling kindly at me again. "And you are?"

"Rachel. Rachel Fletcher."

"Fletcher! Interesting. I have another Fletcher this hour, too!"

"Hey, Brother Clawson!"

A second later, an extremely hyper girl rushed in to gush about how excited she was to have Brother Clawson as a teacher again, and while she continued to babble at him, I casually looked around the room to see who all was in my first class of the day.

I was surprised to see that the class was clearly a mix of sophomores, juniors, and seniors, but what made my eyes really fly open was seeing a blond-haired boy two desks up and a couple of rows away from me, hunched over his desk with his scriptures flipped open.

"Dallin? No way!" I whispered. He couldn't have heard me—he couldn't have—but two seconds later, he lifted his head, turned, and looked at me. I looked away and flipped nervously through my own set of scriptures.

"Hey, Ackerman!"

I jumped again. That voice was familiar. Very familiar. I turned my head to see who had just entered the classroom barely ahead of a group of noisy girls, and my heart jumped and skipped at the incredibly handsome, familiar face.

Jason! Jason West was in my first class of the day!

Dallin turned halfway around in his seat and grinned while Jason slid into the desk behind him. It was the best seat in the room for Jason to have chosen. I could easily see him without having to turn my head at all. Wonderful. Perfect. His dark, nearly black hair was wet and shiny. I'd heard he'd been practicing with the varsity football team all summer, and he had the muscles and tanned skin to prove it. He'd carried in a backpack, too, and was wearing a maroon T-shirt with "Central High Football" on the front of it in gold lettering.

Nice scenery. Very nice.

"Wow—look at that eye! It's not so huge anymore!"

Dallin laughed. "Yeah, it's getting better."

"So how come you didn't try out for football?"

Dallin shrugged. "Didn't feel like it. I made the golf team instead."

Jason almost gasped. "But you were on the sophomore team last year, and you were good! I saw you play! You easily would've made junior varsity. Probably varsity!"

Dallin only grinned and shrugged again. "Maybe."

"I heard the coaches talk about you once. They were pretty disappointed you never showed up to try out."

"I know. They called my dad about it."

Jason laughed and punched Dallin lightly in the shoulder. "See—I told you you were good! What did your dad say?"

"Said it was up to me. He already knew I wanted to try for the golf team."

"Why'd you pick golf over football?"

Dallin laughed. "Because you don't get beat up on a golf course! Besides—I'm not that great at football. I'm not freakishly good at it like you are!"

Jason laughed back. "Yeah, right!"

"If I went for football, I'd sit on the bench and never play, but on the golf team, I'll actually get to play. That made the decision easy."

Jason nodded, and then out of nowhere, he turned his head and looked directly at me with those huge blue eyes of his before flashing me a smile. I blushed and smiled tentatively back.

"Hey, Rachel!"

I couldn't believe he remembered my name, and before I could squeak out more than a "hi," Dallin turned and looked at me, too, and waved a hello. And then Brother Clawson hurried up to the front of the room from where he'd been hello-ing with a group of students and turned around to face us all with a huge smile before sitting on the front edge of his desk.

"Good morning, everyone! And to you sophomores, welcome to Central High! And to you juniors and seniors, welcome back! I'm Brother Clawson, and this year, we're studying a book of scripture that was buried in the ground for hundreds of years here in the Americas. Can anyone tell me what book that might be?"

Most everyone mumbled "Book of Mormon."

Brother Clawson grinned and gave us the thumbs-up signal. "See, I knew you guys were smart! Okay—we should probably start off with a song and a prayer—"

And with that, my first day of high school seminary was underway.

Brother Clawson decided to do something I hadn't done since elementary school: He went around the room and made us introduce ourselves and tell something unique about ourselves or something interesting we'd done that summer. I was dreading my turn, not wanting to say anything. I wasn't going to talk about *It*, even if everyone in the room was thinking of *It* in connection with me. The only other thing I could think of was, "My mom's hanging out with Dallin's dad." I wondered what

Dallin would do if I said that, and then in true horror, I wondered if Dallin was going to mention it and prayed he wouldn't. Thankfully he didn't, and he said he and his dad had gone to Hawaii for part of the summer with his brother, Brandon, and his wife, Natalie.

Jason laughed and said he hadn't done anything interesting all summer because of football practice.

Brother Clawson smiled. "Well, I'd say that's unique in and of itself. Not everyone gets to play football for Central High all summer long!"

By the time Brother Clawson worked his way around the room to me, my heart was pounding, because the only other thing I could remember about summer was babysitting Ryan, but I wasn't about to bring that up, either. So I floundered and said I hadn't done anything interesting all summer, and that there wasn't anything unique about me. I hoped Brother Clawson would leave it at that. Instead, he cleared his throat dramatically.

"Well, that's not true. We've got Central's resident poet right here in our class. Her poems are amazing! I just know you're going to be published someday!"

I wanted to sink under my desk. *Note to self: Never write poetry during seminary ever again!*

"You write poetry, Rachel? That's cool."

If it wasn't for Jason's comment and Dallin's surprised look followed by his smiling and nodding at me, I was sure the class would've exploded with laughter.

"Yep, she's always scribbling in her notebooks. She's got millions at home."

My heart stopped at that way too familiar voice behind me. I didn't have to turn around to be sure who it was, although everyone else did.

"Hey, Fletch!" Jason again.

Brother Clawson smiled and nodded at Ryan. "So you must be the other Fletcher in the class. You're . . . Ryan. Ryan Fletcher?"

Ryan nodded and loudly said, "Yep."

"Related to our poet Rachel here?"

I sighed. *Yes, unfortunately.*

Ryan grinned back at Brother Clawson. "Unless our mom is lying to one of us."

I finally dared to glance behind me. Ryan had dropped himself noisily into the only empty desk in the back of the room—the one directly behind mine. A plastic cola bottle with a twist-off cap and dirty remnants of bits of the label was on his desk, and watching him sip from it before glaring at me challengingly, I had a feeling there wasn't any cola in it.

"I thought you weren't coming!" I whispered angrily.

Ryan grinned and held up a ten-dollar bill.

"What's that?"

"Incentive. From Mom."

I gasped. I was shocked. Truly shocked. "Mom's *paying* you to go to seminary?"

"Who would've guessed—you *are* smarter than you look!" Ryan chuckled and pocketed the money. "Yep, ten bucks a class. That's an easy fifty bucks a week."

I narrowed my eyes at Ryan's grin. "Smirk while you can. I'll be sure to let Mom know if you don't show up!"

I turned back around and closed my eyes when Ryan kicked the back of my chair hard. I prayed that he wouldn't do anything worse for the rest of the class.

CHAPTER ELEVEN

Thankfully, Ryan only slumped in his desk, sipped on his drink, and stayed pretty quiet for the rest of the hour. He disappeared out the door before I did, and after catching up with Teresa, who squealed and giggled when I told her Jason West was in my class, I tried to forget about Ryan and his pop bottle so I could focus on my first class inside Central High itself. I had the usual subjects that year—English, math, and U.S. history—but best of all, I had creative writing with Mrs. Townsend for the last hour of the day.

Creative writing was a mixed-grade class, like seminary. I didn't know anyone well in the class, and I was glad. I wanted to focus on learning about poetry and fiction and writing my own poetry and fiction without any distractions and hopefully wow Mrs. Townsend while I became the best writer she'd ever had in her class.

That was the dream, anyway. Even so, I didn't want to be the geek who entered the classroom first, so I loitered in the hall until at least ten students filed in before grabbing one of the seats in the back. Unlike Brother Clawson, however, Mrs. Townsend stayed seated at her desk with her head bent low, writing fast with a pen, and didn't acknowledge anyone coming into the room.

I glanced around the room at the prints of famous paintings hanging all over the walls: Claude Monet's *The White Water Lilies* with the weeping willows and bridge arching across the middle of the painting. And one of a field of red flowers with a woman in a yellow hat carrying a blue parasol with a small boy walking beside her also wearing a hat. It was titled *Les Coquelicots*. And a print of *The Lady of Shalott*, by John William Waterhouse, sailing mournfully in a small boat down the river to Camelot. There was also a painting of William Shakespeare on the wall and quotations of his like "Neither a borrower nor a lender be" and "To thine own self be true."

Be Your Own Kind of Beautiful.

I nodded to myself and leaned my elbows on my desk with my chin in my hands, staring thoughtfully at Monet's water lilies painting. I jumped when the bell rang.

Mrs. Townsend set her pen down before standing up to move to the front of the room, dragging a stool behind her. She was tall and thin with short, dark brown hair, and as she seated herself on the stool, she adjusted her glasses on the end of her nose before folding her arms and smiling a closed-mouth smile at us.

"Well, you've nearly survived your first day of school. Think you can make it through one more class?"

Mrs. Townsend received a few chuckles and "yeahs" for that, and after a quick read-through of the roll, she handed out the syllabus.

"As you know, this is a creative writing class. Maria Denny on the front row, please read the course description."

"Students will increase their skills in writing prose, poetry, and short stories."

"Exactly. We'll be spending the first semester on poetry, though, so prepare your minds for that. Now, let's see—Mitch Leatham. Please read the course objectives."

"To provide time and guidance for creative writing, thus for self-expression, and time for prewriting, drafts, and group and teacher editing."

Mrs. Townsend nodded. "If nothing else, I hope this class will indeed provide you with time each day to put down your creative thoughts and time for me to guide you in helping to make something out of those thoughts. Creative writing can do many wonderful things. It can have a positive effect on mental health, particularly expressive writing and journaling. Writing about your deepest thoughts and feelings, especially regarding a traumatic event, can be quite therapeutic. Some of the best creative writing there is comes from the darkest moments in a writer's life." Mrs. Townsend looked at the clock briefly before glancing at the roll in her hand again. "Russell Stevens, please read the types of daily assignments."

"Students will write in response to discussion, pictures, music, poems, and stories. They will then polish first drafts and aspire to publish."

Mrs. Townsend nodded again. "Exactly so. There are several contests coming up that you will be required to enter for your grade, both poetry and short story contests, so be thinking about that. Rachel Fletcher, please read the last paragraph of class conduct."

I jumped and nervously cleared my throat. "Students must write on demand and not wait for inspiration or the right mood. Such a wait can be very long indeed. Ideally, students should feel able to risk a little—to risk honesty and sharing."

"Exactly so again. Waiting for the creative mood to strike is ridiculous. If one waited for the mood to strike in order to do other things in life such as washing dishes, cooking meals, or cleaning your room, these things likely would never get done. A good writer disciplines himself or herself to spend a certain amount of time a day, preferably at the same time each day, to simply write. My hope is to help you get into that habit by writing every day at this same hour in class in response to whatever we discuss." Mrs. Townsend tossed the roll onto her desk, folded her arms, and looked at each of us in turn. "So. Let's begin! Take out a piece of paper. Maybe three. And your pens."

I took out a red notebook from my backpack that I'd bought specifically for this class and gripped my pen, waiting.

Mrs. Townsend slowly looked at each one of us. "I need to get to know all of you and see what kind of writing talent you have. Or at the very least, I need to get to know your writing style as it currently exists.

So." Mrs. Townsend stood up abruptly, pushed her stool to the side, and wrote on the chalkboard:

"These I have loved":

"These I do love":

"What am I?":

Mrs. Townsend turned back around to face us, holding her chalk behind her back. "Now, respond to these three statements. Tell me what you loved as a child. Anything you want. And then tell me what you now love. Then tell me what you are. List them out for me. Be creative."

Mrs. Townsend hurriedly scrawled three fast, short, free-verse style poems on the chalkboard about herself to illustrate all three statements and then nodded to us.

"Now, write me three such poems about yourselves. Don't worry about rules. Just tell me about yourselves."

I stared at the blue lines on the white paper before me for a moment and then gripped my pen against the first line of blue.

These I have loved.

Warm, early morning breezes,
Sunlight turning crystal to rainbows,
The first sign of peaches, and the taste
Of the first one ripened.
Bedazzling arrays of dancing, colorful
Flowers, skipping in new shoes,
Pink and lavender hair ribbons, and
Jouncy, long curls.
Soft fur, and wide-eyed, lacy-covered
Dolls, and popsicles melting in the sun.
A surprise just for me on a nonessential
Day, and soft bristles being
Run through my hair.

These I do love.

Breathing untouched mountain air,
The smell of a new book. The safe feeling

Of a familiar place, and the peaceful
Feeling of a favorite spot—my own oasis.
Photographs of well-loved faces, faded
And old.
A pleasant sound—soft music, a
Soothing voice, rippling waves on a tranquil
Summer's evening, and the sound
Of nothing—absolute quiet.
A friendly smile, a stolen glance,
The feel of new clothes, and the feeling
Of comfortable old ones.
A happy ending, a freshly dusted
Room, and a soft bed to sleep in.
Happy dreams of fantasies come true.
All of these have been and will always
Be those I love.

What Am I?

What am I? I am a bridge—I help others get across the rough seas in their lives.
What am I? I am a broom, used to get rid of unpleasant things whether I want
to be used or not.
What am I? I am a fire that will die unless attention is occasionally given to it.
What am I? I am an island in the middle of a tumultuous sea that threatens
to drown me.
What am I? I am the last rose fighting to survive as winter storms approach.

I jumped when the bell rang.

"Congratulations. You made it through your first day of school. Please hand me your work at the door. You'll receive it back tomorrow, and we'll write again."

I handed Mrs. Townsend my three poems and smiled briefly at her before hurrying down the hall to meet up with Teresa.

CHAPTER TWELVE

I'd been looking forward to Labor Day ever since I'd found out two weeks before that Robert and Wendy were coming to spend the long weekend with us. I'd called Robert to fill him in about what had been going on between Mom and Mr. Ackerman, but he'd cut me off before I could get very far.

"I know, Rachel. Mom already told me. That's why Wendy and I are driving up for Labor Day weekend."

I couldn't wait for Robert and Wendy to arrive on Friday, partly because I figured that meant Mr. Ackerman wouldn't be coming around since we'd have extra family with us, but mostly because I was hoping Robert would convince Mom to nix her thing with Mr. Ackerman.

Robert and Wendy had been in the house for only an hour, though, before Mom announced we were all going out to dinner. At one of the fancy restaurants in the city, no less.

"So let's all change into our Sunday best and get ready to go. Our reservations are for seven o'clock."

No one had said the word *Ackerman* at all until Robert pulled his SUV into the parking lot of the restaurant.

Ryan had been slumped in the backseat beside Mom and me when he sat up and stared at a vehicle near the door to the restaurant. "Hey—that looks like Ackerman's Lexus!"

And it did, too. Mr. Ackerman drove a really shiny, brand-new, silver four-door Lexus that looked suspiciously like the one at the restaurant.

"Mom!" I choked.

Mom squirmed uncomfortably before squaring her shoulders. "It looks like the Ackermans' vehicle because it *is*. We're having dinner with them tonight."

"What?" Ryan exploded.

"I wanted Robert and Wendy to meet Joe, and Joe asked his oldest son, Brandon, and his wife, Natalie, to join us as well so that we can all get to know each other a little."

I couldn't speak a word. Neither could anyone else in the car. Ryan mumbled something that could've been cursing, but no else could even breathe. At least, I knew I couldn't. Robert sat gripping the steering wheel with a stunned look on his face.

Wendy was the first to make noise by nervously clearing her throat. "Well, this should be . . . interesting."

I felt a bizarre level of comfort upon walking into the dimly lit restaurant to see Dallin, his brother, Brandon, who was every bit as blond as Dallin, and his wife wearing the same stunned looks on their faces as I was sure we still had on ours. Mr. Ackerman was wearing a strained smile when he jumped up to welcome us as one of the waiters ushered us to a table.

"Elaine!"

Mr. Ackerman gave Mom a brief hug while Robert stiffened beside me, watching. I saw Brandon and his wife stiffen as well with widened eyes, and I wondered how much—or, more likely, how little—they'd been told about Mom and Mr. Ackerman's "thing."

Awkward introductions and handshakes went around the table as Robert, Wendy, Ryan, and I sat across from Dallin, Brandon, and Natalie. Mom seated herself by Mr. Ackerman, who pulled her chair out for her as she smiled up at him nervously.

Lame, stilted, uncomfortable conversation limped around the table. I was sure everyone was hoping someone would scream "Fire!" so we'd all have an excuse to run away like crazy. But of course, no such luck. After catching Dallin look over at me once with a small smile, I looked away, grabbed my water glass and nervously swallowed half its contents, and then kept my eyes on my plate or my own family members.

I'd never considered myself to be psychic in any way, but anyone could plainly see by the way Mom and Mr. Ackerman kept nervously smiling at each other with eyes that sparkled too much that they'd cornered us for something more than just to meet and eat expensive food all dressed up in a fancy restaurant. As soon as the waiter had taken our orders and removed the menus, my suspicions were confirmed.

Mr. Ackerman cleared his throat and took hold of Mom's hand, causing just about everyone to stiffen and stare at the two of them again. Then he smiled at all of us and launched into a speech about how he'd never expected to meet anyone special again, and how amazing Mom was, and how much she meant to him. I couldn't listen to anything else after that due to the silent screaming echoing in my head.

"I've asked Elaine to marry me."

Mom smiled hopefully around the table at everyone. "And I told Joe yes!"

My whole body shook. Hard. I kept my eyes down on my clenched hands in my lap, willing myself not to cry. If I let myself, I knew I'd never stop. *"I'm sorry, honey. There was nothing anyone could have done. Your father was killed instantly."* I never wanted to feel that horrifying shock again, and yet here it was, drowning me all over again.

Mr. Ackerman wouldn't stop talking. "There's not going to be any fuss. We'll just be married at Elaine's ward house. Probably in the Relief Society room."

And neither would Mom. "And just a small dinner with family afterwards. Something like this!"

Robert looked as if he'd seen ten ghosts. "When—how—how did this happen?"

Mr. Ackerman kept his smile on his face. "I proposed to Elaine a week ago. In the temple, actually."

Mom kept her smile glued to her face, too. "Joe and I have been going to the temple together a lot lately. Last week, while we were in the celestial room after the session, Joe asked me to marry him."

"And you never told anyone?" Wendy blurted out.

Mom continued smiling. "We wanted to wait and tell you in person all at once."

"Have you set a date?" Brandon had finally found his voice, too.

Mr. Ackerman nodded. "Yes, actually, we have. We've already talked to our bishops, and we've made arrangements to be married in two weeks."

Shocked gasps and one- and two-word exclamations were passed around the table while everyone just kept staring at Mom and Mr. Ackerman.

"And then what happens?" Robert again.

"We decided it would be easier if Joe and Dallin moved in with us. We've got more room, and Dallin can have your old room."

"But you've only known each other for two months!" That was from Natalie.

Questions started to really fly hard and fast at Mom and Mr. Ackerman from everyone after that. Mostly from my side of the table, but Dallin's brother threw in a few good, concerned questions of his own. The whole situation was so bizarre and awkward that within minutes, I felt strangely lightheaded, as if at any second I was going to pass out and slide under the table. Or dissolve into hysterical tears. I wasn't sure which one would be worse, but I was afraid one or the other was going to happen to me before the night was over.

I looked hatefully at Mr. Ackerman, but as I watched him look around the table at everyone and then back at Mom, I could see something that almost made me feel sorry for him. He was nervous. I was sure about that, but when he looked at Mom, I would've had to have been blind not to see that he was in love with her and that he was ready to do anything for her.

My stomach sank as I glanced at Ryan, who was slouched beside me.

He was staring vacantly ahead, dry-eyed, his hands shoved deep into his pockets.

I feel nothing. I could almost hear the defiant words forming inside his head.

———•———

The night went on painfully for too long, and no one ate much of their dinner. I felt a surge of mean satisfaction watching Mr. Ackerman pull out his credit card to pay for nine expensive, hardly touched dinners. Somehow I was able to contain myself until Mom said her good-byes to Mr. Ackerman and we'd all climbed into Robert's SUV before the dam broke and I was crying. Hysterically.

"How could you do this? How?"

Mom turned around in the front seat beside Robert and put her hand on my knee worriedly. "Rachel, sweetie—it's going to be all right—"

I shoved her hand away. "All right? No, it's not! You don't even know this guy!"

"I know he's kind and good and makes me happy—"

"Don't—don't! I don't want to hear it!" And then I screamed that she didn't know what she was doing—that she didn't love Dad anymore, and how could she do this to Dad, to me, to all of us. Wendy shushed me and put her arm around me while I cried on her shoulder. Mom tried to deny my accusations, but I cried louder and tried to drown out her words.

"Rachel, honey—please—I've prayed to find someone. Someone who would make our family whole again. Mr. Ackerman is so good and wonderful, and he really wants for his family to be a family with us . . ."

"Just stop it, Mom! Just stop it!" I bawled.

Mom turned back around and stared ahead, quietly wiping her eyes. Robert drove silently while Ryan slouched on the other side of Wendy, staring out the side window.

Mom cleared her throat and looked into the rearview mirror. "Well, Ryan, you haven't said anything. What do you think?"

Ryan didn't turn his head from staring out the window. "I don't see how you can marry him. He's easily ten of the most boring people I know."

I couldn't believe that was all Ryan had to say on the subject, but he closed down completely and refused to talk to anyone after that. He jumped out of Robert's SUV to go hibernate in his room even before Robert had turned off the engine.

Robert and Wendy stayed up half the night talking to Mom, but none of what they said made any difference. Mom was marrying Mr. Ackerman in two weeks. Period.

I got up early Saturday morning and tried to talk to Mom about what I was sure had to be nothing more than a bad dream, but Mom stiffly assured me that last night was not a dream at all and that screaming at her wasn't going to change anything.

"This conversation is over, Rachel. Now, I need to head into the city to make a few wedding arrangements. You're welcome to come with me if you promise to be pleasant."

"I'll promise to be pleasant if you promise not to marry Mr. Ackerman."

"You know I won't do that."

"Then I can't promise you anything, either, so no, thanks."

Wendy couldn't stand seeing Mom go off alone, and because Ryan had disappeared as usual, that left Robert and me alone in the house.

Robert sat beside me on the couch in the living room while I dully flipped through television stations with the remote before he gently took the remote out of my grip and switched the television off. "So where do you think Ryan took off to?"

I shrugged. "Who knows and who cares?" I rubbed my eyes with the heels of my hands. "I can't believe Mom is actually doing this!"

Robert rubbed my shoulder awkwardly. "It's going to be okay, Rachel."

I shoved his hand away. "Easy for you to say! You're not the one who's going to have to live with him! I don't want a stepfather! I can't believe Mom could even think of doing this!"

"Mom's lonely, and she's still young. She shouldn't have to live the rest of her life alone already."

I stared in horror at Robert's set face. "Are you saying you're okay with this?"

Robert shook his head sadly. "No, I'm not. I think it's too fast and too soon. But it's not my decision, and it's not my life."

I turned back to stare stonily at the television with my arms folded tightly across my chest. "He's nothing at all like Dad. The total polar opposite, in fact. He's quiet, and he's never funny." I could feel my whole body starting to shake again. "He doesn't belong in this family. He doesn't belong in my life, and I don't think he belongs in Mom's life, either." I couldn't say anything else because I was crying again. I wasn't going to like Mr. Ackerman or let him be part of my life. Ever. I would never betray Dad like that.

Robert pulled me into his arms and let me cry all over his shoulder. "I just can't believe she's really going to do this!" I blubbered. "Without telling any of us or asking us what we thought about it. She just said yes without thinking how this would affect the rest of us!"

Robert held me and patted my back. "It's hard when you're not a kid anymore but you're not an adult yet. You know what that means?"

"No," I sniffed.

Robert drew back to look at me seriously. "That means, like it or not, Mom isn't always going to include you in every big decision she has to make. She's not required to. She's an adult, and she's your mom, so she doesn't have to ask for your permission to do anything. Not even to get married, even though it's going to affect your life, too."

I sniffed hard again. "It would have been nice if she would've at least asked me how I felt about this and given me some warning, instead of throwing this at me and everyone else at once, especially when I'm going to have to live with him!"

Robert nodded and handed me the box of tissues on the lamp table beside him. "True, this whole thing might have been smoother if Mom had asked us how we feel about the changes coming up, especially you and Ryan, since you still live here. But the fact remains that either way, whether she talked to you first or not, you still wouldn't have any say in the whole thing." Robert tried to smile as he wiped a few new tears off my face. "This is Mom's decision, and as long as you live here, you're going to have to deal with that."

I blew my nose hard in a wad of tissues and wiped the tears that wouldn't stop coming from my eyes. There was something about the resolved, albeit unhappy, tone in Robert's voice that made cold realization force me to see this whole nightmare was pretty much final. Cut and dried.

"I still wish she would've given me some warning instead of blurting it out in public like that. In front of Dallin and everyone else! It would've been nice to know that she at least cared about my opinion, and yours and Ryan's, enough to ask us first before saying yes!"

Robert frowned. "Who's Dallin?"

I wiped my eyes again with more tissues. "Mr. Ackerman's son. He sat across from you at dinner last night. He goes to Central High, too. I have a class with him, and now he's going to be living here, too!" The thought drained the blood from my face. For the first time since the horrible announcement had been made, I thought of Dallin and wondered how he felt about the whole thing: getting a stepmom and having to move into our home and deal with me and Ryan.

"Well, Ryan will be here, too. Speaking of, how's Ryan doing? He looks like he's lost weight, and his eyes were all bloodshot. I couldn't get him to talk to me . . ."

Ryan. I mouthed the word silently as I pictured his inevitable stumbling into the house later that night and all the nights to come before the wedding and after. I covered my face with my hands when I felt tears clouding my eyes again.

CHAPTER THIRTEEN

There are too many
"why's"
In this world
Curling snake-like
Surrounding every tree of innocence
And lying in every puddle of grass
Waiting for careful footsteps
And then—
The cry follows like a screaming shadow.
Why?
There are too many
"why's"
In this world
And not enough "yes's,"
Lung-felt sighs, happy Cinderella endings,
Satins, smooth on purpose
And tree barks, rough on purpose.
There are too many
"why's"
In this world.

I stared at the words before rubbing my eyes and leaning my head on my arm. Ryan had kept himself in line until Wendy and Robert left Monday afternoon, but he'd stumbled into the house at 3 A.M. the next morning, leaving a mess in the bathroom that kept me up for an hour cleaning up both him and it.

I sighed as Dad's face swam before my eyes.

"Where are you going, Rachel?"

"I'm running away!"

"Running away? Can I come, too?"

Dad smiled, his arms reaching for me.

"Be your own kind of beautiful, Rachel."

I jumped when I felt someone tap my shoulder, my pen flying from my fingers to land behind me on the carpet. Brother Clawson was standing beside me looking down with a kind but concerned smile.

"Rachel, would you read Second Nephi, chapter 2, verse 27?"

Face definitely aflame, I shoved my blue notebook to the side of my desk, ignoring the curious stares, smirks, and giggles from everyone else in the room as I furiously scrambled for the right page in my scriptures.

"Um, Second Nephi . . . ?"

Brother Clawson continued to smile at me kindly. "Chapter 2, verse 27."

I could still feel everyone's stares, but I kept my eyes bent low over my scriptures. "'Wherefore, men are free according to the flesh; and all things are given them which are expedient unto man. And they are free to choose liberty and eternal life, through the great Mediator of all men, or to choose captivity and death, according to the captivity and power of the devil; for he seeketh that all men might be miserable like unto himself.'"

"Thank you, Rachel." Brother Clawson patted my shoulder and moved back to the front of the room to lean against the edge of his desk, where he picked up an old broom handle and twirled it in his hands.

"Agency is an incredibly precious gift our Father in Heaven has given to us. So precious that a war was fought in heaven over it." Brother Clawson stopped twirling the stick, smiled, and laid it down on the carpet in front of him. "But with this gift of being able to choose, as with any important gift, there's responsibility. When we make a decision, something else happens." Brother Clawson looked up and pointed at Jason. "Jason. Come grab the end of the stick pointing at you and pick it up."

Jason jogged forward and did just that.

"Now, what happened to the other end of the stick?"

Jason handed the stick back to Brother Clawson. "It came up, too, with my end."

Brother Clawson nodded. "Exactly. You can't pick up one end of a stick without picking up the other end at the same time. So if one end of a stick is Choice, what would the other end be called?"

"Consequence," Dallin called out.

Brother Clawson nodded at Dallin. "Exactly right, Dallin. When we exercise our agency to make a choice, we also pick up the choice's consequence at the same time. So when we make a good choice, like reading our scriptures, we pick up the great consequence of learning more that will add to our knowledge and help us continue to make wise choices. But when we make poor choices, or 'transgress,' then we have to deal with those consequences." Brother Clawson ran his hand from one end of the stick to the other. "No doubt about it. There is always a consequence for transgression. You have control over your decisions but not over the consequences. That's a fact most people forget when they choose to make a bad choice, because basically no one is ever prepared for the consequences of sin." Brother Clawson nodded slowly and tapped one end of the stick against the carpet. "The sad thing about getting involved in any type of sin is that the sin can easily turn into an addiction, be it chemical, alcohol, pornography—whatever. And once you're dependent on any type of addiction, the ability to choose disappears. Even if you want to stop and would if you could, you feel as if you've lost the ability to choose for yourself. Few things are worse than feeling hopeless, as if there is no way out because your ability to choose is gone."

Brother Clawson laid the stick across his desk and turned back to all of us with a smile. "Our Father in Heaven has given us some advice to help us make wise choices and stay away from potential addictive pitfalls. Can someone read Alma 37:35?"

Jason raised his hand. "'O, remember, my son, and learn wisdom in thy youth; yea, learn in thy youth to keep the commandments of God.'"

Brother Clawson nodded at Jason. "Our Father has promised us blessings beyond our wildest dreams if we simply are obedient and keep His commandments. You're better off learning now to keep the commandments so that doing so will be part of your nature as you grow in the gospel. It'll make it easier to make wise, good decisions and not be fooled into making poor choices."

Brother Clawson had looked at me and Ryan, who had chosen to slouch in the seat directly behind me again today with his old, dirty plastic pop bottle that he'd sipped on during class. I still couldn't believe Mom was paying Ryan to go to seminary, but when I'd cornered her about it the first day of school, she'd only shrugged miserably and said she'd do whatever she had to for Ryan.

"He needs to go to seminary. I'm sure he'll thank me someday for getting him there."

Glancing over my shoulder at that dirty pop bottle, I didn't have to guess where the seminary money was likely going. As horrifying as it was to know that Ryan had more than just soda in his pop bottle every day at school, at least he never drank enough during class to make him clearly and obviously drunk. He at least had enough sense to be that careful. Today, though, I had worse things to worry about. I squirmed in my seat, shocked that I'd been caught sleeping in class—something I'd never done before in my whole entire life—while my heart pounded, wondering what would happen to me as a result. Would Brother Clawson call my mom? Torture me after class? Kick me out of class? I'd already had to deal with the humiliating consequence of being caught sleeping in class by the teacher and everyone else. There couldn't possibly be a much worse consequence for my sleepless decision last night, thanks to Ryan. I glanced behind me at the offender, but Ryan only stared out the window, his scriptures closed, seemingly oblivious to everything going on around him.

"Both of those verses are scripture mastery scriptures, so you probably ought to mark them." I reached for my pen and then remembered it was somewhere on the floor behind me. I leaned down to grab it but couldn't see it anywhere.

"Looking for something?"

I jumped at the sound of Ryan's voice, and when I turned around, there was my blue pen, hanging out of Ryan's right nostril.

"Gross! Not anymore!" I reached for my backpack to scrounge for a new pen, but Ryan laughed loudly and leaned forward, tossing the pen onto my desk before tugging at my hair.

"Ouch! What was that for?"

"Sorry. Thought I saw something in your hair."

Ryan lurched out of the room while the bell was still ringing, even before Brother Clawson dismissed class. I had stuffed my notebook and scriptures into my backpack and just made it out the door before Brother Clawson could stop me when I felt a hand on my arm.

"Hey, Rachel—wait up."

I was sure I'd been caught by Brother Clawson, but my eyes widened in surprise when I turned around. It was Dallin. "What do you want?"

"You've got gum in your hair."

I stared at Dallin's unsmiling face. "What? No, I don't!"

"You do. In the back. Right in here somewhere."

Dallin reached to touch the back of my head, but I drew back sharply and felt the back of my head myself. "I don't feel anything!"

Dallin stuck his hand in his pocket. "Well, I can guarantee you there's gum in there."

"How do you know?"

"I saw Ryan do it. I just thought you should know."

I ran my hand through my hair and glared at Dallin. "I still don't feel anything!"

Dallin shrugged. "Whatever. See ya."

I stared at Dallin's back as he pushed the seminary building doors open and jogged to catch up with Jason West. For all I knew, he'd stuck a wad of something in my hair. *Stupid, dumb boys!* I irritably shoved through the doors myself, running my hand self-consciously again through my hair.

CHAPTER FOURTEEN

S o, is it going to be a salad again, Rachel?"

I nodded at Teresa as we shoved our way into Central High's cafeteria.

"Well, I want a hamburger, so give me your backpack so I can save us some seats, and I'll meet you over at that table, okay?"

Teresa stretched her arm to point towards a table near the back of the room. I nodded again and stood in line to build a chef's salad. My jeans had been feeling too tight lately. Likely due to too many Friday night pizzas with Teresa. She didn't have to worry because she never gained an ounce, no matter how much candy and pizza and soda and chips she ate, but all I had to do was look at a piece of pizza and I could feel my thighs expand.

The salad line turned out to be shorter than the burger line, so I stabbed at the green leaves and tomatoes with my fork, being careful not to use too much dressing, and munched down a few bites at our table, waiting for Teresa.

I looked up to take a swig of milk, just in time to see Jason West and a few of his varsity football friends sit down with their lunches a few tables away. I watched Jason laugh and smile his beautiful, big smile, my milk carton hovering near my mouth. I'd never seen such blue eyes on anyone before. It wasn't fair. Boys shouldn't have such incredible eyes, but Jason did. There was nothing anyone could do about it. I couldn't help sighing. In my opinion, the perfect senior class gift that my class could grace Central High with would have to be a bronzed, life-sized statue of Jason constructed on the top of our school.

"Don't even dream about it. He and Angela are practically married."

I'd been watching Jason with my milk carton an inch from my mouth for a good solid minute, whole-heartedly enjoying my reverie of him, when Teresa startled me enough that I nearly dropped my milk carton into my lap.

"Thanks for the encouragement," I grumbled, setting the milk carton safely back down by my salad while Teresa settled in at our table.

Teresa glanced over her shoulder before turning back to me. "There's Angela now. She's going to go sit by him. See?"

I watched while Angela did indeed go squeeze herself in next to Jason, putting her arm around him to whisper something in his ear that made him look at her and smile, causing my own smile to fade fast.

"They're practically soul mates." For a girl who was supposed to be my best friend, sometimes Teresa was really crummy at it.

"Okay, okay," I sighed. "So maybe I don't have a chance, but I don't care. I'm going to fantasize about him anyway." I stabbed at my salad determinedly with my fork.

"As long as you realize that nothing could ever happen," Teresa stated just as firmly. Some best friend.

Now, I loved Teresa dearly. She'd been my best friend forever, so I didn't feel bad or guilty if I said mean things about her to myself. Sometimes Teresa was such a realist she could make me physically sick.

"So how's your choir class?"

"It's okay," Teresa shrugged. "We're already working on some songs for the Christmas concert."

"Oh, yeah? Some good songs?"

"Yeah, some of the songs are pretty cool. We're doing the "Hallelujah Chorus" from *Messiah*, too. And guess what? Ms. McPhee, the choir teacher, is taking over the musical this year."

"Really? How come?"

Teresa shrugged again. "She wants to make sure the leads go to good singers."

"Has she picked a musical yet?"

"Yeah—*A Funny Thing Happened on the Way to the Forum.* It's supposed to be funny."

Jason looked up then, and my heart leaped into my throat. He was smiling! I smiled back, but Teresa kicked my foot under the table and looked pointedly over my left shoulder.

"Didn't you see her walk by a minute ago to grab some napkins?" Teresa hissed softly.

I didn't turn around but shook my head slightly and sat stiffly in my chair. Angela's blonde curls and her perfectly slender body bounced past our table towards Jason. She'd been standing behind me a few yards waving at him. I felt ten pounds fatter just watching her glide back over to Jason.

Teresa stared hard at me while I stared glumly back. "Don't you see? It's useless to like him. Entirely hopeless."

Yes, Teresa. I could see.

CHAPTER FIFTEEN

Mrs. Townsend liked to spend the first five minutes of class having us all write "nonstops," which sometimes meant writing whatever we wanted to for the first five minutes of class—journal writing, poetry, the beginnings of a short story, anything—and sometimes she'd have something written on the chalkboard for us to respond to. This time, she'd written something on the board.

"Art is a way we can break bread with the dead. Creative writing can be used to make some sort of sense of death and loss and feelings following such loss, leaving a type of memorial behind, perhaps re-creating life to produce the work of genius."

I wasn't sure what Mrs. Townsend was hoping to get from us—from me—but faster than I thought I would, I scribbled down in my red notebook:

> *Death*
> *Comes out from corners—*
> *Unexpected,*
> *Cold, frightening, and cruel*
> *Tightens its grip and*
> *Pulls and squeezes till nothing is*
> *Left but*
> *Death itself.*
> *Leaves behind nothing but an empty*
> *Shell,*

Tears, bitterness,
Injustice, anger.
It never comes at the right moment—
Always too soon, leaving blows of shock and deep sorrow,
And fear of wondering who will hear its call and feel its pull
Tomorrow.

She'd liked the free-verse poems I'd written the first day of school and had written the comments, "*Beautiful* moods and images, Rachel," and "These are all excellent, Rachel. They carry the feeling of truth in metaphor." I'd been pleased and relieved to know that so far she seemed to like my writing style.

"The first five minutes are up, class. Please pass your papers forward, and we'll begin talking about haikus and cinquains, and then you'll all write a few for me."

I liked the Japanese haiku form: Three lines of poetry containing five, seven, and five syllables, respectively, usually having a seasonal reference as well.

Campfire flickering—
Face caught mesmerized in flame
There against the night

First Dawn of today—
Dew glistening on a leaf
Shines, caught by the sun

The cinquain, however, was more challenging.

"The American poet Adelaide Crapsey developed this poetic form, which is related to, but not copied from, Japanese literary styles, such as haiku. Ms. Crapsey's five-line stanzas of cinquains are always unrhymed and have twenty-two syllables: five lines of 2, 4, 6, 8, and 2 syllables, respectively." Mrs. Townsend read Ms. Crapsey's cinquain "Triad" to us and then looked up from her poetry book to smile without opening her mouth. "Let's write some, shall we? Try to draw from your own life experience, if you can."

I stared at the blue lines on the white pages before me as my pen slowly scrawled across the page.

These be
Three ugly things:
Running blood . . . long believed
Lies . . . knowledge that the truth was kept
Silent.

Picture
Faded, not old
Frozen laugh, timeless smile
Long remembered, forever mourned
Sadness.

"Pass your haikus and cinquains to the front and take out another piece of paper. I want everyone to make a note of this, so there will be no room for excuses later. Please write down the numbers 1 and 2." Mrs. Townsend repeated the two numbers slowly. "Can anyone tell me the significance of these two numbers?"

No one could, so Mrs. Townsend smiled. "*One* represents the first month of the calendar. Now can anyone tell me?"

A girl in the back raised her hand. "Oh—January 2."

Mrs. Townsend nodded. "And what is January 2?"

Mitch Leatham called out, "The day we come back from Christmas break."

Mrs. Townsend smiled again and sat on her stool in front of the classroom. "Very good. It's also the date of something else in this class: the last possible date to hand in your own original piece, either poetry or a short story, as your final project for the semester."

Before too many groans could escape from the entire class, Mrs. Townsend continued. "And before you resolve to just throw any old thing down on paper, let me remind you that your piece needs to be of a quality high enough to submit to the creative writing contest this year among all the high schools in the state, as most assuredly, they *will* be submitted to the contest as your final project for your first semester in creative writing. I expect this class to produce exceptional work." Mrs. Townsend crossed her arms, drumming her fingers on her arms. "I'll be expecting a first draft in a few weeks and then a second draft by Thanksgiving. Central High has traditionally been well represented in this contest, and I would like to see that tradition upheld. Be assured that your grade depends upon it." Mrs. Townsend stopped her drumming fingers to smile at our opened mouths and whimpers of pain before speaking again. "Don't worry about winning the competition. Just let your imaginative juices flow and enjoy writing about whatever you desire. There *is* prize money involved, so if nothing else I've said has inspired you so far, hopefully that will do the trick."

CHAPTER SIXTEEN

I'd stared at all the paintings in Mrs. Townsend's classroom the rest of the class period, thinking about our assignment, praying for inspiration, and hoping I'd be able to figure out something to write about that would be special. Unique. Even if it didn't win a prize, I was determined to make sure that my piece would at least be something more than just a writing assignment for a grade in creative writing.

I still had the assignment on my brain while I walked home with Teresa when out of nowhere, the clouds ripped in half. Within minutes, Teresa and I were both soaked to the bone.

"Your house is closest, Rachel. Can you give me a ride from there?" Teresa gasped as we both ran through the storm.

"Probably—unless we drown first!"

I could see Mom's car in the driveway as we ran across the lawn. When we made it to the front porch, I turned to Teresa, strands of wet hair hanging in my eyes, and calmly said, "Does my hair look okay?"

Teresa giggled. "You should've used one of those hairsprays that protects against environmental elements." We were both laughing hard as we hurried into the house. I kicked the door shut with my foot before motioning Teresa to follow me down the hall.

"I'll ask my mom if I can borrow her car. You can blow-dry your hair—"

We both froze in mid-step at the sound of Ryan's slurred, sing-song sounding voice.

"Well, well, well, if it isn't Drippy," Ryan said, looking glassy-eyed at Teresa's wet hair and then turning to face me, "and Dippy." Ryan was slouched on the couch, half hiding a can of something behind a throw pillow. He was clearly buzzing from whatever he was drinking, and even though he gave something a kick underneath his feet, I could see a couple of silver cans peeking from under the couch, and a couple more under the television set.

Of all the stupidly bold, idiotic stunts—I glanced at Teresa, who was staring at Ryan with a deer-in-the-headlights look on her face.

I glared at Ryan, but he only glared darkly back with his bloodshot eyes. He clearly wasn't pleased to see me and have his binge interrupted, but that was fine with me, since I was never too pleased to see him, either, and certainly didn't like catching him drinking out in the open like this when I had a friend with me.

"Shut up, geek," I greeted him. "Where's Mom?"

Ryan turned away and stared blankly in front of him. "Not here."

I'd purposely kept myself out of any and all wedding plans, and since that was all Mom had on her mind now, we'd hardly spoken since the Labor Day Fiasco Dinner.

"Is she doing wedding stuff with Mr. Ackerman?"

Ryan didn't answer or look up. I threw my wet backpack down on the floor and angrily strode over to Ryan to stand in front of him. "Hello, is anyone home?" I yelled.

Teresa didn't say anything and instead made a beeline for my bedroom. For a person who could usually talk a mile a minute, she could never squeak out a syllable in front of Ryan. I made a face at Ryan's black glare before turning and following Teresa down the hall.

Once we were safe inside my room with the door firmly shut, Teresa's vocal cords moved into high gear. "Sorry I took off like that. It's just that your brother makes me so—*nervous.* Maybe if he was ugly I wouldn't get so stressed out around him."

I frowned as I searched for a brush and my blow-dryer. "But Ryan *is* ugly."

Teresa laughed. "You only say that because he's your brother. Other girls at school don't think so."

"They don't know him like I do."

Teresa sat on my bed, and after we blow-dried and brushed out her hair, mine had pretty much air dried, so she turned me around to brush through my hair without the blow-dryer. We hadn't spoken since we shut my bedroom door.

Teresa hesitantly spoke up. "Rachel—can I ask you something?"

"Sure. What?"

Teresa was silent for a few seconds before quietly asking, "Is—is Ryan okay?"

I stiffened. "Why do you ask?"

"I don't know. He's—he's different now."

I didn't answer.

Teresa tried again, just as quietly. "Um, can I ask something else?"

I shrugged and looked at the floor. "Go ahead."

"What was Ryan drinking? I saw some cans on the floor, and they kind of looked like . . ."

Teresa paused, and I tensed up tight as a drum, waiting—and then I'd jumped as the brush she'd been running through my hair snagged and stuck, causing me to yelp in pain.

"Hey—there's gum in your hair!"

"What?"

Teresa frowned and carefully removed the brush. "Yeah, it's definitely gum. Not a big wad, but enough to be a pain. I think I'm going to have to cut it out of your hair."

"Cut it out? Can't you brush it out?"

Teresa laughed. "No way. Look, it's only going to be a little piece. No big deal."

I sighed and dug out some scissors and winced at the snipping sound before Teresa presented me with the evidence. A blob of grayish-looking gunk had indeed been stuck in my hair. I thought of Dallin and cringed.

Teresa stood up and stretched before reaching for her book bag. "This has been fun, Rachel, but I've really got to get home. Do you think you can still give me a ride?"

"Yeah, I think I know where my mom's keys are."

I found the keys on the kitchen counter, and without saying anything to Ryan, who was still sitting in a stupor in front of the television, I gave Teresa a ride home. When I got back, Ryan was still on the couch, but now he had his arms folded with a scowl planted deeply on his face as he watched me walk through the front door.

"Know what I wish?"

"No," I said, tossing Mom's keys on the lamp table.

Ryan's words slurred as he tried to focus his eyes on me. "I wish we weren't going to Central at the same time. Having you there is ruining my senior year. I hate that you're in my seminary class, even if it *is* filled with a bunch of rejects." Ryan took another swig from the silver can in his fist. "I guess you fit right in."

"I love you, too, Ryan." I grabbed one of the throw pillows and chucked it at his head.

Ryan grabbed the pillow after it landed at his feet and easily beaned me in the face with it, laughing loudly and too long. "Loser. You can't even throw straight from four feet away. No wonder you're such an embarrassment."

I glared at him in disgust. "And you don't think you're an embarrassment to me?"

"I'm not the one falling asleep in seminary!"

"That's thanks to you, jerk! At least I'm not a stupid drunk!"

Ryan's eyes darkened even more. "I'm not a drunk!"

I rolled my eyes. "Oh, sorry—I meant 'closet alcoholic'!"

Ryan threw the empty can in his hand in my direction, but it bounced off the lamp shade. "At least I'm not a fat hog like you!"

Oh, of course. Ryan always pulled the fat card on me when he couldn't find a decent comeback. Even so, my Achilles heel hurt when it was stabbed like that, so of course I stabbed back. "At least I don't have to be paid to go to seminary, *and* I can walk a straight line at any given moment of the day, *and* I don't stink all the time, like you, you stupid alcoholic!"

"You stupid—" Ryan tried to jump up and lunge for me, but he tripped all over his feet, crashing into a lamp table before landing with a loud, hard thump on the floor.

I moved to stand in front of him with my hands on my hips, glaring angrily down at him. "You made me look stupid in seminary today. I realize you're used to looking stupid all of the time, but I'm not, and I don't appreciate being dragged down into your world, such as it is."

Ryan tried to focus his eyes on me. "Talk about the pan . . . telling the kettle . . . telling the pan—saying—"

"You'd be able to say it if you weren't stinking drunk!" I marched angrily into the kitchen and grabbed an empty trash bag before snatching up the beer cans all over the living room. "You wouldn't be able to make it without me, you know that? You think anyone else would do for you what I've been stupid enough to do? You don't care, though. You're too busy hiding in your room, destroying your liver, drinking yourself into a stupor everywhere you go. You wouldn't last a day if I didn't change your diapers all the time!"

I kneeled down to grab the cans from under the couch, but Ryan crawled over and grabbed a handful of my hair, jerking me hard into a sitting position.

"Ouch!" I screamed. "You're scalping me!"

"Don't ever talk to me like that again!" He let go of my hair and gave me a hard shove. Before he could do anything else, I grabbed the bag of cans and ran into my room, slamming the door hard. I squeezed my eyes shut tight and leaned against it with my heart thumping, praying that Mom would be home soon.

CHAPTER SEVENTEEN

We'd gone to Jackson Hole last summer, just the four of us, right before school started. Dad loved Grand Teton National Park and the hike around Jenny Lake.

"Let's take a breather here for a second and take some pictures. Rachel, stand by Ryan in front of that wooden fence so Jenny Lake will be in the background."

I moved to stand near Ryan, who pretended not to notice that I was near him.

"Okay, move in closer, Rachel—"

I did, and a second later, Ryan turned quick and yelled "Rarh!" in my face. I screamed and jumped and then laughed at Ryan's laughing face as Dad snapped the photo.

"Watch out—there's a mama bear with twin cubs coming down the trail!"

I panicked, screaming, but Dad moved fast, shoving us all up on top of a huge boulder just off the trail. I trembled and bawled, clinging to Mom, while Dad and Ryan excitedly took pictures of the black bear and her cubs. The cubs had appeared first, galloping down the trail as people screamed and dodged them as if it was all a fun game.

"Don't come near us—don't come near us!"

The mama bear had appeared next, lumbering wearily behind them. I hadn't been able to stop shaking and crying long after they'd moved on.

Dad had wrapped me up tight in his arms. "Rachel, honey, I'd never let anything happen to you. Do you want us to say a prayer?"

I nodded and bawled some more and only stopped after Dad said the prayer, the four of us sitting in a tight circle on top of the boulder.

Ryan and Dad laughed in the hotel room that night when we watched the news and saw the story of the mama bear and her cubs on the loose.

"Mug shots of a bear—you'd only see something like that on TV in Jackson Hole!"

I cried again, and Dad hugged me again.

"You're safe now, Rachel. You're safe—"

I turned around to smile at Dad but saw a stranger in a blue uniform instead. Beyond him through the living room window, red and blue lights were flashing over and over and Ryan's voice was screaming, "He was on his way to pick you up from your stupid friend's house!"

And then I was awake, shaking so hard I thought I'd never stop.

———•———

I have tried to search
These pages
Trapped inside the blackest cover
Without a flashlight for comfort.
Perhaps I am crazy—
Ready to be locked tight as a drum
Inside some glass cage
But not even braces
Could suffocate my words.
They would've dripped through my fingers
Out the tips
Anyway.
Rivers and rivers dripping, tripping to the Biggest Sea—
One I could never drown in,
Although some have refused their
Rings of life preservers
Like stale cups of coffee.
So I will collect them—
Cradle them dearer
More precious

Than any baby
And sleep on a shore
Without end.

It was Saturday, and after my visit to the cemetery with my blue note-book to tell Dad all about my creative writing class and all the great poets I was learning about and the poetry I was writing and then praying and wishing he would answer me about the wedding coming up faster and faster, hardly more than a week away now, I knew I needed some serious cheering up.

I grabbed the phone and dialed Teresa's number the second I arrived home.

"Let's go see a movie tonight." I needed to get away from the house, my family, the wedding, and everything that was going to descend after that and escape for a while.

I could almost see Teresa raising her eyebrows in surprise. "Really? Okay, sure. What's playing?"

"Who cares? Let's just pick one once we get there."

"Okay, Rachel. Whatever you say. Do you think you'll be able to get the car tonight?"

"I'll talk to my mom and make sure of it."

———•———

Ryan and I had been facing each other in the kitchen for a solid five minutes now with poor Mom acting as the referee standing between us, fighting over Mom's car.

"I need the car. I mean, I *really* need it," Ryan insisted darkly.

"You've got a car. Why do you need Mom's?"

"I've got a headlight out in the front, and I got a ticket for it the other day."

Mom stared at Ryan. "What?"

Ryan shrugged irritably. "It's no big deal, but I don't want to get stopped for it again!"

I almost said I'd seen the car on my way back from the cemetery that morning and that the right headlight was "out" because it had been smashed out and that the right front end looked a little crunched, but Ryan was glaring at me so darkly that I kept my mouth shut tight.

"That's your problem, not mine. Mom told me yesterday that I could borrow her car tonight if I wanted to!" I whined. Mom turned away from us, so we both turned as well to lean across the kitchen counter, imploring Mom like two lawyers facing a judge.

Mom sighed. "I'm sorry, Ryan, but Rachel's right. I did tell her she could take the car."

"Great! Thanks, Mom," I said happily.

Ryan gripped the kitchen counter tightly with both hands. "But I need it! You don't understand—I promised I'd have it."

"Well, I'm sorry, Ryan, but you shouldn't make promises like that until you talk to me first." With that, Mom tossed the keys to me and left the room.

Once she'd left, Ryan let me have it. "Spoiled brat. You *always* get your way."

I tried to walk away, but he followed me down the hall. I didn't turn around but kept on walking. "Yeah, right. Just go away—"

He cut me off angrily. "All I want is the stupid car keys for one night until I can get my car fixed, but no—you get them to do something stupid with Teresa."

I whirled around and faced him and actually looked him in the eye. "What's going on tonight that's so important that you need the car?"

"None of your business," he shot back coldly.

"You're just going to go get wasted at a party tonight, right? It's probably your turn to buy the beer, right? With your seminary money?" Ryan glared at me and wouldn't answer.

"Yeah, I thought so. Well, I'm doing all of us a favor. I'm not about to let you wreck Mom's car, too!"

Ryan scowled at the floor with his fists jammed into his Levi's pockets before whirling away from me, slamming his bedroom door shut behind him.

"I'm glad you wanted to go to a movie tonight, Rachel. Your depression lately is nearly killing me. Are the Ackermans really that bad?"

We were sitting in the theater listening to stale elevator music, waiting for the movie to start, while Teresa stuffed her face with buttered popcorn and diet cola.

I frowned. "The Ackermans?"

"Yeah. You know—the wedding and everything? It's almost here. I thought that's why you've been quiet."

I'd wanted to forget about that today and almost had. "I have to use the bathroom." I stood up and left before Teresa could say anything else.

When I came around the corner by the candy counter, there was only one guy in line waiting for popcorn. He looked up when I came into view. *Jason.* I felt shivers go down my spine and barely smiled at him. He looked at me in surprise, and then he smiled.

"Hey, Rachel!"

My heart pounded in my ears. "Hi, Jason," I breathed softly. I thought my legs might buckle, so before that could happen, I hurried on to the bathroom. I stared at myself in the mirror, checking to see if there'd been anything weird on my face when I walked by him. *How did my hair look?* I grimaced at my sad reflection. *Yuck,* I moaned inwardly. I shouldn't have worn a ponytail, and I definitely should've opted for some makeup. I stayed in the bathroom until I was sure he must've bought his popcorn and left. It wasn't until I hurried back into the theater and scanned it to make sure I couldn't see Jason anywhere that I realized I hadn't used the bathroom. I told Teresa what had held me up, and she threw a kernel of popcorn at me.

"You get a perfect opportunity to talk to him, and what do you do? You run and hide in the bathroom."

"Well, what am I supposed to do? Turn into Sexy Cindy again?" I froze the second the words were out of my mouth. I'd never let myself speak about the prank call and the night *It* happened. Not to Teresa or anyone else.

"Shush!" Teresa glanced over her shoulder. "He's practically right behind us," she whispered.

"What?!" I gasped. I turned around briefly and saw him cuddled up with Angela. For some reason, it depressed me worse than I'd expected to see him with his arm around her. *You're being stupid.* After all, what did I expect would happen—that he'd fall madly in love with me tonight and dump Angela? Well, sure, it would've been nice, but I wasn't a gorgeous blonde like she was, and our conversation at the candy counter hadn't exactly been sparkling.

I shook my head, forcing my thoughts aside, and punched Teresa's arm. "Why didn't you say something?"

"I thought you knew. You saw him at the candy counter," she said, keeping her voice low.

"I didn't think he was going to see *this* movie."

"Well—" Teresa began, but the movie started, so we both shut up. I tried to focus on the movie, but all I knew was that it was extremely long. The longest movie in history. I practically dragged Teresa behind me at a dead run to the car when it was over. At least, she thought so.

"I'm sure he didn't hear us. He was too wrapped up in Angela," Teresa insisted once we were safely inside Mom's car.

I couldn't help acting like a geek. The idea of him possibly overhearing us talking about him *and* finding out about my prank call as Sexy Cindy was enough to make me want to die.

"I still laugh when I think of your prank call to him."

"Shush, will you?" Even though the windows in the car were rolled up and I'd just started the engine, I was sure Jason and Angela and everyone outside walking from the theater to their cars could hear her.

"He's not going to hear us!" Teresa laughed.

"Yeah, well, I don't want to talk about it." I fumbled with the seat belt. "Just *thinking* about it makes me nervous. I must've been really insane to do it."

We were both quiet until Teresa carefully spoke again in a low voice. "Rachel, it's okay to laugh about stuff that happened before . . . you know. Your dad loved a good practical joke like that. He would've thought it was funny."

I stared out the windshield of the car, gripping the steering wheel. "Yeah, he would've." And I meant it. I knew Dad would've gotten a kick out of it.

Then a horrible thought crossed, unwelcome, into my brain. I looked over at Teresa in horror. "Hey—you don't think Jason recognized my voice, do you? I mean, he's been so nice to me in seminary."

"How could he? You've never talked to him much before."

I sighed. Typical Teresa. Always the realist. "Thanks for reminding me," I grumbled as I put the car into reverse and slowly backed out of our parking spot.

"Hey, considering the prank call, it's probably for the best." Teresa poked my arm and grinned. "Do you want to prank call him again tomorrow night?"

I almost snorted. "Are you crazy? I'm not ever doing that again. He'd figure something out if I did."

Teresa's eyes were sparkling. "Wait—you could 'accidentally' dial his number again, bring up how this happened once before, laugh about it, and just start talking to him instead."

"No way. Dumb idea." I was quiet for a second, thinking. "Even if he didn't hang up on me, he might eventually want to meet me, and then what?"

Teresa frowned. "Oh, yeah. I hadn't thought of that." We were both silent. "Well, he probably wouldn't ask to meet you. It would be funny—"

"Forget it," I interrupted. "It was fun to talk to him, even if it was as Sexy Cindy, but my acting career is definitely over."

CHAPTER EIGHTEEN

"Where are you going, Rachel?"
"I'm running away!"
"Running away? Can I come, too?"
"Don't come near us—don't come near us!"
"You're safe now, Rachel. You're safe—"
Be Your Own Kind of Beautiful.

The evening of Mom and Mr. Ackerman's wedding, I lay on top of my bed, staring dry-eyed at the ceiling after I'd made it home from school.

"Rachel, are you getting ready? Robert and Wendy are going to be here in half an hour!"

I sighed and threw my legs over the edge of my bed. Then I slid down until I twisted myself into a praying position. A prayer was probably a good idea. Like I'd done each night for months, I begged Heavenly Father to help Ryan get better. I was still reading my scriptures every morning and night, and still fasting nearly every Sunday. It was hard to go to church, thanks to the usual looks Ryan got, but I held my head up, gritted my teeth, and kept attending. Besides going to all the Young Women's activities, I'd even helped spearhead a service activity, and it had been a good one. I'd rounded up a bunch of girls to go to a rest home where we'd given the women manicures using crazy colors of nail polish topped off with tiny flower stickers and rhinestones. The ladies had a good time, and we'd coaxed them into confessing stories about their torrid teenage love affairs. I'd prayed for forgiveness for falling asleep in seminary not just once but a handful of times now, thanks to Ryan, and again promised I'd do my best to stop doing that. I'd horrified myself by falling asleep in creative writing a couple of times, too, but Mrs. Townsend was pretending not to notice. I wasn't sure why, but she'd chosen not to throw me out of class or report me or anything.

I sighed. Nothing had broken up Mom and Mr. Ackerman, and Ryan hadn't improved. At all. I ended my prayer, saying that since Heavenly Father had chosen not to break up Mom and Mr. Ackerman like I'd requested, now I was asking for strength to deal with the challenge of becoming a twisted Brady Bunch family, and again I asked that Heavenly Father would heal Ryan.

"Rachel! Are you ready?"

" . . . amen." I stood up and sighed resignedly. "Yes, I'm ready!"

I threw on the new peach-colored dress Mom had bought for me and secured my hair out of my face with a barrette. By the time I'd brushed my teeth and applied a little mascara and lip gloss to my face, Robert and Wendy had arrived and Mom had already left with Mr. Ackerman.

———•———

At Mom's request, I sat on the front row of the blue cushioned chairs in the Relief Society room of our ward house between Robert and Wendy. Even though Robert had his arm around me and Wendy held my hand, I kept my eyes glued to the carpeted floor throughout the ceremony.

Ryan sat as far away from everyone as he could get, resting his head back with his eyes closed. His new suit already looked wrinkled, and his tie was sloppily tied and crooked. His hair was messy, too, but I knew he couldn't have cared less. Dallin was seated on the front row as well with Brandon and Natalie. Dallin's suit looked new, too, but it wasn't wrinkled, and his tie was tied properly and was nice and straight. Ryan's hair hung in his eyes and needed cutting desperately, but Dallin's hair had been recently trimmed and was cut in a current style, unlike Ryan's bedhead, no-style look.

Dallin looked up and caught me watching him. He smiled, but I quickly looked down at my hand Wendy was holding.

"You may kiss the bride!"

I wasn't about to watch Mr. Ackerman kiss Mom, and I gripped Wendy's hand harder instead. When I did finally look up again, Mom and Mr. Ackerman had turned around to face all of us, hand in hand, smiling at each other, now officially Husband and Wife. Robert squeezed my shoulders and gave me an encouraging smile, but I couldn't decide if I felt more like laughing or crying.

We all converged on another restaurant for dinner after our own unique Horror Picture-Taking Show in front of the ward house. It was bizarre being seated in a private banquet room with not only a few unknown relatives of Mom's but a bunch of unknown Ackerman extended family members as well. I was lucky enough to be seated by Robert and Wendy, far away from any Ackermans, while Ryan sat across from us, picking at his food as if it were a plate of dead rats. I could see his hand shake when he'd reach for his glass of water, which he'd refilled three times already. His eyes were bloodshot, but I knew he hadn't been crying. I looked away from Ryan to answer Robert's nudge and "You okay?"

"It's just that I always thought the next family wedding I'd be going to would be mine or Ryan's, not Mom's."

Robert chuckled briefly and nodded as he took another bite of salad. "You realize that today's the easy part, don't you? The real stuff, the hard stuff, starts happening now. There's going to be a lot of changes for you. For all of us. Are you ready for that?"

I shrugged uncomfortably and jabbed at the prime rib on my plate. "I don't know."

"Everything's going to be different now, Rachel. Count on that."

I wanted to ask Robert if the sadness that had been in the pit of my stomach since It happened would ever go away. All I knew was that the sadness had become worse ever since Labor Day.

"I just wish my life could go back to how it used to be. Before everything."

Robert nodded. "I do, too."

I crumpled my napkin hard in my lap and glanced around before speaking again, my voice low and soft. "I still think he'll walk though the front door any minute, you know? And that everything will go back to the way it was before."

Robert reached over and briefly squeezed my hand. "That life is gone now, Rachel. We're never going to get it back, no matter how much we wish for it."

Of course, Robert was right. He'd been right about everything, especially the fact that Change was the theme in our twisted Brady Bunch house from that day forward. Mr. Ackerman and Dallin had spent the previous weekend moving all their stuff into our house. Mom had warned Ryan and me that she was going to let Mr. Ackerman have Dad's old study, so before any Ackermans could touch any of Dad's things, I had stood in the doorway of the study one more time and soaked in the feel of the room and wished for the millionth time that I'd see Dad sitting at the desk before I curled up in one of the study's comfy chairs and allowed myself to have one last good cry. Dad's pocket digital camera was still in the top drawer of his desk, so after flipping it on, I snapped shot after shot of different parts of the room before I solemnly boxed up the garbage can basketball hoop, the pictures of our family from vacation trips, all of his pens and pencils and notebooks, and everything else that reminded me of Dad that I didn't want anyone touching. Once Mr. Ackerman and Dallin had arrived, I'd stayed in my bedroom with the door shut. I kept Robert's old bedroom door shut once both of them had left, but it didn't take me long to realize that everything really had changed for good.

The first thing I learned the hard way was not to leave my room in the morning in my ratty old pajamas, or worse, in one of my old, long T-shirts. I never knew who I might see walking down the hall. It'd been unnerving early Friday morning after the wedding to come down the hall to find the bathroom door open and Dallin brushing his teeth in nothing but a towel. I'd whipped around and headed back to my room before he saw me, but as a result, I made sure never to leave my bedroom in the morning without a robe on or without brushing my hair. And I learned not to forget to do the necessary scanning in my bedroom mirror to see if anything weird had grown on my face while I was asleep. That meant moving my makeup out of the bathroom and into my room in case something gross appeared on my face overnight.

I'd forgotten to make room for Dallin's bathroom stuff, and that first Friday morning after the wedding, once I was assured that Dallin had left not only the bathroom but the house as well, I dared to leave my bedroom to take a shower. I hung my bathrobe on the back of the locked bathroom door and turned around to see a green toothbrush and tube of toothpaste squeezed into one corner of the counter along with a can of shaving cream, a disposable razor, and some weird sort of liquid face soap. There was also a bottle of aftershave that I picked up and inspected by carefully twisting off the cap and taking a sniff. "Nice," I said out loud. I caught myself blushing in the mirror and hurriedly twisted the cap back on and shoved the bottle back into the corner.

I cringed at the mess of Ryan's stuff everywhere all around the sink, and when I opened the bathroom mirror, I cringed again. Ryan had removed his things from inside, so now my stuff appeared to take up every shelf. I sighed and scrunched my stuff to free up the bottom shelf before moving Dallin's items onto it.

Ryan and I kept our toothbrushes on a toothbrush holder mounted securely above the sink. I stuck Dallin's green toothbrush into the holder as well, since there was plenty of room, and as I watched its green handle swing back and forth, bumping against my red toothbrush and Ryan's blue one, I knew that, officially, life would never be the same again.

CHAPTER NINETEEN

Ryan stumbled home earlier than usual Saturday night. Mom and Mr. Ackerman were out for dinner and a movie, and Dallin had taken off with some of his friends as well, so no one was around to witness Ryan's mess. I sprayed down the bathroom with Lysol after I'd shoved Ryan into his bed and prayed that Dallin wouldn't smell anything weird.

The next morning, though, we had our first set of fireworks. I was in the bathroom brushing my teeth when I heard Dallin's voice calling from inside Robert's old bedroom with the door thrown open wide.

"Has anyone seen my MP3 player?"

I stopped scrubbing my teeth and tensed, listening to Dallin's footsteps move down the hall before he rapped on Ryan's bedroom door. I could just make out Ryan's groggy-sounding "What?" before Dallin opened Ryan's door.

"Hey, Fletch—have you seen my MP3 player?"

"No. Why would I?"

I hurried out of the bathroom, wiping my face on a towel. "Where did you last see it?"

Dallin glanced at me before pointing back towards Robert's room. "Here in my room."

Ryan rolled from his stomach onto his back. "You sure? You probably left it at your house."

Dallin frowned as he watched Ryan. "No, it was here by my bed Friday morning. I saw it. Have you seen it, Rachel?"

Actually, I had, but I was too afraid to tell Dallin it was most likely gone forever. Some of my things had mysteriously disappeared shortly before new bottles of booze showed up inside the toilet tank, so I had my suspicions as to where my things had gone. And why they were gone. I'd been consistently letting Mom know when Ryan hadn't made it to seminary, so he rarely got more than twenty or thirty dollars a week. And, of course, Ryan was still jobless. Not that he would've held onto a job even if he could've gotten one.

"If you borrowed it, that's fine. I'd just like it back now—"

Ryan grunted angrily. "Look, man, it's not my fault you can't keep track of your own stuff. Maybe it got lost in the move—who knows. Stuff like that happens all the time."

"It didn't get lost in the move." Dallin stared hard at Ryan's back. "Look, I'm fine with you borrowing my stuff, but it'd be nice if you asked first or at least put it back when you're done. I promise not to take any of your stuff without asking—"

Ryan threw off his covers with a muffled curse. "I'll find it for you so you'll shut up and I can go back to sleep." Ryan stomped into Robert's old room, and soon both he and Dallin were turning over the bed mattress, looking under the bed, and pulling apart the bed covers and searching in drawers. Of course, the MP3 player mysteriously stayed lost, but Dallin at least had relaxed and actually seemed embarrassed for accusing Ryan of anything.

"Forget about it. It'll turn up. I probably left it in my car or something."

Ryan nodded and ran his hands through his hair. "Yeah, probably."

"Thanks for looking, though."

Ryan nodded and shuffled back to his room and fell right back to sleep as if he had the clearest conscience in the world.

I stood in the hallway with Dallin watching Ryan sleep, twisting the towel in my hands nervously. "I'm sure my mom will get you a new one if it's been lost in our house," I tried.

Dallin shook his head. "I don't want your mom to buy me anything. I'll find it, or I'll buy a new one myself."

He turned and walked back into Robert's room, but before he could close the door all the way, I said, "Um, maybe you'd like to get some sort of a locked box for your room. Just so you can keep track of your stuff here, maybe."

Dallin looked up sharply at me, but I hurried into my room before he could say anything else.

By Monday evening, a large black foot locker had been added to Robert's old room. Dallin had a nice stereo, and I noticed that his CD collection wasn't sprawled around the stereo and speakers anymore. In fact, a lot of his stuff wasn't lying around his room anymore, making it look as bare as a hotel room, and the sight made me sad.

I tried not to think too much about Dallin and how weird and hard this whole situation had to be for him, too. He seemed to be taking care of himself and handling all of the changes and healing up from everything as quickly as his bruised eye was. Because he was on Central's golf team, he didn't get home from practices and matches until some time in the evening, and he usually hung out with his friends as much as he could. I hardly ever saw him at home, so it wasn't too hard not to think about him.

I'd been wearing my birthday hoodie from Teresa a lot lately, now that fall was officially underway and I usually ended up having to walk home from school. Dallin had made himself scarce all week, and since Mr. Ackerman was an attorney and had some big cases going on, I hadn't seen too much of him, either. He usually didn't make it home until eight o'clock at night and sometimes later. Mom had taken dinner to him a couple of times and left Ryan and me to fend for ourselves, which was fine with me, because I preferred to stay out of Mr. Ackerman's way as much as possible. At the same time, though, it was strange to have two more people in the house and yet not see them often at all. Mom was happier, though, and I had to admit that it'd been nice not to hear her crying herself to sleep every night.

I shook that thought out of my head as I left Central High for the day, zipping up my hoodie and throwing my backpack over one shoulder. Mrs. Townsend had reminded us again about needing to turn in our first draft of our semester project soon, and I was still fudging around with it, trying out different ideas for a poem but tossing each one that I started. Teresa had left school early due to a doctor's appointment, so I was on my own for the hike home.

I dug my hands deep into my hoodie's pockets and shivered against the cold wind blowing. It'd been raining hard earlier, and the gutters were raging with water. I glanced up at the black clouds in the sky as I crossed the first main street towards home. It was going to rain again soon, likely within minutes.

A car honked as I hurried across the street. "Idiot—pedestrians have the right of way!" I grumbled under my breath. I didn't even look up at the car, but my heart beat faster when I realized it was cruising along slowly behind me, and I heard its horn honk again. I walked faster, praying that whoever it was would just go away, but the car pulled over sharply beside me, right into the overly full gutter, and the next thing I knew, a tidal wave of extremely cold and dirty rain water hit my entire left side, soaking me from the waist down.

I couldn't help it. I jumped and screamed. Pretty loudly, too. The passenger window of an old blue Ford Mustang rolled down, and a familiar face leaned over whoever was sitting on the passenger side of the front seat.

"Rachel! Oh, man—I'm so sorry—are you okay? Didn't you hear me honk?"

Dallin. I stood and just stared stupidly at him. "I—I didn't know it was you!"

"You want a ride home? Oh, man—I really am sorry!"

My heart beat faster when I saw that it was Jason West in the front passenger seat, grinning and trying not to laugh at my soggy self.

I couldn't get in—not all wet, with Jason West in the front seat! "Oh—no, that's all right—I don't mind walking—"

Jason smiled and threw open the door. "It's going to rain again in about two seconds, and you're soaked, so get in!"

I was ready to climb into the backseat, but I was stopped short by the sight of Chad and Zachary, two of Dallin's friends who were juniors on the golf team, too. Both guys were known to be a dangerous combo of being too flirty and too smart-mouthy. And way too cute, too.

Jason jumped out of the car and grabbed my backpack out of my hands before yelling over his shoulder, "Dallin, pop the trunk for Rachel's backpack." I couldn't seem to make my feet move. Jason slammed the trunk down, grinned, and swung the front passenger door open wider. "Go ahead and get in the front seat."

Dallin's car was small. There couldn't possibly be enough room for Dallin, Jason, and my big, sopping wet backside in the front seat! "Um— the car's kind of full—"

Dallin smiled and motioned me forward. "It's okay, Rachel. Get in!"

I smiled hesitantly back and was soon sandwiched between Dallin and Jason West on the car's bench seat. I kept my eyes straight ahead and tried to scrunch myself into a tiny ball, gripping the dashboard, but Dallin's right shoulder kept bumping me on one side, and Jason's left shoulder bumped me on the other.

Teresa's going to die! I thought to myself, trying not to nervously giggle.

Dallin looked over his left shoulder before carefully moving the car from the gutter back onto the road. "Um, I'm sorry I'm getting your car seat all wet," I tried.

Dallin looked over at me and grinned sheepishly. "I'm sorry I almost drowned you."

"Yeah, he can't help it that he's such a bad driver!"

Dallin looked in the rearview mirror at Chad. "You want to walk home, don't you?"

Chad only laughed before leaning forward to tap me on the shoulder. "So, you're Rachel?"

I jumped and turned to look at Chad's grinning face. "Yeah."

Zachary was leaning back in his seat with his eyes half shut. "Are you hating having to live with Dallin or what? I know I would!"

"It's okay."

Chad laughed. "Look how lucky you are to have such a nice stepsister, Dallin. You can tell us the truth, Rachel. He's a complete slob, right?"

"No, he's not—"

Chad only laughed harder. "You paid her to say that, didn't you?"

"Hey!" Dallin laughed.

Jason turned around to throw something at Chad. "Hey—did you know that me and Dallin and Rachel all have seminary together? Clawson's Book of Mormon class."

Zachary opened his eyes all the way. "Oh, yeah? He's a pretty cool teacher. You like him, Rachel?"

I nodded. "He's nice."

"Fletch is in there, too."

"Really?" The surprise in Zachary's voice and the loud guffaw from Chad annoyed me. "So how's Fletch? We haven't seen him in a while."

I tensed up but forced a smile and said, "Fine." Dallin had pulled up into our driveway by then, and Jason opened the door and retrieved my backpack for me.

I leaned back into the car before Jason could hop back in. "Thanks for the ride, Dallin."

Dallin smiled and switched the car into reverse. "No problem. Tell your mom I'll be home for dinner, okay?"

I nodded while Jason, Chad, and Zachary yelled, "Bye, Rachel!" Even though it was raining pretty hard by then, I stood on the porch and watched Dallin drive away.

During dinner that night I was still reeling over riding home beside Jason West. It was the first time all five of us had sat together for dinner in the dining room since the wedding. I had to give Mr. Ackerman kudos for trying hard to strike up a friendly conversation between himself and me and Ryan. Dallin pleasantly filled him in on his latest golf matches and school classes, and Mom made an appropriate fuss over his putting abilities and command of calculus.

"And how about you, Rachel? How's school going?"

I looked up at Mr. Ackerman's smile. "Um, fine."

"Which class are you enjoying the most so far?"

I shrugged and twirled my fork in my pasta. "Creative writing, I guess."

"Creative writing? Now, that sounds fun! Are you writing short stories?"

"No, we're doing a poetry unit right now."

"Really!" Mr. Ackerman actually looked interested and not at all as if he was faking interest to be nice.

I nodded. "Yeah. We're studying poets and learning how to write different forms of poetry."

"Do you like poetry, Rachel?"

"Oh, she loves it. She's been writing poems of her own for years now!" Mom gushed, a little too excitedly. I could feel Dallin's eyes on me now, too, and when I looked up, he was watching me curiously.

"Is that true, Rachel?" Mr. Ackerman pressed.

I nodded again hesitantly.

Dallin smiled. "Watch out, Rachel. My dad loves poetry. He might ask you to read some of your stuff to him!"

"What?"

Mr. Ackerman chuckled. "Don't listen to Dallin. I wouldn't ask you to do that, but maybe you'd let me read something you've written sometime?"

I shrugged. "Maybe."

"I've written a poem or two of my own. Maybe you could read one of mine in exchange for me reading one of yours?"

It was definitely an interesting idea. "Yeah, that could be okay."

Mom sat there beaming at both of us. "I think that would be wonderful!"

Mr. Ackerman shifted his eyes to Ryan on my right. "And how about you, Ryan?"

Ryan didn't look up from slumping over his hardly touched food. "What about me?"

Mr. Ackerman's smile looked tight now. "How are your classes going?"

"Oh, they're going."

Mr. Ackerman couldn't get Ryan to say anything more about school. He got even less out of him about football. But he wasn't going to give up.

"Ryan, your mother's told me how much you love camping. You know, Dallin and I have always liked to go camping, too. I've been thinking it would be fun to take the two of you camping up in the mountains, maybe next weekend before the weather gets any colder—"

"No, thanks." Ryan was curt and cold.

"Ryan!" Mom gasped, setting her fork down.

Ryan only glared at Mom while she stood up to refill the water pitcher. "I've got a football game Friday night and every Friday night!"

Mr. Ackerman's smile tightened up even worse. "Well, we could make it just a day trip and leave early Saturday morning—"

"No, thanks."

I knew Mr. Ackerman was trying to win Ryan over, and I was just as sure that Mom had pushed him to take Ryan camping in hopes of bonding with him. I also knew it was going to take more than the offer of a camping trip or reading poetry with me to make us all one nice, big, happy, twisted family.

Mr. Ackerman stopped smiling and set his fork down before looking intensely at Ryan. "Ryan, is there something I've done to offend you?"

Ryan looked up at him briefly. "You haven't done anything to make me want to poke you in the eye with a stick. Yet."

I tensed, waiting for Mr. Ackerman to yell something about being respectful, but instead he stared at Ryan for a second and then burst out laughing. "Fair enough!"

Mom had been standing near Ryan gripping the pitcher of water with both hands, but when Mr. Ackerman laughed, she laughed and set the pitcher down. Then she moved behind Ryan to put her arms around him and hug him.

"That's my Ry-Guy!"

Ryan tolerated Mom's over-affection better than I thought he would, and the sight of Mom with her arms around him like that, tousling his hair with her hands and giggling in his ear while Ryan kept laughing and saying, "Stop it, Mom!" made the sadness in my stomach relax and a warm feeling I hadn't felt in a long time chase down my spine.

As I turned my head from Ryan and Mom back to my plate of food, I caught a brief glimpse of Dallin's face and my heart stopped. Dallin hadn't spoken at all but sat silently watching Mom and Ryan laugh together, Mom's arms still around Ryan, with a look of unbearable longing etched into his face.

CHAPTER TWENTY

W ell, since we're all together again, I think we ought to discuss the need for a few new rules in this house."

Dinner had gone relatively well a few nights before, and since we'd all made it back to the table at the same time Saturday afternoon for lunch, Mr. Ackerman was clearly feeling more confident about how our twisted Brady Bunch situation was going.

"Rules? Like what?"

I knew that tone in Ryan's voice and tensed, knowing there would be fireworks. Ryan had been forced to go to the dentist the day before to have some seriously needed work done on his teeth and he was still in pain, which made him an even worse crab to deal with than usual.

Mr. Ackerman smiled at us all and cleared his throat. "Elaine and I have been talking, and now that there are five of us living here, Rachel and Elaine shouldn't have to be stuck doing all the dishes and cooking and housework. Everyone needs to be pitching in."

Ryan stopped picking at his food to lean back in his chair, eyeing Mr. Ackerman defiantly. "I've got football practice after school."

Mr. Ackerman nodded. "I know. And Dallin has golf. That means the two of you will have to help out more with dishes on the weekend. In fact, Elaine and I have already been planning a rotating sort of job chart."

I raised my eyebrows at that. "Job chart?"

Mr. Ackerman looked at me and smiled. "That's right, Rachel. Each person will be responsible for a different room in the house for a week, and then the assignments will rotate. There will be specific things that will need to be done in order to clean each room."

Ryan shook his head and slumped back over his dinner plate to pick at his food again. "Whatever."

Dallin looked at Ryan briefly before turning to Mr. Ackerman. "Are we going to start taking turns cooking dinner again?"

"Excuse me?" Ryan said.

I turned and noticed the black look Ryan was giving Mr. Ackerman, but Mr. Ackerman only nodded and smiled. "All of you need to fend for yourselves more. You'll be going off to college in no time. You'll thank me later for helping you learn to improve your cooking skills. I took turns with my two sons cooking for years, and it worked out well. Right, Dallin?"

Dallin laughed. "Oh, sure, except that Brandon's a lousy cook—"

"I don't have time for that!" Ryan burst out.

Dead silence reigned afterward. I waited for Mom to say something, but she didn't.

Mr. Ackerman's smile was looking more and more forced. "Well, you'll just have to make time, Ryan."

Ryan shook his head slowly and turned his back on Mr. Ackerman to glare at Mom. "Mom, is this for real? You never made us cook or do stupid job charts before!"

Mom tried to smile brightly. "I think it's a great idea, and I'm on board with the plan."

"Then count on cold cereal when it's my turn!"

Mr. Ackerman kept his smile pasted on. "That'll be fine for a start."

I looked across the table at Dallin, but he'd become interested in the napkin on his lap.

Mr. Ackerman cleared his throat again. "Another thing. I think a curfew is in order for all of you—"

"Curfew?" Everyone but Mr. Ackerman jumped at Ryan's explosion.

Mr. Ackerman set his fork down firmly and stared unflinchingly at Ryan. "Both of my sons have always had curfews while living with me.

I think it would help if everyone made it a priority to be home on week-nights by 10:30 and 11:30 on weekends."

I nodded silently, but Ryan guffawed loudly and threw down his fork. "You've got to be kidding me!"

Mom reached over and touched Ryan's arm worriedly. "Ryan, no one else is having a problem with this, so why can't you accept it? These changes are going to help everyone!"

Ryan really started to laugh then, but Mr. Ackerman didn't like his loud laughing at all.

"And what is so funny, Ryan?"

Ryan shrugged and looked at Mr. Ackerman defiantly again. "You said we were going to 'discuss the need for new rules in the house,' but it sounds like you've already gotten everything figured out and decided without us. Probably without Mom, too."

"Ryan!"

Ryan yanked his arm free of Mom. "Just admit it, Mom. You've never cared about this kind of stuff before, but now he's here, and wham—cleaning, cooking, curfews. This isn't you at all, Mom!"

Mom tried to be firm. "It is, Ryan. It's me now."

Mr. Ackerman wiped his mouth with his napkin and pushed his plate forward. "I think it's important that we discuss what the consequences will be for those of you who choose not to get on board with the program here."

Ryan shrugged again and leaned back on his chair until only the back two legs were touching the floor. "Doesn't matter."

Mr. Ackerman looked at Ryan evenly. "What?"

Ryan folded his arms. "You can't tell me what to do, and you can't punish me for anything."

Mom gasped. "Ryan!"

"Dad would never have smothered us with rules and junk like this!"

Mr. Ackerman raised his voice louder over Ryan's. "If you haven't noticed, things are different now!"

"Maybe, but you're not my father!"

I had known one of us would use the dreaded "you're not my parent" line at some point, and I guess I knew it would be Ryan who did it first. Dallin was actually getting along well and politely with Mom, so I couldn't imagine seeing him scream such a line at her. But Ryan—well, he was a horse of a different color.

Everyone was silent for a few seconds before Mr. Ackerman quietly continued. "No, but I *am* your stepfather, and as long as we're all living here together, you're going to have to get used to the fact that things aren't exactly as they were before."

Ryan rolled his eyes and let his chair thump back loudly onto all four legs. "I'm not brainless. I realize that. We're a 'blended' family now. I don't know how I've kept from throwing up on myself at just the thought of it. But 'blending' is one thing. 'Changing' is something else. You don't want to 'blend' us all nicely together. You want to change everything and turn us into whatever freak show you had going on at your house before!"

Mr. Ackerman gave up on being calm. "Ryan, that is enough!"

Ryan laughed and looked pleased with himself. "Enough? I haven't even started yet!"

Mom looked like she might cry any second. "Ryan, please! Just stop it!"

Ryan shoved his chair back and stood up. "Fine. But only because *you* asked me, Mom. I don't have to do anything *he* says!" A second later, Ryan had stormed out of the house, slamming the front door hard, leaving behind only uncomfortable silence for the rest of us.

CHAPTER TWENTY-ONE

I watched the clock that night, waiting for Ryan to come home. He broke Mr. Ackerman's suggested 11:30 P.M. weekend curfew, but luckily for both Ryan and me, Mom and Mr. Ackerman had gone out for the evening and hadn't returned home yet. Dallin was out on a date, but he'd received clearance to get home late because he was taking his date to a play out of town. Teresa came over for ice cream and a movie but left by 11:30 P.M., so once she was gone, I had the house to myself. I flipped channels on the TV in the living room with the remote, nervously waiting for Ryan to arrive home, and prayed frantically that he'd get home before Mom and Mr. Ackerman. Miraculously, Ryan staggered into the house, slamming the front door behind him, at 12:30 A.M.

"Hey . . . Rachel! Where is everybody?"

"Don't yell. No one's here to care but me!"

"Darn. Too bad. I was ready for a good ol', knock out, drag down fight!" Ryan tried to bounce lightly from foot to foot boxer style with his fists up, punching at the air, but he tripped all over his feet and stumbled until he landed in a heap on the couch, smacking into my shoulder.

"Ow! Get off me, jerk!" I shoved him hard, but Ryan only laughed and tried to sit on me. I shoved his side with one hand and his face with my other hand and this time managed to make him land on the floor.

"Oooh—my face! Don't touch my face!"

"Then don't fall on me!"

Ryan moaned. "My mouth is killing me. Stupid dentist, drilling all my teeth out of my face. Oh, man, I'm going to be sick!" With that, Ryan slowly pulled himself back up on his feet by gripping the couch and the lamp table. Once he'd stopped weaving back and forth, he lurched his way down the hall, his hands outstretched to balance himself against the wall on either side of him, until he made it to the bathroom. I winced at the sounds until I heard the toilet flush. I sighed and ran my hands through my hair before following him into the bathroom. This time, there wasn't much of a mess on the floor but enough that I had to run for the paper towels.

"If you have to insist on doing this, just once, could you please make sure everything makes it into the toilet?"

"Just once, could you just shut up?"

I bit my tongue and kept cleaning while Ryan stayed on his knees, moaning into the toilet bowl.

"You should've been there, Rachel."

"I have no desire to be at any of your stupid drinking parties!"

"No—not there!"

I frowned. "Then where?"

"The dentist—Dr. What's-His-Face. He totally destroyed my mouth. I think he used a hammer. You know that water thingy he puts in your mouth? He kept spraying me in the face with it."

I kept my back to Ryan and grabbed more paper towels. "Who cares?"

Ryan moaned and flushed the toilet again. "I swear he was sculpting a statue of the devil outta my teeth. I even asked him to please stop scraping if the white part of my teeth disappeared, but he ignored me. I'm sure he learned how to drill in prison."

I squatted down beside Ryan to roughly twist and yank his dirty shirt off over his head, catching a nice chunk of his messy hair in the collar in the process.

"Ow! You're worse than that stinkin' dentist! Just look at my teeth now—" Ryan stuck his face close to mine and opened his mouth wide.

I nearly threw up myself at the strong stench coming from Ryan's mouth. "Ryan—gross! You smell like death!"

"Just look—look at my teeth! They're all bloody little stumps now. I'm never going to be able to eat solid foods again," Ryan moaned.

"You're going to be fine. Just—"

But Ryan was back to heaving again. I threw his dirty shirt aside to grab his head and force it back into the toilet bowl, barely saving him from throwing up all over himself. I sighed, relieved, and sat up to brush my hair out of my face—and froze.

Dallin was standing in the bathroom doorway, just as frozen as I was, looking at both Ryan and me with a surprising mix of both disgust and pity. My heart pounded as I stared back at Dallin, truly petrified, but after watching Ryan moan and slump onto his side on the bathroom tile, Dallin shook his head and went back down the hall to Robert's old room, quietly closing the door behind him.

CHAPTER TWENTY-TWO

If all fingers hadn't been pointing at me—
Some barely lifted off their arm rests
Others jabbing like spears—
The fire would've have eaten my heart anyway,
Burning to the crisp of a fried pig's tail.
They say
"You need to learn to be you
No matter what they think,"
But how am I supposed to dodge
Those eyes spitting ricocheting bullets
So I can fling toward home?
Impossible.
Everyone pretends to stand on an island
Uncaring of the sea of faces close as a hula-hoop.
It's a lie.
Everyone looks over their shoulder
Wondering if the fish are leaping to bite.
True safety
And eyes closed to caring
Is only found six feet deep.

Before King Benjamin gave up the kingdom to his son Mosiah, he talked to his people about service. What thought-provoking truth did King Benjamin teach his people about service in Mosiah

2:17?" Brother Clawson was standing in his usual place in front of his desk, leaning against it until he was basically sitting on it. "Yes, Jason."

I looked up from my blue notebook to see Jason put his hand down. "That when you're in the service of your fellowmen, you're in the service of God."

Brother Clawson nodded. "Good paraphrasing. And yes, that's exactly right. We're actually serving God when we're serving others. Now, please turn to Matthew 5, verses 44 through 46."

Dallin beat Jason raising his hand. "I've got it."

"Great. Go ahead and read it, Dallin."

"'But I say unto you, Love your enemies, bless them that curse you, do good to them that hate you, and pray for them which despitefully use you, and persecute you. That ye may be the children of your Father which is in heaven . . . For if ye love them which love you, what reward have ye?'"

"What do you think that means?" For some reason, Brother Clawson was looking at me as if he thought I might venture to answer. I stuffed my hands deep into my hoodie's pockets. Or maybe he was staring at Ryan, who was slumped in a stupor behind me.

Jason had his hand up again. "I think it means if you're serving and doing good for people you already love and who love you, then there's no real reward, but that serving those we have a problem with is where the real reward starts."

Brother Clawson turned his head from my direction to smile at Jason. "Very true. We tend to have an easy time serving people we love. What's not so easy is to serve people we have a hard time loving. And I believe the real reward of service comes when we serve and learn to love those we know don't love us."

And then Brother Clawson was back to looking in my general direction. "Unconditional love means you love someone more than you hate the things they do. Things you know are causing that person to commit sin. Unconditional love doesn't require a person to approve, support, or even accept wrong behavior from someone he or she loves. It simply means we must continue to love that person as a son or daughter of God."

Brother Clawson smiled and shook his head. "It's almost scary how easy it is to feel anger, resentment, even hatred towards someone in your life who has chosen to wander into the dark mists of Lehi's vision. That's when it's important to pray for help, because that's when people in our lives who are struggling need us the most, even though they'd never admit it. Unconditional love, I believe, is a spiritual gift that can be gained through humble prayer and faith."

Brother Clawson finally moved his eyes from my direction to look over the rest of the class. "And what is this reward that we can gain through serving and loving those who aren't easy to love or serve?"

Jason had his hand up yet again. "Well, I guess the ultimate reward: Living forever with Heavenly Father and Christ. And our families."

Brother Clawson nodded. "Yes. And what else?"

The class was silent for a full ten seconds before Dallin hesitantly raised his hand. "Not just *learning* to love someone who's hard to love, but finally *loving* that person you thought was hard to love. And maybe being loved back."

"Very good, Dallin. Very good." Brother Clawson nodded again before standing up to pace the front of the room thoughtfully. "I often think perhaps the reward is also . . . perhaps . . . accomplishing having taken another step towards becoming more like Christ."

———•———

As usual, Ryan came alive the second the bell rang and hurried out the door before anyone else in class had even closed up their scriptures. By the time I made it out the seminary building doors myself, after meeting Teresa in the foyer, Dallin and Jason West had long since disappeared into Central High.

I had my head down, zipping up my hoodie to block out the nip in the air when Teresa poked me. "Hey, isn't that Ryan?"

"Where?"

Teresa nodded towards my left. "Out there in the parking lot. Wonder what he's doing?"

I could see Ryan leaning against a green Jeep with a couple of guys I'd never seen him bring home. My breath caught strangely in my throat when I saw Ryan pouring something into the plastic cola bottle he'd had with him in seminary.

I waited until we'd made it into Central High before stopping just inside the doors. "Um, go on without me, Teresa. I'll talk to you at lunch, okay?"

Teresa frowned and shrugged. "Okay, I guess. See you at lunch!"

I hugged my books to my chest and waited by the lockers near the back doors until Ryan finally pushed through Central's back doors. By then, the halls were deserted, and I knew we'd both be late for class.

"I saw what you did!"

Ryan glanced over at me but kept on walking. "What? Oh, it's just you."

I hurried to step in front of him. "You can't do this—not at school!" Ryan ignored me and tried to push past me, but I grabbed his arm. "I've seen you fall asleep in seminary!"

Ryan glared at me. "So what? You've crashed in there, too!"

"Not for the same reason you do!" Ryan shoved me aside, but I jumped in front of him again. "Why do you do it? I know you don't care what it's doing to everyone else, but why are you doing this to yourself?"

Ryan had been sullen throughout my angry nagging, but now he turned ugly and started shouting, inserting ugly curse words everywhere he could in his tirade against me. "Because I like it, and because I can. And because I want to, and because I feel like it. And because no one's been able to stop me yet. I can do whatever I want, so leave me alone!"

Ryan turned away, but I moved in front of him again. "Do you hear anything that's said in seminary? Anything at all? Did you hear what Jason and Dallin said when Brother Clawson talked about keeping the commandments—"

"Maybe there's something Ackerman and the great Jason West could learn from me. Maybe something like knowing when to SHUT UP!"

"You know you can't keep doing this, Ryan. You know what,—"

Ryan turned on me viciously. "Know what? Know what? Know what? If someone doesn't like it, THEY SHOULD GO AWAY!!"

I stared back at his black, angry glare, his face mere inches from mine. "Why can't you just say it?"

"Say what?"

"That you've got a problem, and it's messing up your life!" I was still too much of a coward to call Ryan's "problem" what it was.

"The only problem I have right now is you!"

I snatched the dirty cola bottle out of Ryan's hand. "Well, if you're not going to own up to it, I'll do it for you! I'm sick of dealing with it—I'll take this stuff right to the principal myself!"

Ryan glared hatefully into my face enough to make me wish I could bite back my threat, but it was too late. A second later, Ryan reached behind my head, yanking the hood of my jacket hard up onto my head and so far forward that my eyes were covered and I couldn't see.

"Ryan! Stop!"

A second later, Ryan had jerked viciously on both ties of my hood so that only the tip of my nose and my mouth were poking out of my hood. The noose around my nose and mouth tightened, and I knew he'd tied a firm knot.

"Ryan! Stop it—now!"

Ryan easily pushed me into the row of lockers behind me, forcing me to bend my knees. Although I struggled against his shoulder pinning me to the lockers, I couldn't tell what he was doing.

"Let's see you try to go to the principal's office now, stupid tattler!"

Ryan easily snatched the cola bottle out of my hand and stomped down the hall.

I tried to stand up straight and take a step forward myself, but the second I did, I was wrenched to a stop. Panicked, I felt the strings of my knotted hood and followed both in horror to where they'd been knotted to the door of a locker, threaded into the holes where a pad lock could double secure the locker.

I threw my books down and clawed at the knot with shaking fingers. I couldn't see a thing due to the dark blue hood over my eyes, but I kept clawing, and in sheer frustration that was turning into tears, kicked the locker over and over.

In seconds, I was crying, yelling, and kicking for all I was worth. When I felt someone grab my shoulders, I was sure it was Ryan back to torture me again, so I shoved back hard.

"Hey—I'm trying to help, Rachel!"

Jason! I froze, trembling, while Jason tugged on my hood's strings as he worked on the knot.

"I'd ask who did this to you, but I think I can guess."

"You're right," I mumbled.

Jason sighed. "He's done a good job, I'll give him that much. Hold on—I'm going to have to get something to cut this with. Shop class is just down the hall—I'll be right back."

My legs were trembling from being unable to stand up straight for so long. I leaned my back against the lockers to give them a rest until Jason returned a few minutes later and within seconds, I could finally stand upright again.

"Hold on—I'm going to try and untie the knot on your hood."

Jason worked at the knot under my chin for a whole minute before it was obvious to me the knot wasn't going to budge. "Just cut it!" I whimpered.

"It'll ruin your hoodie."

"I don't care—I can't see!"

"Okay—I'll cut the knot. Hold still so I don't cut you."

I held perfectly still, except for the shakes I couldn't control. In a few seconds, Jason had the knot cut, and he pushed the hood off my head.

Jason's face was way too close to mine. "You okay?"

I nodded, too embarrassed to look him in the eye, and turned and wiped my eyes with the sleeve of my hoodie.

"I'm going to take this knife back to the shop class, and then I have to head back to the seminary building. You want to come with me?"

I nodded while Jason reached down and picked up my books before he jogged off to return the knife. When he came back a minute later, he didn't hand my books to me but carried them easily under one arm and walked beside me while I snuffled and tried to stop crying. When we arrived at the back doors by the cafeteria, Jason shoved one of the doors with his shoulder and held it open for me to walk through.

"Thanks," I mumbled.

Jason only nodded. I walked beside Jason in complete silence and waited in the seminary building's foyer until he returned with a thick blue textbook added to the stack of my books under one arm. We'd been back outside a few seconds when Jason nodded towards the small set of bleachers by the school's baseball diamond beyond the parking lot. "You want to sit down and decompress?"

"We'll miss first period!"

Jason shrugged. "That's okay. I think we'll survive just this once."

I numbly walked beside Jason through the parking lot before sitting down beside him on the bottom row of the bleachers, our stack of books between us.

"So, what happened?"

I shoved my hands deep into my jacket pockets and didn't look up. "Ryan happened."

"Why'd he tie you to a locker?"

I hesitated for a moment, and when I spoke, my voice was small and quiet. "Because—because I was going to tell about his . . . problem."

Jason was silent for a long moment. "I guess he didn't like that."

"He doesn't think he has a problem."

"Most people who drink don't."

I looked up at Jason's unsmiling, serious face. "I guess . . . . I guess you've known about this for a long time."

Jason shrugged. "I don't really hang out with Ryan, but I've seen him drunk at a few parties. I was there the night he punched Dallin in the face, and he'd definitely had too much to drink that night."

I could feel my stomach tighten at Jason's casual, knowing tone about Ryan and wondered if Dallin had told him about seeing me on the bathroom floor dealing with Ryan the other night.

We were both quiet for a long minute while I stared uncomfortably at the empty baseball diamond before I finally spoke again. "So—how did you happen to find me? Could you hear me screaming all the way to your next class?"

Jason laughed. "No. I was halfway to English before I realized I'd left my book under my chair in seminary. I was on my way back to grab it."

"So I'm not the only one who's not always quite awake during seminary, huh?"

Jason laughed again. "I guess not."

"You're sure you're okay with missing your English class?"

Jason grinned. "I have a good tutor. She'll catch me up during study hall."

We were both silent again before I coughed nervously and carefully edged my books out from underneath Jason's blue book. "I think I'm going to go to the bathroom and check my hair and face and everything now, if that's okay."

"Sure." Jason nodded, looking at me carefully. "You sure you're okay now?"

I nodded and stood up. "Thanks. For 'decompressing' with me."

Jason grinned. "No problem."

I smiled back. "And thanks for rescuing me."

"I'm sorry I had to destroy your hoodie."

"Oh, no, it's fine. I'd still be kicking at the locker screaming like a freak if you hadn't come along."

Jason laughed. "No big deal."

I hugged my books to my chest while Jason walked silently beside me until we were back inside Central High. Once the back cafeteria doors had closed behind us, I stopped and faced him. "Well, thanks again, Jason. For being so nice and helping me and everything."

Jason smiled. "Anytime, Rachel."

I turned to walk away from him, but after taking a few steps, I turned back around. Jason had started to walk in the opposite direction, but he turned around when I called out to him. "Hey—one more thing. Can you do me a favor?"

"Sure. What?"

I clutched my books tightly to my chest and chewed the side of my bottom lip nervously for a second while Jason watched me, waiting. "Don't tell anyone about this—about Ryan—and him tying me to the locker. Especially not Dallin, okay?"

I didn't wait for Jason's response but hurried down the hall and didn't stop until I was safe inside the girls' bathroom.

CHAPTER TWENTY-THREE

This smile isn't real.
I found it stuck behind my bureau.
I nod at him, her, you—
You shouldn't answer.
Your face is ground easily inside my shoe.

"All right, class. Nonstop time is over. Today, we're going to learn the English sonnet."

I jumped at the sound of Mrs. Townsend's voice right by my left ear. I hadn't put much down on paper during our nonstop time before I'd drifted off. It wasn't completely my fault. Everyone had been too quiet, and it was too warm in Mrs. Townsend's classroom. I looked up nervously, but Mrs. Townsend merely looked over the end of her glasses at me and smiled without opening her mouth before slowly walking back to the front of the room.

Mrs. Townsend had liked my cinquains. By one of them, she'd written, "*Woo!* Packs a punch. Good images." Her final comment for all of my cinquains and haikus had been, "The ring of truth is in all of these, Rachel." I wasn't sure how I was doing compared to the rest of the students in class, but it was a relief to see good comments from her on my poetry. I wanted to believe she honestly thought my stuff was good, but I couldn't be sure if she was just doing her teacherly duty by being nice and encouraging. She still hadn't sent me to the principal for falling asleep in her class a few times. I wasn't sure why, or for that matter, why Brother

Clawson never reported either me or Ryan falling asleep in class, but I wasn't about to question it or complain.

"Shortly after the Italian sonnet was introduced, many English poets, such as Sir Philip Sidney, Michael Drayton, Samuel Daniel, the Earl of Surrey's nephew Edward de Vere, and of course, William Shakespeare, began to develop their own native form of what is known as the English sonnet. Sometimes it is referred to as the Shakespearean sonnet because he was the most famous person to use it. The form consists of three quatrains followed by a couplet. The couplet should introduce an unexpected sharp thematic 'turn,' which we call a 'volta.' The usual rhyme scheme for the English sonnet is *a-b-a-b, c-d-c-d, e-f-e-f, g-g.*"

Mrs. Townsend asked us each of us to take a turn reading a sonnet aloud from our poetry textbook until everyone had read one out loud.

"You're getting the idea by now, I hope? Good. Let's try some, shall we? I'll expect each of you to create one truly profound sonnet to turn in that will tell me something deeper about you."

I'd studied the blue lines on the white page of my red notebook and even scratched a few words down that I knew were worthless drivel before giving up and tossing the notebook into my backpack when the bell rang. Luckily, we didn't have to turn in our sonnets until the next morning, so hopefully I'd get inspired to share something deep about myself tonight at home. In a sonnet, no less.

"Don't forget I'll need the first draft of your creative writing piece for the high school writing contest next week." Mrs. Townsend only laughed at the answering moans and mutterings. "Groan all you want, class, but you'll thank me once the deadline to turn it in is almost here and you're already more than halfway finished. And don't forget—this project is a big part of your final grade in this class. Those of you who decide to turn in shoddy work or nothing at all will reap the consequences on your report card. It's your choice."

I still had no idea what I was going to write about. All I knew was that I'd be writing a poem. It wouldn't be in an established form like haiku or the sonnet, but it'd definitely be in Rachel form.

119

I was halfway out the door when it finally happened.

"Miss Fletcher, may I see you for a moment, please?"

I stiffened before turning around to look at Mrs. Townsend, who was again smiling with her mouth closed, peering down at me over her glasses perched on the end of her nose. I nodded dumbly and stood stiffly by her desk while the other students filed out the door. A few paused to eye me curiously, but I stared stonily back until only Mrs. Townsend and I remained.

Mrs. Townsend didn't stop smiling, but before she could open her mouth and ream me for falling asleep in class all the time, I cut to the chase and apologized and promised to buckle down and try harder and do better work, since I was sure she was being overly kind grading my poems so far. I was only halfway through my spiel when she cut me off mid-sentence.

"Relax, Rachel. That's not why I wanted to talk to you."

I frowned, confused at her smile.

"I just wanted to tell you how much I've been enjoying your pieces. You're a hard worker, you've got drive and energy, and you're teeming with thoughts and ideas. You're really starting to get a handle on poetry."

I was sure my eyes were popping out of my skull. "You think so?"

Mrs. Townsend actually chuckled. "I do. You're developing quite a voice that's all your own." She paused until our eyes met. "I will be very pleased to enter your work in the high school state creative writing contest this year," she said seriously. "You have some real talent, and I think others need to know it. Including yourself, rough as it may be right now."

I nodded without speaking, and a minute later I was being crushed and pushed along among the waves of students in the hall. So I wasn't in trouble, and I wasn't failing creative writing. In fact, Mrs. Townsend hadn't mentioned my trips to dream land at all.

CHAPTER TWENTY-FOUR

Am I afraid to face the dark of night?
Or is it something deeper that I fear?
All near me changes with the end of light;
The suffocating shadows press too near.
The need to sleep is strong, but then, I'll dream—
To me, an awful, unprotected trance
Where all strong forces gather to team
Against my soul, and on my grave they dance.
I cannot hide—inside my dream I'm caught;
My body, helplessly in bed I'll lay.
Escaping? No, although so hard I've fought;
My freedom only comes with light of day.
Perhaps it's just a childhood scar in me;
I always fear whatever I can't see.

The eighth line was awkward and I knew it, but I couldn't figure out a better way to rhyme something with "trance." I sat with my elbows on my desk in my bedroom, frowning with my chin in both hands, and stared into space while my *Be Your Own Kind of Beautiful* Mormonad stared back at me. I looked at the mirror beside it and studied myself. My face was round. Too round. Like the rest of me.

I sighed and pushed my red notebook away before laying my head down on my crossed arms on my desk. Just a quick power nap and I'd be fine. I yawned and closed my eyes. Twenty minutes. That's all I needed.

"Wake up, baby—we're here!"

*I yawned and looked out the window of the backseat of Dad's truck.
"Where's here?"*

Dad laughed. "Here is Green River, Utah."

*Ryan leaned out the other window in the back, laughing and shaking his
head. "Wow—look at this place. We are definitely not in Kansas anymore, Toto!"*

*Dad pointed out the window as we drove down what was easily the only
main road in town. "Look at those cliffs! The guidebook says they're called the
Book Cliffs. Pretty cool, huh, kids?"*

*Mom leaned out the window herself to take a few pictures. "You kids just
wait until we see Range Creek Canyon tomorrow. Archaeologists are finding all
kinds of Fremont Indian ruins and rock art and things in there, and we get to be
some of the lucky few to see it all first! Amazing that the owner of the property
was able to keep it all a secret for so long before selling the land to the state."*

*Dad laughed pretty hard at that. "You really think the people in this town
haven't already seen it all, Lainey? I doubt it's been a secret to them."*

"Why do you say that, Dad?"

*Dad turned and grinned at me. "No one keeps a secret for long in a small
town like this. And I should know—I grew up in one!"*

*We still felt lucky to be some of the first to get a grand, private tour in fancy
SUVs in the canyon. We bounced slowly under the hot sun along the rough,
winding trails that led steeply down into the desert canyon, stopping all over the
place to take pictures and inspect hidden Indian rock art panels and squint
through binoculars at the mountains, looking for stick and mud-walled granaries
hidden in crevices high up in the cliffs and walls of the canyon.*

"Look there, Rachel—do you see? See that granary, way up in that cliff?"

*I did my best to zoom in with my binoculars onto the cliff Dad kept pointing
at, but I couldn't see a thing. And then—suddenly—*

"I see it, Dad—I see it!"

Dad laughed and clapped." I knew you would!"

*"It's hard to find the cool stuff here. It's not obvious and all over the place
like in Mesa Verde."*

"Nope—that's why I like it here. Hidden treasures everywhere that you have to work to find. You have to keep your eyes open or you'll miss something."

Dad nudged me to point out a panel of rock art directly behind me. I jumped, knowing I wouldn't have seen it at all if he hadn't pointed it out to me.

I stared solemnly at the rock art while Ryan snapped photos of it with Mom. "What is it, baby? You look too serious."

"I guess I'm wondering what kinds of beautiful things and mysteries are right in front of me that I don't ever see. In things, and people. In everything."

Dad stared at me, shaking his head. "Wow. Amazing."

"What?"

"You've grown up a little, right in front of my eyes."

I couldn't stop gazing at granary after granary on the trail, all of them so incredibly high up the jagged cliff walls. Tons of them were hidden all over the cliffs surrounding the canyon. There were even remains of villages on cliff edges a thousand feet above the valley floor. "What would cause people a thousand years ago to do something like that? What were they afraid of that caused them to build homes in such bizarre places?"

"I don't know, but people will do crazy things when they're afraid. Things they'd never do otherwise."

I stared at Ryan, but his eyes looked funny. Bloodshot. And he was stumbling backwards away from me, pointing and screaming, "He was on his way to pick you up from your stupid friend's house!"

And then a sound like a gunshot jolted me awake, and I was trembling hard all over.

CHAPTER TWENTY-FIVE

I t'd only been my thick poetry textbook that I'd sent flying to the ground off my desk, but even so, I couldn't stop my heart from pounding. I squinted at the clock by my bed. Eleven o'clock. I crept into the hall to peek inside Ryan's room. Of course, he wasn't there, clearly out breaking Mr. Ackerman's curfew again. Mom had to have been doing some serious intervening to keep Mr. Ackerman from punishing him. It wasn't fair. I knew if I'd been thumbing my nose at the new rules, I would've been grounded for years by now.

Mom and Mr. Ackerman had gone out for the evening again and still hadn't returned yet, and Dallin's bedroom door was closed. I wasn't sure if he was home or not, but if he was, he was either sleeping or listening to music with his earphones on with the light off, like I knew he'd been doing since he found me cleaning up Ryan on the bathroom floor. I couldn't blame him. I probably would have done the same thing if I were him.

I turned back to Ryan's room, and this time I flung the bedroom door open wide. As usual, it was a huge mess with dirty clothes and garbage everywhere and rumpled blankets and pillows on the floor.

It's not fair! Dallin and I were living the rules, rules I was trying hard not to resent, but Ryan hadn't done anything. He broke curfew every night, he never took his turn to cook, and he never cleaned whatever room in the house was his turn to clean. He hadn't done anything, and yet nothing was happening to him. Nothing.

I turned on my heel. Flipping the bathroom light switch on, I angrily yanked the top off the toilet tank. Two glass bottles of beer and a bottle of some other sort of alcohol were lined up inside. I stared for a good solid minute at those bottles until something inside me snapped. The next second, I yanked one of the bottles out and wrenched the top of it until I finally managed to get it open. With a quick flip of my wrist at the sink, I poured the entire thing down the drain. A minute later I'd dumped the other two down the drain, too, and angrily thrown the empty bottles onto Ryan's bed.

It wasn't the first time I'd disposed of Ryan's stash in the bathroom, but this time I went wild and searched the house as if I was on an Easter egg hunt gone horribly wrong. I found two more beer bottles and emptied them in the sink before tossing them onto Ryan's bed.

The loud slam of the front door made me jump, and my heart pounded fast. It was Ryan, of course. I hurried out of his room and stepped into the bathroom doorway. A few seconds later I could hear him doing his usual stumbling and muttering and cursing as he banged into things on his way down the darkened hall towards the bathroom.

"Get out!"

Ryan gave me a hard shove into the hallway before crashing to his knees in front of the toilet, but he was too late. Again. I ran for the paper towels and tried to wipe up the floor, even though Ryan kicked at the back of my legs, yelling for me to get out again.

"Be quiet, Ryan! You don't need to wake everyone up!" I was angry, and yet stupid tears were blurring my vision. I wiped furiously at my eyes before turning to glare at Ryan hunched over the toilet. "You're so mean to me—I don't know why I bother to help you at all. You obviously couldn't care less!"

"Then why don't you just shut up and leave? I don't need you!"

Ryan couldn't say anything else, because he got really sick after that. So sick that I had to toss the towels aside to kneel by him and hold his head while he kept being sick. Finally he pushed me away before slumping onto the bathroom floor, closing his eyes and moaning.

I sat on the floor beside him and buried my face on my arms and allowed myself the luxury of a few good sobs before the hair standing up on the back of my neck warned me I wasn't alone with only a passed-out Ryan for company.

I slowly raised my head to look in the open doorway that was now filled with Dallin standing there looking pretty horrified.

"Oh, just go away!" I buried my face back on my arms, but I could tell he hadn't left. The floorboards creaked a little, but only because he'd shifted his weight from one leg to the other. I lifted my head up again. He was still standing there, just looking at me. Sadly. Kindly, actually. I stared back, and a second later, he'd walked over, crouched down on the floor beside me, and gently pulled me against his chest and wrapped his arms around me while I cried and cried some more. I don't know what would've happened if he'd just walked down the hall as he'd done in the past. Who knows how things would've turned out if he had. But luckily for me, he hadn't. Instead, he kept patting my back awkwardly and saying softly, "It's okay, it's okay," even though we both knew it wasn't.

It felt—different—strange—having Dallin, someone who wasn't really family, holding me and trying to comfort me. Even though it felt nice in a confusing kind of way, sitting on the bathroom floor together like we were, I started to feel weird about the whole situation. I pulled myself together as quickly as I could and let Dallin help me up into a standing position again.

I couldn't look at Dallin, so I kept my eyes lowered and smoothed my hair with my hands. "I thought you were asleep."

"No—I just got home."

Dallin still had on his shoes and jacket, so I knew he wasn't lying. "How long have you been standing there?"

"Long enough."

I bit my bottom lip and crossed my arms, rubbing my upper arms before I turned my back on Dallin to step over Ryan. I leaned down to roll Ryan over onto his back, but he was so far gone it was like trying to move a sack of bricks. I looked up at Dallin who just stood there, watching me. "Would you mind doing me a favor? Help me get Ryan to bed?"

Dallin hurried over to me and easily wrenched Ryan up into a sitting position before crouching a bit to throw him over his shoulder like a sack of potatoes. I ran ahead of him to turn the light on in Ryan's room so he could see where to dump the body.

I watched Dallin hesitate in the doorway, looking around the room and at Ryan's bed with all the empty bottles scattered everywhere. I shoved the bottles off the bed onto the floor, laughing nervously. "Sorry it's such a mess in here. You'd think Ryan turned into a werewolf in here, but he's human, really. At least I think he is . . ."

Instead of moving into Ryan's room, Dallin looked hard at me again before he turned around and headed back for the bathroom.

"Hey! What are you doing?" I hurried after Dallin and watched in shock as he unceremoniously dumped Ryan back onto the bathroom floor.

"I'm doing all of us a favor," Dallin said firmly.

I could only gasp. "What?"

"Let Ryan wake up in here on the floor in his dirty barf clothes."

"I can't believe you!" I angrily moved towards Ryan, but Dallin gently took hold of my arm and pulled me back.

"If you don't stop babying him all the time, he'll never stop this. Never. He has to deal with the consequences of what he's doing to himself, even if it means waking up from passing out on the bathroom floor with puke all over him."

I yanked my arm from Dallin's grip. "Fine. Don't help, then!" I tried to move Ryan again, but he was useless, dead weight with spaghetti legs.

Dallin sighed and shook his head. "Forget it, Rachel. Just leave him there. He's probably thrown up as much as he's going to, so it won't hurt him. Who knows? Maybe it could actually help him."

I was feeling so used and abused tonight that I gave Ryan a defeated shove and wearily climbed to my feet. I pushed past Dallin, who followed me out to the kitchen. He sat on one of the bar stools while I poured myself a glass of water and reached for a box of crackers. I crunched one down before holding the box out to Dallin.

"Want one? The smell was making me sick. It had to have grossed you out, too."

Dallin smiled and reached for a cracker and silently crunched along with me.

"Those bottles I saw on Ryan's bed—did he drink all that tonight?"

I shook my head and swallowed some water. "No. I raided his hidden stashes and poured it all down the sink."

Dallin looked shocked. "Really?"

I smiled ruefully back. "Yeah. I do stuff like that when I'm in a rage, thanks to him."

"You think it's going to help him?"

I shrugged and bit into another cracker. "It'll keep him from drinking anymore tonight. And tomorrow."

Dallin shook his head and looked across the kitchen counter at me seriously. "You'll never control the problem, because you can't control him. He has to make the choice to stop and get help himself."

I laughed bitterly. "But that's the problem. I don't think he *can* choose to stop anymore. Even if he wanted to stop. And the sad thing about that is I'm not so sure he even wants to yet. Or if he ever will."

"Whether or not you think he can make his own choices anymore, you have to let him deal with the results of messing up like this. Otherwise, he'll never feel the urge to change."

"It's not exactly nice—leaving someone who needs help lying on the bathroom floor!"

Dallin shrugged. "Think of it as tough love, then. I've listened to you take care of him night after night, and nothing's changed. You might as well try leaving him to take care of himself and see what happens."

I shook my head slowly. "I don't know. We'll see, I guess." I set my empty glass in the sink before turning back to look at Dallin curiously. "How's your eye, by the way?"

Dallin smiled and lightly touched his eye. I could still see some light blue and yellow bruising around it. "It's healing okay. I'm glad it doesn't look like a rainbow anymore."

"Are you going to have to have more surgery?"

Dallin shook his head. "I doubt it. It should be okay now. I still have to go to the doctor a few more times, though."

"Does it make it hard to golf?"

"It was kind of hard at first, but it's not a problem anymore."

I nodded and glanced at the kitchen clock. "Well, it's late, so . . . I guess I'll head for bed." I walked back down the hall to my room before turning to call to Dallin before he disappeared inside Robert's old room. "Hey—Dallin. Thanks."

Dallin raised his eyebrows. "For what?"

"For listening, and—" I shrugged my shoulders, embarrassed, while Dallin watched me, waiting. "And—just for caring, I guess. So, thanks."

Dallin smiled and said, "See you in the morning," before quietly closing the bedroom door.

I sighed heavily as I stepped into my own room and closed the door.

My sonnet was still lying on the top of my desk, waiting for me. I read it through again before changing the last line:

I always fear whatever I don't want to see.

CHAPTER TWENTY-SIX

Thinking about the hoodie incident and my raiding of Ryan's stash worried me the next morning while I was getting ready for school, but I basically worried for nothing. Ryan was confused and annoyed over the empty bottles in his room, but since he couldn't remember anything from the night before, it was impossible for him to accuse anyone of disposing of his poison.

I was fixing my hair in the bathroom when Ryan limped in hunting for aspirin, still wearing the clothes he'd had on the day before—even his shoes and socks. His eyes were bloodshot and angry.

"Is it just déjà vu, or are you wearing the same thing to school again today?"

Ryan only scowled back but grimaced from turning his head my way and rubbed the back of his neck with one hand.

"What's wrong with you?"

"I woke up in here last night! You try sleeping for hours on this floor and see if your neck doesn't feel like someone stomped on it!"

"How stupid. Why in the world would you fall asleep in here?"

Ryan ignored me while he sat down on the closed lid of the toilet and stared into space as he gulped down his aspirin and water. Slowly he stood up to lean against the towel closet in the bathroom. I gave him a shove and angrily wrenched open the closet before grabbing a hand towel and slamming the door shut.

"Excuse me would've been nice!"

"Yeah, well, not tying me to a locker and not pulling my hair and not calling me stupid and not throwing up all over this bathroom would've been nice, too!"

Ryan winced and put his hands over his ears. "You don't have to scream! What's wrong with you, Rachel? Good grief—do I need to get you some Midol?"

"You're a huge jerk. Did you know that?"

"What did I do?" Ryan had the gall to look surprised.

"The usual jerky things you always do when you come home plastered, of course!"

"I don't remember," Ryan mumbled.

"You don't remember a lot of things. Must be nice to indulge in a habit where you can be a creep to everyone and later just say 'oh, sorry, I don't remember,' and think that excuses you from being a gigantic loser!"

I slammed out of the bathroom and finished fixing my hair in my bedroom while I listened to the muffled sounds of Ryan removing the lid of the toilet tank, followed by a few curse words before the lid was loudly slammed back into place. Even though Ryan complained to Mom and Mr. Ackerman that he wasn't feeling good, Mr. Ackerman hardly looked at him as he calmly read the paper over breakfast.

"I'm sorry you're not feeling well, Ryan. Be sure to take it easy today at school. Hopefully you'll be well enough for football practice after school."

That was all Mr. Ackerman had to say to Ryan, but his tone and piercing look made it clear he wasn't about to allow Ryan to stay home. It didn't matter, though. Ryan didn't show up for seminary, so I knew he was working off his hangover somewhere, just not at home.

By Friday night, I had nearly chewed off all my fingernails, wondering when Mr. Ackerman would do something about Ryan consistently breaking curfew every night, but I didn't have to wait much longer. I knew everything around our house was going to change even more when I dragged myself out of bed late Saturday morning and saw Mom putting groceries away in the kitchen. At least, I thought it was Mom. The woman with her back to me had red hair in a funky modern cut, while my mom had always been a sedate brunette, but everything else about the woman looked like Mom. Pretty much, anyway.

"Mom? Is that you?"

Mom turned around to face me and laughed. "Rachel, honey! Of course it is. Who else would it be?"

Mom was wearing a new outfit, too. I'd never seen Mom in cargo jeans before, and her shirt was a different style than I'd ever thought she'd consider. She even had new shoes on. Boots, actually. I couldn't remember ever seeing Mom wear any type of boots in my entire life.

"I honestly don't know. What in the world did you do to your hair?"

Mom lightly tossed her head with a grin. "Do you like it? I wanted to surprise Joe!"

"But—but you have brown hair! You've never dyed your hair a different color before!"

Mom burst out laughing again. "Then it's time I gave it a try, don't you think? I don't know what came over me, really. I went to get my hair done and was just going to cover up the gray as usual, but then I thought it would be fun to try something new. Who knows? Maybe next time I'll try being a blonde, like you!"

I couldn't stop staring. "I—I can't believe you'd do this! Did he make you do this?"

Mom couldn't stop laughing today. "Of course not, silly! I just think I was finally ready for a change, that's all."

I had to fight not to cry when Mr. Ackerman emerged from Dad's old study. His face lit up at Mom's transformation.

Mom smiled shyly at Mr. Ackerman. "Well, Joe, what do you think?"

"Wow—you look amazing! Absolutely stunning!"

Mom looked so thrilled I had to turn away. "You like my hair?"

"I love it—I knew you'd look great with red hair!"

Mom's smile faded when she saw the look on my face and quickly hugged me. "Sweetie, it's just hair! It'll grow out, and I can dye it back. I'm still me, you know!"

Mr. Ackerman laughed, but I didn't think any of it was funny, or stunning, or amazing. And I was definitely not loving any of it.

Dallin found his way to the kitchen next and had the nerve to light up, just like his dad. "Wow—look at you!"

Mr. Ackerman had his arm proudly around Mom. "Doesn't she look great?"

"Yeah—awesome!"

Mom laughed and ruffled Dallin's hair. "I knew I liked you, Dallin!"

When Ryan stumbled into the kitchen, he didn't even notice anything until Dallin pointed out the new "hot babe" in the kitchen. Mom giggled, but when Ryan looked up from slouching over his usual aspirin and water at the kitchen counter, he only squinted and looked Mom over before rolling his eyes.

Mr. Ackerman moved to stand in front of Ryan. "Well, Ryan, what do you think of how your mother looks?"

"No comment."

Mr. Ackerman looked like he was going to say something, but instead he put on a big smile and turned back to Mom. "Well, I think you look great, Elaine!"

Mr. Ackerman was beyond thrilled with Mom's new look, but I hated it. I was ready to storm out of the kitchen, but Mr. Ackerman made us all sit down around the kitchen table so we could "talk."

"It's becoming painfully obvious to me that we all need to be reminded about the house rules: Everyone needs to pitch in with the cleaning and follow the job chart, take their turn making dinner, and most important, make curfew." Mr. Ackerman used words like "we" and "everyone," but he kept his eyes fastened on Ryan, who slouched back in his chair with his arms folded, rolling his eyes, and looking at everyone as if he thought he was superior and we were all stupid. Then Ryan turned to point a finger at Dallin.

"You hear that, Ackerman? Get yourself home on time, will ya?"

Mr. Ackerman shot Ryan an annoyed look. "Dallin is not the problem here!"

Ryan only grinned wickedly back. "Oh, then I guess it's Rachel's fault. Did you have to get your stomach pumped after she attempted to cook Thursday night? I thought for sure we were eating cat vomit."

Mom rubbed her temples under her new red hair. "Ryan, please!"

And now Mr. Ackerman was pointing at Ryan. "Ryan, you better listen up—"

"No, I think *you* need to 'listen up!'" Ryan slammed his hands down on the table, making everyone but Mr. Ackerman jump. "I don't know what planet you're living on, but you don't get to have any control over me, got that? You can't make me do anything. Stop trying to be my father. You're not him, and you never will be, okay?" Ryan turned to glare at Mom. "Mom—you want me to do something, you tell me, but don't hide behind him."

Poor Mom looked like a frazzled rope in the middle of a tug of war. "Ry-Guy, please—I want so much for all of us to be a family. Won't you just try?"

Ryan burst out with a bitter laugh. "We're not 'a' family, Mom. That's the problem. We're two families now living under one roof. This guy thinks now that he's married to you, he can tell me what to do. Doesn't work that way."

"Ryan!"

Mr. Ackerman put up his hand to stop Mom. "No, Elaine. Don't let yourself get all upset." Then Mr. Ackerman clasped his hands in front of him on the table before turning to look carefully at Ryan, lowering his voice when he spoke again. "Ryan, you're right. I can't 'make' you do anything. However, be aware that if you continue in the direction you're going, things are only going to get harder for you. Not easier."

Ryan rolled his eyes and looked away. "Whatever."

"Your mother and I are aware that your grades have been slipping fast and that you're dangerously close to being thrown off the football team."

Ryan laughed before turning back to raise an eyebrow at Mr. Ackerman. "Been snooping my grades on the Internet, huh?"

Mr. Ackerman shook his head in exasperation. "We're concerned about you, Ryan! A couple of your teachers called and e-mailed us this week—"

Ryan swore under his breath.

"Regardless of whether or not you pull your weight around here, you know very well you won't be kicked out of this family. However, that wonderful high school and football team you love so much won't be so kind and forgiving. If you don't pull yourself together, not only will you find yourself booted off the varsity team but you won't be graduating, either. So maybe you ought to rethink how you spend your time in the evening and instead spend some time studying instead of hanging out for all hours of the night with your . . . 'friends.'"

My head had been turning back and forth, following the three-way, heated tennis match of words in silence. I glanced across the table at Dallin. He looked decidedly uncomfortable, as if he wished he could be anywhere in the entire world but sitting here in the middle of all of our twisted Brady Bunch drama. As for me, all I knew was that every day my world was turning more and more into a much different place than I ever thought it would be.

"Um, if it's okay, can I be excused?"

I left the table without waiting for an answer from anyone, nearly knocking the chair over in my hurry to get out. I ran down the hall to my bedroom, snatched up my blue notebook and a pen, and headed out the front door.

CHAPTER TWENTY-SEVEN

It stands,
A cola bottle
Pregnant with bubbles and foam.
A slight tap in the right direction—
Down
It falls—
End over end
Sometimes pointing its mouth toward Heaven
And sometimes to Hell.
Circling, circling
And then the shattering—
Drops, dirt-colored
Fly in unheard of places
And splinters
Sharp like ten thousand needles
Sprinkle everywhere
Cutting toes, ankles, heels—
Even fingers that stoop to grasp.
In the end, there is only
A redness
Thick and oozing—
No amount of Comet
Will remove its stain.

I sighed and set my notebook and pen aside to zip up my hoodie before reaching out to brush a few strands of grass off Dad's headstone.

"I'm sorry I haven't been back here sooner, Dad. Things have been so crazy at home, you wouldn't believe it. I wish you could see Mom's hair—"

The loud snap of a twig being crunched underfoot behind my back made me jump to my feet and my heart thump loud in my chest.

"Sorry—I didn't mean to scare you!"

Dallin. My face was flushing hot, and I nearly writhed with embarrassment, wondering if he'd heard me talking out loud.

"I don't appreciate being spied on!"

Dallin's eyes were wide, and he put his hands up as if he were surrendering. "I wasn't—honest! I totally did not expect to see you here!"

"How long have you been creeping up behind me, listening in on me?" I demanded.

"I don't creep, and I wasn't listening!"

"Why else would you be here except to spy on me?"

Dallin ignored me and walked slowly over to where I'd been sitting and looked at Dad's headstone with his hands stuffed in his jeans pockets. "This is your dad's?"

I nodded warily and bent down to pick up my notebook and pen.

Dallin looked over at me with a frown. "What's that?"

I hugged the book protectively close to my chest. "Nothing. None of your business!"

"Is that the book you write in during seminary?"

I shrugged. "Sometimes." Dallin turned back to look at Dad's headstone. I took a step towards him. "Why are you here?"

Dallin didn't even turn to look at me. "Your dad's not the only person buried in this cemetery." Dallin stepped around Dad's headstone and walked away without looking back over his shoulder. I watched him weave around the headstones and trees until he disappeared behind a big, old oak tree. Curiosity got the better of me, and after walking past a dozen rows of grave markers and rounding the oak tree, I saw him again, squatting in front of a large flat, white stone, using his pocket knife to cut the grass growing around it. I walked slowly towards him, hugging my notebook to my chest, before stopping hesitantly beside him. I looked down at the stone and caught my breath:

Margaret Brown Ackerman
Loving Wife and Mother

"I . . . I didn't know your mom was buried here, too."

Dallin didn't look up from cutting at the grass with his pocketknife. "My dad wanted her buried close by so Brandon and I could come here anytime we wanted. I used to walk through this cemetery every day on my way home from school when I was a kid so I could sit here for a while. Now I stop by whenever I can."

I looked silently at Dallin's mother's birth and death dates and was stunned. "You were only ten years old when she died!"

"Yeah, I was," Dallin said softly with a sad smile.

I sat down beside him and watched him work for a minute before I dared to ask. "How did your mom die?"

Dallin stopped cutting and looked at me briefly. "She had breast cancer."

"Oh. I'm sorry." I didn't know what else to say. What else can you say to something like that? "You must miss her very much."

Dallin nodded. He finally brushed off the knife and folded it back into his jeans pocket. "I miss just *seeing* her the most, you know? Just having her around and knowing she'll be at home. I miss that a lot."

I nodded before asking another question softly. "What was your mom like?"

Dallin smiled. "She was probably the most patient, calm person in the entire world. Even during her cancer. She always took everything in stride without freaking out over anything. She was our family's rock. She was amazing on the piano, too. I miss hearing her play." He leaned forward to brush a few strands of grass off the headstone before turning to me again. "She liked to hug a lot, too. I think she hugged me and my brother, Brandon, about a million times a day." Dallin smiled and shrugged. "My dad says I look a lot like her. She had blonde hair and blue eyes, like me."

I tried to picture what Mrs. Ackerman must've looked like—a woman's face with blonde hair and Dallin's beautiful eyes. "I wish I could have met her."

"You'd have liked her. Everyone did." Dallin looked at me curiously. "So what was your dad like?"

I couldn't help smiling. "He was funny—loud—crazy. He could make everyone laugh so easy. He gave everyone nicknames, too. He called my mom Lainey on their first date, instead of Elaine, and he barely even knew her. He was the first one to call Ryan 'Ry-Guy.' He called him that the second he and Mom decided to name him Ryan." Dallin was looking at me so intently that I had to look away. "He made everything fun and was just a lot of fun to be with. Basically, he was the complete opposite of your dad." Dallin burst out laughing while I scrambled to extract both feet from being crammed down my throat, truly horrified I'd said something so stupid to him. "Not that your dad isn't a fun person, too. I didn't mean it to sound like that!"

Dallin laughed. "Yeah, my dad's a regular standup comedian!"

I laughed, too, and tried again. "Your dad is really nice. I know my mom likes him a lot. Loves him, I mean. I guess."

Dallin nodded, and we were both quiet for a long moment. "My dad was sad for a long time. I hated seeing him like that. It's awesome to see him happy again. Your mom's been really good for my dad."

I nodded slowly. "It must've been hard to have to leave your house and move into ours."

Dallin shrugged and kept smiling at me. "Sort of, I guess, but it hasn't been so bad. I would've been moving out soon enough anyway. I'm just glad my dad won't have to be alone now."

"Yeah."

"I guess all this has to be harder on you and your family, since your dad didn't pass away as long ago as my mom did."

I looked down at my lap and nervously fidgeted with my pen before I spoke again, quietly and slowly. "I didn't get to say good-bye. Or I'm sorry, or I love you, or anything. I mean, one second, we were us, our family, and the next—" There were no words to describe what we became next. I could see the flashing red and blue lights in the living room again, and I could hear Mom sobbing softly while Ryan stared blankly in front of him.

"He was on his way to pick you up from your stupid friend's house!"

Dallin leaned towards me worriedly and touched my arm briefly. "You cold?"

I was shaking, but I rubbed my arms and forced a smile. "No, I'm fine."

Dallin watched me carefully for a second until I stopped shaking. "That's got to be hard. I can't imagine what that must've been like."

It felt strangely cathartic to sit and talk about our parents—all four of them—with Dallin. I knew I'd never be able to get Ryan to talk with me like this, but Dallin—he understood. It was bizarre, sitting there in the cemetery, realizing that Dallin comprehended things about my life now that not even my best friend Teresa could ever really understand.

"I'm sorry I got snotty with you earlier. I didn't mean to—you just startled me . . ." My voice trailed off, because even though Dallin was looking at me kindly, I didn't want to admit that I talked to my dad here a lot. Maybe too much.

"I always feel better after I've been here. I don't think it's weird to talk here. I'll bet most people do."

There was something about Dallin—a combination of the way he kept looking at me, and knowing that he knew, too—that he was dealing with this, too—that made my tongue have a life of its own. "It's just weird, you know? I'd just like to ask God—why. I mean, I've been raised with the whole idea that God has a plan for everyone. And I believe that— I really do. It's just—I can't make any sense out of why my dad had to die. Why *my* dad? He died for no reason. It doesn't fit into any plan."

Dallin shook his head and spoke softly. "Not everything is going to make sense while we're here. You know that."

"Yeah, I know, and I hate it. It's not fair."

"It's not, but God never promised anything was going to be fair here. That's something I know beyond a doubt. It's the whole 'I never said it was going to be easy, only that it was going to be worth it' deal."

I stared hard into Dallin's eyes. "Do you believe that?"

Dallin looked back just as seriously and nodded slowly. "Yeah, I do. More and more. But I have to keep reminding myself of it every day."

I shook my head and sighed. "You seem almost okay with everything that's happened to you. How do you do that? Just be okay and keep going?" Dallin looked surprised, and once again I was trying to yank my feet out of my face. "I'm sorry—you don't have to answer. It's none of my business how you're dealing with your mom being gone."

Dallin smiled. "No, it's okay." He looked down at his own lap for a second before looking at me wonderingly. "You want to know something? You're the first person to ask."

My eyes widened at that. "Really?"

Dallin nodded and looked at his mom's headstone again. "I was just a kid when my mom died. I guess most people think I'd be used to it by now. Over it, I guess, just because I'm not crying all the time or getting thrown out of school and into jail or anything like that." Dallin turned his head to look at me seriously again. "I'll tell you one thing, Rachel. You never 'get over' losing your mom or dad. Life is never the same again, and you'll miss your dad every day for the rest of your life. That's just a hard given."

I could feel tears starting in my eyes, and I turned away to swipe at them. "So what do you do to keep from losing it?"

Dallin looked at me kindly again and took a deep breath. "Well, just like you, I went for a long time wanting to know how God could let this happen, and why He had my mom get sick, and why He took her away from me. It took me a long time—lots of prayers and scripture reading and thinking about it a lot and talking to my dad and my brother—before

I decided that maybe it wasn't just that it was God's plan for my mom not to be here long, like everyone kept telling me, but maybe that it was also part of *my* plan to not have my mom here for very long."

Dallin stopped and slowly nodded his head before looking kindly and seriously at me again. "I'm trying not to see my mom's death so much as a tragedy but instead as part of a plan. A plan I don't understand but still a plan. Definitely not an accident but something carefully decided by Someone who knows more than I do. Someone who knows what I need and what my mom needs and what everyone else needs. I mean, I'm learning and growing in ways I never could've imagined. This has all been incredibly hard, but I think it's going to benefit me in ways I can't know or understand right now." Dallin looked down for a moment before looking up to smile at me again. "I even memorized a scripture that I've used whenever I'm feeling ready to quit."

I raised both eyebrows at that. "A scripture? What scripture?"

"D&C 58:2–5: 'Blessed is he that . . . is faithful in tribulation. . . . Ye cannot behold with your natural eyes, for the present time, the design of your God concerning those things which shall come hereafter, and the glory which shall follow. . . . For after much tribulation come the blessings. Wherefore the day cometh that ye shall be crowned with much glory; . . . Remember this, . . . that you may lay it to heart, and receive that which is to follow.'"

I nodded slowly. "I like that."

"I had no control over what happened to my mom, and there's nothing I can do about the past, but I can do a lot now with my own life. I can make something of it. Something both my mom and I will be proud of."

I had to turn my head away. That's where Dallin was lucky. He had nothing to do with what happened to his mom.

Dallin reached out to touch my arm gently. "You okay, Rachel?"

I shivered. "Yeah. I just miss my dad."

Dallin nodded and patted my arm awkwardly for a moment. "I miss my mom, too. But I feel pretty lucky. My dad's happy now, and I have a really nice stepmom."

I looked back in surprise. "You like my mom?"

Dallin smiled and nodded. "Sure." Dallin looked back at his mother's headstone briefly before turning back to me again. "I'm also learning more about the Atonement than I ever would have by now. I don't understand it on a very deep level and probably never will before I die. But I do at least know that it's real. And that it is powerful, and that it can heal." Dallin looked at me carefully, waiting until my eyes met his.

"You know, Rachel, no one in the world has gone through what you have. Sure, you're not the only person who's lost a parent, but no one experienced the exact circumstances of your dad's death exactly as you did. Not even your brothers. Everything about you and your relationship with your dad makes your situation unique. That's why Christ is the only one who can help you get through this or any of your trials. He experienced the exact trials and the exact pain you're going through when He was in Gethsemane, in the exact way you're experiencing it and going through it every day. You don't have to explain why and how you hurt to Him. He already knows. That's why He's the one who knows how to heal and comfort you, if you'll go to Him for help. Sometimes He sends that comfort and help through other people, and sometimes it comes in pretty unexpected and unique ways. That's why it's important not to push people away who want to help. And that's why understanding and using Christ's Atonement can help so much."

As truly great as it had been to sit and talk with Dallin, I left him alone soon after that so he could have some time alone to think about his mom. I'd sat so long in front of my dad's headstone that I was stiff and sore when I unpretzeled myself back into a standing position and headed for home. No one heard me when I quietly entered the house, but I could hear laughing coming from the kitchen and realized it was Dallin talking with Mom.

"Here you go, Dallin."

I hid against the wall just out of sight and watched Mom from behind the kitchen counter set a sandwich on a plate in front of Dallin, who was seated on one of the bar stools. "Wow. It's been a long time since anyone made me a peanut butter and honey sandwich!"

Mom smiled. "Your dad told me how much you liked peanut butter and honey when you were little."

Dallin nodded and picked up one half of the sandwich to examine it. "I still do. Holy cow—you even cut the crust off!"

Mom laughed. "Yep."

Dallin looked at Mom with a truly happy smile. "Thanks, Mom. I mean—Elaine—sorry—"

Poor Dallin looked pretty flustered, but Mom was beaming and looking like she was going to cry, all at the same time. "You can call me Mom if you want to, Dallin. I'd consider it a huge honor if you did. I know you love your mother very much."

Dallin nodded and spoke quietly. "Yeah, I do."

I could see that look of hopeful longing on Dallin's face again. I turned away when Mom reached out to smooth his hair, but I didn't move to hurry down the hall until Dallin had disappeared into Robert's old room. I'd thought I could make it to my own room undetected, but I was wrong.

"Rachel, is that you?"

I stopped but didn't look over my shoulder. "Uh-huh."

"Hold on. Come see me for a minute."

I sighed and turned around to face Mom in the kitchen. "What?"

Mom looked at me worriedly. "Are you still mad that I dyed my hair?"

I sighed again. "I just don't see why you felt you needed to change something else!"

"It's just hair and clothes, Rachel! You've done the same thing yourself, you know."

I gasped. "What have I done?"

"You've bought new clothes and wanted a new haircut when you've met some cute boy you wanted to impress!"

I blushed and looked away. "Okay, fine, if you think you need to cut and dye your hair and buy new clothes to impress Mr. Ackerman."

Mom shook her head and moved forward to look at me closer, her arms folded. "This is about more than just hair and clothes, isn't it?

I shrugged and looked away. "Yes and no."

Mom frowned. "Yes and no? What does that mean?"

"It's just yet another change in a long line of changes."

"Such as?"

I looked back at Mom and wanted to scream at the look of bafflement on her face. "Well, for one thing, you're always going out to plays all the time!"

"I like going to the theater!"

"You never liked the theater before!" I accused.

"I never *went* to the theater before, mostly because your dad didn't care for it. I had no idea I'd enjoy it this much. It's so nice to have someone to go to plays and things with who honestly enjoys them."

I shook my head angrily. "You're being different to make him happy!"

Mom shook her head back. "That's not entirely true, Rachel. You learn new things from everyone you meet in life, and you develop new interests. It helps make life more interesting."

"It's more than just that. There's all of these rules around the house. He's changing what you like to do, and how you look, and how you do your disciplining stuff, and you're just—"

Mom waited for me to continue. "I'm just what?"

"You're different now!" I could feel my throat closing off, but I wasn't about to let myself cry. "It was hard enough losing Dad, but now—I'm losing you, too."

Mom looked shocked, and a second later she'd forced me into a tight hug. "Honey—you're not losing me—you're not!" She pulled away to look into my now tear-stained face and kept her hands on my shoulders. "I'm still your mom, and I always will be. Just because I'm having some fun trying new things and getting a new hairstyle and a few new outfits doesn't mean that I love you any less or feel any differently about you!"

Mom grabbed me up into a hug again. "Clothes and hair and going to the theater could never change my relationship with you. The only change I hope ever happens to our relationship is that it grows stronger and better. That's all."

Mom pulled away again and grabbed a tissue for me. "The wonderful thing about life is that it's filled with the promise of many wonderful, meaningful relationships that you'll have the opportunity to discover and have, hopefully for a long time." She smiled and brushed my hair back from my face with her fingers. "I will love your father forever, and having a chance to love someone again is something I never imagined would happen to me. Joe feels the same way and has told me the same thing. But even so, new relationships can never replace the ones I have now. No one can take your father's place, and no one can take yours, Rachel."

I nodded and let Mom hug me again. "Okay, Mom. Okay."

When Mom was finally convinced I was okay, she smiled conspiratorially at me. "I want you to know—I've been introducing Joe to some new things, too."

"Oh, yeah? Like what?"

"We've been dancing. Ballroom dancing, actually."

I couldn't help laughing. "No way!"

Mom laughed, too. "It's true. Your dad was such a great dancer, and Joe—well, he's a terrible dancer, but it's so sweet that he tries for me. He does it to make me happy."

"So what's his dancing like?"

"Well, he dances sort of like this—"

I laughed until I hurt, watching Mom imitate Mr. Ackerman stiffly trying to concentrate on his feet and count and dance, all at the same time, and getting messed up and stepping all over Mom's feet in the process. Mom laughed, too, and I realized it'd been a long time since both of us had laughed together. And that I'd missed it. A lot.

CHAPTER TWENTY-EIGHT

Every day I was being reminded that my life was a constant yo-yo. Having a bad day turn out good, like Saturday, didn't mean that life was going to stay on an upswing. I held my breath when I had a good day, waiting for the moment when things would turn sour and I'd feel my life spinning, flying back to the ground again. With Ryan around, I was guaranteed that nothing would stay great for long.

Ryan was still breaking curfew; he was just being sneakier about it. Mr. Ackerman retaliated by booby-trapping the front door every night, so Ryan returned fire by using his bedroom window as his new front door. When he came home at all, that is. He'd turned Mr. Ackerman's speech on "shaping up" against him and often claimed to be sleeping over at friends' homes to do some intense "studying" to make sure he'd be ready for a test or to work on some project to make good enough grades to graduate.

It was hard leaving Ryan to rot on the bathroom floor at night when he did come home, but I felt guiltier over my relief when he didn't come home at all. I should've been more worried about where he was and what he was doing, but somehow he usually made it to slouch in a desk behind me in seminary at least a couple of times a week. Between that fact and my prayers every day begging that Ryan would be watched over and somehow healed from his problem, I was able to make myself sleep a few hours each night.

And Dallin—Dallin had been so great lately. I looked up from scribbling in my blue notebook during seminary to watch him carefully redpencil something in his scriptures. It'd been so nice to have someone in the house to talk to who understood what I was going through. It had felt wonderful not to feel quite so alone anymore. Dallin was still busy with golf matches and his own homework and friends, but we'd been running into each other at the cemetery more often, and he'd been going out of his way to talk with me more whenever we were both at home, and it'd just been nice. Really nice.

"Could I have someone please read First Nephi 7:12 for me?" Brother Clawson smiled at Jason's as-usual swiftly raised hand. "Jason—thank you."

"'Yea, and how is it that ye have forgotten that the Lord is able to do all things according to his will, for the children of men, if it so be that they exercise faith in him? Wherefore, let us be faithful to him.'"

Brother Clawson turned to look us all over with a broad smile. "Isn't that amazing? The Lord is able to do all things according to His will for us, if we exercise our faith in Him. If we don't exercise sufficient faith in God, we're truly denying Him the opportunity to help us." I could hear Brother Clawson pause, but I was already back to thumbing through my blue notebook. "Another scripture I love that goes along with this is First Corinthians 10:13. Rachel, will you read that one?"

I jumped at the sound of my name and scrambled for my scriptures, unopened and off to the side of my desk. "'There hath no temptation taken you but such as is common to man: but God is faithful, who will not suffer you to be tempted above that ye are able; but will with the temptation also make a way to escape, that ye may be able to bear it.'"

Brother Clawson smiled kindly at me as I looked up from my scriptures. "Elder Neal A. Maxwell once stated that 'the Lord knows our bearing capacity, both as to coping and to comprehending, and He will not give us more to bear than we can manage at the moment, though to us it may seem otherwise. Just as no temptations will come to us from which we cannot escape or which we cannot bear, we will not be given more trials than we can sustain.'"

Brother Clawson looked slowly around the room at all of us. My heart pounded strangely when his eyes settled back onto me. "It takes faith to believe we can overcome our own temptations. And it takes much faith to believe those we love can eventually overcome their own temptations if they will come unto Christ. And it takes even more faith to believe they can successfully cope with whatever suffering might await them in the process. But there is hope and the realization that we are, each one of us, a child of God with the greatest potential in the world. We all have the potential to survive the pain that comes to us during this life, sometimes due to our own poor choices. God has faith we can overcome temptation. So then should we."

I looked away as Brother Clawson continued. "I think whenever we, or someone we love, is going through something difficult, we can feel forsaken and have a tendency to say, 'O God, where art thou?' God can free any of us at any time from our pain and suffering, and yet, often He does not. Why do you think that is?"

I watched Dallin hesitantly raise his hand before Brother Clawson nodded to him. "I guess—mostly because this life is supposed to be a test. It wouldn't be much of a test if we were rescued every time things got hard."

"Yes, that's true." Brother Clawson folded his arms and nodded before turning his eyes towards me again. "When we, or someone we love, is going through something hard, we seem to quickly forget that there is purpose behind the struggles and challenges in our life. It's natural, I think, to want to rescue those we love from their pain, even if it's due to their own poor choices. Mostly because we're going through pain ourselves, watching that person we love, and in helping him or her, we're hoping to ease our own pain as well. The problem with that, though, is that sometimes when we do so, we rescue that person from the very experience they need for their own good in order to change, overcome trials, and ultimately progress in this life."

Teresa was waiting for me after class, leaning against the wall outside the classroom tapping a pencil against her leg. "I didn't see Ryan come out. Is he still in there?"

I shook my head as I walked over to her. "He didn't show up today."

"Again?"

I frowned and nervously pushed my hair off my shoulders. "Yeah. I think—" One second later, I was rudely shoved from behind and turned to glare at whoever had rammed into me.

Jason's face looked so surprised I couldn't help laughing. "'Scuse me, Rachel—sorry about that!"

"That's okay, Jason."

Dallin smiled and waved at me as he and Jason walked out the seminary building doors.

Teresa grinned and waited until both Dallin and Jason were safely outside the seminary building before speaking. "Did you hear who Jason asked to Homecoming?"

My heart sank into my sneakers. "Don't tell me. Angela Barnett."

Teresa grinned as we pushed through the seminary doors and walked towards Central High. "Nope. It wasn't Angela Barnett."

That fact made my mouth drop open. "Really? Who'd he ask instead?"

Teresa's grin grew even wider. "Kathy Colton!"

Kathy Colton was a sophomore, too. I didn't know her well, but I did know that she wasn't exactly popular, although she was smart and nice and relatively well liked. Even so, I couldn't picture her with a football star like Jason West. At all. "Kathy Colton? How do you know?"

"Missy and Heather told me. They saw him ask her in the library. She's his English tutor, and I guess he made a big scene about asking her."

"Kathy Colton is Jason's English tutor?"

"Apparently."

"She's not Mormon, is she?"

Teresa looked surprised at my question, and the fact annoyed me. "I don't think so."

We'd made it to Central's doors by the cafeteria, and it felt good to give one of the doors a hard, vicious push. "So he's liking Kathy Colton now?"

Teresa hurried inside behind me. "Well, he doesn't dislike her, that's for sure. Missy and Heather have study hall at the same time as Jason and Kathy. They've seen them doing their tutoring thing together, and I guess they always look pretty cozy."

Of course. Jason *would* have to like a girl who wasn't Mormon. And Kathy Colton was pretty, too. She didn't need to wear makeup at all, and rarely did, and she was still pretty. And she never had to wonder if she looked fat in anything.

"Does Kathy like Jason?" I couldn't help it. I had to ask.

Teresa laughed. "That's what's so funny. Missy and Heather said even though he flirts like crazy with her, she acts like he's a great big annoyance she has to deal with. Maybe Jason likes the challenge. Who knows?"

Of course again. Jason would have to like a girl who wasn't Mormon and who apparently disliked him anyway. Of course.

"So—do you know who Dallin's taking?"

I shrugged outwardly, but on the inside, the question unexpectedly made my heart jump. "I don't think he's asked anybody yet."

"Really? Hey—wouldn't that be cool if Dallin asked you, and you doubled with Jason and Kathy?"

The idea made my heart jump strangely again, but I shook my head and forced a laugh as we weaved around a clump of students coming towards us down the hall. "I don't think Dallin would ask me to Homecoming!"

"Why not?"

I rolled my eyes and gave Teresa a shove. "We live in the same house. It'd be too—weird!"

Teresa laughed and shoved me back. "It wouldn't be for me. I'd love it if Dallin asked me. He's hot."

I couldn't help raising my eyebrows at Teresa. "He is?"

"Like you haven't noticed!"

I thought about the Homecoming dance the rest of the day and wondered what I'd do if Dallin asked me to go. We'd definitely been doing some serious bonding lately, talking about our parents and religious stuff and scriptures and Ryan and school and everything, but I couldn't be sure it wasn't all just on a brother-sister level. Dallin hadn't done anything that could definitely make me think otherwise.

I stopped wondering whether or not Dallin might possibly ask me to Homecoming almost the minute I arrived home after stopping by the cemetery to sit by Dad's headstone for a while.

"Rachel, come see! What do you think?"

Mom dragged me down the hall to take a peek into Robert's—Dallin's—bedroom. I couldn't move past the doorway, tightly gripping my backpack slung over one shoulder.

The room was overflowing with balloons and twirled streamers of crepe paper in Central's colors of maroon and gold. A big white banner was taped across one of the walls with "Dallin—Valerie says yes!" painted in big gold and maroon letters.

Stunned. That about summed up how I was feeling. "I—I had no idea he was even planning on asking anybody."

"Isn't it cute? That Valerie is so sweet. She called me up to ask if it would be okay for her to come over and decorate Dallin's room to answer his invitation to go to the Homecoming dance. She brought one of her friends with her, but I couldn't resist asking if I could help. We had such fun. Just look at the cake they made with all the little golf clubs on it!"

I frowned as I studied the writing on the cake. "'Good luck on Thursday'? What does that mean?"

Mom looked at me in surprise. "Dallin's part of the golf team representing Central at the high school state championship tournament. Don't you remember? Joe's made arrangements to get off work. It's a two-day tournament, you know. I'm going to go with him. I haven't ever seen Dallin golf, but Joe's told me how talented he is."

I couldn't stop staring at that cake. "I didn't know." Dallin wasn't one to talk about himself, but I still felt bad that not only had I never asked him about his golfing or even tried to see him play but also that he'd never mentioned that he was going to be in any high school state tournament at all. Valerie, however, apparently seemed to know all about it.

"Well, he's going to be playing in the tournament on Thursday. Do you want to get out of school and go with Joe and me to see him play?"

I chewed my bottom lip for a second. "I don't know. I've got a lot going on at school."

"Well, if you change your mind, honey, let me know." Mom gave me a brief hug and then turned to laugh at the massive amount of candy tossed all over Dallin's bed, desk, and basically his entire room, including the carpet. "Just look at all this candy—"

I'd seen enough by then and turned away to walk into my own bedroom, shutting the door firmly behind me.

At dinner that night, Mom continued to rave about Valerie and Dallin's decorated room. Mr. Ackerman had to work late, but the rest of us made it to the dining room for dinner.

"Dallin, are you and Valerie going alone, or will you be doubling with one of your friends?"

Dallin didn't look up from his plate of spaghetti. Spaghetti I had made, since it was my turn to cook dinner. "Um, Jason and I were thinking of doubling."

"Jason West?" Dallin looked at Mom and nodded. "Well, that should be fun!" Dallin smiled and went back to fighting with his spaghetti while Mom turned to beam at Ryan. "And what about you, Ry-Guy? Are you taking anyone to Homecoming?"

Ryan shrugged, slumped in his chair beside me. "Hmm. Maybe. Don't know yet."

Mom laughed and poked him with her fork. "Well, you don't have much time if you're going to ask someone!"

Ryan turned and gave me a hard shove. "What about you? Anyone ask you yet?"

I grabbed for my fork as it flew from my hand from Ryan's shove, but it clattered noisily onto my plate instead. "Um, no," I mumbled.

Ryan leaned in and cupped a hand around his ear. "What? I don't think I caught that."

I shoved Ryan's head away from me. "I said no! No one's asked me, okay?"

Ryan laughed, but Mom hurried in with an apologetic smile. "It's just the first dance of the year, honey, and you're only a sophomore. There will be lots of dances for you to go to. You just wait!"

Ryan snickered. "Yeah. Girls' choice!"

"Shut up, Ryan!"

Dallin didn't look at me once during dinner and excused himself early from the table before the rest of us were finished eating.

"Sorry—I've got a big test tomorrow, so I'm meeting up with some friends for a study group at Jason's."

Mom smiled at Dallin. "Just be home by 10:30, okay?"

Dallin nodded and finally glanced at me with a brief smile as he rose from the table before hurrying from the room and out of the house.

I was supposed to work on my persona poem for my creative writing class, but I sat at my desk that night and stared at my reflection in the mirror instead. So Dallin was taking Valerie What's-Her-Face to Homecoming. It was stupid to feel hurt about it or even to care. Really stupid. Why did I care at all? It was really, really dumb. I was just a stepsister to him, after all. A little stepsister, and a freakish one at that. I looked at my reflection harder, with slitted eyes. A fat, freakish stepsister.

I angrily flipped to a clean page in my blue notebook and pounded out my words:

> *Born to a family of sticks*
> *I tried to apologize my thickness away*
> *But that was as useless*
> *As strewn green peas under the kitchen table.*
> *Or the milk thumped over too many times at dinner.*
> *Perhaps I should've become a gymnast*

After all
Even if my neck would've snapped—
The only skinny part of me.
I could've stood it better
Than being led to the scaffold
On our yellow bathroom tiles
Doomed to whip myself with a white measuring tape
Standing with bowed head
Atop a groaning scale.
Touching raw fish—
Being forced to eat a dead fish's eyeball—
Would've been happier.

I sighed and laid my head down on my desk, and as I stared off into space, out of the corner of my eye I caught sight of my old Mormonad and that daisy in the middle of all of those gorgeous red roses.

Be Your Own Kind of Beautiful.

I sighed and sat up. Turning back to my red creative writing notebook, I found the page I'd titled "Persona Poem."

"Persona poems are also called 'dramatic poems.' One of the two main types of persona poems are dramatic monologues, in which only one person speaks. Some good examples of poets who have used this style are Sylvia Plath and Robert Browning. Your next assignment is to follow Sylvia and Robert's lead. Write me a persona poem. Tell me something about yourself that is impossible for you to tell anyone out loud. Something, perhaps, that you don't want to admit to anyone."

I stared long and hard at the blue lines running across the white page before me and then in a rush threw down line after line:

Love Poems

I've always hated those kinds of poems—
Love ones—
Because they were
Sappy,
And smothered with overly felt emotion,

155

Emotions that were untouched,
Not even breathed upon before in me.
But now,
Because of you,
Those stupid poems are starting to mean
Something.
Sometimes,
When I look at you,
A feeling like an overpowering ocean wave
Grows unbidden inside me.
I want to let it crash softly down on top of me,
Soaking my skin,
But I open my eyes and look at you,
Standing somewhere on your shore,
And I'm afraid.
If I let the wave release All,
If I look at you,
And you see what I've held,
Just a twitch of your eye
In the wrong direction,
Or worse—
A laugh of strangled teasing—
Would destroy me.
So now,
I find myself joining many long loved
And dead poets
Before me,
And I write a stupid, sappy poem
For you.

CHAPTER TWENTY-NINE

Since both Teresa and I were passed over for the Homecoming dance, Mom and Mr. Ackerman gave me the green light to invite Teresa to commiserate with me over movies and pizza.

"We'll be out late tonight, but make sure Teresa's home by midnight, okay?"

I nodded at Mr. Ackerman and watched him help Mom on with her coat. Mom was wearing a fancy dress, and Mr. Ackerman was wearing one of his expensive suits. "Going to a play tonight?"

Mr. Ackerman shook his head. "Nope. We're going out for dinner and dancing." Mr. Ackerman frowned when I giggled and Mom coughed.

"Have a nice time!"

Mom waved and told me again to be good before Mr. Ackerman closed the front door behind them.

I was busy straightening the living room, waiting for Teresa to arrive, while Dallin did whatever he needed to do to get ready for the dance. I jogged down the hall to grab a few more pillows from my room and passed the bathroom just in time to see Dallin through the open door. He was wearing his gray Sunday suit and had a blue tie in each hand.

I stopped and leaned against the door jamb. "The darker one."

Dallin turned his head towards me in surprise. "What?"

I smiled. "The darker blue one. Looks better with the suit."

"Yeah?"

I nodded. Dallin always looked good in his suit, and he'd put on just enough cologne. I could smell it, but he clearly hadn't drowned himself in it. "Did you remember to get Valerie a corsage?"

"It's in the fridge—thanks for reminding me!" I watched Dallin easily wrap and twist the darker blue tie around his neck.

"You look really good. Nice, I mean."

Dallin looked at me briefly and smiled. "Thanks."

Silence reigned for a few awkward seconds before I stabbed the air with another sentence. "So, are you picking up Jason, or is he coming to get you?"

Dallin frowned but didn't move his eyes from the mirror. "I'm not going with Jason."

"How come?"

Dallin shrugged and fussed with his tie. "He decided to go with Brad and Jeff."

"Really? I can't see Kathy Colton liking going with them."

Dallin didn't answer for a few seconds. "He's not taking Kathy after all."

I could feel my jaw drop a bit. "I thought he asked her!"

Dallin looked at me briefly again and shrugged. "It didn't work out. He's taking Angela Barnett."

"Oh. So—you and Valerie are just going to go by yourselves?"

"Looks like it."

I didn't know what else to say, and since Dallin seemed intent on checking his tie and hair, I turned to go back to the living room. "Well, I hope you have fun."

"Rachel!"

My heart jumped and I turned back. "Yeah?"

Dallin looked at me almost solemnly before he finally tried to smile. "I hope you have fun tonight, too."

I smiled and nodded once before moving down the hall to my room for the extra pillows. I carried them into the living room just in time to see Dallin grab the corsage before sailing out the front door. I peeked through the living room window as he climbed into his Mustang and drove away and felt my heart sink even more than when I'd heard Jason had asked Kathy Colton to Homecoming.

———•———

I was glad Teresa had been given the okay to come over. Even though we stuck in a DVD both of us had wanted to see for a while now, we were too busy stuffing our faces with pizza and diet cola and talking about everyone we knew to pay any attention to the movie.

Teresa took a swallow of diet cola and nodded after I told her the gossip Dallin had filled me in on about Jason West. "Yeah, I heard Angela accepted his invite in his English class. How gross was that, prancing around in her drill costume in front of the whole class? Kathy Colton's in his English class, too, you know. I'm sure she just loved every minute of that."

"Yeah, I'll bet." I wondered how I would've handled something like that and hoped I wouldn't have ruined the rest of my high school career by bursting into tears.

"The sad thing about it is that I think Jason is really liking her."

I swallowed a bite of pizza and frowned. "Why do you say that?"

"I'm just going by what Missy and Heather told me from seeing her tutor Jason in the library every day."

I sighed and reached for another piece of pizza. Jason was nice to me, too, but I doubted it would ever enter his mind to invite me to a school dance. Or out on a date. Or anything other than a ride on a rainy day if he saw me stranded, without an umbrella, walking home in a storm. I couldn't stop the tiny smile on my face. Dallin would definitely stop and give me a ride, even if stopping meant accidentally spraying me with gutter water first.

Teresa was looking at me curiously, so I hurried and asked, "So how's your choir class?"

Teresa shrugged. "It's good. Ms. McPhee is really pressuring all of us to try out for the musical, though."

"When are the tryouts?"

"Some time in November."

"Are you going to try out?"

"I'll probably have to for my grade." Teresa reached for another slice of pizza, too. "So—how's your creative writing class going? Are you liking it?"

I wrinkled my nose and picked a piece of green pepper off the slice in my hand. "Yeah, it's all right. Pretty fun, actually."

Teresa grabbed a pillow from under my feet and tossed it in the air a few times. "I heard there's some big writing contest going on between the high schools. And the winner gets a big cash prize. Is that true?"

I laughed. "I don't know that the cash prize is going to be that big, but yes, there *is* a high school writing contest that's coming up soon. Any high school student in the state can enter."

"So—are you going to enter it?"

I shrugged without looking up. "Everyone in creative writing has to."

"Have you written something yet?"

"I'm working on something." I was, too, but so far, inspiration hadn't hit me yet. I was still hoping and praying that a creative bolt would strike me soon.

"Hey—I heard Central came in second in state at the golf tournament!"

"Yeah, they did." I hadn't gone to the tournament in the end, but Mom and Mr. Ackerman had made a huge fuss over Dallin and took him out for a celebratory victory dinner Friday night. Just the three of them. I didn't mind. I hadn't gone to the tournament, and neither had Ryan.

Ryan had snorted when Mom asked if he wanted to go. "Stand around quietly and do the golf clap? Sounds boring."

I'd said I couldn't miss any classes. "I should've gone, but it was an all-day thing."

"Really? Then I would've gone for sure!"

I sighed loudly. "What can I say? I'm a terrible stepsister."

Teresa laughed and raised an eyebrow at me. "So, tell me. How's life with the Brady Bunch?"

"Fine, I guess."

Teresa shook her head and chuckled. "It must be so bizarre, having someone from our school living with you!"

I shrugged. "It's been good, actually. Dallin's cool. I like having him for my stepbrother."

"So would I!"

I gave Teresa a hard shove. "It's not like that! He just treats me like a friend. It's nice, though. Especially since Ryan's so—"

Teresa looked at me expectantly. "Ryan's so, what?"

I shook my head and looked away. "Ryan's got problems. It's been great to have Dallin to talk to. He's the best."

"What about his dad? Are you getting along with him okay?"

"I guess. We don't really talk ever. But he's been nice to me. I can't complain. It could be worse." I sighed and pulled my knees up tight under my chin and hugged my legs to my chest. "I know I compare him to my dad too much."

Teresa was silent for a moment before looking at me. "Life is nothing but comparisons, you know? I think it's impossible not to compare."

I rubbed my forehead wearily. "I've just got to try and stop comparing what I think is wrong with him with what was so right about my dad."

Teresa nodded. "I think it would be hard for anyone not to do that." She looked at me curiously again. "So, what do you call him? I'm guessing you don't call him Dad."

I shook my head firmly. "No. I can't do that."

"So what do you call him?"

"I try not to have to call him anything, but so far I call him Mr. Ackerman."

Teresa burst out laughing. "Mr. Ackerman? He's not your teacher, for crying out loud!"

"I know, but I feel weird calling an adult by his first name. My mom wants me to, but I just feel weird about it."

"Hmmm." Teresa drummed her fingers on the floor and squinted off into space, obviously concentrating deeply. "Maybe you could call him 'Pops' or 'Papa Joe,' or something like that." Her eyes lit up after a moment and she jumped, making me jump as well. "Wait—I know! Call him 'Joey'!"

Now I was the one laughing hysterically. "Yeah, he'd love that!"

Teresa laughed, too, before drilling me with more questions. "So—do they make out in front of you?"

"What? No! Of course not. Don't be gross!" I grabbed a pillow and smacked Teresa in the face with it. I didn't even want to *think* about that kind of stuff.

Teresa giggled and brushed the hair out of her eyes. "They don't do anything in front of you guys?"

"I've seen them hug, hold hands, that kind of stuff. It just feels wrong to see even that much, though."

Teresa nodded slowly. "I wonder if my dad died if my mom would get married again. You're lucky your mom got together with someone nice like Dallin's dad and that you have someone cool like Dallin for a step-brother. With my luck, if this had happened to me, my mom would've married some guy with the most horrible kids ever, and my life would've become a nightmare."

I could see Ryan sprawled on the bathroom floor and that disgusted, horrified look on Dallin's face again and inwardly cringed. "Yeah, I guess I'm the one who got lucky."

Teresa picked at the half-eaten piece of pizza on her plate. "So—Dallin took Valerie?"

I took a swallow of diet cola. "Yep."

"Does he like her?"

"I have no idea."

"But you said you guys talk all the time and everything!"

"Not about that kind of stuff!"

I didn't know what kind of look was on my face, but Teresa was looking at me strangely. "What?" I sounded defensive and I knew it.

"You're not—I mean—are you liking Dallin, Rachel?"

I tried to laugh, but it sounded hollow. "Yeah. How stupid would that be!"

"I don't think it would be stupid to like Dallin! He's hot!"

I rolled my eyes at Teresa's excitement. "We're living in the same house together, so yes, it would be stupid. Too hard and weird and awkward. Just not good. Besides, he's clearly not interested in me in that kind of way." I'd finally said it out loud and hated even the mere sound of the words. I uncurled my legs and stood up. "Do you mind if we stop this movie and put in a funny one instead? I could stand to laugh right about now. I'm going to go to the bathroom, so do you mind getting the movie set up?" I didn't wait for Teresa to reply as I hurried out of the room.

CHAPTER THIRTY

I had no idea if it was like this all over the state, or all over the United States, for that matter, but in my own little corner of the world, the Sunday following any high school dance meant another chance for the guys and girls who'd asked someone or had been asked by someone to show off their fancy dresses, new suits, corsages, and boutonnieres. I was dreading going to church as a result, but I knew there was no way I'd be allowed to stay home.

Luck was not with me. When I made it to church and into the Young Women's room, I was greeted with having to watch a few of the Mia Maids and Beehives making a fuss over some of the fancy dresses a few of the Laurels were wearing. My Laurel class only had seven girls in it, but once we all made it from opening exercises to our classroom, after viewing a rainbow of fancy dresses and wrist corsages, I had the indescribable joy of realizing I was the only Laurel in the ward who hadn't been invited to the dance.

Perfect. Just perfect.

Our teacher made a brief fuss over all the fancy dresses but thankfully moved on to the lesson and shushed all the girls from babbling on and on about the dance.

And then it was time for Sunday School.

I dragged my feet behind the rest of the Laurels in their fancy dresses down the hall to our classroom. As soon as the five guys in our class, including Dallin, had filtered in wearing their boutonnieres pinned to their suit jackets, it was again horribly apparent that not only was I the only girl who hadn't been invited, but I was the only Central High student in our ward who hadn't gone to the dance.

Brother Parker, a youngish dad in his early thirties, was our teacher. He smiled and said hello to everyone as he entered the classroom. I kept my head down, buried in my scriptures, and didn't look up at either him or the rest of the guys and girls in the room.

"Wow, Rachel." I looked up in surprise to see Brother Parker smiling at me. "I don't think I've seen that dress before."

I actually hadn't worn it before. It was just a simple, straight-skirted dress with short sleeves and a hem that hit just below the knees, but I'd liked it when I'd tried it on a couple of weeks ago because I thought it made me look thinner. And I thought the dark blue color looked good on me and would look great with my dark blue heels.

Brother Parker was still smiling at me. "I like it. You look really nice."

I wasn't sure what the compliment was all about, because I didn't need any charity. I could handle being the only one not asked to the dance. Unlike my Laurel teacher, though, Brother Parker didn't say a word about any of the obviously fancy dresses the rest of the girls were wearing. He didn't even seem to notice they were wearing corsages and dance dresses or that the guys were wearing boutonnieres. Instead, after smiling at me again, he turned to the rest of the class and said, "Okay, everyone open your scriptures." It was nice of him, but definitely unnecessary. I looked up once to catch Dallin looking at me. He smiled and nodded, sitting between Paul and Brian, and so I did the same back.

Sunday School let out early, so I hurried into the chapel to save a bench for myself, Dallin, Mom, and Mr. Ackerman. Two Laurels—Sarah and Tricia—followed me in and sat a few rows behind me, blabbing about the dance and their dates. I had my blue notebook with me and opened it to a fresh page before touching my pen to the paper.

> *I've been here*
> *At this stop light*

Too long,
This stop light
That won't let me turn left,
But I don't want to turn right
Or keep putting on ahead
Toward some unknown,
Unfelt
Golden gate.
I sit
Knees clenched tight
As the teeth on a Nutcracker soldier doll.
I cock my ear like a gun
At the sweating face before me.
He'll never know
I left him,
My foot pressed all the way down
On the gas
Like a sledgehammer
Years ago.
There are rows and rows
Of heads
In front of me and behind me,
And I'm wondering
If the hands who chiseled out
These benches from once happy trees,
Glossing them over with embalming fluids
Are laughing or crying now.

I didn't pay much attention to the constant giggling and whispering behind me until I heard Dallin's name, and then my ears perked antenna-like, and I had to force myself not to turn around.

" . . . yeah, Dallin's cute. We could use more cute guys like him in the ward."

"Did you see Jason West dancing with Kathy Colton last night? I thought Angela was going to burst her spleen watching them."

"I know! I thought it was funny. My mom would never let me wear a dress like Kathy had on."

"My mom wouldn't, either. She looked good in it, though."

"Did you see Ryan Fletcher last night?"

"Yeah. He was totally wasted. I felt so bad for his date."

"I can't believe she went with him. I mean, everyone knows he drinks like a fish."

"He's turning out to be such a waste."

I gripped my pen, stunned to realize I was trembling.

"Move over!"

I nearly jumped to the ceiling when Ryan appeared out of nowhere and gave me a shove. The buzzing conversation behind me stopped abruptly, too.

"I said, Move over!"

It would be hard not to smell the alcohol on Ryan, but he only gave me a lopsided grin before slouching on the bench in his wrinkled suit and messy hair. I had to fight not to slouch myself when the older couple sitting in front of us turned around at Ryan's noise to give him the usual disapproving frown and pointed stare before turning back around again.

"You don't have to scream!" I whispered to Ryan angrily.

Ryan ignored me and pointed towards the sacrament table. "Hey—there's good ol' Paul and Brian! I need to say hi."

I tried to make Ryan sit back down, but he jerked out of my grip and stumbled up the aisle, tripping against the edge of one bench, until he made it to the sacrament table to bellow hello to poor Paul and Brian, who were busy trying to finish setting up the sacrament. More people were in the chapel now, and everyone's eyes were fixed on Ryan as he continued to bother Paul and Brian, who to their credit, were doing their best to try to be nice and make him sit down.

"Hey—I can help—just gimme a second here—gimme a chance—"

I couldn't move—couldn't stop watching, horrified, while Ryan clumsily tried to straighten the white cloth on the sacrament table, but I could've done a better job blindfolded. Anyone could have. And then, the girls behind me started buzzing again.

"They're not going to let him pass the sacrament, are they?"

"They're not that stupid!"

"He touched the sacrament table! Watch for lightning—It's going to hit the church any second, I bet!"

Both girls were snickering, making play-by-play comments over Ryan's embarrassing antics with Paul and Brian.

My ears were throbbing from the buzzing of shocked voices all over the chapel. My heart was pounding. Where was Mom? Where was Mr. Ackerman? And Dallin—where was he?

And then there was a crash as Ryan turned abruptly from messing up the sacrament table cloth with a strange jerk and knocked over a stack of hymn books on a folding chair by the table and crashed to the floor. Both girls behind me burst out laughing, but I'd had enough and seen enough. I could feel tears starting to flow, and my heart was pounding as I finally remembered how to make my legs work. I jumped up from the bench and ran out of the chapel and outside the church itself. I waited until I was past the parking lot to a grassy area with trees where we sometimes had church picnics before I sank to my knees and let myself cry.

It wasn't fair—I'd prayed and fasted so often for so long, and yet— nothing. Nothing was changing. Heavenly Father wasn't listening to me. At all. I didn't know why, but I was sure He wasn't.

"I'm done," I whispered out loud.

I'd been crying too hard to hear anyone approach, and I jumped when a white piece of cloth floated into my lap. Dallin quietly sat down beside me with his legs stretched out before him crossed at the ankles, his arms stretched out behind him, acting for all the world as if it was perfectly normal for him to be sitting there beside me while I bawled.

"Thanks," I mumbled. I wiped at my face with Dallin's handkerchief before handing it back to him.

"Keep it."

"How did you find me?"

"Sarah and Tricia said they saw you run out of the chapel and out the side door."

I nodded dully. "I should probably go back in and see if Ryan's destroyed the chapel."

"Your mom and my dad took him home. I've got my car here, so I can give you a ride home if you want."

"I don't want to go home," I mumbled.

"You want to go back inside?"

"Definitely not!" I said hotly. Dallin nodded, and we were both silent for a few minutes until I sighed. A loud, ragged sigh. "You know what really bugs me? If my brother was trapped underneath a crumbled building, everyone would race to the rescue and climb over each other to get out there with a shovel and dig him out. But because the rubble he's trapped under is his stupid drinking, everyone just talks about him and my family behind our backs instead. Or if I'm at church, right in front of my face."

"Being buried under a building that's just crumbled is one thing. Choosing to drink and having to deal with the fallout is another."

I glared at Dallin's calm face. "I don't see any difference at all! A person who gets buried under a building chose to go inside. The person had no idea the building was about to crumble. Anyone who chooses to drink has no idea if they have the gene or abnormal chromosome or whatever it is that makes a person unable to stop craving alcohol the first time they drink!"

Dallin picked a blade of grass and chewed thoughtfully on it. "Well, walking into a building is generally considered safe to do. Picking up alcohol to drink for any reason isn't the smartest thing to do from the start."

"Neither is talking smack about people. In church, no less!"

Dallin sighed and nodded. "Okay, you win. I'll give you that one."

We were both quiet for another minute before I spoke again. "Do you have any idea how hard it is to have to hear people say things about my brother? It's getting harder and harder for me to come to church every Sunday."

Dallin turned towards me with a determined, serious look on his face. "Don't stop going to church, Rachel. I can promise you that's not the answer."

"Then what *is* the answer? I've been asking Heavenly Father to help Ryan, but He's not! He's not listening to me, and He doesn't care!"

Dallin shook his head slowly. "Just because He's not answering your prayers the way you want Him to doesn't mean He's not listening, and it definitely doesn't mean He doesn't care. Maybe you're asking and looking for the wrong miracle, Rachel."

I had no idea what Dallin meant by that, but after blowing my nose unattractively into his handkerchief, I let him pull me to my feet and walk me to his car so he could drive us both home.

CHAPTER THIRTY-ONE

I expected fireworks when Dallin and I arrived home on Sunday, but apparently Ryan had passed off his "odd behavior" as being dizzy from a head cold and having taken too much medicine. Dallin and I could hear him griping to Mom from his room where he was lying down on his bed in sweat pants and a T-shirt, drinking juice through a straw.

" . . . Who cares that we missed church? I saw the program. Brother Dalton was going to speak. I've still got a scar on my forehead from the last time he talked and I dozed off and banged my head against the bench in front of me!"

"Joe and I are very concerned about you, Ry-Guy. You need to take better care of yourself . . ."

I sighed and walked into my bedroom while Dallin shook his head and closed himself off in Robert's old room.

Ryan made himself scarce most of the following week and only made an appearance in seminary twice. Dallin had been getting together with Valerie to supposedly study for a supposedly big calculus test, so I hadn't seen much of him all week, either.

"You need some cheering up, Rachel. You've been a sad sack all week. Come with me to Central's football game tonight!"

I knew how much Teresa liked going to the football games, and in truth, so did I. "Who are we playing?"

"South High Panthers. It should be a good game. They're a good team!"

Teresa drove and picked me up that night. The parking lot located between Central High itself and the football field was a crazy mess of cars trying to park. Once we finally snagged an empty spot, finding a spot in the bleachers on Central's side wasn't any easier, but we managed to find a space to squeeze into near Teresa's friends, Missy and Heather. I smiled and nodded hello to both of them before casually looking around to see who all was there while I rearranged the blanket I'd brought, trying to fight off the chill in the air. I could see Kathy Colton sitting with her friends a few benches below and to the right of me, shivering with her jacket zipped up tight to her chin. She didn't look too excited to be at the game, but I was sure she was there to see Jason. Why else would she and probably most of the girls in the stands be there? Including me, I thought to myself glumly.

Teresa shoved me and pointed at the locker room doors at the back of Central High. "Here comes the team!"

The pep band blasted as loud as they possibly could, and seconds later, everyone on Central's side had jumped up to stomp, scream, and cheer while the football team in their maroon and gold uniforms jogged onto the field. It only took me a second to find Jason West, clutching his football helmet under one arm with the rest of the team. I watched him yank his helmet on, and after listening to some last-second advice from the coach, run onto the field to take his usual place as quarterback.

I had pulled the blanket tighter around me in order to jump to my feet with Teresa, Missy, and Heather and not lose it while I screamed and cheered until my throat burned and ached. Jason was amazing on the field, easily one of the best football players Central had ever seen. I couldn't believe how far he could throw a football and how quickly he'd jump back up again when a Panther would slam him to the ground. The only play South High seemed to want to do was a quarterback sack, and I wondered how much longer Jason's body was going to be able to take the constant throws to the hard, cold ground. Ryan was out there, too, and for someone whose position required him to block anyone who came near the quarterback, he clearly wasn't doing a great job at all. I could feel myself tense up, wondering how much Ryan had drunk before the game and wishing I'd checked his stashes before leaving the house.

I didn't have to wait long to find out how much more Jason could handle. In the last minute before halftime, Jason was busy jumping and running around the field, dodging Panthers, clearly looking for someone to throw the football to.

Teresa nudged me with her elbow, her eyes on the football field. "Hey, how come Jason doesn't throw the ball to Ryan?"

"Because Ryan's not even paying attention—good grief!" And he wasn't, either. Who knew what Ryan was doing out on the field. "Oh no—"

"Oh no? What's wrong?"

"Jason's trying to run the ball himself!"

"So?"

I watched with my heart in my mouth while Ryan made a clumsy, slow grab for a Panther, missed, and just let himself trip over his own feet until he'd crashed to the ground.

One second, Jason was gripping the football, weaving around Panthers for the goal line, and the next, the two Panthers coming at him on either side leaped—one of which Ryan had inexcusably let slip by— slamming into him from both sides, whacking poor Jason hard while the football snapped high into the air. All of Central's side of the bleachers jumped to their feet, gasping in horror in unison. Jason's legs twisted sharply at a strange, painful looking angle, and then he was on the ground and piled on by Panther after Panther.

Referee whistles were blowing like crazy while the rest of Central's team ran to the pile of Panthers and Jason. By the time all of the Panthers peeled off, poor Jason was lying on his side, clutching his right knee and rocking in pain.

"Holy cow—poor Jason!"

I nodded silently in agreement. My eyes bulged while the coaches surrounded Jason. A minute later, the ambulance in the school parking lot sped onto the field, and EMT people were loading Jason onto a stretcher and carrying him off of the field.

Unbelievably, once the ambulance had screamed off with Jason, since it was now halftime, the drill team had the nerve to prance out and shake their stuff to a pop song in the middle of the football field as if nothing horrifying and dramatic had barely happened. Even Angela was out there beaming and snapping her head around in time to the music.

Sadly enough, upon glancing around, I could see that a lot of the students in the stands were sitting up and taking notice of Angela and the rest of the drill team doing their thing, as if they hadn't just watched Jason get carried off in a broken, painful heap moments before.

The more I had to see those girls twirling, kicking, and doing splits in those short, sparkly skirts, and watch everyone—especially the guys—in the bleachers gawk with eyes glazed over at their trim little figures, I couldn't help wondering what it would be like to be part of a group like that and be noticed by everyone like they were. I stared hard at the tiny figures jumping around on the football field before me. Of course, there was the matter of weight. Everyone on the team looked good, and although to myself I was an absolute elephant, Mom always said I looked just fine. Still, I knew I needed to lose some serious pounds. And then I was wondering what would happen if I were to lose weight, try out for the drill team, and actually make it. I could almost see Jason's eyes watching me twirl in one of those sparkling skirts next year. And Dallin—what would he think if I made the drill team? I glanced over at Kathy Colton and saw her watching the drill team with a worried frown and a strange, faraway look on her face. I felt the guilt hit, knowing that she at least was clearly thinking about Jason, not Angela or the drill team at all.

CHAPTER THIRTY-TWO

Halloween arrived, and of course Dallin was invited to a party. Angela Barnett's party, no less. He'd decided to take Valerie to the party, even though he claimed they were just friends.

"Sure. Guys only take girls to parties who they consider to be 'just friends,'" Teresa said, rolling her eyes when I told her.

"I think he's just trying to find reasons to stay away from our twisted home and twisted Ryan." *And his freakish stepsister, too,* I thought miserably.

Teresa rolled her eyes at me again. "Whatever, Rachel. Hey—I know we had plans for Halloween, but my parents are taking us all out of town to a resort where we can go swimming and out to eat at this great, fancy restaurant my parents love. They hate trick or treaters and thought this would be more fun, since I don't have a date and my brothers and sisters don't have big plans. Don't be mad, okay?"

Great. Just great. I watched Dallin hurry out the door to pick up Valerie after dinner, while Ryan claimed he'd been invited to a party, too.

Mr. Ackerman frowned silently at Ryan's grin and continued to frown at the front door after Ryan left before turning to Mom. "He still hasn't fixed that broken headlight on his car, you know. He could easily get pulled over for that, even if he doesn't do anything else."

Mom nodded. "I know. I've mentioned it to him several times already."

"Maybe we better take away his car keys until he gets it fixed."

"I'll talk to him about it again, Joe."

Mr. Ackerman only sighed and shook his head before digging his fork more forcefully into his meatloaf.

"May I be excused?"

I left the table and shut my bedroom door firmly behind me and leaned against it, frowning as my eyes wandered over everything in my room.

Be Your Own Kind of Beautiful.

I sighed and reached for my red notebook and took another stab at the next draft I'd need to turn in for the high school writing contest. Mrs. Townsend liked the poem I'd finally decided to write for my first draft, but she kept telling me I could do better.

"You're imitating other well-known poets, which is a first step towards finding your own voice, but I'd like to see something more original for your contest entry. I just know there's something better inside you than this, Rachel. Your work in class proves that. Keep working on your entry. I know you can make it better."

I sighed and worked on the piece for a while but ended up scratching out every new line I tried. I rubbed my eyes wearily and tossed the red notebook on my bed, reaching for my blue notebook instead.

> *I can't quite grasp the back final pole*
> *Of this runaway train.*
> *I can see its trail*
> *And the dances it creates*
> *But I'm left choking*
> *Eating the dust of sweetest wine*
> *Flung in my face.*
> *I'm chasing rats in a circle maze all day.*
> *If I leap into one position*
> *Sylvia screams it's hers,*
> *But William Carlos won't let me touch*
> *His piece of sky.*
> *There must be an empty cloud somewhere*
> *In a shape saved just for my bare feet*

To leave a print no one else
Will match.
Not even stars on Broadway.
Perhaps a cloud is asking too much.
Maybe one small star in the Milky Way
Will be thrown from heaven
Like a baseball
Fitting neatly
Into my eager glove
And then maybe I'll know
And the crowd will cheer—
Happy I've finally found the key
To buy my own ticket.

I easily jumped a mile when Mr. Ackerman knocked on my door before I called out to him to come in.

Mr. Ackerman stepped only a few feet into my room. "No plans for Halloween, Rachel?"

I smiled back tightly, gripping my pen. "Nope."

"So you're just going to stay home tonight?" Mr. Ackerman pressed.

I looked him back straight in the eye. "So?"

Mr. Ackerman smiled. "So, I'd think a sixteen-year-old girl like you would want to be out with friends or going on dates instead of hibernating in her room."

I could feel my insides tensing. "Yeah, well, in case you haven't noticed, I never get asked out."

Mr. Ackerman tried to backpedal and blabbed on for a minute before he turned and left my room. Once the door was safely shut behind him again, I stood up too fast from my desk and made it wobble, knocking my math textbook off the desktop to land sharply on my bare toes. Before I could begin to fathom what I was doing, I snatched up the textbook, my toes throbbing in pain, and cocked my arm back. One second later, the textbook was airborne—to smash hard against the wall directly in front of me.

177

Mr. Ackerman knocked on my bedroom door again, this time more lightly than before. "Rachel? Are you okay in there?" he asked softly.

"Yeah," I called back, trying to force my voice to sound as cheerful as possible. "I just dropped something."

"Sounded more like you *threw* something."

I forced a laugh through the door and did my best to assure Mr. Ackerman that all was well, fine, and good, before I heard him slowly walk away after wishing me a good night and a Happy Halloween. I sighed and threw myself on my bed, face down, and stayed that way until I fell asleep.

"*Bobby—are you saying Ryan's drunk?*"

"*Pretty hard to miss, don't you think, Lainey?*"

"*Then why didn't you do something? Say something?*"

"*He probably wouldn't remember it. Don't worry—his hangover will be enough punishment tomorrow.*"

"*Bobby, I can't believe you're acting like this isn't a big deal!*"

"*And I can't believe you are, Lainey! Good grief—all teens experiment when they're young. Even Mormon kids!*"

"*Well, I didn't! My parents would never have let me get away with a poor excuse like that. 'Everyone else is doing it,' so that makes it okay?*"

"*Look, Lainey, I'm not going to drive him away over this. Besides—I played around with alcohol a little when I was fifteen and lived to tell about it.*"

"*Did your parents know?*"

"*They did eventually.*"

"*And they didn't do anything, either?*"

"*Actually, my dad sat me down with a case of beer and said, 'If you're going to drink, then drink up. We'll see if you still think drinking's so wonderful after you've had all this!' And he made me sit and drink a whole case of really bad, warm, cheap, disgusting beer. I threw up so much that night that I never wanted to touch the stuff again.*"

"*Well, Bobby, then I'd say you were unusually lucky, in more ways than one! I can't believe your father would think doing such a thing wouldn't be harmful!*"

178

"My dad grew up rough. He didn't handle me or my brothers and sisters with kid gloves."

"We should've tried to do something about Ryan. A long time ago."

Dad's eyes were turning away from Mom, and now he was looking at me.

"Where are you going, Rachel?"

"I'm running away!"

"Running away? Can I come, too?"

Red and blue lights screaming, twirling around and around—bloodshot eyes, angrily drilling holes into mine.

"He was on his way to pick you up from your stupid friend's house!"

I awoke with a start when the phone rang and checked the clock by my bed. Three o'clock in the morning. I waited for it to ring a few times before stumbling down the hall to answer it myself.

"Hello?" I said sleepily.

"Get Mom!"

It was Ryan, and he sounded pretty sloshed. The background noise behind him, though, didn't consist of the usual party sounds of talking, laughing, and ear splitting rock music. In fact, the voices and code-talk and serious bustling noises sounded suspiciously like a police station in full swing.

"Where are you?"

"Just get Mom!"

I hated knocking on Mom's bedroom door to wake her up, but once she'd gotten on the line, her quick hysterics made it clear my suspicions were right. Even before she shrieked, "The police station?!"

Mom and Mr. Ackerman were dressed and out the door in a record-breaking three minutes. Dallin's bedroom door didn't open at all, and I could only assume he'd fallen asleep with his headphones on again.

I waited, trembling in my bed, sitting up with my legs pulled in tight to my chin under the blankets, hugging my knees to my chest. Two hours later I was still awake, and after grabbing my robe, I quietly made my way down the hall in the dark to get a drink of water. I'd just set my empty glass in the sink when I heard the front door open. I froze.

"Well, Ryan, I hope having to spend most of the night in jail taught you something about the insanity of drinking. Has it?"

I crept to the kitchen doorway and flattened myself against the wall where I could see into the living room but not be seen. I nearly choked when I saw Ryan. He was a mess. Rumpled, dirty clothes, and egg-beater hair. He even had bruises on his face to go with his usual bloodshot eyes. I watched him stumble to the couch before crumpling into it, hunching over his knees with his head in his hands.

Mom's eyes were swollen from crying, and she was still sniffling away, wiping at her nose and eyes with a tissue. Mr. Ackerman had his arms folded and was frowning at Ryan with a disappointed, angry glare. Ryan didn't say anything, and after a few quiet seconds filled with nothing but my hammering heart and Mom's sniffling, Mr. Ackerman walked to the couch, sat down beside Ryan, and put his hand on Ryan's back.

"Ryan, we need to talk about your problem—"

I jumped when Ryan angrily shoved Mr. Ackerman's arm off his back. "Dude—I can see you and hear you. I don't need to *feel* you!"

"Ryan!" Mom gasped.

Ryan glared at both Mom and Mr. Ackerman. "Look—okay, you caught me. I got drunk, but so did a lot of other kids at the party. The police just showed up this time because it got a little crazy. I wasn't the only kid who got thrown in jail!"

Mr. Ackerman shook his head. "Unlike the other people at the party, I'm not their father or stepfather. And this clearly isn't the first time you've been drunk."

"What? How would you know?"

Mr. Ackerman snorted angrily. "Ryan, give me a little credit! I'm not blind. The signs are as obvious as day, mostly because they keep happening over and over and over again."

"Signs? What signs?"

"Moodiness, for starters. And the horrendous smell that floats around you and lives in your room. Your grades have gone down drastically, too—another sign."

"I'm a senior—I'm taking hard classes!"

"You don't spend time with Brian and Paul from the ward anymore. Your mother told me you used to be the Three Musketeers with them."

"So I have other friends I hang out with. So what?"

Mr. Ackerman shook his head at Ryan's angry face. "You're never home, and if you do somehow make it home, it's well after curfew. Money and things are disappearing all over this house. Your eyes are constantly bloodshot, your weight has dropped, you claim you're sick and tired all of the time—"

"I know I'm sick and tired of you right now!"

Mr. Ackerman ignored the interruption. "And let's not forget your constant evasiveness and defensiveness about every and any question asked of you!"

"Whatever!"

Mr. Ackerman ran his hands through his hair in frustration. "Ryan, I was a teenager once, too. Do you think you're the first teenage ever to pick up a beer? I'd have to be deaf, dumb, and blind not to see that you clearly have a drinking problem!"

"I don't have a problem! *You* guys are the ones who have a problem sticking your faces into everything I do! Leave me alone and mind your own business!"

Mom started crying again. "Ryan, we care about you—we love you!"

Ryan only rolled his eyes and ran his hands through his hair, too. "Look, if it's such a big, stupid thing to you, I'll stop drinking. I promise, okay? Consider me as having had my last beer. It's not a big deal. I can stop any time I want!"

Mom shook her head worriedly, wiping tears off her face. "But you don't stop, Ry-Guy. That's the problem. Don't you see that?"

"Fine! I'm done with drinking, okay? I'm done!"

Mr. Ackerman sighed, and when he spoke again, his voice was quiet and low. "I know you've gone through a rough time since your dad's accident. I know that."

Ryan's head jerked towards Mr. Ackerman, and I saw him glare at him hatefully. "You *know* that? What do you know? You don't know anything! You have no idea what I'm going through!"

Mom pulled herself together and spoke just as quietly. "I know that if you keep choosing to drink, you're giving up control in exchange. The power of choice is something you should never give up. You need to make decisions that increase control over your life, not ones that will take that control away!"

Now Ryan was glaring angrily at Mom. "Really, Mom? Well, maybe if you had taught me better, I wouldn't have gotten into drinking in the first place!"

"Ryan!"

"You've never tried to educate me about anything important!"

Mr. Ackerman's voice was louder now and more angry. "Ryan, listen to me—"

"Listen to you? I'd rather staple my tongue to a moving garbage truck!"

"Ryan, I want to help you!"

Ryan snorted arrogantly at Mr. Ackerman. "Help me? You're not a doctor. You're an attorney. Do you save lives? No, like every other attorney out there, you ruin them!"

I kept myself frozen in the kitchen when Ryan stumbled down the hall while Mom cried harder and Mr. Ackerman tried to comfort her.

"I'm—I'm sorry, Joe. I know Ryan's been drinking a little, but I—I assumed it was grief over Bobby. I—I thought it would—I don't know—go away after a while."

"I don't think his drinking is just going to go away, Elaine. We've got to do something about this, or something worse than just having to bail him out of jail in the middle of the night is going to happen."

Mom fought hard to keep her sobs under control. "Bobby was so—so sure Ryan would out grow this, like—like Bobby did when he was a teenager. We just kept saying we'd help him out one—one more time. And—and Ryan kept saying things we wanted to hear, all the right excuses every time."

Mr. Ackerman's voice was quiet again. "This has to stop, Elaine. You know it does."

Mom sighed raggedly. "I—I wish I knew if he's acting this way because his father died, or—or simply because he's a teenager."

"Does it really matter? Either way, his problem has to be addressed, Elaine. I can't keep ignoring what's plainly in front of me anymore."

"He said he'd stop drinking!" Mom wailed.

Mr. Ackerman shook his head sadly. "I think he would've promised anything to get us off his back. I don't think reasoning can have any effect on him anymore. We're going to have to do something to make him see he has a serious problem with drinking."

"I—I just don't want to do anything that would take away his agency!"

"What exactly do you think the alcohol is doing?"

Mom cried harder, fighting to get her words out between desperate sobs. "I—I just don't understand how—how any of this happened—Bobby and I were good, loving parents. We—we did everything the Church asked us to do. Bobby always wanted to promote good—good family relationships by giving Ryan the benefit of—of the doubt when he came home drunk. Having a child who can't stop drinking—that—that wasn't supposed to happen to us!"

Mr. Ackerman had his arm around Mom and let her cry on his shoulder for a minute before speaking again. "Do you at least agree there has to be a change? That something has to be done about Ryan?"

Mom didn't answer, but I could hear that she was still quietly crying.

"It's bad enough to have a child who has a problem with drinking, but it's going to get worse if we can't work together towards finding a solution. I would hope that if it was my son who couldn't stop drinking and I had died, that someone would be strong enough to step in and help my son for me."

I slowly let myself slide down the wall until I'd sunk to my knees and cried quietly on the floor of the kitchen long after Mom and Mr. Ackerman had gone to bed.

CHAPTER THIRTY-THREE

It was strange seeing Jason limp into seminary on crutches now. He'd been out for a while after knee surgery, and the rumor all over school was that he probably wouldn't ever play football again. Every time I saw him on his crutches and thought about Ryan buzzing from who-knew-what before the game, I'd see that Panther easily swing around Ryan to storm Jason with the other mean Panther, and my stomach would tie up painfully into too many knots. *Why Jason?* I was sure he knew Ryan had messed up, and why he'd messed up, and yet, he still said hello to me with a cheerful smile every day when I entered Brother Clawson's class. As if nothing had happened to him or his knee at all.

And now,
I stand alone,
waiting.
The audience is gone—
Their hands are too busy,
Too full of other names
To dully recall
The knife handles they once held,
Gouging and stabbing at my soul
Until it ran away—
Leaving this shell.
If one cared to press their ear against
My ear, mouth, or eye hole

Nothing would be heard.
Not even the echo
Of the sea.
Not even of a small pond.
It hardly matters.
One more nobody
Drifting feather-like
through an ocean
Of nobodies
Ever hurt anything.

"Rachel, will you read Ether 12:27 for me?"

I jumped at the sound of Brother Clawson's voice and as usual, scrambled for my unopened scriptures before clearing my throat. "'And if men come unto me I will show unto them their weakness that they may be humble; and my grace is sufficient for all men that humble themselves before me; for if they humble themselves before me, and have faith in me, then will I make weak things become strong unto them.'"

Brother Clawson was watching me with that horribly kind look on his face again. Ryan hadn't shown up for seminary in days. Sometimes Brother Clawson would ask me if Ryan was going to be late, and other times, like today, he didn't mention Ryan at all.

"What does this scripture mean to you, Rachel?"

My mind went blank as Jason and Dallin and everyone else turned to look at me, waiting.

I don't know. Why don't you ask someone who knows?

"It means—" I scanned the words of the scripture again frantically. "It means me—you—anyone—even someone who seems to be beyond hope—can overcome anything if we turn to Christ for help."

Brother Clawson looked at me solemnly. "Do you believe that, Rachel?"

"I want to."

Brother Clawson nodded with a strange look in his eyes. Respect, I think. "Thank you for your honesty, Rachel. Desire to believe is the first step to truly believing. I think most of us have the desire to want to believe something before we actually believe in something. Alma addresses this very point in Alma 32. Will you read verse 27, Rachel?"

I nodded and hurriedly flipped through my scriptures. "'If ye will awake and arouse your faculties, even to an experiment upon my words, and exercise a particle of faith, yea, even if ye can no more than desire to believe, let this desire work in you, even until ye believe in a manner that ye can give place for a portion of my words.'"

Brother Clawson smiled. "You see? If you're having a hard time believing in something, test it for yourself. If you desire to believe you can not only overcome a weakness but turn it into one of your strengths as well, then try turning to Heavenly Father in prayer for help. Obey the commandments connected to that weakness. Experiment. Test. Try. Prove. See if you don't end up not only gaining a testimony of this principle but finding that you actually *have* overcome that particular weakness in your life."

The class was nodding and marking their scriptures, including Dallin and Jason, but Brother Clawson's answer hadn't caused me to want to nod and mark my scriptures.

But what if your weakness is that you don't have faith that God will ever help someone you love to stop doing something? Something wrong?

I wanted to voice my question out loud, but I couldn't. I kept my eyes down on my scriptures, but when I looked up again, Dallin was looking at me with so much unexpected compassion that I looked away out of fear I'd start crying and pretended I hadn't seen him looking my way at all.

CHAPTER THIRTY-FOUR

I'd been thinking about Brother Clawson's lesson that night while I sat curled up on the couch, numbly surfing television channels with the remote in a ratty old T-shirt and pajama pants. Mom and Mr. Ackerman were out for the evening, and Dallin was out with his golfing buddies. Ryan was supposedly still at football practice, but who knew for sure what he was doing.

Shortly before seven o'clock, I was forced to answer the door when someone rudely pushed the doorbell at least half a dozen times.

"Hey, Rachel. About time!"

Seconds later while I stood holding the door and gaping like a fool, the entire Laurel class from my ward pushed their way into my house, followed by our Laurel advisor, Sister Jensen.

"What—what's going on?"

Sarah rolled her eyes and grinned. "It's activity night, dork!"

I could only stare at Sarah stupidly. "Okay. And so why is everyone here?"

Tricia was behind Sarah and burst out laughing. "Oh man—you forgot, didn't you?"

Like an electric shock to the head, I remembered stupidly volunteering my house for some sort of service project at least two months ago, back when I'd thought being Super Mormon Girl would help make things better in my life.

"Um, actually I did!"

Sister Jensen hurried to the rescue. "Oh, I thought I'd reminded you on Sunday, Rachel. Did I forget?"

Actually, she hadn't. I'd just forgotten again, even with her reminder. Luckily, the project consisted of making care packages of candy and cookies for our ward's missionaries and sending little feel-good letters in the packages. Because the rest of the girls had brought everything for making chocolate chip cookies, all I'd agreed to provide was the kitchen.

"I'm sorry I'm such a mess, but the kitchen is clean, so I'll get out all the stuff we need, and we can get going."

I couldn't believe all six of the other Laurels had come, but after one casually asked where Dallin was, it was obvious what had brought all of them over to my house.

"He's not home."

"What about Ryan?" Sarah persisted.

Someone snickered, but I just shrugged and busied myself getting out the measuring cups and spoons. "Football practice."

The actual cookie making and baking went okay. Sister Jensen wasn't against us putting on some music, and even though the noise level was pretty loud in the kitchen with the giggling, yelling, and out-of-key singing, she kept a smile on her face and dug into the service project, too.

It took us an hour and a half to get the cookies baked, letters written, and candy, letters, and cookies carefully packaged in the missionary boxes and loaded into Sister Jensen's car.

"My goodness, I didn't realize it was this late. Your kitchen still needs to be cleaned up, Rachel!"

I waved away Sister Jensen's concern. "Oh, that's no big deal. I'll take care of it."

Sister Jensen didn't want to leave until the kitchen was looking decent again, but after being assured by the six smiling girls in the kitchen that they'd clean up the mess and that everyone had a ride home because two of the girls had driven themselves over, Sister Jensen finally climbed into her own car with the boxes and drove home.

I felt a wave of panic hit as I watched Sister Jensen drive away. I didn't want to be alone in my house with my Laurel class. It was stupid to feel that way, but I did.

Sarah was the first to corner me with an insincere, probing smile. "So, Rachel—what's it like living with Dallin?"

Unconsciously, I took a step backwards from six pairs of eyes waiting and watching me.

"It's good. I mean, it's fine. Dallin's really nice."

Tricia grinned eagerly. "Really? How nice?"

"He's—"

"Hey! Looks like I missed the party!"

My heart froze when I heard Ryan's overly loud voice, followed by the front door slamming shut. At least a couple of the girls had the decency to look a little scared, too, although the rest grinned at each other.

When Ryan rounded the corner and swaggered into the kitchen, I was relieved to see that although he was clearly buzzing from something, he wasn't falling-down drunk. He'd drunk enough to be loud and obnoxious, which he easily could be when he was sober anyway, but not enough to make him stumble and fall and end up bonding with the toilet.

"So what's everybody doing?"

"They're all just leaving—" I tried to push everyone towards the front door, but Ryan blocked the way.

"Leaving? No way. Hey—I learned a new game tonight. It's really fun. Wanna learn?"

"No!" I said firmly, glaring hard at Ryan.

Sarah stepped up with a grin. "Well, I do!"

Ryan rubbed his hands together with a grin of his own. "We need some candy first. Rach—don't we have a bunch of leftover Halloween candy?"

"I don't know—"

Ryan ignored me, ransacking the kitchen cupboards until he grinned, holding up a large bag of Skittles. "This'll work perfect!"

Before I knew what was happening, Ryan had made everyone sit in a circle around the kitchen table with a mixing bowl full of Skittles in the center of it.

"Now we just need some dice!"

"Dice?" I frowned at Ryan suspiciously.

"Yeah. Hmmm—where's our Yahtzee game?"

"I have no idea—"

But Ryan was off and running and soon came back triumphantly shaking the Yahtzee cup filled with dice. "We'll only need one for this game, though."

Sarah smiled brightly at Ryan. "So what's the game?"

Ryan grinned back and settled himself on a stool beside me. "Well, it works like this. You throw the die. If you get a 6, 5, 4, 3, or a 2, that's how many Skittles you have to put in your mouth and start chewing, but you can't swallow."

"What if you throw a 1?" Tricia asked.

"If you throw a 1, you can finally swallow what's in your mouth. Ready? Rachel, you throw first."

I didn't want to play at all, but Ryan's glare made me obediently shake the die, luckily only rolling a 2.

"Okay—grab two Skittles and chew, but you can't swallow. And by the way, keep the game going fast. Shake, grab your Skittles, and move the die on."

Janie unfortunately shook a 6 and had to pop six candies in her mouth. Mandy was next and had to chew four. By the time the die came to Ryan, everyone else had at least three Skittles in their mouths, but Ryan grinned and passed the die on to me.

"I'm just going to referee this and make sure no one cheats!"

I could've sworn the die was rigged. No one seemed able to throw a 1, and soon our cheeks were bulging like squirrels', but Ryan was relentless, laughing his head off that none of us could manage a 1. And when I finally did throw a 1, gratefully chewing and swallowing the wad of Skittles in my mouth, the second Janie threw the die down, Ryan grabbed my arm.

"Oh, yeah—forgot the last rule. You have to stop swallowing once the next person throws the die, so stop swallowing, Rachel!"

I knew I had to be rotting out every tooth in my head, and my jaws were tired from all the chewing. Poor Mandy finally had enough and bolted from the table to run to the kitchen sink, where she gagged out all the Skittles she had in her mouth. Ryan, of course, couldn't stop laughing.

I ran to the kitchen garbage and spit out all the Skittles in my mouth, too, and hurried to check on Mandy, who was still leaning over the sink.

"You okay?"

"I need some water!"

I poured big glasses of water for Mandy and all the rest of the girls, who were now all gagging and spitting Skittles into the kitchen garbage can.

"Hey—everyone say Skittles!" Ryan had Mom's new digital camera held out in front of him, and before I could do more than scream, Ryan jumped forward to snap photo after photo of the girls hunched over the sink and garbage can in pure misery. Ryan only laughed harder. "That's a great one of you, Sarah—and the group shot of you all is totally priceless. Can't wait to get these out on the Internet—awesome!"

"I'm sorry—so sorry!" I couldn't stop nervously wringing my hands after trying unsuccessfully to snatch the offending camera and wishing I could strangle Ryan.

Of course, everyone raced out of the house as if it were on fire, and the second everyone had peeled out of our driveway, I turned to Ryan to light into him good, but he only laughed even harder.

"Ryan! What was all of that for?"

"Serves them right. They came here looking for a freak show, and they got to star in one instead! You've gotta take a look at some of these—look at Tricia here—and look at this—I switched it to movie camera mode. Is this Academy Award contending footage or what?" Ryan couldn't get control of himself, he was laughing so hard.

"Why do you have to do stuff like this, Ryan? Why?"

Ryan laughed off my angry ranting all the way into his bedroom where he slammed the door in my face and cranked up the music on his stereo loud enough to deafen himself and block out my pounding fists.

By the time I made it back into the kitchen to clean up the Skittles mess, I jumped at the sight of Dallin munching on a handful of Skittles and staring thoughtfully from the brightly colored mess in the sink to the rainbow of colors in the garbage can.

"So what happened here?"

I turned on the garbage disposal and shook my head. "Ryan was being an idiot, as usual. I'll never be able to go back to church now, that's for sure!"

"Why is that?"

I sighed and moved the offending bowl of Skittles as I sat down at the kitchen table and rested my elbows on the table with my head in my hands. "It's bad enough that he acts like a jerk in seminary and at church, when he actually shows up, but then he has to do this stupid thing here tonight, making all the girls from my Laurel class play his stupid game. And then take pictures of them, too!" Dallin moved to sit across from me at the table, still munching on Skittles. "You should've seen how sick everyone got, and all he did was laugh and snap photos. Why does he have to be like that? Why can't he be normal—"

I was in the middle of telling Dallin what happened, interspersed with plenty of name calling on my end regarding what a jerk, idiot, and loser Ryan was, when Ryan appeared around the corner and leaned against the kitchen door jamb with his arms folded.

Ryan looked all casual and uncaring, but his eyes were dangerously mean. "Talking smack about me again? Don't let me interrupt. I'd like to know how everyone really feels about me."

I glared back at Ryan. "Just go away!"

"Aw, don't get yourself all bunched up over this, Rachel. I know you don't like anyone in your class, anyway." Ryan picked up the bowl of Skittles and held it out to me with an evil grin. "Come on, Rachel. Have some candy!"

I gave him my best withering glare and didn't move.

"What do I have to do to get you to come over here, Rachel? Wave a Twinkie around on a string?"

And then Dallin did something unforgivable. He burst out laughing at Ryan's comment. Ryan was as surprised as I was, but he had the nerve to look pleased. "You think that's good? Me and Robert used to call her the 'Incredible Bulk' when she was a kid."

"Sometimes I really hate you, Ryan!"

I knocked the kitchen chair over backwards in my hurry to get out of the kitchen and ran into my room to slam the door, hearing nothing but Ryan's mean laughter echoing down the hall.

CHAPTER THIRTY-FIVE

If I'd been pretty sure Ryan had been drinking the night Jason was injured on the football field, by the night of the last game before Central's shot at the playoffs for the high school football state championship, anyone would've been able to tell Ryan was playing "impaired." Still, I knew how much the coaches liked Ryan and how willing they were to give him chance after chance after chance, followed by the benefit of the doubt far too many times. So when Ryan came storming into the house after the game, slamming the front door and throwing his gym bag and car keys across the room, his announcement was a shock, although it truly shouldn't have been a surprise, and actually should've happened a long time ago.

"I've been kicked off the team!"

Mr. Ackerman and Mom had gone to the game and were waiting up for him, watching television in the living room with me.

Mr. Ackerman calmly bent down and smoothly pocketed Ryan's car keys before raising his eyebrows at Ryan. "Why were you kicked off the team?"

"I don't know. Why do you think?"

Mom rushed in to try and help. "Don't be a smart mouth, Ryan!"

Ryan glared at her before turning back to Mr. Ackerman. "You want to know? You want to know? Coach said he knew I was smacked, that I couldn't walk straight, and that he was done with me." Ryan threw himself into one of the recliners and raked his fingers through his hair. "Really nice to plan and prepare for all these stinking football games, getting ready to go to State, and then have it yanked!"

Mr. Ackerman's voice was still calm. "And whose fault is that?"

"The stupid coach's, for kicking me off!"

Mom's voice was calm now, too. "I know it feels like they're punishing you, Ryan, but I think they want to help you."

Ryan looked from Mom to Mr. Ackerman suspiciously. "Wait a minute—you're both acting too calm about this. You knew this was going to happen, didn't you?"

Mr. Ackerman took hold of Mom's hand and of the conversation. "Your coach is one of the teachers who has called in concern over you and your behavior."

"Why didn't you tell me?"

"We tried, but you weren't interested in listening. We warned you this could happen, but you didn't seem to be too worried or to care very much about it."

"What did you tell Coach?"

Mom sighed. "We told him to do whatever he had to do for the good of the rest of the team. That in the end, whatever he decided would most likely be the best thing for you, too."

Ryan responded in the only way he seemed to know how to anymore: curse and run away. After treating us all to a string of obscenities that mostly didn't make any sense, he gave us another string when he looked for his car keys and couldn't find them, not realizing they were now in Mr. Ackerman's pocket.

"Who cares if I'm kicked off the team? Dad's not here to see me play, anyway. Football doesn't matter to me anymore."

Mom's eyes filled with tears, but Ryan only stormed down the hall to his own room, slamming the door shut behind him.

CHAPTER THIRTY-SIX

M r. Ackerman held on to Ryan's keys and told Ryan the next morning that he was doing it for his own good.

"We can't take the risk anymore that you could harm yourself or anyone else. Your mother and I will restore your car keys when we have proof you've stopped drinking."

I thought Ryan would fight his punishment more, but apparently he decided to try a new tactic. For the rest of the week, he stayed home and claimed to be doing his homework in his room. I'd find his scriptures lying innocently in the living room on one of the lamp tables, with a pen resting on the open pages. He even went so far one day as to interrupt a conversation between Mom and Mr. Ackerman to say, "Hey, I read this really great scripture. Totally goes with what you're talking about," before launching off to paraphrase the scripture. Mom beamed and Mr. Ackerman nodded, but I was sure Ryan was just doing his best to convince them he was doing better in order to get the two of them off his back and have his car keys returned.

I was nervous to go to church on Sunday due to the Skittles Incident, and unfortunately, I had good reason to be concerned. Every girl in Young Women was buzzing about it, and none of the Laurels would talk to me or even look at me. Sister Jensen knew something was up and tried to ask everyone in class, but the other six Laurels only shrugged and said, "Nothing."

"Well, Rachel, will you please tell me what's going on?"

All I could do was shrug and say, "Nothing," too.

I wasn't about to subject myself to the other Laurels during Sunday School, though, and instead wandered out into the parking lot and over to the grassy area that had become a favorite spot of mine, my red creative writing notebook in hand.

Mrs. Townsend's next assignment due Monday was a villanelle piece. "This type of poetic form is nineteen lines long. Only nineteen. The stanzas need to be written in groups of three lines, or 'tercets,' and only two end-line rhymes are allowed. Also, the first and third line of the beginning stanza *must* alternate as the third line in each successive stanza. These two lines will then form a couplet at the end of the poem."

Mrs. Townsend's eyes briefly scanned our confused faces before she burst out laughing. "I can see that we'll need to look at some examples. Dylan Thomas's villanelle, 'Do Not Go Gentle into That Good Night,' is one of the most famous English examples of this French form of poetry. Let's look first at his poem, written for his aging father, and then we'll examine a few others."

I'd been struggling all week with my villanelle, tossing aside each idea I'd attempted to put on paper, but now, the words flew from my pen as fast as I could speak each one out loud:

I would've tried harder, but all was dead.
You even twisted glass in my heart to make the blood flow,
You cried, I was numb—I could only turn away instead.
Everything seemed lightened, but I knew different in my head.
I didn't want to run—where could I go?
I would've tried harder, but all was dead.
I walked to you—I thought I did—my feet were lead.
Your eyes and hands begged, your voice was low;
You cried, I was numb—I could only turn away instead.
Look in my eyes—you searched—but nothing could have been read.
Was it tears I saw? Your eyes held something I must've known long ago.
I would've tried harder, but all was dead.
And now there is blood—so much of a killing red;
"The earth trembles," you whispered. "The storms and winds forever blow!"
You cried, I was numb—I could only turn away instead.

"Your heart! The glass! You have to feel—and hurt!" you said.
Everything happened, yet I was empty. It has ended, I know.
I would've tried harder, but all was dead.
You cried, I was numb—I could only turn away instead.

"How come you're not in Sunday School?"

I jumped at the voice near my ear and slammed my notebook shut. It was Dallin, of course, leaning against the tree I was sitting under, scrutinizing me as if I was under a microscope.

"I could ask the same question of you."

Dallin nodded. "You could. I got a message on my cell phone from Brandon during priesthood, so I went to my car to call him back. That's my excuse. Now what's yours?"

I shrugged. "I just don't feel like going."

"And?"

"And what?"

"Does this have something to do with the Skittles deal on Wednesday? Because I meant to tell you that I deleted the pictures from your mom's camera. And the movie camera stuff, too."

"You did?"

Dallin grinned at my stunned face. "I did."

"How?"

"I saw it sitting by Ryan's bed the next morning when he was in the shower. Only took me maybe five seconds to do it. I doubt he'd had a chance to download anything onto the Internet."

"Well, thanks, Dallin. I mean it. Thank you." And I did mean it. It was incredibly great of him to step up and do something nice for me. "But Skittles have nothing to do with why I'm sitting out here. I don't care about that."

Dallin raised his eyebrows. "Really?" He wasn't about to give up, so I sighed before turning to face him.

"I don't know. I guess I just thought we're all taught at church to be nice and friendly and brave and true and all that. I mean, why go to church and read and memorize scriptures if everyone's just going to ignore what's being taught?"

Dallin nodded thoughtfully and didn't speak for a few moments before crouching down to sit on the grass beside me. "It's all pretty simple, actually."

I raised an eyebrow. "Simple?"

Dallin nodded again. "Everyone's at different levels of learning all the time. Everyone grows—figures things out—changes—at their own speed. And sometimes that speed is pretty slow. Like in school. A teacher teaches everyone in class the same thing at the same time, but not everyone's going to get an A, right?"

I shrugged. "I guess so."

Dallin smiled. "See? Everyone learns stuff at a different rate. Some people figure out something new really fast. Other people need to have an idea beaten into their head a million times before it sticks. You should know that from dealing with me, right?"

I couldn't help laughing. "Yeah, you're pretty hard to deal with!"

Dallin laughed, too, before turning serious again. "I'm sorry the girls in the ward aren't the nicest around. They're not perfect, but neither are you."

"What? I'm not?"

Dallin grinned. "Sorry. And by the way, neither am I. I'm sorry I laughed at Ryan's Twinkie comment."

I was shocked. Truly. "You are?"

Dallin nodded. "Yeah. I thought the line was funny. That's all I was laughing at. I wasn't laughing at you."

"Yeah. You weren't laughing at me. You were laughing beside me."

Dallin burst out laughing. "So you *can* be funny!"

I grinned back. "Sometimes, I guess."

"Are you going to go to sacrament meeting?"

I frowned and looked away. "I don't know."

"If I promise to beat anyone up who even looks at you weird, will you come?"

"I may hold you to that, you know!"

The idea of Dallin beating up someone at church made me laugh all over again, but Dallin only grinned as he helped me to my feet and walked with me back inside.

CHAPTER THIRTY-SEVEN

I'd turned in my villanelle poem before my creative writing class started on Monday, and by the end of the class period, Mrs. Townsend handed it back to me with her comments noted in her usual tiny, perfect cursive handwriting. "Vivid, painful imagery. This has such a note of heartfelt pain. I hate to carp—but in truth: the rhyme scheme is villanelle—alas—but the rhythm isn't. Should we care? No."

For some reason, Mrs. Townsend's comments irked me. Rhythm? I couldn't remember her saying anything about any particular rhythm the poem was supposed to have. I was deep in thought on the living room couch, rereading my poem to myself out loud, telling myself my villanelle had perfectly fine rhythm, when Ryan burst through the front door and angrily flung himself into one of the recliners.

I looked up at Ryan's angry face. "What's wrong with you?"

"Nothing's wrong with me, but everything's wrong with Mr. Reynolds!"

"The school counselor?"

"Duh! Who else?"

"Why'd you have to talk to him?"

"My stupid grades, of course!" Ryan threw his gym bag across the room. "He's a jerk, and you know why?"

I sighed. "I'm sure you're going to tell me!"

"First off, he pretends he's human, but everyone knows he's got a monkey brain. He wants everyone to believe he can think, but all he does is annoy every living being he's ever come in contact with!"

"So I'm guessing he wasn't willing to help you figure out a way to work with your teachers so you'll be sure to graduate?"

"Of course he was no help at all! He's obviously in love with all of my teachers. And why should he care if I graduate or not? His pay will be the same either way!"

I set my poem aside to watch Ryan as he talked, and for a moment, my heart hurt for him. He'd lost more weight, causing his jeans to hang loosely on his hips. His legs were visibly bouncing, and I could see his hands shake. His longish hair was matted to his forehead from sweat, and although his eyes were bloodshot, I figured it was from having a hard time sleeping lately and not from his usual drinking. Mr. Ackerman was watching him more closely, and he'd taken over my job of raiding Ryan's stashes. I knew Ryan's recent anxiety and hostility were due to a forced, cold-turkey cutoff from alcohol more than from his low grades or anything else going on with him.

"Have you tried talking to your teachers yourself?"

Ryan glared at me before turning sarcastic. "What a brilliant idea, Rachel! Wow, I can't believe I didn't think of that!"

"Sorry."

"I've tried all I'm going to with them. I can't stand any of their smells anymore." Ryan's voice turned low, and he stared off into space, his hands still shaking and his legs still bouncing as he talked out loud to no one. "I don't know why I even care. None of it even matters anymore anyway. Who cares about stupid grades and stupid football? I had to bury my dad. How can they think anything they say means anything to me? How in the world could they think school could really matter to me at all? Nothing matters anymore!" Ryan ran his fingers through his hair again. "If only he hadn't died—it's not fair—none of this would've happened—none of it!"

Ryan's words made my insides turn cold. "So, your bad grades are Dad's fault. Everything's all his fault, for dying? So now you don't have to try anymore or do anything anymore? I can't believe you're actually going to try and blame your drinking and your bad grades and who knows what else on Dad!"

Ryan's voice raised frantically, his eyes looking almost wild now. "Don't talk to me about Dad! Don't ever say the word *Dad* to me again!" He put his head in his hands and moaned, his whole body shaking now.

"Ryan—"

"Leave me alone!" Ryan struggled out of the recliner and stumbled down the hall to his room but made a jerky detour to the bathroom to be sick. I had to force myself to stay seated on the couch, unconsciously rearranging myself to sit on my hands.

I was still seated on the couch, on my hands, long after Ryan had closed himself off in his bedroom.

202

CHAPTER THIRTY-EIGHT

Saturday afternoon after I'd spent some time at the cemetery followed by taking my turn at cleaning the bathroom, I passed Dallin's bedroom, glancing in to smile briefly, and then had to stop and take another look.

"What are you doing?"

Dallin had all of his golf clubs lined up on the floor and was carefully inspecting one of the smaller clubs, rubbing it gently with a cloth.

"Just cleaning my clubs before I go play."

"Isn't golf season over?"

"At school it is, but I'm going to keep playing until it's too cold outside." Dallin finished wiping the club and then placed it in his golf bag before gathering up the rest of the clubs to put them back in the bag as well, covering the bigger ones with furry covers that looked like socks. He smiled at me as he slung his golf bag over one shoulder. "I'm going to the driving range at Hill Valley Golf Course to practice my swing."

"Oh. Well, have fun." I moved out of the way of Dallin's bedroom door and followed him to the living room. Dallin reached for the doorknob to the front door and paused, turning around to look at me curiously.

"Would you like to come with me?"

My mouth dropped open. "To play golf?"

"Not to play golf. Just to hit a bucket of balls at the driving range. We wouldn't be playing a round of golf at all."

I couldn't help laughing. "I've never played golf before in my life!"

"That's okay. I can teach you."

My heart pounded, and I couldn't stop the grin that matched the one on Dallin's face. "Well—all right. I'm just going to let Mom know, okay?"

"I'll meet you at my car."

I ran to the bathroom to run a brush through my hair before yelling to Mom that I was going to the golf course with Dallin.

"Have fun, dear!"

I'd never been to a golf course, but Dallin had clearly been to Hill Valley a million times. He smiled and said hello to everyone who was working at the clubhouse and then paid for a bucket of balls before holding open the clubhouse door for me. Pointing to the right, he said, "Driving range is this way."

Dallin had rented clubs for me to use, along with the bucket of golf balls. I grinned as I took the rented clubs from him. "I guess you don't want me to ruin your fancy clubs, huh?"

Dallin laughed. "I'm taller than you. My clubs would be way too long for you to use. You need clubs that fit your height. You'll be able to hit the ball a lot better with shorter clubs."

Dallin went through the motions of showing me how to hold a golf club, standing beside me holding one of his own clubs. "Okay—before you can hit a golf ball, you need to hold the club right. A good grip will make the difference between a good shot and a bad shot, and a good round of golf and a bad round of golf."

I watched Dallin demonstrate how he curled his fingers around the grip of the club, making sure to hold the club just so.

"I use an interlocking grip, with my right pinky between my middle and first finger of my left hand. See?"

I nodded and tried to do the same. Dallin shook his head and showed me how to grip the club again. "Your hands are small, so you can just grip the club more like you would a baseball bat. Hold the club lightly, though. The more relaxed your grip is, the straighter and farther you'll hit the ball."

"If I hit the ball at all, you mean!"

Dallin laughed and handed me a golf ball. "You'll hit the ball just fine. I have every reason to believe you will!"

I tossed the golf ball lightly in the air once. "Oh, yeah? How come?"

Dallin grinned and grabbed another golf ball out of the bucket. "Because I'm the one teaching you, of course!"

He went through the mechanics of showing me how to swing, but being as uncoordinated as I was, when it was my turn to imitate what he'd shown me, I failed miserably.

"You need to keep your knees bent." Dallin launched off then into a speech about creating triangles and following through and back swings and not breaking the wrists and a bunch of other things that didn't make any sense to me at all, but I nodded and tried to concentrate, trying hard not to grin, because he was clearly enjoying having the opportunity to show off his expertise.

"And then, you just—"

"Why don't you show me how you hit a golf ball?"

Dallin stopped in surprise and then grinned before placing a golf ball on a blue tee. I stood in awe as Dallin swung and hit golf ball after golf ball with his smooth swing, watching the club move in a perfect circle. I was shocked at how far he was able to hit the ball and to see the golf ball always fly like a bullet and as straight as an arrow.

"Wow!"

Dallin shook his head, watching the golf ball fly. "Not really. That last shot swung too much to the right. I need to work on my follow through."

I couldn't help it. I swung my golf club lightly to swat him in the back of the legs, making him jump a little. "What are you talking about? You're good at this—really good! Did your dad teach you?"

Dallin laughed and poked me back with his golf club. "Nah. My dad doesn't golf."

"He doesn't? How'd you get into golf?"

"My mom was a really good golfer. We used to go golfing together when I was little. She took me golfing for the first time when I was about five and entered me into all kinds of junior leagues and had me take lessons from pros. My dad kept me in lessons and junior leagues and junior tournaments after she passed away."

I nodded, impressed. "No wonder you're so good!" I watched Dallin set another golf ball on the tee. "I'm sorry I never saw you play. I mean, I'm sorry I didn't go to the tournament."

Dallin looked up at me in surprise. "It's no big deal, Rachel. I don't play so others can watch me. I just love to play the game, period. It's fun to be on the golf team, but I'd still play whether I made the team or not."

"Did Valerie come see you play?" I wanted to bite back the words the second they flew out of my mouth.

Dallin didn't seem to notice a thing. "I don't know. I never saw her."

"I'm sorry."

Dallin only laughed. "It's not a big deal. She's just a friend."

I could feel myself blushing all over, and having Dallin watch me made it even worse. I tapped my golf ball on the grass nervously with my rented club. "I thought maybe you two were—you know—going out or something."

Dallin waited until I dared to look up at him again. "She's fun to hang out with, but that's all." I had to try hard not to grin like a fool. I couldn't help it. Hope springs eternal, and it was doing so for me. Dallin laughed and poked at me again with his golf club. "Enough stalling. Your turn to hit one!"

"Don't hold your breath!" I swung badly without a golf ball anywhere near me, but I did even worse with one on a golf tee directly in front of me. I swung three times, each time more horribly awkward than the last, but the golf ball didn't move from the tee an inch. Not even a half inch.

"You have to keep your head down and your eye on the ball. And you need to follow through with your swing."

"I thought I was!"

"Nope. Sorry. And you keep straightening your knees. You gotta stop that!"

Dallin tried to explain more of the scientifics of golf, but it was all confusing to me, and I guess it showed on my face, because Dallin burst out laughing.

"Here. Let me show you."

The next thing I knew, Dallin had stepped up behind me to wrap his arms around me, holding his hands over mine gripping the golf club. I was shocked, but at the same time, it felt nice to have his arms around me like that, even if it was just to show me how to swing a golf club properly.

"Now, watch what I do, and see—feel how the club is supposed to go. See how this arm needs to stay straight?" My heart was pounding as he slowly raised the club, his hands on top of mine, and gently and slowly swung it through to make it hit the golf ball. Even though I was between him and the ball and he'd done his swing in slow motion, I was surprised at how far the golf ball flew. It was nerve wracking, and yet it felt way too nice having Dallin help me like that, so I stayed confused for a few more swings before Dallin laughed and said I needed to try it by myself. And this time, I hit the ball.

"Good job! You're getting it!"

The happy, pleased look on Dallin's face made me glad I'd finally, successfully hit one of the golf balls on my own, although I was disappointed he didn't try to help me hit a golf ball again.

Dallin would hit a few and then he'd watch me hit a few, coaching me along and making a big deal every time I hit a ball that went a decent distance, even though all of my shots curved too much to the left.

"You're doing great! I can't believe you've never done this before."

I laughed. "I can! Definitely!"

Once the bucket of golf balls was empty, Dallin bought another bucket. I hit a few more, but after a while, I stopped to rest my arms and watch Dallin's perfect swing.

I sat on the grass, quietly watching Dallin for several minutes before I dared to break Dallin's concentration. "Do you ever feel sad playing golf now? I mean, now that your mom's not here to see you?"

Dallin turned to look at me with a smile. "Actually, I never feel sad at all."

"Really?"

Dallin nodded slowly and tapped his golf club on the ground. "I always think of her when I play and how excited she'd be that I'm still doing something we had so much fun doing together. I can see her watching me, cheering me on. My dad has this picture of her—he took it of her at the last tournament she came to see me in right before she got sick. I'd just made a great shot, and he took an awesome picture of her face all smiling and excited, cheering me on. It's my favorite picture of her. Just thinking of her cheering me on like that makes me play better. I know she's going to look in on me playing as much as she can. I always try to play my best in case she's watching."

I looked down and plucked at a few blades of grass. "I wish Ryan felt that way."

Dallin walked over to me. "It hasn't been as long for him since his dad died as it's been for me. Or for you, either." Dallin reached down and grabbed my hand, easily swinging me to my feet. "So—let's see that incredible swing you have a few more times. There are three golf balls left, and they've all got your name on them."

Luckily for me, I hit all three. I couldn't help grinning as Dallin cheered and yelled "Woo hoo!" after each hit. Dallin held his car door open for me and stopped to buy us each a Big Gulp at the 7-Eleven on the way home. It'd been such a fun Saturday with Dallin that I couldn't make myself stop smiling. I wished the day could go on forever like this, just driving around with Dallin, laughing and singing with the songs on the radio.

All too soon, Dallin eased his Mustang into our driveway. "Thanks for taking me to the driving range with you, Dallin. And for teaching me a little about golf."

Dallin grinned. "Anytime, Rachel."

Hope rose even higher as Dallin opened the front door for me and I floated back into the house.

CHAPTER THIRTY-NINE

The fact that Saturday had been such a fun day with Dallin and the fact that Sunday was thankfully uneventful should've been a loud and clear warning that my yo-yo life was about to take a downward turn.

Monday had started out normal enough. Seminary, first period, and second period had gone well, meaning nothing unusual had happened. Third period, however, was different. The door to the classroom was closed, with a full-sized sheet of paper taped to the door. On it were the words, "Central High Shakespearean Festival Today. Meet downstairs in the drama classroom, room 103."

I knew that next semester everyone at Central would be studying a few Shakespearean plays in all of the English classes and that the drama class had agreed to kick things off by performing a little Shakespeare for everyone in the school, but I'd forgotten the supposedly big event was happening today. I glanced at my watch and groaned. Five minutes to the hour! I hustled back downstairs, arriving at Room 103 with two minutes to spare but was forced to a stop when I stepped into the room.

The drama classroom contained a built-in mini stage, which took up a good portion of the classroom. The room was large, though, and lots of folding chairs had been placed in neat rows for the festival. Even though only third-period English students from each grade were supposed to be in the drama room right now, clearly the room was housing a ton of uninvited festival crashers. The room was bulging with people. I had to push and shove my way in, mostly due to students trying to come in behind me who were shoving me along. My eyes darted all over the semidark-ened room full of loud, noisy students before I finally spied a lone chair towards the back. I snagged it a second before the girl shoving behind me, who was one second away from winning the award for the rudest high school student ever, could grab it herself.

I gave the girl an annoyed glare as she shoved her way around me and then craned my neck to see who all was crammed into the room sardine-style with me. Before I could find anyone interesting, the lights dimmed and Miss Goforth, the drama teacher, took center stage to welcome every-one and introduce the program.

" . . . so let's begin our festival with the opening scene from *King Lear.*"

The curtains to the mini stage opened, and out walked three guys in sixteenth-century costumes. I was impressed with how good the costumes were, although I wasn't that impressed with their acting. Within moments, though, the three were joined by King Lear and his three daughters. The older two, Goneril and Regan, were dressed in dark purple and blue gowns with their hair piled high on their heads with gold circlet crowns. Each of the older two sisters had guys playing their husbands. I hardly noticed the third and youngest daughter dressed in a white gown until she stepped to the side and away from the others to say to us, the audi-ence, "What shall Cordelia speak? Love, and be silent."

I stared at the girl in the white dress. She wasn't just pretty. She was what anyone would term beautiful. Her hair flowed past her shoulders in big, loose waves, with only her gold circlet crown to keep it in place. She was familiar—I knew I knew her, and yet I couldn't figure out who she was until she spoke her next line, which again was said just to the audi-ence: "Then poor Cordelia! And yet, not so, since I am sure my love's / More ponderous than my tongue."

The drama room was so quiet no one dared to sniff or cough. As Cordelia finished her line, my eyes bulged as I realized who the beautiful girl was who didn't seem to be acting at all but just seemed to *be* this Cordelia, King Lear's daughter. *Kathy Colton!*

I couldn't believe the transformation. I glanced around the room, and based on the overly rapt attention she was getting, no one else could believe it either. One of the spotlights on Kathy from the back of the room caught the glow of a blond head in its path, sitting near the far left wall of the room several rows in front of me. I didn't have to look twice to see it was Dallin's head, and by carefully skootching my chair forward a few inches, I could easily see Dallin's profile. My heart jumped and then stopped. Dallin was staring at Kathy, as transfixed as everyone else in the room. *Especially the guys*, I thought to myself glumly. I watched Dallin watch Kathy until the room burst into applause. I looked back at the actors then, and although everyone else bowed and curtsied as if to say, "Well, of course we're great and deserve tons of applause," Kathy blushed and smiled and actually seemed surprised that everyone was clapping and cheering.

I hardly paid attention to the rest of the performances. Dallin watched the rest of the scenes, leaning back in his chair between Chad and Zachary, his arms folded and a half-interested look on his face. He wasn't into the rest of the scenes like he'd been with the first one. I tried to tell myself he'd only sat forward on his chair, watching Kathy—everyone in the *King Lear* scene, really—with intense interest because their scene was first. That was all.

I absently clapped along with everyone else as the actors in the *Macbeth* scene bowed and smiled. Then Miss Goforth took the stage to announce the finale.

"Our final scene is from *Romeo and Juliet*."

The curtains opened, and there, seated on the edge of a table covered with a large fancy blanket and pillows as if it were a bed, sat Kathy Colton. This time, she had one braid down her back and a dark red skull cap on her head. Her dress matched the color of the cap, with puffed long sleeves and tiny gold threads that ran down the dress, winking and sparkling from the spotlight shining on her. The gown was incredibly gorgeous, but again, Kathy was oblivious to it as she stared sadly and intently at a tiny glass bottle in her hands, before lifting it high into the air with one hand to speak to it.

I glanced at Dallin. He wasn't leaning back in his chair with his arms folded anymore. I sighed sadly as I saw his eyes watching Kathy closely as he leaned forward and adjusted his chair so he could see her better. The room was as quiet as death, and to see everyone staring at Kathy, who was so focused on being Juliet that she didn't even care who was watching her, made me want to scream.

"My dismal scene I must act alone. / Come, vial. / What if this mixture do not work at all? / Shall I be married then tomorrow morning? / No, no! This shall forbid it."

And then, before I knew what was happening, I fell under Kathy's spell, too, and couldn't keep from shaking my head. She was talented. Really talented.

"How if, when I am laid into the tomb, / I wake before the time that Romeo / Come to redeem me?"

I looked at Dallin again, and my heart sank. *You'd just love to be Kathy's Romeo, wouldn't you?* I shook the thought out of my head. Dallin was impressed with her acting, like everyone else in the room. That was all.

Kathy's face was full of horror—real horror—as she cried, "Methinks I see cousin's ghost / Seeking out Romeo, that did spit his body / Upon a rapier's point. Stay, Tybalt, stay! / Romeo, I come! This do I drink to thee." And then she drank whatever was in the glass bottle, sank onto her table bed, and closed her eyes, looking as if she truly had just died.

No one moved for a good three seconds or even made a sound. But then, the room erupted into loud applause, and Kathy sat up and jumped off the table to curtsy and smile shyly at everyone before the curtains drew together. I glanced at Dallin once more, just in time to see that he was one of those on his feet, still clapping loudly and cheering with an amazed look on his face.

I couldn't stop seeing that amazed, basically adoring look on Dallin's face in my head the rest of the morning. It was still throbbing in my forehead when I met Teresa for lunch in the cafeteria.

"What's wrong, Rachel? You seem so depressed!"

"It's nothing. I just saw the Shakespeare plays. Have you seen them yet?"

"No, but I've heard everyone buzzing about how great Kathy Colton is in them. Is she?"

I shrugged and stabbed a fork into my salad. "I guess. Dallin definitely thought so, anyway."

Teresa kicked me under the table and nodded over to my right. "Speak of the devil—there's Kathy now." Teresa's eyes widened as she stared at Kathy along with the rest of the lunchroom crowd. "Wow—look at her hair! And makeup—I don't think I've ever seen her wear that much before!"

I turned around to see Kathy holding a tray of food a few feet away from us, scanning the room for a place to sit before smiling at two girls who were waving at her excitedly from a table in the back. I leaned over the table to Teresa to whisper. "She's in costume. That's how her hair and makeup looked for her first Shakespeare scene."

I watched Kathy move a few steps towards her friends, only to have someone step into her path. I took a sharp, fast breath, and couldn't breathe again when I saw who was smiling at her. *Dallin!*

"Hey—Kathy, isn't it?"

I watched Kathy frown in confusion at Dallin. "Yes—I'm Kathy."

Dallin grinned back. "I'm Dallin."

"Hi." My heart pounded as I watched Kathy smile shyly back at Dallin, clearly flirting with him.

Dallin only grinned wider in return, with eyes that were sparkling too much. "Hi. Hey—great job on the plays you did today."

Kathy actually looked surprised as she stuttered, "Oh, well, thanks!"

"I guess you're doing your plays again after lunch?"

"Um, yes—we all are!"

"Well, good luck. You'll do great!"

Dallin grinned again before nodding and walking past Kathy, who

turned and watched him with a look of shock on her face as he walked
out of the lunchroom.

Teresa nudged me with a sympathetic smile. "Don't worry about that.
You know how Dallin is. He's nice to everyone. He's probably gone up
and said 'Good job' to everyone in the drama class today."

"Yeah, maybe."

I watched Kathy sitting with her friends and felt envy and jealousy
and a lot of other crazy feelings as I watched guy after guy approach her
table and say hello and "Good job." And then, worst of all, Jason West
himself on his crutches glided through the crowd over to her before plopping himself down beside her, trying to stare down any guy who dared to
say hi to Kathy—as if he owned her.

Teresa choked back a laugh. "Too funny. He's scared off her friends,
too!"

I watched Kathy's two friends hightail it out of the lunchroom but not
before giving Kathy a thumbs-up behind Jason's back. I sighed as I
watched Jason and Kathy google and flirt at each other.

Teresa watched me carefully over her milk carton. "So, do you hate
Kathy Colton now?"

I tried to give her my best shocked look. "What do you mean?"

Teresa rolled her eyes. "I know you've liked Jason West forever!"

I shrugged and stabbed at my salad again. "I don't know. She can't
help that she's dangerously pretty."

"Dangerously pretty? What does that mean?"

I didn't look up from absently pushing salad leaves around in my
salad bowl. "She's dangerous because she's pretty and doesn't even know
she's pretty. And she's nice, too. Girls who *know* they're pretty are
dangerous, but pretty girls who *don't* know they're pretty and are nice, too,
are worse." I stopped to take a bite of salad, but it tasted like chalk.

Teresa leaned over the table to grab my arm. "She's just getting a lot of
attention because of the plays." I looked up to see Teresa grinning at me
Cheshire Cat style. "Hey—tryouts for *A Funny Thing Happened on the Way*

to the Forum are after school today in the auditorium. You ought to try out. Who knows—maybe you, too, can get a fan club like Kathy's!"

I turned around again to see Jason staring intently at Kathy. He was under her thumb. Definitely. Probably happily. What in the world had made me think I ever had a chance with him, just because he was nice to me? He was only nice to me because of Dallin, anyway. He'd never looked at me like that. Ever.

And Dallin—well, who knew? I didn't expect him to look at me as intensely as Jason was looking at Kathy, but I did wonder what it would be like to at least have Dallin look at me the way he'd looked at Kathy today, both onstage and just now in the cafeteria. Like I wasn't just his freakish stepsister he felt sorry for and had to be nice to. I looked over at Jason and Kathy one more time and realized that it wasn't enough for me to wonder what it would be like. I wanted to *know* what it would be like.

CHAPTER FORTY

I'd made my decision during lunch, and now was the big moment. There was no turning back now. I'd never forget the look on Teresa's face when I told her what I was going to do after school. That look alone almost made me decide to give it up as the stupidest idea I'd had yet.

"I can't believe you, Rachel!" Teresa was so floored that she actually seemed to be mad at me. And that surprised me. "I was just joking during lunch. You're not really going to do it, are you?"

"Why shouldn't I? Tryouts are open to everyone, not just for the drama and choir classes." I took a deep breath and tried to keep my voice from shaking. "I want to do this, Teresa."

Teresa studied me for another minute. "Well, I'm trying out tomorrow because I have to go to a doctor's appointment now, so I guess 'Good luck' is all I can say."

———·———

"Rachel Fletcher?" The thin, nasal, feminine voice startled me. I nearly jumped out of my chair and into the lap of the kid sitting next to me. I'd been staring at the poster in the auditorium: "November 16 and 17: Open School Tryouts for *A Funny Thing Happened on the Way to the Forum*" and hardly heard Ms. McPhee's voice above the noise of my heart beating.

"Yes—I'm here." My heart was really pounding now.

"You're next. Front and center on the stage, please." Somehow,

I managed to keep my feet from tripping me as I made my way to the front of the auditorium and up the stairs onto the stage. I could feel the other girls in the room sneering at me. At that moment, I was wishing I'd eaten more salads and not so many fries and chocolate milkshakes. I could feel my heart thumping in my chest and in my head, and I was sweating and sticky and trembling, all at the same time.

The choir director, Ms. McPhee, and the musical's student director were sitting on the front row of the theater-style chairs in the auditorium, a small table in front of them. A healthy smattering of students was seated in the auditorium behind them waiting for their turns to try out for the musical.

Ms. McPhee looked me up and down before she spoke, making my heart beat even faster. "Now, which part are you reading for?"

"Ph-Philia," I stuttered.

"Philia?" she said sharply. I nodded. "All right. I'll read Senex's lines, and you read Philia's on page 28. Start at the top of the page when you're ready."

My fingers were shaking as I flipped through the half dozen pages of the script I'd been studying for the past hour, waiting for my turn to hopefully speak in front of all of these people.

"Take me." That was all that was typed neatly by "Philia." Those two little words sounded incredibly dull falling from my lips and flat onto the stage. I could almost hear the splat they made when they hit the floor.

"What did you say?" Ms. McPhee's voice was still as sharp as a razor.

I jerked my head up to stare wide-eyed at Ms. McPhee. I knew my face must have been as red as it could get. "Oh, I'm sorry—I said, 'Take me.'"

Ms. McPhee and the student director looked at each other, and the student director rolled her eyes. My hands shook harder, and I looked back down at the script in confusion. I could hardly read the words in front of me.

"No, no. My lines are, 'What did you say?' Didn't you look at Senex's lines below Philia's?"

"Oh. Oh, yes. I see. Oh. I'm sorry." I was babbling like an idiot, and the worst thing about it was that I couldn't seem to make myself stop. I laughed nervously.

The student director narrowed her eyes at me. "Are you part of the first year drama class?"

"Well, no, but the poster doesn't say only drama students can try—"

"I know," she interrupted, obviously annoyed. "I just wanted to know for sure whether you were or not." She rustled through some papers on the table. "How about your song?"

"Song?" I said stupidly. No one had ever mentioned there'd be singing involved with this!

Ms. McPhee and the student director looked at each other again. Ms. McPhee sighed loud and long. "My dear, this is a *musical*. Philia *sings* in this play. Do you have a song prepared?"

Why was I putting myself through this torture? I wanted to die. Become invisible right that second. Why couldn't a light fixture break loose and fall on me and put everybody out of this misery?

"Can you sing the school song?" Ms. McPhee continued.

"I think so," I whispered.

"Okay. Shelley, go play it on the piano." The student director rolled her eyes at me again before seating herself at the piano. Somehow, I squeaked and choked my way through the first verse of the song. I wanted to die. Just die. Right then. It would've been so much easier to just pass out cold, smacking the hardwood floor with my skull. Anything was preferable to such torture as this.

"Fine, fine. We'll let you know. Thank you for trying out." Ms. McPhee didn't even look at me as I hurried off the stage and out of the auditorium as fast as I could go.

———•———

"So, how did the tryouts go?"

I'd only been home a matter of minutes—seconds, maybe—when Teresa called.

"How do you think?" I grumbled.

"Oh boy. That good, huh? Hey, well, at least you tried. So—what song did you sing?"

I gripped the phone tighter. "You knew I'd have to sing?"

Teresa didn't say anything for a few seconds. "Well, sure. The play's a musical, right?"

"I wish you'd reminded me," I muttered.

"Well, what song did you sing?" she pestered.

I rolled my eyes and sighed. "You're never going to believe it."

"Tell me, tell me!" I could hear her clapping her hands together.

"Promise you won't laugh?"

"Of course!"

"The school song."

It took me a second to realize Teresa was trying to smother her laughter by covering the phone receiver.

"Stop it! How was I supposed to know I was going to have to sing? I've never tried out for any dumb play before!" She still hadn't stopped laughing, so I pushed buttons on the phone and whacked the kitchen counter with it a few times before she gasped "sorry" over and over. "You *did* promise not to laugh, you know," I grumbled, which was no help, because she only laughed harder.

"Okay, I'm sorry, Rachel, really. But hey—I still really am impressed that you tried out. I mean, you've never been one to dare to get up in front of a group to do anything, not even to bear your testimony in church, so I think it's cool that you tried out. So, what did your mom and Joe say about you trying out?"

I shrugged and slumped on the kitchen stool I was perched on. "Not that much, actually." I didn't add the reason they hadn't said much was because they didn't know what I'd done yet. And that I intended to keep my debacle a secret.

Of course, since my day was already on its downward spiral, I should've known it had a few more feet to go before I'd hear the clunk that I'd hit rock bottom.

"I have some good news, and I have some rotten news."

We were all seated around the dining room table, trying to enjoy dinner together. I stopped with a forkful of Rice-a-Roni halfway into my mouth when Ryan spoke up.

"Well, let's hear the good news first." Mr. Ackerman frowned suspiciously at Ryan's twisted smile.

"I don't think I'm going to flunk English after all."

"Oh, Ry-Guy, that's wonderful!" Mom was absolutely beaming at Ryan, who grinned back at her. Then he turned and looked at me. I tried to get back into my dinner, but my stomach felt all tight, as if I'd been trying to eat a plateful of live bugs.

"And now, for the bad news." I didn't dare look up, although I could feel Ryan's eyes sneering down on me. "Imagine my surprise—no, my horrified *shock*, to find out that old Dipstick here tried out for the school musical!"

"Ryan!" At least Mom tried to reprimand him.

Mr. Ackerman smiled, and even Dallin looked surprised. "Rachel, that's great! Why didn't you tell us before?"

"Well,—" I began, my mind racing to try and think of something intelligent to say.

"I think probably the fact that she had to fumble her way through the school song had something to do with it." Ryan definitely had an evil grin on his face now.

"Why don't you shut up? For once?"

"What are you talking about?"

Ryan turned to Mom's confused face. "She didn't even have a song prepared. Half the school is still laughing about it."

"Really, Ryan. You should've stood up for your sister." Mom frowned at Ryan, wiping her mouth with a napkin.

"And let her embarrassment affect *me*? No way."

"So what did you do?" Now Mr. Ackerman was frowning at him, too.

220

"I laughed and said I was sure she had to be adopted."

I threw down my napkin, told Ryan I hated him, and stomped down the hall and slammed my bedroom door. Mom tried to soothe me later on with the usual motherly spiel about "how wonderful it was that I at least tried out." Nice try, Mom, but no cigar.

I'd thought I would've cried over the whole thing, but I lay on my bed dry-eyed and stared into space at nothing. I had homework I needed to do, but I didn't care about any of it. Not even about my poems. Who cared about those? No one would ever read them but me and Mrs. Townsend, anyway. Even if I had a shot at the writing contest, nobody would see the poem but the judges. No one would even know I'd done anything.

When I heard the tapping on my door an hour later, I was sure it was Mom again.

"Please go away, Mom."

"I'm not your mom."

Dallin. I rubbed my eyes wearily but stayed flat on my back on my bed. "I don't feel like talking to anyone, Dallin."

Dallin opened the door anyhow. "That's okay. I just thought you might like some of this." He had a bowl of ice cream that he held out to me with a sympathetic smile. "It's really good!"

I sat up and tried not to smile. "What's this for?"

"Just because."

Dallin handed me the bowl and sat down at my desk before looking around at all the knickknacks and stuffed animals and books I had all over my room. "I think this is the first time I've ever been in here!"

"You haven't missed out on anything that spectacular."

I wasn't sure if Dallin had heard me. He'd been staring intently at my Mormonad poster.

"*Be Your Own Kind of Beautiful.* I like that. Where'd you get the poster?"

"My dad gave it to me. For my twelfth birthday when I entered Young Women."

Dallin nodded slowly, his eyes glued to the poster. "Your dad was a very smart man. Wise, I mean."

I shrugged and set the bowl of ice cream beside me on my bed. "In some things, I guess he was."

Dallin turned to look at me kindly. I wasn't sure if I liked his look or not. "You know, Rachel, you really are special—"

"Special? Ugh. Don't call me that!"

Dallin laughed. "No—I don't mean it like that. What I mean is . . ." He stopped and frowned, trying to find the right words, but then Mom yelled down the hall, "Dallin, phone for you!" and the moment was over.

He had one foot in the hall when I called out to him. "Thanks. For the ice cream. And everything."

He smiled and nodded. "See you in the morning, Rachel."

CHAPTER FORTY-ONE

L uckily for me, enough other hopeful actors made fools of themselves during the two days of tryouts to make my own ugly moment quite forgettable in comparison. By the end of the week, the actors had been picked, and other than Ryan's continual snide comments and jokes regarding my attempt at an acting career, my life went back to its own twisted form of normal.

Mrs. Townsend had given us a break from writing more poems in order to focus on our contest entries, because the second-draft deadline was fast approaching.

"Instead, let's read and dissect the poetic works of some of the greatest poets of our time. Perhaps it will inspire you to give your work that extra something it's missing in time for the contest deadline. Your next assignment is to give me your impressions of 'Thirteen Ways of Looking at a Blackbird,' by Wallace Stevens."

Thinking I had the house to myself, I'd tiptoed to the door of Dad's old study. I hadn't set a foot inside the room since Mr. Ackerman had taken it over, but since he and Mom were out for the evening, I dared to peek inside. Ryan was in his room with the door closed and Dallin was studying with friends, so with no one to stop me, I took a deep breath, gripped the doorknob, and slowly pushed the door open.

The room didn't look all that different, which surprised me. Mr. Ackerman had added his own pictures and personal things, including a few filing cabinets and a couple of fancy wingback chairs, but the main difference was that everything was clean, tidy, and orderly. Mary Poppins would definitely have been proud. I closed the door quietly behind me and walked slowly over to the desk to look at the framed pictures Mr. Ackerman had on it. Dallin had shown me the picture of his mom that he liked so much—the one of her cheering him on at his last golf tournament with her. Mr. Ackerman had a different framed picture of her on the desk, one of her smiling with one arm around a nine-year-old Dallin and the other arm around a teenage version of Dallin's brother, Brandon.

I walked slowly over to the bookcase behind the desk and carefully pulled out the black photo album Dallin had shown me before and thumbed the pages until I found Dallin's favorite photo. I studied his mother's pretty face and marveled at how much Dallin looked like her. My breath caught in my throat a bit at the photo of Dallin's mother hugging a ten-year-old Dallin, both of their faces turned to the camera, close together with big smiles. It was the sweetest mother and son photo I'd ever seen. I sighed and shut the photo album before returning it to the bookcase. I turned from the bookcase to snuggle into Dad's old couch, pushed against one wall of the room. I had Wallace Stevens's poem with me, and after staring around the room, I read it through. Frowning, I read all thirteen stanzas again. And again. And after ten times of reading it, I still couldn't figure out what Mr. Stevens was trying to say. At all.

I'd brought my red creative writing notebook with me, intending to write down my thoughts and impressions, hoping to wow Mrs. Townsend with my (of course) correct interpretation of Stevens's poem, but all I knew for sure was that the poem had a lot of blackbirds in it.

"Stupid poem!" I yelled, throwing my notebook with the poem shoved inside down at the floor.

"Dropping things again, Rachel?"

Mr. Ackerman stood in the doorway, smiling hesitantly.

"Oh—yes, something like that."

"Mind if I come in?"

I stood up quickly. Guiltily. "No—I mean, I'm sorry—I shouldn't be in here. I'm invading your space."

"No, no. It's fine. Just fine. Sit back down." Mr. Ackerman waved me back to the couch and walked over to my notebook. The poem slipped out and fluttered back to the floor, but Mr. Ackerman caught it neatly in one hand.

"Poetry! Mind if I take a peek?"

"Go ahead. It isn't mine, anyway."

"'Thirteen Ways of Looking at a Blackbird.' Wow! I haven't read this one in a long time."

"We're studying it in my writing class this week. We're supposed to write down our impressions and thoughts and stuff like that."

Mr. Ackerman sat down on the couch beside me. "Really? Well, tell me what you think of it."

"I hate this poem. I really do," I blurted out, louder than I meant to.

Mr. Ackerman jumped and looked at me in surprise. "What? Why?"

"Because it's impossible to figure out. There's no satisfying interpretation of it anywhere. Believe me—I've tried to figure it all out, but all I've been left with is more questions than I had before I read it the very first time. In fact, every reading of it frustrates me more. I can't find any answers—" I raced along, babbling at Mr. Ackerman's stunned face, but I couldn't stop. I ripped apart every one of the poem's thirteen stanzas, trying to figure each one out and coming up with nothing that satisfied me. I ended with, "Nothing makes sense. Nothing *ever* makes sense. I'm so sick of not understanding anything . . ."

I shut my mouth while Mr. Ackerman stared at me for a few seconds, looking just plain baffled before he shook his head. "Wow—well, maybe I'm doing something wrong, or maybe I'm just not as bright as you, but I didn't grasp that from the poem at all. I don't know for sure, but I think maybe that was because I didn't expect to grasp it. Not all at once, and certainly not on my first reading. So instead, I focused on that top, 'first layer' of the poem. I really like all the different pictures—images—the poem has. Any of those stanzas would make an amazing painting, don't you think?"

"I guess," I said, folding my arms to almost glare back at Mr. Ackerman. "But it doesn't change the fact that I don't understand anything."

Mr. Ackerman laughed and gave me a light nudge in the shoulder. "A poem wouldn't be worth anything if you could figure it out in one reading, right? The fact that you have to stop and take another look at it, and read it over and over again, is enough to prove the poem is something above and beyond the ordinary, one you'll never forget."

I didn't respond, so Mr. Ackerman continued.

"A lot of people would say this poem is stupid because they didn't get it in seconds. We're all used to getting everything we want in seconds, whether it's food, entertainment, or just going from one place to another. We're a microwave society. Who wants to slow down and read something that was written years ago that you're going to have to read over and over again and sit and think about for a while before you can even begin to understand it? I love writing poetry myself, and I'm always amazed at other poets' talents. I think that's why I love poetry: it forces me to slow down and see and think in a world that says we have to hurry, hurry, hurry all the time."

I looked down at my hands and still didn't respond. I could feel Mr. Ackerman's eyes on me as he quietly continued. "I also think, since the poem's title has the word 'looking' in it, that maybe we're supposed to learn how to *look*. Maybe to learn how to see something we haven't seen before. Or maybe to see something we've seen our whole lives in a new way. Maybe in the way we should've been seeing it all along."

I nodded slowly. "I—I think I know what you mean, but I still don't— I don't understand. Not just about the poem." I took a deep breath and looked up at Mr. Ackerman, my heart pounding as I dared to say anything to him about what was inside of me. "I mean, I know what we believe— that I'll see my dad again, that he's probably busy doing tons of stuff and having a great time hanging out with my great-grandparents, but I'm sorry—I want him here, with me—with my family. I just want to know why—why it had to be—him. Why *my* dad—and why Ryan, and why—" I couldn't begin to make Mr. Ackerman comprehend all of my questions and agonized "why's" that had been growing deep inside me for months now, mixed with so many intense feelings that I didn't know if I'd ever be able to sort it all out.

But as my frustration threatened a wave of tears, Mr. Ackerman quietly put his arm around me and said, "It's okay, Rachel, it's going to be okay," over and over while I cried on his shoulder without making a sound.

"I'm sorry, Mr. Ackerman—" I tried to pull myself together as I awkwardly wiped the tears off my face with the sleeve of my shirt.

He smiled. "Sorry? For what?"

"For acting like a big baby—"

Mr. Ackerman shook his head and patted my shoulder with his arm that was around me. "You weren't acting like a big baby, Rachel. I'm honored—touched, really—that you trust me enough to tell me how you've been feeling about your father, and Ryan, and everything." Mr. Ackerman handed me a tissue from the box on his desk. "And another thing—will you promise to do something for me?"

"I guess."

"Would you mind calling me Joe? Mr. Ackerman makes me feel so old. Or as if I'm your schoolteacher instead of your stepfather!"

I thought of Teresa and couldn't help laughing. Mr. Ackerman—Joe—laughed, too, and I was amazed to realize how nice it felt to talk to him, an adult in my life that I was starting to believe honestly cared about me, too.

"You know, Rachel, it's okay not to understand everything at once. Take Stevens's poem. I've learned enough to know that any poem I read will mean something different to me in ten years than it does right now. So I'd be stupid to only read any poem once in my life and leave it at that, right? I'm not going to beat myself up trying to figure out every secret meaning in any poem, especially on a first read. I'll find all kinds of new ideas and things every time I read it. And that's pretty wonderful. I guess that's why I like poetry so much. And why I enjoy reading the scriptures so much, too. I find something new every time I read them. Something that helps me get through whatever I'm going through at the moment, you know?"

I nodded. "I guess."

Joe gave my shoulders a squeeze. "I don't think you should expect to figure out everything and have all your questions answered all at once. Poems and scriptures will mean something new and different to you six months from now. Even ten years from now. All of your life experiences will mean something new and different to you over time as well. Not because the poem, or the scripture, or the life experience will have changed, but because *you* will have grown and changed. So you can't read something like a poem only one time and expect to understand every-thing about it all at once. You have to keep that in mind whenever you read anything or experience anything of value."

"I suppose you may be right," I sniffed, wiping at my eyes. It was something to think about, anyway.

"You know what I'd really like to do?"

"What?"

"I'd love to read one of your poems."

I slowly went through my creative writing class notebook, looking for a writing assignment I felt okay about having Mr. Ackerman—Joe—take a look at, and decided to start with my sonnet.

"Wow—good job, Rachel! You make the rules work!"

I let him read my villanelle next, even with its lousy rhythm. Joe made a fuss over that one, too, and so for the finale, I let him read my cinquains.

"Oh—those are powerful, Rachel! Really powerful. Excellent—just excellent!" Joe took the sandwich approach and showed me his expertise in poetry by pointing out my weak lines and offering suggestions before padding it all with more compliments. "I'm so glad you're taking a writ-ing class. I think it's wonderful that you tried out for a school play, but it's clear you have a talent for writing poetry. I hope you'll never stop writing."

I didn't say anything, so Joe hesitantly continued on.

"You know, Rachel, if God didn't want us to realize our own potential, develop our own talents, and be true individuals with different talents and abilities, He would've made us all look the same, have the same personalities, the same talents, etc. If we all needed to be the same in every way in order to make it back to Him, He would've made us the same. But He didn't. He wants us to be unique individuals, different from everybody else, not carbon copies of everyone around us."

I looked up in surprise at Joe, and could almost see my dad smiling back at me.

"Be your own kind of beautiful, Rachel."

"Would you like to see some of my poems?"

I smiled slowly back at Joe and nodded. "Sure."

Joe's poems weren't half bad. He asked me for my honest opinion, and he took both my compliments and my criticism well, nodding and agreeing with some of the things I said. And I could tell he was sincerely pleased with the lines I pointed out as being especially good and strong, and he was impressed that I found some weak spots in his writing. It was nice, sharing something important to me with someone who completely understood because the same thing was important to him, too.

"This has been wonderful, Rachel. Really wonderful! It's nice to be able to talk with a fellow poet!"

"Poet? Aspiring poet, maybe, but I'm not a real poet."

"Yet!" Joe grinned.

"Well, thanks for thinking so. And thanks for your help. And for listening to me."

"Anytime, Rachel. I mean that. I'm here for you whenever you need to talk, whether it's about poetry or not."

As great as it was to hear Mr. Ackerman—Joe—say those words, to see him looking at me in a way that reminded me of how my own dad used to look at me made my heart hurt, because just like my dad, he truly meant every word.

CHAPTER FORTY-TWO

By the time Thanksgiving arrived, not only had I completed and handed in the second draft of my creative writing contest entry, but it was finally getting easier for me to call Mr. Ackerman Joe. Mom and Joe invited Robert and Wendy and Brandon and Natalie to spend the holiday with us. I'd been counting down the days, looking forward to seeing Robert again more than I was looking forward to a few days off from school.

I couldn't help it. The moment Robert stepped inside the house on Thanksgiving Day with his big grin that reminded me so much of Dad, I threw myself at him and hugged him tight.

Robert laughed and hugged me back. "I guess I don't have to ask if you've missed me!"

"I've missed you every day, Robert!"

Robert laughed. "Well, tell me how you've been. And Ryan. How's Ry-Guy?"

I shrugged. "He's about the same."

Robert raised his eyebrows, studying my face. "Hmmm. Well, I'd like to see for myself. Where is he, by the way?"

"I don't know. Somewhere, I guess."

Brandon and Natalie arrived only minutes later, and Dallin and Joe had hugs for both of them. Mom joined in and insisted on giving them big hugs like she'd given Robert and Wendy. It was in the middle of all the hugging that Ryan finally decided to lurch from his room.

I could hear Robert and Wendy's quick intake of breath as if they'd seen a ghost, and I guess in a way they had. I looked at Ryan and tried to scrutinize him the way everyone else was. His clothes were rumpled and hung loosely on him. And he was skinny. Too skinny. His face actually looked sunken in, and his bloodshot eyes were hollow, black holes in his face.

I could see the shock Robert was trying to hide as he smiled too brightly and said, "Hey, Ry-Guy!"

Ryan stared woodenly at Robert. "Hey yourself."

Mom smiled and moved to put her arm around Ryan, but he sidestepped her and folded his arms. "Ryan, you remember Brandon, Dallin's brother, and his wife, Natalie?"

Ryan hardly even glanced at either of them. "So, where's the turkey? I don't see a turkey anywhere."

I could tell by the look on Dallin's face that he was dying to say something about exactly where the turkey was, but Joe smiled patiently at Ryan and stepped towards him.

"It's a tradition in my family to go out for dinner at a nice restaurant on Thanksgiving. I thought we'd give your mother a break and let her enjoy Thanksgiving by not having to cook."

Ryan glared at Joe and kept his arms folded. "We've always had Thanksgiving dinner here at home."

Mom laughed and dared to shake Ryan's arm a little. "I'm excited to eat out for a change. I love not having to cook on Thanksgiving!"

Ryan turned his head to glare accusingly at Mom. "That's funny. You always told Dad you loved cooking a turkey for us here at home."

Thankfully, Robert jumped in to save the awkward moment. "Well, I think it's going to be great to just sit around a table together without anyone having to do anything but talk and eat. Mom deserves a break!"

Wendy smiled at Joe and took Robert's arm. "So where are we going?"

"I've made reservations at a new steakhouse in the city called McGregor's."

"We're not going to the steakhouse on 45th?"

Dallin nodded at Brandon before looking at Joe in surprise. "Yeah—we always have Thanksgiving dinner there. They've got the best food in the city!"

"I thought it would be nice to try something new. Maybe even start a new tradition."

Mom smiled at Joe, who moved to stand by her and Ryan. "I think that sounds wonderful, Joe!"

"Whatever!" Ryan mumbled loudly.

"So what time are the reservations?"

"We've got about a half hour before we need to leave, so let's all get dressed up a little so we can head out!"

Natalie and Wendy shared my room with me in order to get ready. I wasn't thrilled about getting dressed in front of them, since both women would drown in a size five, but I was able to hide most of myself in the closet while I yanked on my navy blue dress. When I emerged from the closet, both women beamed at me and made a huge fuss over my outfit.

"It's the perfect dress for you. It really flatters your figure, Rachel!"

I laughed and tugged at the skirt self-consciously. "You mean it hides my fat well!"

Wendy's mouth dropped open. "Hides your fat? What are you talking about?"

And Natalie joined her with wide-open eyes. "You're not fat, Rachel!"

I rolled my eyes and laughed. "You don't have to be nice. I know I am!"

Wendy shook her head, both hands on her hips. "If you think having curves means you're fat, you're seriously mistaken, Rachel! Plenty of women would love to have your figure."

"Well, I'd give it to anyone who wanted it if I could!"

Natalie only laughed, her eyes sparkling. "I don't think you'd say that if you could see how other people look at you."

"Other people? Like who?"

"Well, like Dallin, for one!"

I stared at Natalie with my mouth hanging open. "What?"

Wendy laughed. "Oh, come on, Rachel. You're a cute girl, and I'm sure lots of boys at your school think so, too."

I grabbed a pillow and threw it at both women. "Oh, shut up! I don't believe either of you!"

Before either could do more than duck from the pillow, Robert beat a few hard, fast knocks on the door. "You girls ready in there? You're holding up the show!"

I wasn't able to say anything else before we loaded up in cars and headed to the restaurant. We'd never dressed up for Thanksgiving as a family before, but it was kind of fun to get fancied up for once. Everyone looked nice, too. Dallin was wearing his gray suit, and I had to hide my grin when I saw he was wearing the darker blue tie I'd suggested he wear to the Homecoming dance.

Ryan, however, had to be difficult. He was still wearing his jeans and sneakers and had only thrown on a rumpled suit jacket. Luckily, Robert took him in hand before he could sneak out the door and made him change into a nicer pair of pants and shoes to go with his rumpled suit jacket. Ryan and I rode with Wendy and Robert, who took turns asking me questions about school.

"This is so lame!"

All three of us jumped at Ryan's loud outburst.

"What is, Ry-Guy?"

"This stupid dinner. At a restaurant. And dressing up. Just everything."

"Would you rather stay home?"

Ryan glared at Robert defiantly through the rearview mirror. "Yes, I would!"

"Please, Ryan—can't we just have a nice Thanksgiving together? Please?"

Ryan barely glanced at Wendy's pleading face before grumbling something thankfully unintelligible before remaining silent for the rest of the drive.

The restaurant was incredibly fancy. So fancy that I was glad Joe had asked everyone to get dressed up. The waiters even held our chairs for us as we sat ourselves around the large, round table covered a huge white tablecloth and sparkling silverware.

"I'm so glad everyone was able to come. Please order whatever you want. It's my Thanksgiving Day treat to all of you!"

Our waiter started with Ryan, who was slumped in his chair, staring off into space. He hadn't even opened his menu.

"And what would you like, sir?"

"Nothing."

Joe looked up from his menu to smile at the waiter. "How about you come back to him at the end? Ryan, why don't you open your menu and see if there's something there you'd like?"

Ryan glared at Joe and didn't touch his menu.

Robert was seated beside Ryan and smiled too big at the waiter, his hands gripping the menu too tightly. "I guess I'll start then. I'll have the prime rib, well done, with a side salad."

The waiter walked around the table taking everyone's orders until he made it back to Ryan again. I was a tense bundle of knots as I watched Ryan. He still hadn't opened his menu.

"And what would you like, sir?"

"I want a Thanksgiving dinner. Turkey, stuffing, mashed potatoes, pumpkin pie, etc."

"I'm sorry. We don't have a turkey dinner on the menu."

Ryan shook his head before glaring at the poor waiter. "How can you not serve turkey today? It's Thanksgiving!"

Robert leaned towards Ryan, trying to smile. "Ryan, how about you get some prime rib like me? How does that sound?"

Ryan only glared back. "I'm not two! I can order for myself!"

"Then do it! You're holding everything up!"

"All right then. Fine." Ryan looked up challengingly at Joe. "I can get anything I want?"

Joe nodded slowly. "Yes. Order what you like."

Ryan finally opened his menu, scanning the items quickly. "Wow! The

Porterhouse steak alone is forty dollars. Is that your most expensive steak?"

"It is, sir. It's a quality cut of beef, and—"

"Sounds great. I'll take that. With a side of lobster. And a full salad with both rice and vegetables. And the baked potato . . ."

I was mentally adding up all of the items Ryan was ordering and was horrified to realize his meal alone was going to reach over seventy dollars easily. Without tax. I glanced nervously at Joe, and although his mouth was twitching in an angry line, he only nodded when Ryan looked up at him defiantly with an evil grin when he was finished.

"I hope you can eat all of that, Ryan. We'll all be more than happy to sit and wait while you do."

Ryan slouched deeply into his chair with a scowl and kept his face turned away from the rest of us while we all did our best to keep the small talk alive until our food arrived. His forehead was damp with sweat even though the restaurant itself was too cold for me, and he couldn't stop nervously bouncing his legs and tapping his fingers on the table. Robert tried to coax Ryan into talking, but Ryan only gave him a few one-word answers before Robert finally gave up and kept us laughing with his and Wendy's adventures as semi-newlyweds. Brandon and Natalie added in a few stories, too, and by the time our food arrived, I was relieved that the only irritating thing Ryan had done so far was order a mountain of expensive food.

By the time the rest of us had stuffed ourselves sick, Ryan had only picked at his steak. He didn't attempt to touch his vegetables or salad, or even the lobster or the rice. When the waiter came by to pick up our empty plates, Ryan shoved his 99-percent full plate away from him.

"I'm done."

Joe stopped talking to Mom to call across the table. "I don't think so, Ryan."

"I said I was done!"

"We'll wait until you've eaten your meal. How about some dessert for the rest of you?"

Ryan glared hatefully at Joe. "I'm not eating any of this!"

"Then why in the world did you order it?"

Mom leaned forward from her end of the table, her eyes pleading. "Let's just get a doggie bag so we can go, all right, Ry-Guy?"

"You ask for a doggie bag, and I'll toss it in the trash before we leave!"

Joe wiped his mouth slowly and deliberately with his napkin before setting it on the table to stare Ryan down with his courtroom face. "We're not leaving until you eat that steak."

I was so used to expecting the unexpected from Ryan that it didn't surprise me the way it did everyone else to see Ryan angrily stab at his steak and then wolf down a good chunk of it in only a few bites.

"Satisfied? Can we go now?" Before Joe could answer, Ryan's eyes bulged strangely before he swallowed hard once and then bolted from the table for the men's room. Robert ran after him while the rest of us sat in dead silence as Joe calmly paid the bill and led us all out to the lobby to wait for Robert and Ryan. Ryan was as white as a ghost and shaking when he came out of the rest room and headed straight outside for Robert's SUV without a word to any of us.

Ryan slumped in the backseat with the side of his sweaty face pressed against the window.

Wendy looked at Ryan worriedly before turning back to Robert, who was staring straight ahead, clenching the wheel as he drove. "What happened?"

"He threw up." Robert took a deep breath and shook his head before looking at Ryan in the rearview mirror. "Ryan, I don't know everything that's going on with you, but I do know that you look like death. And I mean before you threw up. You need help, man. Some serious help!"

"I don't need any help—I'm fine!"

Robert shook his head and looked at Ryan again. "No, you're not, man. Have you taken a good look at yourself in the mirror lately? You're a mess—"

"Why don't you worry about yourself and leave me alone?"

Ryan and Robert argued the whole way home while Wendy and I remained silent.

Ryan exploded out of the SUV the second we arrived home and slammed his bedroom door shut behind him once he'd made it inside the house. I stayed in my room for a while, slowly changing out of my dress. I knew Mom and Joe would be busy filling everyone else in on the details of Ryan's misadventures. I didn't think I had the stamina to live through it all again. When I finally emerged from my room, I could hear Dallin talking quietly with his brother in the kitchen.

"So, are you going out with anyone?"

Dallin laughed softly. "Nah, not yet."

"Not yet? What does that mean? You liking someone?"

"I don't know."

"Oh, boy. Who is she?"

I took a slow step forward, hiding in the shadows in the hall, my ears straining to hear their quiet voices.

"Did you know Alex or Brett Colton?"

"They went through Central a few years before me, but yeah, I know who they are."

"They have a little sister, Kathy. She's the same age as Rachel. I'm thinking of asking her to the Christmas dance . . ."

I froze where I stood, certain both of them could hear my heart pounding, but neither of them heard me turn on my heel and head back for my room.

Natalie's parents lived nearby, so Brandon and Natalie opted to stay overnight at their home. Robert and Wendy had chosen to stay in a hotel, much to Mom's disappointment. In the end, though, it was for the best that both couples decided not to be around that night. I faked a headache and stayed in my room for the rest of the evening. I only glanced briefly at Ryan's bedroom door after brushing my teeth before closing my own door and crawling into bed.

"Where are you going, Rachel?"

"I'm running away!"

"Running away? Can I come, too?"

I smiled up at Dad but was blinded by red and blue lights screeching, screeching—and when I could finally see again, there were only angry bloodshot eyes, piercing straight into mine.

"He was on his way to pick you up from your stupid friend's house!"

"No!"

I was awake, sitting up in bed and breathing hard and fast. My heart was already beating rapidly, but it pounded harder when I heard the crash of breaking glass and realized it came from Ryan's room.

CHAPTER FORTY-THREE

Although I'd scrambled out of bed as fast as my shaking legs would let me, stumbling and tripping over everything in my dark bedroom as I rushed frantically for the door, by the time I finally wrenched the door open, Dallin had beat me to Ryan's room and had thrown his door open and turned on the light. I couldn't help it—I screamed.

Glass from Ryan's large bedroom window was in pieces all over the bedroom floor and all over Ryan. Blood was trickling down his face where he'd cut his head and was running down his arms, too. His hands were splattered with blood, and Ryan—he was sitting in the middle of all that glass with the blood dripping down his face, looking incredibly dumbfounded. He was drunk. Horribly, horribly drunk. So drunk I could smell it thick all over him.

Ryan stared at the blood on his hands in confusion. "I'm—I'm bleeding!"

"Yeah, man, you are—"

Dallin tried to move forward to help Ryan, but Ryan shoved him away, leaving red smears on Dallin's T-shirt.

"Lemme alone—go away!" Ryan tried to stand on his own but floundered, clawing at the air strangely until he managed to get himself into a crawling position on all fours. I winced, seeing his hands digging into the broken shards everywhere, but Ryan didn't seem to notice or care as he slowly crawled through the glass toward his open bedroom door. I jumped when I heard Mom scream before breaking out into hysterical sobs in the hallway. Joe was there a second later, and more out of fright and panic than anything else, he dug right into Ryan.

"You—you're drunk! You promised to stop this drinking, and of course, like idiots we gave you another chance, and now look at this window—"

Ryan stared numbly at Joe, his eyes trying to focus on him, before he did something I'd never seen him do before. Halfway through Joe's rant, Ryan crumpled back down on the floor and cried, shaking hard without making any noise, rocking back and forth with his head in his bloody hands, moaning, "Help me—please help me! Please, please—*please!*"

Ryan couldn't stop shaking and mumbling about not being able to handle what he called the "despair beyond despair" anymore. As Joe and Dallin braced themselves on either side of Ryan and helped him up, I could feel my whole body trembling as I stared wide-eyed, wanting to move and do something but not being able to do anything but listen to the glass breaking into more pieces under Joe and Dallin's feet and Mom quietly sobbing beside me.

"Okay, okay, Ryan—we're here for you. You know we are! We're going to get you some help, okay? It's going to be okay, Ryan. Let's get you into the bathroom—Elaine, I think we're going to need to get him to the hospital for stitches—"

Dallin and Joe carried Ryan between them, barely making it to the bathroom before Ryan threw up violently again and again before passing out cold on the bathroom floor.

"Elaine—call for an ambulance!"

I could hear Joe calling for Mom, but I'd finally remembered how to move and was already running down the hall for the phone.

———•———

Mom and Joe rode in the ambulance with Ryan. Dallin and I waited up for hours in the living room, neither of us saying anything. I couldn't stop shaking, curled up on the couch, so Dallin put a blanket around me and brought me some water.

"It's going to be okay, Rachel. Ryan's going to be okay."

What else could Dallin say? What else does anyone say in bizarre, unbelievable moments like this?

Mom and Joe made it home shortly before 5 A.M., and sat down with Dallin and me in the living room. Joe spoke eerily slowly, his voice too quiet, as he looked solemnly at us.

"Ryan's blood alcohol content was dangerously high, so our doctor recommended that he be admitted to the hospital's detoxification program. We're really lucky our hospital has a wing especially for people who struggle with alcohol—"

"How long will he be in the hospital?" I blurted out.

Joe looked at me for a long moment before answering. "I honestly don't know. A few weeks, I'm sure. He needs all kinds of help right now. Help we can't give him here at home."

"How many stitches did he get?" It was a strange question for me to ask, but I couldn't force the sight of all of that blood out of my head.

"Twenty in his head, and twenty in each hand."

I stood up and let the blanket drop to the floor as I walked slowly down the hall to my room. Even with my door shut, I could hear Mom sobbing in the living room with Joe.

" . . . I've done everything wrong with Ryan—everything! I—I wanted to do more, but Bobby—he thought Ryan would outgrow it. Oh, I can't blame him—it's my fault for not doing more—I—I shouldn't have let him go anywhere without knowing who he was spending time with—"

"Stop it, Elaine—this isn't helping you or Ryan! Forget about placing blame. We can't waste any more energy on that—"

"I'm a failure, Joe—I—I tried to raise my children with gospel values, tried to do everything I'm supposed to, and—and somewhere along the line I failed—I failed Ryan—"

"You're not a failure!"

I could hardly understand Mom through her horrible sobs. "Then why is my son an alcoholic? Why?"

I couldn't stand anymore and buried my head under my pillow, Mom's wailing "Why?" echoing loudly in my head.

CHAPTER FORTY-FOUR

I had a pounding headache that refused to leave the rest of Thanksgiving weekend. The next morning I sat by Dad's grave for a while, staring heavily at his headstone. By the time I returned home, everyone had rushed back over to the house because of Joe and Mom's calling with the news of Ryan's hospitalization.

"The doctor said due to Ryan's heavy, continuous drinking, he'll probably have a hard time drying out and may suffer some intense withdrawal symptoms, including seizures and hallucinations."

"How long will that last?"

"The doctor thinks it could last a few days. He'll treat Ryan with a few medications to help him through the detoxification process more easily."

Mom couldn't stop nervously clenching her hands together, sitting on the couch beside Joe who kept his arm around her. "No one's allowed into the detoxification unit to see Ryan for the first seventy-two hours. They won't even let me in, his own mother—" Mom's voice broke before she buried her head on Joe's shoulder to cry again.

"It'll be fine, Elaine. He'll be fine. We'll be able to see him on Sunday, remember? After the first seventy-two hours, visitors are allowed for a few hours every Sunday."

Robert looked worriedly at Mom before sliding to the edge of the recliner, gripping the edges with both hands. "I think maybe we should have a family prayer together."

Brandon looked up at Robert from across the room and nodded. "I think that's an excellent idea."

Mom raised her head and tried to smile as she nodded, wiping at her face with her hands. "Oh, yes, Robert—of course. That's what we need to do now!"

We all knelt in a circle in the middle of the living room while Robert offered a sincere, truly heartfelt prayer, asking that Ryan be watched over. He even asked that the doctors would be guided and blessed to help Ryan and that we would receive the strength we needed to get through this together as a family. As one family.

After the prayer, my head was hurting so badly I felt sick to my stomach, so while everyone else sat quietly together in the living room, I opted to take a long, hot bath. Force of habit made me take a pair of jeans and a T-shirt in the bathroom with me, even though I had the back of the house to myself. Or at least I thought I had. I was busily scrubbing at my hair with a towel as I made my way from the bathroom to my room and nearly jumped out of my skin when I saw Dallin sitting at my desk, obviously engrossed in something. I shrieked, Dallin jumped, and then he guiltily slammed shut whatever it was he'd been reading.

"What—what are you doing in here? In my room?" I could see a hint of blue on the desktop and felt my heart seize up when I realized I'd left my blue notebook out and open on my desk that morning.

I ran into my room and angrily snatched up the notebook. "Don't you dare touch my things! Who said you could be in here, reading my stuff?" Before Dallin could answer and before I knew what I was doing, I threw my towel at him as hard as I could, hitting him nicely in the face with it.

Dallin struggled to free himself from the towel. "Hey! I'm sorry, Rachel—I'm sorry, okay?"

I could feel angry tears forming, tightening up my throat. Just thinking about the poems I'd written lately—poems about myself, and poems that were obviously about Dallin—made it even harder not to cry. "Yeah, just sorry you got caught, I'm sure! This is private—my private thoughts! How could you? I don't go snooping around in your room!"

At least Dallin had the decency to look sincerely sorry. "I wasn't snooping, and besides—you left it out and open on your desk!"

"That doesn't make it okay for you to come on in and read it without even asking!"

"I'm really sorry—it's just that you're always writing in this thing, so I was just curious to see—"

I didn't want to hear anymore, even though Dallin did seem to feel bad. At least, he seemed to feel bad that I was so upset. I sighed and waved my hand at him. "Okay, I'll give you thirty seconds to make fun of it, so hurry and get that over with and then just leave, okay?"

Dallin stared at me for a moment in surprise. "Why would I make fun of it? Your poems are good—seriously!"

I turned away and snatched the wet towel off the floor. "Stop being nice."

"I'm not just being nice! I mean it. I'm being completely honest here. I'm totally and sincerely impressed. Really!"

I could almost believe Dallin was being sincere about his general take on my poems, something Ryan certainly never would have been. I sighed in defeat before crumpling onto my bed and rubbing my eyes. Dallin stood in front of me for a moment, looking down at me worriedly with his hands stuffed deep into his jeans pockets, before carefully sitting down on the bed beside me.

I wiped my face with the towel before glancing at Dallin. He was watching me too closely and seriously, so I tried to muster a laugh. "Sorry I hit you in the face with my towel."

Dallin smiled. "I'm sorry I read your poems without asking." I nodded and wiped at my face again with the towel. And Dallin—he really shocked me by putting his arm around my shoulders. "Ryan's going to be okay, Rachel."

I shook my head, but I didn't push his arm away. "You don't know that."

Dallin shook his head slowly and frowned. "No, I don't."

I sighed and wiped at my face again. "I'm just sick of bad things happening to me, you know? To all of us—my whole family. First my dad, and now Ryan—" I sighed raggedly again and turned to look at Dallin. "It's not fair, you know? I mean, my family's always been good LDS. We go to church, read scriptures, have testimonies, hold callings. All of that good stuff. Robert went on a mission and got married in the temple and everything, so why does bad stuff like this have to happen to us?"

Dallin shook his head at me sadly, making my heart jump when he moved his arm from around my shoulders to push a wet strand of hair out of my eyes. "You don't get it, Rachel. Doing all of that doesn't guarantee bad things aren't going to happen. That's why you've got to have faith and believe in Christ and everything He did for us. It makes getting through all of this stuff here a little easier when you do."

I lifted both eyebrows at Dallin. "Oh, yeah?"

Dallin smiled. "Yeah. It's kind of like getting ready for a snowstorm."

I frowned. "What are you talking about?"

Dallin kept smiling. "Where we live, we know we're going to have snow in the winter. No one should be surprised around here to see snow fall a few times a year. So to me, the hard stuff that comes along is like a snowstorm. Going to church, reading scriptures, gaining a testimony—all of that is like putting on a coat, gloves and hat, and good boots so I'm ready at any time in case a storm hits. If one thing in this life is certain, it's that snowstorms are guaranteed to hit everyone because life is a test, not a Disneyland vacation. If you're not prepared with a strong testimony and faith, it's like heading into a snowstorm in just your jeans and a T-shirt. When you do that, you're cold and miserable and yelling at God for 'making' you cold and miserable. But for those who've got their coat and gloves and hat and boots on, not only are they not yelling at anybody during a snowstorm but they're out making snowmen and sledding, and skiing and snowboarding down the slopes. And they're shoveling snow and digging out people's cars. They can stay happy, even in a snowstorm."

I stared at Dallin after he finished his long speech. "So you're telling me to get a better coat and some boots?"

Dallin laughed. "I'm not telling you to do anything. I just know that making the effort to prepare myself to be ready for anything makes a difference."

"I don't think anything could've prepared any of us for Ryan."

Dallin nodded with his eyebrows raised. "He's definitely one in a million."

"Sometimes it's hard for me to remember that Heavenly Father loves him, too."

Dallin laughed again. "I hope it won't be as hard to forgive me for being a snoopy loser!"

"Ah ha, so you admit it!"

Dallin laughed and braced himself with his arms held up in front of his face as I reached for my towel again. How could I stay mad at Dallin? He'd apologized, sat and talked with me, and tried to make me feel better with his mini sermon. And he'd put his arm around me. For more than just a few seconds long half-hug. It wasn't fair that my stepbrother was nice, smart, into spiritual things, way too handsome and cool and he actually cared about my feelings. How could I help liking him? Dallin laughed when I flipped my towel at him. It wasn't fair. It just wasn't.

CHAPTER FORTY-FIVE

Even though I'd had a nice moment with Dallin over the Thanksgiving holiday weekend, I couldn't help the guilty pleasure I felt on Monday when I drove into the school parking lot with Teresa.

"Holy cow, Rach—did you see the marquee?"

I glanced up as I made a fast right turn into the school's parking lot, just in time to see the message centered in bold, black letters on Central's marquee: "Kathy Colton: Will U go 2 the X-mas Dance w/Jason West?"

Teresa punched me in the arm when I laughed. "What's so funny? I can't believe you'd be happy about this!"

I hadn't told anyone about the conversation I'd overheard between Dallin and his brother on Thanksgiving, and although I trusted Teresa with my secrets, I only shrugged and grinned.

"It's okay. Good for Jason. And Kathy."

At dinner that night, Dallin only shrugged when Joe asked him if he was planning on asking anyone to the Christmas dance. Since Dallin insisted on being quiet during dinner, I decided not to pull a Ryan and ask if he'd seen the school marquee that morning.

By Friday, the marquee's message had changed to "Jason West—Kathy Colton says yes!" This time, though, I didn't laugh. Sunday was only two days away, and I was too tense thinking about our family visit to see Ryan to worry about Jason and Kathy or any school dance.

My heart pounded anxiously the entire drive to the hospital after church on Sunday. Dallin and I both went with Joe and Mom, and when we walked into the hospital, it was a surprise to find Ryan sitting up in a chair in his room dressed in jeans and a T-shirt, surfing through channels on the television.

Ryan tossed the remote on the bed and folded his arms to look us over with a small grin. "So, you've come to see the prodigal son."

Dallin smiled big and tried to be nice. "Hey, Fletch. What's up?"

"Oh, you know, just drying out from booze these days. You can imagine my surprise to wake up and find out I'd been dumped here. Boy, it was almost as great as Christmas morning."

No one laughed, but for me, it was a relief to see Ryan still had his sarcasm, even though it wasn't exactly the greatest thing in the world to find in Ryan that was still intact.

Ryan's eyes narrowed as he caught me looking at him. "What are you staring at?"

"Nothing. I—I just thought you'd be in bed, I guess." I had, too. I'd pictured Ryan hooked up to tubes and dressed in a white hospital gown, lying on his bed, weak and tired. But even though he was up and dressed, he didn't look good. His face was a strange reddish purple, and he was irritable and tired. The longer we stayed, awkwardly trying to act as if it were perfectly normal to be visiting him in the detoxification wing of a hospital, the more I wanted to leave. Leave and never come back. Nothing could make me come to this horrible, overly clean-smelling place ever again. It was a relief when Mom finally gave Ryan a tearful hug goodbye, even though Ryan had been unpleasant and meanly sarcastic the whole time.

I waited until we'd silently driven away from the hospital for five minutes before daring to say anything. "Why does Ryan look so much worse now than he did the night he was taken there?"

Joe glanced at me in the rearview mirror and nodded. "I asked the doctor about that, too. He said Ryan's showing the effects of alcohol withdrawal. He's very sick, and it's going to take him a long time to come back from what he's done to himself."

I was still praying for Ryan at night. We all prayed for him during family prayer. It was wonderful not to feel alone in the battle against Ryan's weakness anymore, and although I was truly glad Ryan was finally starting to get some help, even though he clearly wasn't happy about it, I felt horrible realizing how much I wasn't missing having him at home. It was a huge relief having Ryan be someone else's problem. I liked being able to sleep through the night without having any nightmares or being awakened to crashes and bangings or enduring scary scenes in my own home. It felt amazing to be able to just talk and laugh as a family without any stress or tension looming in the air at dinner or breakfast.

It was during that time that I knew I felt peace in my home. It was a shock to realize I'd forgotten what that felt like. And Dallin—he'd been the best. He'd really gotten into decorating the house and a tree for Christmas. He'd laughed at the mistletoe Joe bought before finding a long piece of string to tape it to the archway leading into the living room.

He brought Chad and Zachary over the following Saturday night with a couple of pizzas in hand, only to find Teresa and me in the living room watching a DVD with a half-eaten pizza of our own on the floor. If that had happened when Ryan was home, Ryan would've hit the Eject button on the DVD player and kicked Teresa and me out, demanding that he have the use of the room instead. I wasn't sure what to expect Dallin to do, but after he and his friends stopped laughing and talking to stare in surprise at Teresa and me when they walked through the front door, Dallin only smiled.

"Oh—sorry. I thought you were going to a movie tonight."

"We were, but the movie we wanted to see wasn't playing anymore, so we rented one instead. I'm sorry—I forgot you asked if you could have the living room tonight. We'll just leave—" Ryan would've said something like, "Of course you will!" but Dallin was quick to stop me when I reached for the remote.

"No—no, it's okay. We can go somewhere else—"

Chad, however, shocked Teresa by plopping himself beside her on the couch. "Hey—so what are you guys watching?"

Teresa glanced at him nervously. *"Young Frankenstein,* actually—"

"Never heard of it."

And now Zachary had squished himself between Teresa and me on the couch. "You haven't? It's a classic!"

I scooted over a bit away from Zachary and smiled while Teresa's eyes darted nervously from Chad on her right to Zachary on her left. "We just started it—we could start it over. Or you guys could watch it. We rented a chick flick, too, so we could take that one to my house—"

Dallin laughed and tossed both boxes of pizzas he'd been carrying on top of our box in the middle of the floor. "Would you care if we watched *Young Frankenstein* with you?"

Teresa looked up at Dallin with a big, nervous smile. "N—no, not if you guys don't mind. I mean, we don't want to mess up your plans and everything—"

Chad elbowed Teresa in the ribs, making her jump. "Hey, you're letting us crash your girls' night out deal going on here, so I guess we're even!"

I could tell Teresa was thrilled to spend an evening with Dallin and his friends. She had a huge nervous smile on her face all night, giggled too much at everything any of the guys said, and hardly spoke throughout the movie at all, even when Zachary asked us who we were going to the Christmas dance with.

"No one," I said, leaning down to close an empty pizza box.

"No one? What do you mean?"

I looked up at Zachary's surprised face and shrugged. "Well, we haven't been asked."

Teresa glared over Zachary's head at me. "Not yet, anyway!"

Chad shook his head and reached for his can of pop. "Wow. I can't believe that!"

I could only laugh. "Yeah, I'm sure it's a huge shocker!"

After all the pizza was gone, though, Teresa volunteered to make hot fudge sundaes for everyone. The second Teresa and I were in the kitchen, she finally remembered how to talk again.

"This is the best ever—I'm having so much fun!"

"You are? Then how come you're not saying anything?"

Teresa shrugged happily. "I don't know. I'm afraid of saying something dumb, I guess!"

"You don't need to worry about that. Dallin and his friends aren't rude like Ryan."

I was walking down the hall with a bowl of ice cream in each hand when I heard Chad say my name. That stopped me fast.

"You can't *not* go, Dal. We've made all the plans and everything!"

"I don't have a date, so I can't go, okay?"

"What do you mean? Just ask Rachel."

Chad happened to look over in my direction, so I had no choice but to smile brightly as if I hadn't heard a thing and say, "Here you go!" and hand them each a sundae.

Chad nudged Dallin and grinned at me. "So—go ahead. Ask her!"

"Ask me what?"

Dallin glared at Chad before looking at me exasperatedly. "Nothing. I mean—"

Zachary decided to join in at that point. "Dallin's trying to ask you—"

"I can do it myself!"

I frowned at Dallin and folded my arms, but my heart was pounding. "Do what?"

Dallin sighed and offered me a sheepish smile. "So—what would you think of going to the Christmas dance with me?"

"Are you serious?"

Chad burst out laughing. "Yes, he's serious. Say yes so you can go with us!"

"With us?"

Zachary nodded. "Yeah—we're all going together with our dates. Sort of a triple date, I guess."

I went ahead and said yes so Chad and Zachary would stop putting poor Dallin through so much misery. The second his friends and Teresa had left, though, I put an end to the whole disaster myself.

"Don't worry about taking me to the dance, Dallin."

Dallin turned to stare at me, his arms overloaded with pizza boxes and empty ice cream dishes. "What?"

I snatched up empty pop cans off the floor so I didn't have to look at Dallin's face and see what I was sure would be major relief all over it. "I know your friends shoved you into it. So don't worry. I didn't take you seriously at all."

"But I was serious!"

I stood up and couldn't stop staring at Dallin. He *was* serious. Truly. "Wow. Are you having such a hard time finding a date that you have to ask me?"

Dallin laughed. "No. But I think it could be fun—us going together. Why? Don't you?"

I shrugged and tossed the cans on top of Dallin's heap of garbage in his arms. "No, I think it could be fun, too. But hey—if you change your mind in the morning, it's okay."

"I'm not going to change my mind!"

"Hmmm!" I turned away and walked down the hall to my room. Dallin hurried and dumped his stack of trash in the kitchen before jogging down the hall after me.

"Hey—I'll prove it to you!"

"Sure. Fine. Whatever!"

I closed my bedroom door in Dallin's face and slept in too late Sunday morning. When I finally wakened, I had to rub my eyes at what looked like strangely floating round shadows tied to my desk. I scrambled for the light switch and had to step back and cover my mouth with one hand. Red and green balloons were floating from strings, but they weren't tied to my desk. Instead, they were tied to a breakfast tray that'd been carefully set in the middle of my desk. The tray itself had a big glass of apple juice, two blueberry muffins, and a bowl with a peeled orange inside. A small white envelope with my name printed on it leaned against the bowl with the orange pieces. I cautiously opened it before laughing out loud at Dallin's attempt at poetry.

> *I say what I mean*
> *And I mean what I say*
> *I seriously want to take you to the Christmas dance*
> *So stop saying 'no way'—*
> *I'll pick you up at 6:30, December 16th, Saturday—*
> *Okay?*
> *I'm not a poet*
> *And now you obviously know it.*
> > *—Dallin*

I was surprised at how thrilled Mom was that Dallin had asked me to the dance. Joe seemed to think it was pretty all right, too. Mom took me shopping for a dress, and because the dance was coming up in mere days, I had a hard time finding anything in my size that I liked. I decided on a green, long-sleeved dress that felt a little snug, but Mom assured me it looked great on me because it "showed off my curves."

The night of the dance, though, as I stared myself down in my bedroom mirror, I couldn't stop turning to see how my backside looked and wishing I hadn't picked a dress that had a straight skirt. A nice, big, fluffy skirt would've hidden all of my ugly parts a lot better.

When I heard a light tapping on my bedroom door, I called "come in" but didn't turn to look. Mom had helped me squeeze into my dress and had run for my brush and hairspray in the bathroom to fix any damage the dress caused to my hairdo while yanking it down over my head. I'd decided to wear my hair down in long, loose curls with a small rhinestone barrette in the back holding a lock of hair from each side of my face.

I was still examining the back of my dress in the mirror. "This dress is too tight. My rear end looks huge in this, doesn't it?"

"It does?"

I jumped at the voice that was definitely not Mom's and about died to see Dallin standing in my bedroom doorway with a baffled look on his face. I could feel blood rushing to my face as I laughed nervously.

"I thought you were my mom! And yes, of course it does."

Dallin looked amazing. I couldn't believe he'd bought a new suit, but he had. A nice dark blue one. He had a new tie on, too. And he was still wearing that funny baffled look on his face. Dallin shook his head, looking at me in my dress. "I think it looks great."

My eyes widened, and poor Dallin looked horrified and stumbled around, trying to rephrase. "The *dress*, I mean! I mean, *you* do. You look great in the dress!" Dallin sighed and rubbed his forehead with one hand. "What I mean is, I think you look great."

I laughed at Dallin's sheepish grin. "You're just being nice again, aren't you? I know I'm fat. It's okay."

Dallin shook his head again. "You're not fat. What is it with girls always thinking they're fat?" He sighed and shook his head again. "If 'just being nice' means that you definitely look good in a dress like this, then I guess I *am* 'just being nice.' No one would ever mistake you for a boy. I'd think you'd be happy about that."

I didn't get a chance to respond, because Mom had returned to fuss with my hair. Both Mom and Joe made a huge to-do about how nice we looked before Dallin carefully fastened a pretty corsage of white roses to my wrist, after which I did my best to attach his single white rose boutonniere to his jacket. Dallin opened the car door for me, and as he ran around the car to climb in himself, I couldn't stop grinning. His Mustang smelled like a vanilla pine forest and sparkled inside and out, it was so clean.

We had lasagna at Chad's house in his family's formal dining room. I didn't know Chad and Zachary's dates, Lora and Lindsey, very well, but I knew of them. They were blonde, blue-eyed twins, and both of them played the violin in orchestra and were on the tennis team. Both girls were extremely nice and incredibly funny. The two could easily keep up with Chad and Zachary's jokes during dinner. I hadn't laughed so hard in a long time, and it felt nice. Dallin laughed a lot, too, and smiled at me. A lot. That was even nicer.

When we finally arrived at the Grand America Hotel for the dance and stepped through the hotel's revolving doors into the fancy lobby, I couldn't help sucking in my breath while Lora and Lindsey both said, "Wow!" The ballroom where the actual dance was held inside the hotel was incredible, too. Huge, sparkling chandeliers hung from the ceiling, and at one end of the room a live band was playing on a raised platform.

"Wow—look at all the food!"

I craned my neck to see where Lindsey was pointing. The other end of the ballroom was lined with fancy tables filled with fancy-looking treats.

Lora moaned and patted her stomach. "I'm too stuffed for any of that!"

Zachary grinned and grabbed Lora's hand. "Then let's go dance!"

I smiled, watching Chad and Zachary pull Lora and Lindsey onto the dance floor, but within a second, Dallin nudged me, smiling. "Wanna dance?"

I grinned and nodded back, and even though the song was a fast dance, my heart wouldn't stop pounding. It pounded even worse when the song ended and a slow song took its place. Chad and Zachary kept on dancing with their dates, so Dallin lifted an eyebrow at me questioningly before I nodded and he carefully put his arms around me. I didn't have to worry about conversation for long. Lora was dancing by me and poked me in the shoulder.

"Look over there—isn't that Kathy Colton with Jason West?"

Both Dallin and I glanced in the direction that Lora was pointing. Kathy and Jason were standing by the treat table where Jason was busy stuffing his face while Kathy laughed at him. Kathy was wearing a green dress, too, with her hair up in an interesting sort of a twist. She looked incredible. And Jason—he looked incredible, too. Even with a knee brace on, he looked amazing in his tuxedo. I turned to say something to Dallin and stopped, my heart sinking a little when I saw how he was looking at Kathy.

Lindsey and Chad were dancing on the other side of Dallin and me, and now Lindsey was poking me. "Poor Kathy—here comes the Wicked Witch of the West and her Flying Monkeys."

Angela Barnett was moving purposely towards poor Kathy and Jason dragging her date behind her. A second later, two of her friends and their dates closed in on Kathy and Jason, too.

I could see Angela's date eyeing Kathy behind Angela's back with a big grin on his face, and I rolled my eyes. "Yeah, poor Kathy!"

Dallin laughed. "Yeah, I think Jason's the one to worry about, not Kathy!" Dallin twirled us away so that neither of us had to see anyone by the treat tables anymore. "You having fun?"

I nodded and smiled up at him. "I am. You?"

Dallin smiled back at me. "Of course!"

The song faded into another slow song, and after slowly turning in a silent circle with Dallin, we could both see Jason and Kathy out on the dance floor now. We both burst out laughing when we saw Jason dip Kathy and Kathy almost scream.

"Do you want to go over and say hi?"

Dallin looked away from Kathy and Jason to smile at me. "Nah. He's busy right now." Dallin grinned at me again. "And so am I."

I looked over at Kathy wistfully, who was laughing up at Jason while he smiled happily at her. "Kathy looks really beautiful."

Dallin nodded without looking over at her. "Yeah. Kinda like you!"

I laughed and punched Dallin in the arm and didn't think about Jason or Kathy again.

———•———

After the dance, we all met back at Zachary's house for movies and dessert.

Lora sat down on the couch and kicked off her high heels. "So what are we watching?"

256

Zachary grinned back at her. "Well, since it's almost Christmas, I thought we ought to go with the season."

Lindsey sat down by Lora and kicked off her shoes as well. "Oh, yeah? Which movie did you get?"

"Four, actually. Hope that's okay!"

I couldn't help laughing when the song "Rudolph the Red Nosed Reindeer" blared from the stereo speakers on either side of the huge television in Zachary's family room before the familiar mustached puppet snowman rolled onto the screen with his top hat and vest, holding his umbrella under one arm.

"We'll be watching *Santa Claus Is Coming to Town* next, followed by *A Year without a Santa Claus,* and wrapping it up with my favorite, *How the Grinch Stole Christmas.*"

It was more fun watching those Christmas classics than I'd thought it would be. We belted out the songs together, while Zachary and Chad insisted on saying as many lines along with the puppets as possible. None of us could stop laughing for a full sixty seconds, though, when all six us of said, "I'm not such a loser after all!" with the old Winter Warlock in *Santa Claus Is Coming to Town* as he raced across the screen on a flying reindeer.

I had to try not to giggle as I sneaked looks at Dallin watching the short movies. He watched each show so intently that I had to tap him every time I tried to speak to him. He was so absorbed in the Snow Miser/Heat Miser song that I had to give him a light shove instead, which made us both laugh.

"Are you ready for some cake and ice cream?"

"Sure—yeah—sounds great!"

It *was* great, too. The whole evening was better than I had hoped. I'd been having such a good time that I was sorry to leave Zachary's home and was silent for most of the drive home.

"So, did you have a good time?"

"I did. Thanks for taking me to the dance."

Dallin smiled back at me. "Thanks for going with me."

When Dallin pulled his Mustang into the driveway, he turned to me seriously. "Don't move!"

I didn't get a chance to answer before Dallin jumped out of the car and hurried around it to open the passenger door for me. I laughed as he took hold of my hand with a bow to help me out of the car.

Mom and Joe were snuggled on the couch with only the Christmas tree lights on. The stereo was turned down low on a station playing Christmas music.

Mom smiled when she saw me walk into the living room ahead of Dallin. "You're home! Did you have a good time?"

"Yeah, it was fun—"

"Whoa—what was that?"

I turned to look at Dallin who was only a step behind me. "What was what?"

"Something just hit me in the head!"

It took all four of us a second to realize that Dallin had walked into the mistletoe hanging low from the archway, making it swing crazily, almost hitting Dallin in the head again.

"Watch out for low-flying mistletoe—could be dangerous!" Joe grinned.

Everyone burst out laughing, me with my hand over my mouth, before I noticed that Dallin wasn't laughing anymore but was looking thoughtfully at that funny little sprig of mistletoe. I could hear the beginning of "It Must Have Been the Mistletoe" coming from the stereo, followed by Barbara Mandrell's voice singing the first words of the song.

"Don't worry, Dallin."

Dallin raised his eyebrows and looked down at me. "About what?"

I pointed at the mistletoe he was now batting at with one hand. "You're not obligated."

Dallin laughed. "But I'm not a grinch, either, Rachel."

And before I had a chance to say anything else, Dallin leaned down with a grin. I didn't even think about turning away when his lips gently brushed my cheek, leaving a trace of his aftershave behind and the sure knowledge that my whole face had turned red. Hopefully a nice shade of red.

Standing there under the mistletoe with Dallin, with Barbara Mandrell's voice singing softly in the background, I had one of those moments that asks, What is more satisfying—actually living the moment, or reliving it in memory over and over? I almost laughed as Wallace Stevens's "Blackbird" poem flared into my mind, strangely beginning to make sense to me. "I do not know which to prefer, . . . / The blackbird whistling / Or just after."

I'd never forget how much fun it'd been to go to my first school dance with Dallin. Even if I never saw him again after tonight—which I knew was impossible, since we were stepsibs now—I still knew I'd never forget him, and if years went by and I didn't see him, I would think of this night the second I saw him again and wonder if he was remembering it, too.

If nothing else, I knew I'd never be able to hear that song again without thinking of the Christmas dance, and Dallin, and this exact moment here under the dangling mistletoe. And I knew that nothing would ever be the same for me again.

CHAPTER FORTY-SIX

Since my life was a forever yo-yo, I should've realized that just because nothing was going to be the same again didn't necessarily mean it wouldn't be the same again in a good way. On Sunday, Dallin took pains not to treat me as if anything spectacular had happened the night before, causing me to rethink our mistletoe moment. Maybe it had only been a charity kiss, or mistletoe pressure, or who knew what. Watching Dallin take special care to avoid too much eye contact with me, I felt pretty deflated all through church and afterward at home, especially since Dallin chose to hibernate in his room for the remainder of the day, and I chose to sit by Dad's headstone at the cemetery writing in my blue notebook. Things went from bad to worse when Jason didn't show up for seminary on Monday and Brother Clawson announced that Jason's little sister had been struck by a car over the weekend and was in the hospital, unconscious and in critical condition.

And worst of all, Dallin had a date for Friday night. And Saturday night. As a result, I had a hard time focusing on any school assignments that week, except for creative writing.

"This week's assignment is for you to write a poem to turn in directly after the Christmas holidays. It must have the qualities of alliteration, consonance, and assonance. And don't forget, your contest entry is due January 2, so you'd be wise to finish your entry piece over the holidays as well."

After watching Dallin hurry out the door for his date on Friday night and then being forced to have a déjà vu moment as he ran out the door for his next date on Saturday night, I flipped open my red creative writing notebook at my desk in my room with an angry twist of my wrist and started writing.

Anger

It started warm.
A small, sunny spot
Getting larger, longer
Expanding—almost—
Then it was wickedly, cruelly, unhappily cut,
Stained by a silly falseness that smelled
Sickeningly
Used and stale.
It turned green—
A green so deep, so deep that it was black—
A bloody black that sagged and ripped apart
That green
Into tiny, minute islands of despair;
Deepest green growing rapidly to a fiery rage—
It turned wildly until it hit that stage—
It strangled me.
A never-ending awfulness that was killing me.
It was an illness so frightening—
Can it be inside of me—still?

I sighed and set the poem aside to work more on my contest entry, but the piece I'd been writing insisted on remaining flat and lifeless. I wearily rubbed my eyes and glanced at the clock by my bed. It was after eleven, and Mom and Joe still hadn't returned home yet from some last-minute Christmas shopping.

Christmas. I didn't want to think about the holiday this year. I'd been okay with the preparations for the holiday, but I wasn't sure how I was going to handle the actual day, and then I wondered how I could, knowing Dad wouldn't be there.

I stood up from my desk and stretched before slowly walking down the darkened hall to grab a glass of water from the kitchen. I sipped from my glass and slowly walked into the darkened living room lit only with the Christmas tree lights. I stared at the mistletoe hanging from the arched doorway across from me and felt a horrible urge to yank it down and throw it across the room. Before I knew what I was doing, I marched across the living room carpet and did just that. And then I about jumped out of my skin when I heard low chuckling and slow clapping.

"Bravo. I was about to do that myself."

I peered into the darkened room at the shadowy shape slumped on the recliner by the Christmas tree. Whoever was sitting there was lazily tapping at a shiny silver Christmas tree ornament, making it swing back and forth on its branch.

"Who's there?"

Whoever was sitting there chuckled low again. "Who the heck do you think, stupid? Santa Claus?"

I slapped my hand against the wall by me to turn on the lights, but even before I saw the dark shape bend forward, squinting from the light, I knew who I'd see.

"How—what—what are you doing here?"

Ryan squinted up at me and laughed bitterly. "You think anyone at that hospital is smart enough to know how to keep me there? I have my ways, and people in general are incredibly stupid."

My mind was having a hard time grasping the fact that Ryan was sitting in front of me and that no one knew he was here but me. "Won't you be in trouble for leaving?"

"It's not jail, stupid. They can't make me stay."

I frowned and tentatively moved towards Ryan. "Why'd you leave?"

Ryan stopped laughing abruptly and glared at me almost hatefully. "I'm not staying in some lousy hospital for Christmas! Besides, it may not have been jail, but it was the next closest thing to it. There were so many rules and meetings with other messed-up people it was insane. I hate Ackerman's dad for dumping me there. The only reason I went along with their 'treatment' was to get all those doctors and therapists to stop watching me all the time so I could find my chance to leave. Man, I have to stay out of places like that."

Ryan and I were still up having what almost resembled a conversation when Dallin came home, followed by Mom and Joe. Everyone was as shocked as I'd been to find Ryan at home, which fact annoyed Ryan.

"The prodigal son's returned. You're supposed to be cooking a cow, not having one!"

After a few phone calls between Joe and the hospital the next morning, we all tried to get used to Ryan being home. Even after nearly a month of treatment, nothing could touch his sour disposition, or his crabby, sarcastic remarks.

Although Joe was seriously displeased at Ryan's escape from the hospital when he clearly wasn't "cured" yet, Mom was thrilled that he was home for Christmas. Dallin had decided to remain neutral and did his best to just be nice and try to get along with Ryan.

Ryan came with us to church on Sunday because it was Christmas Eve. He slumped between Mom and me during sacrament meeting, mostly bent over with his head practically on his knees. After church, Ryan slouched on the couch, watching television, while Dallin dared to sit on the other end of the couch with him. Mom and I were busy fixing a Christmas Eve dinner in the kitchen, waiting for Robert and Wendy and Brandon and Natalie to arrive. I could hear Dallin attempting to talk with Ryan, but Ryan only grunted in response. I had no idea what they were watching on television, but suddenly Dallin burst out laughing.

"Wow, did you just see that?"

I poked my head into the living room just in time to see Ryan roll his eyes without turning his head from the television screen. "No—I'm sitting in front of the TV with my eyes closed!"

I sighed and walked back into the kitchen. If nothing else, Christmas was going to be interesting this year.

Once everyone had arrived for dinner and tried not to act surprised to see Ryan at home, we moved everyone into the dining room for our

Christmas Eve traditional dinner of ham and potatoes and a million different salads.

Ryan didn't look well. His skin still had that strange purplish shade to it, and he still couldn't respond to anyone's questions without non-communicative grunting or loud bursts of inappropriate laughter followed by statements filled with arrogant hostility. But at least all of his responses were short one-liners. That is, until Robert made the mistake of commenting on the Christmas music being played on the radio.

"I think it's great that a couple of the radio stations are playing only Christmas music."

Ryan snorted. "Great? If you mean it's been a great big pain, then sure, it's great that only Christmas music has been on every possible station on the radio. I thought for sure I was going insane from it at the hospital."

"You have a problem with Christmas music?"

"I do when stupid radio stations start playing the music nonstop, starting with the day before Halloween! I can only assume their reasoning for laying it on so thick is, 'If a little Christmas music at Christmastime is great, then two months of straight Christmas music would be that much better!'"

Robert actually smiled at him. "It hasn't been that bad, Ryan."

"Are you kidding? I remember when the radio stations would play a Christmas song now and then during December. Then one year a station pulled a stunt called 'The 100 Hours of Christmas.' Talk about indulgence. One hundred stinking hours of sugar sweet Christmas music. Then the next year, the same station played only Christmas music starting the first day of December. Year after that, the Christmas-music-only schedule started on Thanksgiving. And now they can't wait to throw on 'Jingle Bells' the second Halloween is here."

Brandon shrugged and reached for the potatoes. "What's wrong with wanting to hear Christmas music a little early?"

Ryan looked at him as if he clearly thought Brandon's brain was malfunctioning. "Let me explain the problem to you. Here's an analogy: Sometimes I get up in the morning and have pancakes for breakfast.

I pour a little syrup on the pancakes, and it makes me really happy. It just tastes so good. If I use the same reasoning the radio stations have applied to Christmas music, I can only conclude that more syrup would make me that much happier. So I get a big bowl and fill it with syrup and float the pancakes in it. That should taste *much* better. And come to think of it, why drink a big glass of orange juice when I can have a big glass of pancake syrup to drink? We've already established that pancake syrup is *very, very good* and makes me happy. I want to be happy, so at bedtime after I've brushed my teeth with a gallon of pancake syrup, I know I'll be happy, because syrup makes everybody happy, and a gallon of it is sure to fill my life with joy. Then I fill the bathtub with sixty gallons of pancake syrup and just soak in it. It's only logical. If a little pancake syrup on my pancakes in the morning made me happy, soaking in it before bed should make me feel like I'm flying to heaven."

Ryan glared around the table at everyone's silent and bewildered faces. "Exaggeration? No. This is *exactly* the reasoning that has gone into two months of straight Christmas music on the radio."

I was waiting for Joe to explode, but it was Robert who did first. Not with angry words or yelling, though. Instead, Robert exploded with laughter. "Ryan, you are out of control. Completely! That was seriously the funniest thing I've heard you say in a long time!"

"Except in Ryan's case, it'd be beer, not pancake syrup." I couldn't believe I'd said that, but it was true. And I knew I wasn't the only person at the table who was thinking it.

It was so quiet I couldn't stop the nervous giggle in my throat. Hesitantly, everyone else at the table started to chuckle, too, while Ryan kept his black glare on his face. Within seconds of everyone laughing, Ryan angrily pushed away from the table, knocking his chair over as he stomped out of the dining room and into his own bedroom to slam the door shut behind him.

CHAPTER FORTY-SEVEN

I *have a great idea for the Christmas party. You know how our cousins have to annoy us by singing and playing the piano? Well, Mom wants us to sing, too.*

I laughed when Ryan explained his "great idea" to me.

"You with me on this?"

"Sure, why not?"

After all of our cousins had finished wowing everyone with their musical expertise, Mom had looked pleased and surprised when Ryan announced that he and I had been working on a duet as our family's contribution to the Christmas party. While Dad got the camcorder ready, Ryan slipped a CD into the living room stereo. When the beginning chords of Sonny & Cher's "I Got You, Babe" sounded, Ryan and I came sashaying into the living room, me in a long black wig, thick makeup and a tight, fish-tailed dress, and he in a short, shaggy dark wig, fake mustache, huge bell bottom jeans, and a vest on top of a low buttoned shirt. We lip synched and grooved around the living room with microphones, doing our best Sonny & Cher over-the-top impression for all we were worth. Although Mom and all of our aunts, uncles, and cousins were stunned into shocked silence, Dad burst out laughing and kept the camcorder on us.

"I got you, babe!"

I could still hear Dad laughing when I opened my eyes, and knowing it was Christmas day, I pulled my pillow over my head to shut out the sunlight that was fighting its way into my room. Christmas without Dad. I didn't think I'd be able to stand it. I'd made it through Thanksgiving without him, but Christmas—I wasn't sure I'd make it through the day.

Mom banged on my door a few minutes later, forcing me to get out of bed and join everyone else in the living room to open presents. I dragged a brush through my hair but stayed in my T-shirt and pajama pants. Joe was neatly dressed, but Mom had a bathrobe on and Ryan and Dallin were both in sweat pants and T-shirts.

To his credit, Ryan was on his best behavior. At least, he was quiet and only grunted at anyone who tried to talk to him, which was probably the best we could expect. Mom and Joe had bought all three of us some nice things, mostly clothes. Dallin acted excited and appreciative about everything. After the dance, I'd wanted to give Dallin something special for Christmas, but since nothing ever turned out the way I wanted it, I bought a green sweater for Ryan and ended up buying a blue one just like it for Dallin. It was hands-down the most boring gift on the planet, but Dallin smiled and thanked me for it as if it was the best gift he'd ever received.

I was nervous to open the gift Dallin had bought me and was truly awed to see what lay inside the small gold-and-silver-wrapped box. It was a shiny gold bracelet. From a nice jeweler, no less. It was easily the prettiest bracelet I'd ever seen.

Dallin beamed in relief when I thanked him. "I'm glad you like it!"

Ryan didn't have gifts for anyone. "It's kind of hard to Christmas shop from a hospital," he grunted. But Mom rushed to give him a hug before loudly announcing that just having him with us on Christmas was present enough.

I scrambled to take a shower and get dressed, and because I knew more family would be showing up soon, I whispered to Mom that I was going to take a walk before everyone arrived.

"Just make it a short walk, honey. It's really cold outside. Wear your warm coat!"

I'd bought a red rose from a flower shop on Friday that I'd kept in my room. The rose was still wrapped in green tissue paper, and after carefully hugging the rose inside my coat with my blue notebook, I waited for the right moment to sneak out of the house without anyone seeing me before jogging lightly through the skiff of snow on the ground towards the cemetery.

CHAPTER FORTY-EIGHT

The snow was untouched. Not one set of footprints could be found until I slowly walked onto the grounds of the cemetery. I'd stupidly forgotten my gloves and had to use my coat sleeve to brush the snow off Dad's headstone so I could see our family name, *Fletcher*, at the top before gently brushing more snow off until his own first name appeared.

"Merry Christmas, Daddy," I whispered. I wiped my eyes and carefully laid the long-stemmed red rose in front of the headstone. "Red and green. Christmas colors, you know." I tried to smile and fought not to cry. I told Dad that things were going okay—that we were all together. And that I was even starting to like Joe. "I miss you, though, Dad. I can't stop wishing you were here instead." I took a ragged breath and brushed at the snow on the rest of the raised marker until the picture of the LDS temple carved deep into the gray stone appeared as well. I stared at the temple and the words "Families Are Forever" etched underneath for several long seconds before pulling my blue notebook from inside my coat. I opened the book and let my pen take over, my eyes lifting now and then to look at the temple etching. Even though it was cold outside—cold enough that my fingers were already turning bright red—I felt a warmth like burning embers inside my chest as I slowly read the words on the page before me.

"I wondered if I'd find you here."

Dallin. I turned to see him standing behind me with his hands shoved deep into his coat pockets. "You're not spying on me again, are you?"

Dallin smiled and shook his head. "Nah. I've been over by my mom's stone. I brought some flowers for her. For Christmas."

I nodded and glanced at him briefly before looking back at my father's headstone. "Nothing against your dad, but—I don't know. I didn't think Christmas would be so hard."

Dallin nodded and crouched down to sit on the ground beside me. "I know. This has got to be a hard Christmas for you. And for your family. I'm sorry." Dallin reached out and patted me gently on the back. "Are you writing something for your dad for Christmas?"

"Sort of, I guess."

"Would it be okay if I read it?"

I looked at Dallin's solemn face and silently handed him my blue notebook.

From the road
it is simply
a building.
Nothing but an overpowering amount of
cement, bricks, and sidewalks.
But I know better.
Step closer.
Walk up the stairs.
Move softly into its doorway
and you will begin to know.
Close your eyes
and breathe in the scents
Of Security and Warmth,
and Love as big as the ocean,
and as never ending as the tides.
Surely you cannot help tingling all over,
Touched by warm rays the sun could never know.
Allow your fingers to escape from you—let them caress hundreds of lifetimes
locked in every inch of this place.

You are standing in a history
that is tied to thousands of other histories.
Open your ears and do not hear.
Listen—listen to sounds and words
that can touch you,
Perhaps soften you
and make you think of beautiful things
you would never dream of
in your storm-tossed world.
Now—Open your eyes.
Open them and see—See the source of it all,
and you will know what I know.
You will know why this place is different
from every place on earth.
The face before you will smile
Without thick regard for your
awkward imperfections.
I cannot help myself—I fall happily, softly into the embrace
of the One who makes
All worthwhile,
And who whispers I can be
everything and anything.

Dallin nodded quietly, his head bent low over my notebook, before brushing his arm across his eyes. "I know you wrote this about your home and your dad, but it makes me think of my home and my mom, too."

I stared at Dallin and felt my heart hurt for him as realization swept over me. I'd been feeling sorry for myself for days because I was going to have to spend Christmas without my dad, and yet he'd spent seven Christmases already without his mom. Seven. I couldn't begin to imagine how he'd done it. How he could handle any of it. Dallin hadn't talked about his mom very often since that first time or two, but I'd been able to pry a few things out of him. I knew he missed living in his old home. He missed having her there most of all, of course. That was the only reason he'd been able to move into ours, simply because she wasn't there anymore.

"It's not about my dad," I said quietly.

"It isn't?"

I pointed at the title and saw tears in Dallin's eyes as he smiled and nodded, whispering, "*Savior*—of course—I should've realized it was about Jesus!"

"It's—it's how I picture Him. And being in the temple. And in heaven. And meeting Him someday. Just all of that."

"Could I have a copy of it?"

I smiled shyly. "Sure." No one had ever asked for a copy of anything I'd written before.

Dallin shocked me by reaching out for my cold, red hands and rubbing them between his warm gloved hands. "You're freezing! We've got to get you back home. Are you ready to go?"

I nodded and let Dallin pull me to my feet before turning to look once more behind me.

Merry Christmas, Daddy.

CHAPTER FORTY-NINE

Teresa stopped by the day after Christmas to see the bracelet Dallin had given me. And to invite me to go to Brad Hasting's New Year's Eve party with her.

"No offense, but considering he's a senior and he's on the football team, how in the world did you get invited?"

Teresa laughed, twirling my new bracelet around on her arm. "I didn't, actually. Heather and Missy invited me. I think they have biology with Brad or something. Anyway—you know how they are. They know everybody! So—are you up for it?"

I shook my head. "I'm not friends with Missy and Heather, and I don't know Brad at all!"

Teresa shrugged and tossed my bracelet to me. "Who cares? You know the party's going to be crashed by tons of people. No one will know if you're invited or not."

I grudgingly said yes and then regretted it when Teresa called me on New Year's Eve, sneezing and coughing.

"I've got a stupid cold. I want to go, but my mom's not letting me leave the house. Don't worry, though. Heather and Missy are still planning on picking you up for the party."

I wasn't good friends with Heather and Missy like Teresa was, but the idea of staying home on New Year's Eve sounded horrible. Especially since Mom and Joe were invited to a New Year's Eve party themselves and

Dallin likely had been, too. And would probably take a date with him, of course.

I put on my best jeans and a new Christmas sweater, along with one of my favorite pairs of old, comfortable shoes, and brushed my curls out until they were long, loose waves. I was ready when Missy and Heather honked, and I gave Mom a quick hug before I ran out the door.

Missy grinned at me as I climbed into the backseat. "You ready to have some fun?"

I definitely was, even though once we arrived and had to park a block away because of all of the cars lined up and down the street, I had to fight my nerves not to run back to Missy's car and beg for a ride home.

I could hear music blaring from Brad's overly large mansion of a house long before we arrived at the front door and wondered that none of the neighbors had called the police yet.

Heather had barely touched the doorbell before the huge oak front door was swung open wide by a girl I'd never seen before. We'd hardly set foot in the house before the stranger told us to take off our shoes and throw them onto a huge pile in the foyer.

"Sorry. Brad's mom just put in new carpet, and she's sworn to do damage to anyone who dares to leave a stain on it!"

I wasn't excited about walking around in my socks and was glad that at least I had on a pair that didn't have any holes in the toes. I didn't worry about that for long, though, because the house was bulging with people. All teenagers, many of whom I recognized from Central, but a lot were clearly party crashers from other schools.

"There's all kinds of stuff going on. There's karaoke and dancing downstairs, and card games in the dining room. There's a big room upstairs where they've moved the television for watching movies. And there's tons of food in the kitchen."

We moved into the living room where people were standing or sitting with food and drinks, mostly just talking and laughing and flirting.

Heather nudged me with her elbow. "I want a drink. You guys want to get something to drink?"

I didn't recognize anyone in the room and pushed my way through the crowd behind Heather and Missy until we reached the kitchen and grabbed cans of pop. I was glad to have something in my hands and kept taking nervous sips as I eyeballed the room, hoping I'd see someone I knew so I wouldn't feel like everyone could tell I wasn't invited.

"Hey, Rachel! I didn't know you were coming!"

It was Chad. I never would've imagined I could be so relieved to see Chad.

"Missy and Heather were invited. I'm just tagging along."

"Cool!" Chad nodded at Missy and Heather who smiled and said hi. "So where's Dallin?"

My heart jumped for a brief second. "Is he supposed to be coming?"

Chad shrugged. "Don't know. He might, I think. I thought he'd be here by now, though."

Luckily for me, Chad was a talker. Unluckily for me, though, by the time another girl from Central came up to screech "Chad!" and give him an annoying hug as if she hadn't seen him in years and ignore me as if I was less than air, Heather and Missy had disappeared, leaving me to stand stupidly beside Chad who was now happily blathering away with the loud, giggly girl on the other side of him. I suffered through that for the longest thirty seconds of my life before doing my best to gracefully ease away and squeeze through the crowd in search of Missy and Heather. Of course, I couldn't find them. Or anyone else I knew. I did, however, get the chance to say "Oh—sorry! I'm so sorry!" to several people whose feet I accidentally stepped on or whose backs I was bumped and shoved hard into as I squished my way through and around the crowd to finally make it to the basement. After all of that effort, of course Missy and Heather were nowhere to be found. I did enjoy standing against a wall to watch some seriously bad karaoke singing and dancing and wished I had a camcorder on hand. I couldn't help thinking there had to be more than just pop in the glasses of the overly willing performers, although I hadn't seen any telltale signs of alcohol containers in the house.

I squeezed my way back upstairs, intending to go up to the second floor in my quest to find Heather and Missy. The huge oak front door was thrown open, and a crowd was gathered in the foyer looking outside, laughing and pointing. I shivered at the cold gusts of air that easily sneaked into the house. I couldn't see past the stocking-footed herd in the foyer, but I could hear all kinds of commotion outside. As if someone were throwing boulders at the tight line of parked cars in front of Brad's house.

A guy who'd been outside shoved his way back in, laughing his head off. He stopped in mid-laugh to grin curiously at me.

"Hey—aren't you Fletch's sister?"

My heart leaped from my chest to my throat. I must've whispered "yes," because the grinning face in front of me pointed outside and said, "Man, your brother is crazy! I didn't know he was back—"

I didn't listen to anything else he had to say but shoved my way with a vengeance through the wall of teenagers until I was standing on the porch in my socks, staring at what the crowd outside was laughing at.

I could see a tall guy in a Central maroon and gold letterman's jacket standing on top of one of the cars lined up in front of Brad's house. The shadowy figure rocked unsteadily on his feet before jumping down onto the hood of the car and then made a stumbling leap to land sloppily on the trunk of the car in front of it while those on the front lawn laughed and cheered. The shape turned toward the house to hold his arms up in a Rocky movie victory stance, and as the porch light washed over the jumper's face, Ryan's face leered back at me. I watched, horrified, as Ryan leaped up onto the roof of the car before jumping to the hood and onto the trunk of the next car. I screamed when I saw him teeter back and forth crazily before catching his balance, while again, the crowd on the front lawn, porch, and foyer cheered.

"Can't someone stop him?"

"If my car was out front, I would. My car's down the block, though."

"Mine, too, thank goodness!"

Ryan finally did jump back onto the ground, his feet crumpling under him so that he landed funny on the snow-covered grass by the curb, but he found his feet again and lurched towards the house. I tried to shove my way through the crowd to get to him, but Ryan made it past me and pushed his way into the kitchen with his dirty sneakers on before someone nervously told him he had to take his shoes off.

Ryan only glared at the guy pointing at his shoes. "Oh, yeah?"

Luckily someone found Brad, who demanded that Ryan take off his shoes if he wanted to stay, so Ryan grudgingly flopped into a chair to shove his shoes off his feet, mumbling, "Whatever!" By the time I could jostle around the crowd in the living room, Ryan had made it into the dining room where a group of kids was playing some complicated card game that required the use of three decks of playing cards. I watched, horrified, as Ryan lurched into the room and right up to the table.

"Whatcha playin'?"

One of the girls at the table glanced up at Ryan nervously. "Gin rummy."

"Where's the gin?"

Ryan laughed too loud and then reached an arm down to sweep all of the carefully placed cards off the table to flutter crazily to the floor. No one had time to do more than angrily gasp "You idiot!" and "Stupid jerk!" before Ryan turned and smacked the guy beside him in the back of the head with his hand.

"This is a stupid game! You want to play a real card game? Let's play Temple of Doom!"

"Temple of Doom? What's that?"

One of the girls at the table turned to whisper to the boy beside her. "Probably some stupid drinking game, knowing him!"

Ryan whipped his head around to glare at her. "Believe me, little girl, it's not as stupid as your stupid non-gin rummy game!"

Thankfully, one of Ryan's football team cohorts dragged him away. I tried to follow, but the crowd outside the dining room made for slow going. And I wasn't able to get away before hearing the card players grumbling as they gathered up the cards.

"Who was that?"

"Ryan Fletcher. He's on Central's football team."

"*Was*, you mean. He got kicked off."

"Really? How come?"

"Can't you tell? He's a stupid drunk!"

I winced and turned away just in time to see Ryan and Brad disappear out a side door off the kitchen. When I finally made it to the side door myself and cracked it open a slit, I could see Ryan and a small group of guys hunched over a camping cooler. I saw Ryan stand up, laughing, holding a can of what had to be beer.

My heart raced, and I gasped. Loudly. Ryan turned towards me, clutching his poison in both hands, glaring at me as if he dared me to do anything.

"What are you doing? Get out of here!"

"You—you were in the hospital because of this. You could've died!" I was scared. Really scared. And not because of the black, hateful looks from Ryan that should've warned me I ought to back away and run. Ryan moved towards me, calling me horrible names—horrible names—while he yelled at me to get out, but when he finally reached me, I snatched the can out of his hands and flipped it upside down. Ryan made a grab for the can and missed as I jerked my hand away. "I'm going to make you get sober if it kills me!" I screamed.

And then Ryan did something I never thought he'd do. Ever. His face darkened into the ugliest scowl I'd ever seen, causing me to draw back. I was glad I had, because in that same fraction of a second, Ryan took a swing at me. A sloppy swing, but a definite swing.

"I hate you!" Ryan screeched.

Ryan tried again, and this time the swing ended up being a slap in my face. That was enough to finally wake me up from my shock. I whipped around and ran—but not before Ryan grabbed for me. Adrenaline was on my side, though, and I was able to jerk out of his grasp and shove my way frantically through the crowd. I pushed through the living room and up the stairs with Ryan in hot pursuit. The upstairs bathroom was wide open, and a girl was standing in front of the mirror fussing with her hair.

"Get out!" I shrieked. The poor girl stared in bewilderment as I shoved her out the door, shutting it in her face while she yelled "Hey!" back. I gave the lock a violent twist, then leaned against it in relief, only to jump again, my heart hammering fast, when Ryan beat his fists on the door.

My knees buckled and I sank to the floor, leaning my head against my knees. What was I supposed to do now? I was trapped—trapped. In every imaginable way. And then I couldn't stop crying. Someone finally pulled Ryan away, but a second later, a scream made me jerk my head up. Mostly because it was coming from inside the bathroom.

When the scream sounded again, it took me a second to realize it wasn't a real scream. And then new pounding sounded at the door.

"Hey! That's my cell phone—I left my cell phone in there!"

I wearily stood up and saw a tiny, thin black cell phone screaming at me by the sink. I picked it up, ready to slide it out to the girl whining on the other side of the door, but as I stared at the screaming phone in my hand, my thoughts raced. A second later, I'd hit the End button and with shaking fingers dialed my home number instead. I almost hit the End button again when I realized no one would be home and jumped when I heard a voice—Dallin's voice—say "Hello?"

"Dallin? Dallin? You're home?" And then I lost it again, crying enough to last me a month.

"Rachel? Rachel, is that you?"

Somehow I managed a yes through my blubbering.

"What's wrong? Where are you?"

"B-Brad—Brad Hastings'. Ryan—he's here, too. He hit me—"

"He what?! I'm on my way, Rachel, okay? Just hold on—I'm coming over now!"

I heard the phone click off, and I shakily hit the End button myself.

I couldn't believe Dallin was home. I ignored the pounding on the door as I sat on the edge of the tub, trembling.

It seemed like five eternities, but finally instead of pounding, I heard a familiar voice yell, "Get out of my way!" before someone softly rapped on the bathroom door.

"Rachel? It's me, Dallin. It's okay. You can open the door."

I slowly and carefully did, and when I saw Dallin's angry, worried face, I couldn't help it—I threw my arms around him tight and cried again. Dallin held me close and whispered, "It's okay, it's okay." When he did pull away from me, he kept a tight hold of my hand as he pushed our way through the gawking crowd and back down the stairs to the front door.

Ryan was waiting at the bottom of the stairs, though. I clutched Dallin's hand harder, but he only moved to stand in front of me, keeping himself between me and Ryan.

Ryan only guffawed. "So, Ackerman the Great to the rescue!"

"Leave it alone, Fletch. I'm taking Rachel home."

Ryan sneered, folding his arms. "Afraid, huh? 'Cause you know you'd take a beating from me. Last time I put you in the hospital, remember that?" he taunted.

"You're drunk, Fletch. I'm not about to fight a drunk."

"Oh, really? I'm a drunk, am I?"

Ryan tried to swing at Dallin, but Dallin easily blocked him and only had to give Ryan a well-deserved, hard shove that had him sprawling on Mrs. Hastings's precious new carpet at the feet of a bunch of gawking onlookers.

Dallin shook his head at Ryan, who was still on the floor. "You need help, man, not a fight." Then Dallin turned back to me and took hold of my hand again. "Let's go." Dallin had barely closed the front door behind him when he looked down at my feet, stunned. "Where are your shoes?"

"Inside. Somewhere in the pile," I said miserably.

Dallin moved to open the door again. "I'll get them. What do they look like?"

I shook my head. "Just forget it. They're old shoes anyway. I don't want to go back in there."

Dallin looked at me for a second before nodding and running a hand through his hair. "Okay. Well, then put your arm around me."

I could only stare blankly back. "What?"

"You can't walk in socks in the snow. I'll carry you."

My stare had now turned into an unattractive gawk. "You can't!"

Dallin raised an eyebrow at me. "Why not?"

"You'll break your back or slip a disc, that's why!"

Dallin rolled his eyes, and before I knew what was happening, he bent down a little and with one arm under my knees and the other around my back, he easily swung me up into his arms. I squealed and held on while Dallin carried me to his blue Mustang parked crazily in front of the driveway at a bizarre angle, easily blocking any car that might try to drive up Brad's street.

Dallin carefully and slowly put me back on my feet before unlocking the passenger door and opening it for me. He looked at me worriedly, with a small smile. "You okay now?"

I nodded unsteadily, still in shock over being carried. And so easily. By Dallin, no less. "Yeah—I think so."

I shakily climbed into Dallin's car. Dallin didn't shut the passenger door until he could see I was settled in okay, and then he ran around the car to climb in himself. Neither of us spoke for most of the drive. Finally I dared to speak.

"I'm sorry about Ryan—"

Dallin glanced at me briefly. "Don't be, Rachel. You're not responsible for him or his problem. You can't control his drinking, and clearly, neither can he. The sad thing about it is that right now, alcohol's in control, not him."

"But Mom and Joe put him in the hospital to get rid of his problem!"

Dallin shook his head sadly. "It's the whole, 'you can lead a horse to water but you can't make it drink' deal. Just because there are hospitals and treatment centers out there, you can't force an alcoholic to get help. Even if he's actually at a hospital. I think Ryan's proved that point pretty well."

I wiped at my eyes with my sweater sleeve. "I—I don't know what to do anymore."

Dallin reached out and briefly patted my hand. "Sometimes I think all you can do is pray and leave it in God's hands. That's probably the best you can do at this point, Rachel."

I was silent for a while before I spoke again. "I couldn't believe it when you answered the phone. I didn't think anyone would. I mean, I thought you had a date tonight."

Dallin was quiet for a moment. "I did. She got sick and couldn't go."

"Where were you going, you know, for your date?" I instantly felt stupid for prying, but Dallin only smiled.

"I was going to take her out for dinner and stop by Brad's party."

"Oh." I quietly waited until Dallin had finished pulling his Mustang into the driveway and turned off the engine. "So what did you do instead?"

Dallin turned in his car seat and looked at me. "I came and rescued you!"

I laughed and Dallin laughed, and with our faces close together in Dallin's car, we both stopped laughing.

"Thank you for rescuing me. I don't know what I would've done if you hadn't been home."

Dallin reached out and touched my left cheek gently with his hand. "Your cheek is red. Is that where Ryan hit you?"

I looked up shyly, shocked that Dallin was touching my face. "He—he didn't really hit me. I mean, he tried, but it turned out to be more of a slap."

Dallin leaned forward and shocked me again by kissing me gently on the cheek. It was wonderful—magical, really, but when he moved in closer and I leaned forward, Dallin pulled back to sit back hard against the car seat.

Dallin took a deep breath and ran both hands through his hair. "No, Rachel. We can't do this."

"Do what?"

He turned to stare at me. *"This!* I never thought—"

Dallin looked away and didn't continue, so I finally asked in a tiny voice, "You never thought what?"

Turning his head back around, he slowly looked at me. "You're an amazing girl, Rachel. The best. But *this* would lead to nothing but trouble, with us living in the same house together and everything."

I looked down at my hands that were now fidgeting with the edge of my sweater. "So—so you just want to be friends? Brother and sister type of stuff?"

Dallin was quiet again for a moment. "I think if we want to have a chance of staying friends, we're going to have to make sure this never happens again. And I really want us to always be friends, Rachel."

I was silent for a few long seconds before quietly whispering, "Okay, Dallin."

"You want to always be friends, too, don't you?"

I nodded without looking at him. "Sure. Of course. Friends, then." Even though we never would've spoken to each other even once if our parents hadn't turned us into stepsibs. I reached out my hand and made him shake it before I pushed open the passenger door. After scrambling for my house key in my jeans pocket to shove it with shaking fingers into the lock, I ran into the house before Dallin could see that I was crying again.

CHAPTER FIFTY

Early in the afternoon of New Year's Day, Ryan burst into the house like a tornado. Dallin had obviously told Joe and Mom about the night before, because Mom and Joe were ready to corner Ryan and sit him down for a nice long "talk." I crept out of my bedroom to hide in the hallway where I could hear the fireworks for myself.

I listened intently while Mom and Joe stunned me by confronting Ryan directly about his drinking. Ryan, of course, retaliated by first denying any wrongdoing or having done any drinking at all since he'd been back, and when that didn't work, he shifted gears by blaming and criticizing everyone and everything for all of his problems, including his drinking.

"You don't get it. My dad died. That fact is never going to go away!"

I could hear Joe's angry, exasperated voice. "I am so tired of you using your father as an excuse for your drinking! Look at my son. He went through this, too, and he's not a drunk!"

And then Ryan was almost screaming. "Don't you *dare* compare that jerk to me! He's not me—he didn't go through the same thing that I am at all! *Not at all!*"

Dallin stuck his head out of his room at that point, and after looking at each other solemnly for a moment, I tiptoed back into my room. Through my closed bedroom door I could hear Ryan yelling, Mom crying, and Joe trying not to yell. When I couldn't hear anything more, I quietly crept down the hall again and saw Mom and Joe sitting on either side of

Ryan on the couch while Ryan numbly held a couple of teenage alcoholism pamphlets in his hands.

"I can control my drinking. I'm not a drunk. I can stop—I can!"

Joe spoke quietly. "Ryan, we've talked to your doctor at the hospital, and just like we pointed out to you in this literature, you can't. Not on your own. You need more help. You're never going to get well, not while you're here, spending time with your friends who drink."

Ryan tried to protest again, but this time Mom cut him off. "Ryan, your doctor suggested long-term treatment."

"Long-term treatment? You mean you want to send me away?"

Mom's voice caught in her throat funny. "We want to do whatever we have to in order to help you, Ryan!"

"No way. No way! You'll never get me to go there. Never!"

Later on in the day, after Ryan collapsed in his room and fell asleep, Mom and Joe called Dallin and me into the living room.

Joe looked at Dallin and me sitting on opposite sides of the living room. "We've made arrangements to send Ryan to a residential treatment center. We're luckier than most families because we can afford it, and one of the best centers is only a few hours' drive away."

I stared hard at Mom. "You mean—you're sending him to rehab?"

"Yes," Mom whispered.

I shook my head back and forth. "You'll never get him to agree to this. You know that, don't you?"

Joe nodded. "By ourselves, maybe not. But we're hoping that with the help of both of you, and with help from Robert and Brandon, we'll have a chance of getting him to agree."

Dallin turned to look curiously at his father. "What do you mean?"

Joe sighed and looked at us seriously again. "We're going to try something called an Intervention."

CHAPTER FIFTY-ONE

Even with my jumbled, confused, upset feelings loaded with disappointment regarding Dallin that were constantly at the front of my brain, I had a hard time focusing on anything but the upcoming intervention when school started again after Christmas break.

"In order for this to work, no one can breathe a word of this around Ryan. All of the arrangements at the center have been made, but they won't have a bed for him until next week. I wish it were otherwise, but there's nothing we can do about that."

I didn't like the idea of "surprising" Ryan by ganging up on him with the whole intervention idea, but Mom and Joe were on board for it, and actually, so was Dallin. I reluctantly decided to go along with it, but only after Mom and Joe insisted that Ryan's doctor had explained that it was one of the first steps of treatment for an alcoholic.

"This center is especially for teenagers. And he'll be able to take classes there so he'll be able to get his GED—"

I couldn't help cutting Mom off in shock. "You mean, he won't graduate from Central?"

Joe sighed and looked at me sadly. "It's hard to say, but I think it would be wrong to let Ryan believe he'll be able to leave the center in time to graduate with his classmates."

I was still trying to digest this during seminary with Ryan slumped in a desk behind me while Brother Clawson announced a month-long "secret valentine" assignment.

"Just consider it a way to put the scripture 'love thy neighbor' into action," he'd said with a grin. The trick was to do nice things for a "special someone" for one month without getting caught and then to reveal yourself as the "secret valentine" at the end of the four weeks, on Valentine's Day.

I wasn't sure I'd be able to get into the spirit of Valentine's Day at all this year, let alone figure out someone to stalk for an entire month. I tried not to worry about the upcoming family intervention against Ryan by focusing on figuring out a Valentine Victim instead while I waited in the seminary foyer for Teresa to emerge from her class.

"Hey, Rachel. Did you have a nice Christmas?"

Jason. He was smiling and walking easier with his knee brace than he had at the Christmas dance.

I nodded uncomfortably as I tried not to look at his knee. "I'm glad your sister is doing better."

Jason grinned back broadly. "She's doing so great now. It was nice of Brother Clawson to mention it in class." I nodded and looked down at my shoes but looked up again when Jason said, "Rachel—are you okay?" He looked so concerned that I could feel my throat lumping up strangely.

"Jason—I'm—I'm sorry," I tried.

Jason raised both eyebrows in surprise. "Sorry? Sorry for what?"

"I'm sorry about your knee."

Jason shook his head, still in surprise. "You don't need to be sorry about that, Rachel!"

"Yes, I do. I mean, I know it was Ryan's fault. I'm sorry he ruined everything for you."

Jason shook his head again and smiled. "Things happen for a reason, Rachel. I don't blame your brother for anything. How is he doing, by the way? It's good to see him back in school again!"

I was truly astounded. Only Jason could be so kind and forgiving. Not only that—he sincerely seemed surprised that I'd mentioned Ryan in connection with his knee at all. As if he'd never even considered that his injury could be blamed on Ryan. I was still mulling it over when Teresa asked me if I'd picked someone yet for the Valentine assignment, as we walked from seminary to Central High together.

"You mean, your class has to do this, too?"

"I think all the seminary classes have to do it. So, who are you going to pick?"

Almost without thinking, I said a name.

Teresa stopped to stare at me before she burst out laughing. "Of all the people you could choose for this valentine project. As usual, you're crazy!"

"Crazy?" I turned my head to berate Teresa, but she was busy waving and shouting to someone far behind us who'd screamed her name loud enough to wake the dead.

"Crazy" was definitely too harsh a word for her to have used. At first, I'd been surprised at the name that had popped out of my mouth, too, but the more I thought about it, I definitely didn't think my secret valentine pick classified me as being "crazy."

Teresa rolled her eyes after she turned back towards me. "Yeah, like I said, you're crazy! I mean, don't you think you're missing the point? Obviously, the two of you will never date. Isn't everybody else in your seminary class doing secret admirer type of things for someone special they really want to get to know? Someone they could actually, possibly, eventually, go out with?"

I sighed. Considering who my pick was and what he meant to me, someone was missing the point, but I was sure it wasn't me.

———•———

"Well, class, today is the big day: January 2. Time to turn in your contest entries."

I'd continued to work on my contest entry during the Christmas break, and I pulled out my final attempt from my red notebook to hand in along with everyone else's offerings.

Fact vs. Fantasy

The thought
Keeps clanging
In circles

Like an old cowbell
Inside my head,
And once again
I'm Hamlet
Asking
The Question.
It's all very fine
To sit back
Among your lace pillows,
Filling your nose with lavender
But I have to deal with
Gutters bulging with tin cans and leaves
And hair that never turns out right.
I don't believe in snowflakes and prisms
Anymore
But I'm saving my breath anyway.
When Winter comes
Holding its torch high in the night
Burning with its icy grin—
When the sun dares to
Tiptoe back
I'll need it
To draw snowflakes and prisms
On my blurred pane,
At least to remind myself
With their flat images
Like a secret
That Once Upon a Time
They were Real.

I'd tightened up my poem I'd titled "Savior," too, and had set a copy on Dallin's bedroom desk after he left for school that morning. I had another typed copy of it in my notebook, and as Mrs. Townsend walked up my row, on a crazy impulse, I pulled it out of my notebook and scribbled, "Can I enter this one, too?" at the top and placed it in Mrs. Townsend's outstretched hand along with my other piece.

"Thank you, class. Let's talk about the form of poetry called 'bantos' . . ."

We worked silently on the two-line form for the rest of class while Mrs. Townsend silently looked over our contest entries.

> *A dirt road carrying no cars.*
> *A dress left in the back of a closet.*
>
> *An empty house flowing with darkness.*
> *Curtains shut tight behind a small window.*

I was still scribbling down lines when the bell rang, but I jerked my head up in surprise when Mrs. Townsend called out my name.

"Rachel Fletcher. May I speak with you?"

Mrs. Townsend had the ability to make a student nervous with one pointed look over the top of her glasses. My mind raced, trying to think what I'd done wrong in class, and figured she wasn't happy with either of my contest entries. My heart beat hard and then sank as I watched her stand up from her desk and walk unsmilingly towards me. She stopped when she reached my desk, peering over her glasses before removing them with one hand. And then she smiled.

"Miss Fletcher—Rachel. I just wanted you to know how *moved* I was with your piece. I do believe you will represent our school well. I would be very surprised if it didn't place in the contest."

I blushed under her intent gaze as I picked my jaw up off the floor. "Thank you, Mrs. Townsend. I'm glad you liked it."

"I liked them both, actually. I think, with your permission, that I will enter both in the contest."

"Really? You mean that?"

Mrs. Townsend chuckled. "Of course I do. You're a talented writer. I'd be foolish not to."

I shook my head slowly as Mrs. Townsend turned away. Then I looked down at my final bantos and couldn't help smiling.

> *A contented sigh hovering in a darkened room.*
> *A pen resting on stationery.*

CHAPTER FIFTY-TWO

I'd taken the greatest pains to stay as far away from Dallin as I possibly
could ever since New Year's Eve. If he looked over his shoulder at me
during seminary, I didn't notice, because I made sure never to look in
his direction. And after class, between my hurrying out the door to find
Teresa and Jason having tons of things to tell him, Dallin had no chance
of trying to talk to me. After school, I'd go to the cemetery until dinner,
and then I'd either go to Teresa's to study or I'd hibernate in my room
until I went to bed.

And then it was the day before Ryan's intervention.

Arrangements had already been made at Central so Dallin and I could
take the day off to be home for the potential fireworks. We'd even been
asked to have something ready to say to Ryan when we had to take our
turn telling him why he needed help. I hadn't quite figured out what I
was going to say to Ryan yet, so I was hoping to find a moment to talk it
all out with Dad in the only way I could anymore.

I slipped out shortly after dinner. Even though it was only 6:30 in the
evening, it was as black outside as if it were 2:00 in the morning. And
instead of snow, light rain was just starting to fall.

"Lovely," I grumbled, yanking my hood over my head and digging my
hands deep into my coat pockets.

There were a few old people in the cemetery, but I still felt pretty
alone. I walked faster and finally reached Dad's headstone. I brushed the

slushy snow off it and slowly read the phrase, "Families Are Forever" over and over.

"Dad—" I tried to speak, but his name came out of my throat like a cracked whisper. My legs buckled underneath me, and I sank to my knees by the headstone. "I wish you were here, Dad." I squeezed my eyes shut, and when I did, I could see Dad's face smiling in front of me. Just for a brief, brief moment.

"Be Your Own Kind of Beautiful, Rachel."

"Rachel—are you okay?"

I didn't have to open my eyes to know that Dallin was standing behind me.

"You're never going to give up this spying thing of yours, are you?"

"Sorry—I saw you leave, and I was pretty sure you came here. It's dark and it started raining, so I thought I'd better—you know—check up on you."

I sighed and stood up, keeping my eyes down as I brushed the wet globs of snow off my jeans. "I don't know why. You don't need to worry about me."

"Of course I'm going to worry about you, Rachel. We're friends. Friends do that, you know?"

I glanced at Dallin briefly, just enough to see a strange mixture of sadness, worry, and regret on his face. I could feel wet drops pelting my cheeks, but they weren't tears. The clouds had finally waited long enough, and instead of just sprinkling, now it was absolutely raining.

"Come on, Rachel—we'd better get back."

Dallin was still standing in front of me in the now-pouring rain, trying to motion me to walk with him, when a car come blaring noisily up the street—squealing around corners, it was going so fast. Seconds later, it turned with another loud squeal through the open cemetery gates. Dallin whirled around to face the car, keeping himself a protective few inches in front of me.

"What the . . . ?"

I stared at the familiar blue Mustang as it screeched to a violent halt, practically on top of Dallin and me, forcing both of us to jump back and squint at its blinding headlights through the rain. The driver's door flew open and a dark shape, unsteady on its feet, lurched slowly out of the car. I squinted in the rain to see who it was, and the shape chuckled. Then laughed. Loudly.

"Well, well, well. The lovers meet. Not exactly the most romantic place to take a girl, Ackerman, but you never did have much class. At least you've got a nice set of wheels. Though I'd get those brakes of yours checked. They squeal like a girl. Probably just brake dust."

Dallin took a step forward while Ryan stumbled to move to the front of the car before leaning back against the hood. "What—how—what are you doing driving my car?"

I stepped towards Dallin's car myself and peered into the Mustang through the driver's side window. I could see a few crushed beer cans on the floor of the backseat, but other than that, the car appeared to be free of any damage.

Ryan grinned evilly, jingling the car keys in his hand. "Well, thanks to your old man, I still don't have my car keys back. You'd think he would've gotten my broken headlight taken care of by now, but no, it's still busted. And for someone who has a nice foot locker in his room, locked at all times, I can't believe you'd just leave your car keys lying around!"

"They weren't lying around—they were in my room!"

"They were sitting out on your chest of drawers, right under the light switch. Practically in the hall. They could've gotten lost, but I saved them for you."

Dallin walked angrily towards Ryan with his hand outstretched. "Thanks, really—you can give them back now."

Ryan shook his head and gripped the keys in his fist. "Oh, no, I don't think so. Besides, I can see you're mad at me. Pretty dang mad at me. How about I give you both a ride home and no hard feelings, okay? I haven't been able to drive in weeks. You can't blame me for wanting to drive! Plus, your little '68 Mustang is so sweet—no one could resist this, Ackerman. I mean, really. Honestly. Who could?"

"Ryan, I think you better let Dallin drive—"

My voice was hardly more than a whisper, but Ryan heard and glared blackly at me. "No one's talking to you, Rachel. So you can just shut up. And you ought to unless you want me telling Mom and good ol' Joe about you and Ackerman and your secret, creepy cemetery rendezvous.' Though, who knows? Maybe I'll tell anyway. It's about time you were grounded for something."

Dallin held his hand out to Ryan again. "Seriously, man. I can tell you've been drinking. Let me drive us all home so we'll get back safe. The rain is really coming down now—"

"You're right. Get in the car, and let's get home!"

Dallin stared at Ryan. "Are you kidding? Not with you driving. You're drunk!"

Ryan pretended to act hurt. "Drunk? I'm not drunk! I'm not even close to being drunk!" And then Ryan nodded slowly with an evil grin on his face. "Fine. Okay. Do what you want. But—Rachel here is coming with me!"

Ryan had slowly worked his way to the driver's side of the car where I was standing and shocked me by grabbing my arm.

"Hey—leave her alone!"

Dallin tried to run the few steps around the front of the car to where I was standing by the driver's door, but the grass was slick and muddy. Ryan turned around and shoved Dallin as hard as if he were on the football field blocking a runner and sent Dallin sprawling to the ground. I gasped Dallin's name, but Ryan wrenched open the door, shoved the driver's seat forward, and propelled me hard into the backseat before climbing into the driver's seat, slamming the door shut behind him. I slid over to the other side of the backseat and frantically reached forward to try and open the passenger door just as Ryan leaned over and gave the old-fashioned manual lock a smack with his fist to lock it tight before shoving me back with his arm.

"Touch that again, and you'll regret it!"

Dallin was on his feet by then, pounding on the driver's window, demanding that Ryan unlock the door. Ryan only laughed. "Look how funny your little boyfriend looks, Rachel. He's trying to rescue you, but guess what? It's not going to work." Ryan vroomed the engine into life and slowly moved the car forward a few inches.

Dallin stayed with the car and kept pounding on the window. "Ryan—open the door! Just let Rachel out, okay?"

Ryan turned to throw his arm back to keep me from moving while he rolled the window down a few inches. "Nope. She's not moving. You can get in, too, or you can walk home."

"Dallin!" I screamed.

Dallin looked at me worriedly, sopping wet and muddy now, too, before turning to stare blackly at Ryan. "If you hurt her, I swear—"

Ryan laughed meanly before taking a big gulp out of a flask he shoved back inside his jacket. "You've got too much lace on your underwear to do anything to me, Ackerman. Besides—*I'm* her brother. She'll be safe with *me!*" Ryan rolled the car forward a few more inches, faster this time. I screamed "Dallin!" but it was too late—Ryan ground the gears, pounded on the accelerator, and the engine roared to life, making the car shriek as he sped it in the pouring rain out of the cemetery and back onto the main road. I turned and saw Dallin through the back window of his Mustang, standing motionless, staring in shock as Ryan drove us away until I couldn't see him anymore.

Ryan pressed on the accelerator even harder. "You start crying, and I'll give you something to cry about!"

I jerked back around and angrily wiped at my face. My fingers trembled as I secured my seatbelt before I dared look over the driver's seat at the speedometer.

I gasped. I couldn't help it. "Slow down, Ryan! Slow *down!*"

Ryan turned his head to laugh at my panicked face. "I'm barely going over the speed limit, man! Calm down, grandma! I'm not going to hurt your boyfriend's precious car!"

"You just missed our street!" I pointed frantically out the side window as we sped past.

"I didn't miss anything. I thought we'd take the long way home. Just for fun, you know?" Ryan snapped on the radio and flipped the volume up so loudly my ears rang. "We need some tunes, man!"

Ryan was driving faster and faster, hydroplaning and screeching the brakes at every turn. My heart was pounding, and soon I was pleading like crazy for Ryan to please slow down, but he turned and smacked the top of my head.

"I told you to shut up back there! No backseat driving allowed!" Ryan briefly glanced at my panicked and angry face before chuckling. "I know you're mad at me, but I had to borrow Ackerman's car. Imagine my surprise when Robert and Ackerman's brother showed up at the house tonight. For no reason!" Ryan shook his head and pressed on the accelerator even harder, grinding the gears loudly while I winced as if I'd been stabbed. "Too many people in the house right now, and like I said before, Ackerman's dad still has my car keys. Something's up, and I want you to tell me what!"

I didn't say anything, so Ryan looked fiercely at me through the rearview mirror as he nearly rolled the car onto two wheels, screeching around a turn while I gripped the edge of the backseat.

"Tell me, Rachel!"

"Nothing! I mean, I don't know—I mean—"

"What? What do you mean?"

"Just stop the car and let me drive, okay? Just stop the car! I'll tell you—I'll tell you everything if you'll stop the car! But I won't say anything unless you do!"

Ryan glared his blackest scowl at me but didn't say anything back. Instead, he pushed harder on the accelerator again, making the car roar even louder.

"You know what road this is, don't you?"

"I don't know," I whispered.

Ryan stared stonily back at me in the mirror. "Yes, you do. This is Firehouse Road. *The* road. Dad's last road."

My heart stopped as I stared out at sparks of street lights in the dark rain flying past as we sped crazily down the road.

Ryan shook his head slowly. "It should've been me, you know? It should've been me. Would've been better that way—"

For better or worse, the road we were flying down was a rural highway road, and so far it had been strangely empty. But now, I could see taillights coming up fast. I'd never seen a speedometer go so high in my life, but now that we had a car in front of us, Ryan still didn't put his foot on the brake. I yelled at Ryan for the millionth time to slow down, but he only laughed.

"Hey, don't worry. I've done this lots of times! On this very road!" A second later, Ryan swerved into the oncoming lane and swerved violently back over into our lane after passing the frightened driver in the car now behind us.

I was frantically praying for help in my mind when Ryan yanked the wheel violently again to pass another car. All I could see was headlights from an oncoming car and screamed before covering my face with my arms. Brakes from all three cars screeched all over the place, and somehow Ryan made it back to our side of the road in front of the driver he'd passed without hitting either car.

I looked through the back window behind me at the car we'd almost hit head on and sucked in my breath hard. "You've got to stop now—that was a cop! You almost hit a cop!"

"Forget it!"

I turned to look behind me again and was nearly blinded by the explosion of flashing red and blue lights and deafened by the screaming sirens. I couldn't believe Ryan was trying to outrun the police, but try he did. I was still praying hard, shaking all over, my heart in my mouth, while Ryan squealed and swerved the car down Firehouse Road. The police car behind us chased us hard with its screeching sirens and flashing lights.

This can't be real. This can't!

And then another car's taillights were coming up fast, and Ryan was

296

forced to swerve. Only this time, Ryan jerked the wheel so hard he lost control of the car. Firehouse Road had a ditch along a stretch of it, and we'd clearly come to that stretch. Dallin's Mustang bounded crazily into the ditch, blowing a tire as we hit the bottom hard, crunching the front end of the car against the far side. I felt a strange explosion of red pain in my head as the car jerked to a stop. Finally.

When I could breathe again, I pushed my hair out of my face, my fingers trembling hard and fast. I stared at the bright, strange spots before my eyes before blinking hard. "My head hurts." I said that out loud but heard no response.

Ryan was slumped over the wheel, but I saw him move and shake his head dully. And then, a lot of things happened fast.

"Driver! Show me your hands!"

I jumped a mile when I heard the voice before I realized it was coming from the police car's loud speaker. The police officer kept yelling commands until Ryan finally lurched out of the car and into the rain.

I could see more sets of red and blue flashing lights. Three police cars' worth, at least. A few officers were slowly approaching Dallin's poor Mustang. My heart pounded harder when I saw that all of the officers had their guns drawn.

"Driver! Get your hands on top of your head!"

I shakily slid over and pushed the passenger door open, but someone yelled for me to stay in the car. I watched in shock out the back window of Dallin's car while one of the officers turned Ryan around and roughly placed handcuffs on his wrists. But when I was finally allowed to get out of the car myself, I was in for an even bigger shock.

The rain was coming down so hard and fast, soaking me in seconds, that I was sure I'd heard the officer wrong. "What?"

The unsmiling man in the blue uniform only motioned his hand in a circle. "Turn around, miss."

Handcuffs again. On me. If someone had told me I would one day have handcuffs put on me by a police officer, I never would've believed that person. Never. I should've been crying. Bawling hysterically, but I was numb with shock. Too numb with shock.

And then, the questions began. My head was throbbing and pounding too much, and even though my voice was shaking, I was able to answer the officer's questions better than I thought I could.

" . . . I kept telling him to stop, but he wouldn't . . . The car's Dallin's—my stepbrother's—what's left of it, anyway . . . He showed up out of nowhere driving it without anyone's permission . . . He wouldn't give Dallin the keys back . . . he pushed me into the car . . . I saw the police car first and told him he had to stop now, but he wouldn't . . ."

I nodded and mumbled more answers to more questions. Over the police officer's shoulder, I could see Ryan standing in the middle of the road that was blocked on both sides by police cars and flashing red and blue lights. He'd had his handcuffs taken off and was being ruthlessly drilled by a couple of officers himself with sobriety tests, all of which he failed miserably. Then one of the officers made Ryan blow into a strange-looking, hand-held contraption that looked like it had a short straw attached.

"Whoa. Your blood alcohol level is high, kid. I think we better get this one into the hospital." I numbly watched the officer re-handcuff Ryan and put him in the backseat of the nearest squad car.

And finally, after what felt like a million questions and hours and hours, miraculously, the unsmiling officer took the horrid bands of cold metal off my wrists and said I could call my parents.

"I . . . I don't have a phone—"

The officer walked me over to one of the police cars and helped me call home from inside the car with his cell phone. Joe answered on the first ring, and when I heard his voice, I couldn't help it—I burst out crying.

"We'll be right there, Rachel, okay? Just hold on!"

The officer who'd helped me call home directed me to stay where I was in the backseat, but within minutes, an ambulance came screaming into view, its red lights flashing wildly, closely followed by Joe's silver

Lexus, which came screeching loudly to a jerky halt across the street. Three of the car doors flew open, and then Mom and Joe and Dallin were running across the street in the rain to where I was, all of them getting as sopping wet as I was now.

Joe spoke with the officer who'd questioned me before he was finally allowed to approach the police car I was in. I watched him run towards me with Mom and Dallin at his heels before a police officer swung open the door and Joe reached out a hand to help me out of the squad car. "Rachel? Are you okay?"

I nodded shakily at his worried face as I climbed out of the squad car before being swallowed in a tight hug by Joe. "I think so. Dallin's Mustang is probably totaled, though."

And then Mom hugged me hard, too. She was crying hysterically and didn't let go for a long time.

"It's okay, Mom. I'm okay!"

When she did let go, Dallin stepped towards me slowly, worry etched all over his face.

"Rachel?"

I nodded and tried to smile. "I'm okay, Dallin." And then Dallin's arms were around me.

"I'm so sorry—I didn't think he'd take off like that. I ran to the first house by the cemetery and called 911—"

I pulled back to look at Dallin's scared face and tried to smile. "So you're the one responsible for the police chase!"

Mom cried out then, and I turned to see Ryan in handcuffs being helped into the ambulance by two EMTs. Mom tried frantically to run to him, but Joe held her back.

"He—he's bleeding—his head's bleeding!"

"Let the EMTs do their job, Elaine!"

I hadn't noticed before, but Mom was right. Ryan had somehow managed to hit his head on something sharp in Dallin's car and now had blood dripping down the right side of his face. I watched Ryan sway strangely back and forth before being hoisted into the ambulance, followed by a police officer stepping up inside as well. Mom screamed, and this time roughly broke free from Joe and rushed over to Ryan. I'd hardly had a chance to catch my breath again before an EMT jogged over to me and insisted on checking the bump on my head.

"I think she could stand to be checked out at the hospital, too. Just to make sure she's okay."

I shook my head before turning to plead with Joe. "I'm fine—really. I don't need to go to the hospital."

The EMT made me get into the ambulance anyway, long enough to briefly look me over and check my vital signs before Joe signed a waiver to let me go home with him instead of to the hospital. Ryan was lying on a stretcher in the ambulance moaning while Mom sat beside him, talking softly to him and stroking his hair. Ryan only looked at me once before turning his head away and closing his eyes.

Mom rode with Ryan and a police officer in the ambulance to the hospital. It seemed like hours before Joe was able to make arrangements to have Dallin's poor car towed away, and I was finally released by the police officers to Joe so he could take me home.

CHAPTER FIFTY-THREE

Robert was standing in the doorway with Wendy, Brandon, and Natalie close behind him when we finally pulled into the driveway. They were all wearing the same panicked, worried look that Joe and Dallin had on their faces. I wrenched open the passenger door and ran straight for Robert, who caught me up in a huge bear hug while I cried and cried.

"It's okay, baby—it's okay."

Joe drove right to the hospital after dropping off Dallin and me and returned with Mom two hours later.

"Ryan's suffering from alcohol poisoning. They're going to watch him and keep him overnight." Joe rubbed his eyes wearily with one hand while Mom collapsed on the couch by Robert and Wendy. "If they release him tomorrow, I'm going to be busy talking to the police, the hospital, and the judge to see what can be done to get him released to the treatment center as soon as possible."

Robert frowned worriedly. "Is he going to be put in jail?"

"Hopefully not before he goes to the treatment center, since we already had everything in place for him to go tomorrow. I'll just have to see what the police and the judge over his case say."

———•———

"Where are you going, Rachel?"
"I'm running away!"

"*Running away? Can I come, too?*"

I reached for Dad's open arms, but when I looked up into his face, it was Joe's.

I stepped back, but Dad's voice was strong and sure.

"*You're safe now, Rachel. You're going to be safe. I know you'll be safe. Be Your Own Kind of Beautiful.*"

My eyes opened slowly and then squinted nearly shut again from the sunlight streaming into my room. I sat up on one elbow and pushed the hair out of my eyes before peering at the clock on my bedside table. Ten o'clock. *Ten o'clock!*

I jumped out of bed and ran for the kitchen, screeching to a stop when I saw Dallin talking at the kitchen table, mourning over his mangled Mustang with Robert and Wendy and Brandon and Natalie.

Dallin looked up at me and smiled. "I guess you slept through your alarm, too, huh?"

"How come no one made sure I was up for school?"

Robert handed me a glass of orange juice. "Strict instructions. You're not ready to go back to school yet."

Dallin only shrugged. "We were supposed to stay home, anyway, in case we do the intervention thing."

I set the glass of juice down without taking a sip. "Where's Mom?"

Brandon spoke up next. "She and my dad went to the hospital to check on Ryan, and then my dad's going to be busy doing his attorney magic to see what kind of a deal he can work out for Ryan. And for you."

My eyes bulged at that piece of news. "Am I going to go to jail?"

Dallin shook his head and spoke up. "No—no. Don't worry. My dad will take care of everything. He told me the worst that could happen would be that you might have to go to court."

I never thought I'd be glad we had an attorney in the family, but Joe proved he knew his stuff when he and Mom finally made it home.

"Well, the doctor thinks Ryan could use another day in the hospital, so he won't be released today after all. He'll be released from the hospital tomorrow morning instead, and then he'll have to take a trip to the police station for booking. The judge is going to let him wait out his court date at the residential rehabilitation center we've picked out for him. The center agreed to hold Ryan's room, so we'll take Ryan in tomorrow morning after the booking instead, after we've all had a chance to talk to him."

I stared at Joe, my heart beating fast. "After the intervention, you mean?"

Joe nodded at me solemnly. "Yes."

CHAPTER FIFTY-FOUR

M om and Joe had called Brandon and Robert to explain the intervention long before they arrived the night before last. While Joe took care of checking Ryan out of the hospital the next morning, followed by dealing with the necessary trip to the police station, Mom sat us all down in the living room to brief us again.

"We looked into a lot of residential treatment centers and decided to go with Sunnyside because they specialize in helping teens who struggle with alcohol. The doctors and counselors at Sunnyside all stressed the importance of intervention. They called it the beginning step of treatment."

"I thought you said one of the counselors was going to be here," I frowned.

Mom nodded, twisting her fingers together nervously. "Yes, an alcoholism counselor was supposed to come and help, but since we had to move the intervention because Ryan's not ready to be released today after all, we're on our own. I'd thought about inviting more people to come— more of Ryan's friends, kids on the football team, maybe some ward members or teachers, but—I don't know. I just felt that less is more—that just having family here would be enough. And Joe's visited with the people at the center about doing an intervention as a family, so I think we'll be okay."

Mom didn't look okay, though. She looked nervous and scared. And although there was defeat in her eyes, there was a little bit of hopeful determination, too.

"Now, remember, although this is our time to confront Ryan about his drinking problem, it needs to be a caring confrontation. We need to show more concern and love for him than anything else. We want to urge him to accept what this treatment center can offer him. We're not supposed to blame and wound him. We just need to bring to his attention the consequences of his drinking in such a way that he can't avoid the issue anymore. He needs to be brought to the realization that treatment at the center is his best option now."

I wasn't sure how or if this was really going to work with Ryan, but Robert suggested we kneel in prayer and ask Heavenly Father to guide and direct us and to bless our efforts today to help Ryan. After we all stood up again, I was still nervous, but at the same time, I felt more confident that if nothing else, this was the right thing to be doing now to try to help Ryan.

Wendy was sitting on the couch, looking out the living room window, when we all heard the roar of a car engine coming down our street. "There they are. They're here!"

Robert and Brandon had moved our couch, recliners, and a few dining room chairs into a circle, leaving one of the recliners as far away as possible from the front door and the hallway. That chair was for Ryan.

Joe made Ryan walk through the front door first. He had dark circles around his bloodshot eyes as he wearily stepped inside, raking a hand through his messy hair. I could see the line of stitches on his forehead until his longish hair fell back in place, covering the dark threads completely. Ryan stopped in the doorway, though, suspicion narrowing his eyes as he glared at all of us sitting stiffly in the living room looking solemnly back at him.

"What's going on?"

Robert smiled, but his smile looked strained and tense. "Hey, Ry-Guy. Come on in and sit down. We really need to talk to you."

Ryan made a halfhearted effort to dive back out the front door, but Joe blocked him. Ryan was too weak from his hospital visit and sleepless nights to get past Joe, so Joe was able to firmly lead him into the living room and the empty recliner.

Joe sat down beside Mom, facing Ryan, and took a deep breath. "Ryan, all of us are here today because we're your family, and because we love you. We're all deeply concerned about you and the road you're taking in life right now. Ryan, I'm asking you to listen to us, and after we're through, you'll have your chance to respond. Okay?"

Ryan glared suspiciously at Joe and said nothing. I sat on one side of Ryan between Robert and Wendy facing Dallin, who sat between Brandon and Natalie. Mom and Joe sat in front of Ryan at the top of the circle. Everyone was quiet while Joe calmly and slowly explained to Ryan all of the stuff he and Mom had been researching about teen alcoholism and how all of the signs had been clear for a long time that Ryan was indeed a teenage alcoholic and needed help. Now.

Then Joe pointed out how much Ryan had deteriorated in the short time he'd known him. Not just in his failing grades and being kicked off the football team but also intellectually, socially, physically, emotionally, and spiritually.

"I haven't seen you bless the sacrament, Ryan. Knowing you can't do that right now, to me, is incredibly sad. I know it's breaking your mother's heart not seeing you up there with Dallin and Paul and Brian. I want you to be able to do that, Ryan. More than that, I want you to want that for yourself."

I glanced nervously at Ryan. He kept his face turned towards the living room window, avoiding Joe's eyes through most of his prepared speech.

Joe continued to speak calmly and caringly, but firmly, never moving his eyes from Ryan's face. He talked about how any use of alcohol in our home was unacceptable and that he, Mom, Dallin, and I, and Ryan himself had the right to an alcohol-free home.

"Ryan, today could become a major turning point in your life. A chance to reclaim everything worth having. You've been given many great things in life. You've been blessed to come to this earth during the last dispensation when the gospel is here. You came to wonderful parents who love you and raised you in the gospel. You've been taught about your Heavenly Father and His Son who love you and want you to return to them. We all want to see you return to them with honor. The best thing that your mother and I can offer right now to help you reach that goal is to give you the opportunity to receive treatment—treatment at a special place where you can stay and get help. Treatment that will help make everything great in this life and in the next life possible for you again."

Mom was already weeping. When Joe turned to her, putting his arm around her for support, she tried by saying in a trembling voice, "Ryan—Ry-Guy—you know how much I love you—" but then her tears took control and she couldn't go on. Natalie had a box of tissues on her lap and handed them to Mom.

Joe motioned to Robert to take his turn instead. Robert looked nervous, too, but that turned to sadness as he looked at Ryan and quietly said his name. Ryan turned his head slowly and stared blankly at Robert while he walked Ryan through a bunch of the "good days," back when they'd gone camping with Dad, and all the fun the three of them had together, and the fun we'd had together as a family before Dad died. "I could easily visualize a bright future for you then, Ryan. It's been the worst shock in the world to see what drinking's done to you. What it's still doing to you. Every time I see you, I can't believe how much worse you've become since the last time I've seen you. We should've done something a long time ago—I know that. This can't go on, man. This isn't you. This isn't the Ryan you're supposed to be. You deserve better. You're better than this."

Wendy, Robert's wife, tried to look calm and collected, but her eyes darted around the room nervously, and when Robert nudged her to speak next, she jumped and coughed twice, trying to clear her throat before she looked almost fearfully at Ryan. "I'm sorry—I'm really nervous. I didn't think I would be so nervous, but I am. I couldn't sleep last night, trying to think of what to say that could be of any help to you, Ryan." Wendy babbled on some more about what a great kid Ryan was, and how much she wanted to get to know him better, and how she knew he had great potential, and what a shame it would be to throw such wonderful potential away. "Ryan, please, you need help. Don't throw this chance away. Go to those people who can help you, Ryan."

Brandon decided to get his turn over with next. He told Ryan how lucky he was to have parents who would care enough to research out a great residential treatment center like Sunnyside for him—a place that was set up especially for teenagers who have the same problem with alcohol that Ryan had. A place with medical professionals who not only wanted to help him put alcohol behind him but would also allow him to finish his school classes and learn other skills, too. "We love you, Ryan. We all do. We wouldn't do this if we didn't care about you with our whole hearts and souls."

Natalie was as nervous as Wendy and said so right up front. She could hardly dare make eye contact with Ryan, either. She talked about a school friend who had died of alcohol poisoning when she was a teenager. "Family intervention like this might have saved her life. I'm hoping this will help save yours, Ryan. I'm so glad to be able to be a part of this. I know I don't know you well and have only learned a little about you at a few family events since Dad and Elaine got married, but it's been enough to see that you're on a downward spiral. Every time I've seen you, I can tell you've plunged further. I hope this is finally going to be the end to that plunge and the beginning of something better and new."

Dallin took a deep breath and said he wanted to go next. He told Ryan that even though they'd had their differences, he wanted the best for him. That as mad as he'd been that Ryan had wrecked his 1968 Ford Mustang, a car that had been bought in mint condition by his dad when Joe was sixteen, he was shocked to feel relief when he knew Ryan was okay. "It was at that moment I knew that I must care about you, man. I want you to get better so we can have a chance to really be friends. Maybe even brothers. But that can't happen unless you get help. Remember that scripture Brother Clawson talked about in seminary? The one about learning wisdom in your youth? Here's your chance to follow the wisdom you're hearing today, to trade a few months of time that will benefit you for the rest of your life, both now and in the next life. What do you have better to do right now than to take care of yourself so you can have a future?"

All eyes were on me now—eyes that were red from crying as the tissue box was passed around the room among the sniffling sounds. Except for me. I'd slowly taken a few tissues when the box was handed to me, but they remained crumpled in one hand, my eyes dry while I stared at Ryan's hollow expression. Ryan was far gone—so horribly far gone. I could see it. I could see the bewilderment on his face over everyone's tears and pleadings. I could almost hear him saying, "Why is everyone crying? What do they know that I don't?"

I took a deep breath and stared at Ryan until he looked up at me, waiting with his eyes full of surprise and anger and barely sustained tolerance. I wondered if he'd heard anything anyone had said. At all.

"Ryan . . ." I knew I was supposed to tell him how much I loved him, how much I wanted him to get help, but I wasn't sure I could tell him I loved him. I wasn't sure I even did anymore.

"Ryan . . ." I tried again. The room was tense—too tense. And quiet. And everyone was staring at me. "I—You—" I took one last, deep, shaky breath. And then I said what was truly in my heart. "You told me once how much you hated having to go to Central with me in the school, too. That I'm ruining your senior year. Well, you've successfully ruined my entire year, not just my school year. You embarrass me when you come to seminary drunk or pass out in class. It's been—horrifying—having to see you drunk night after night and having to clean you up and clean up the bathroom. And to find alcohol stashed all over the house. And to have kids at school come up and ask me questions about what's wrong with you and hear stories about how wasted you were at some party. I wish I'd used the camcorder and recorded what it's been like for me so you could see for yourself. I'm tired of making excuses for you, lying for you, cleaning up after you, and being embarrassed by you. I'm tired of wishing you weren't my brother!"

I knew I wasn't saying what Joe and Mom had asked me to think about saying, and Mom's horrified look made me stop. I looked down at my shaking fists crumpling the tissues harder and didn't look up again.

Ryan snorted. "Huh. Well, at least there's some honesty from you!"

Everyone was stone quiet until Joe softly asked Ryan what he was thinking.

Ryan glared hatefully at Joe. "What am I thinking? No one cares about me. Consequently, none of you has the right to try and control me or tell me what to do—that's what I'm thinking!"

"You would've been better off if someone *had* tried to control you, man!" Robert nearly spat out the words.

Joe shook his head. "No one ever has it all their own way, Ryan, with no responsibility for their actions—"

And then Mom finally found her voice. And surprised everyone with her pent-up feelings. She was still crying, but she somehow managed to get her words out between her stifled sobs. "You weren't raised this way, Ryan—you know you weren't! You were raised in a non-drinking family, with a religion that is completely against drinking of any kind. Even without our religion, you've been raised in a time in which medical research abounds to show that alcohol is bad for you. So how—why—could you have chosen this? Something you know is wrong and bad for you? You were raised better than this, Ryan. You know better than to do this!" Mom cried harder but pushed the tissue box away when Joe offered it to her as she looked tearfully at Ryan. "I don't know how or when you were first tempted to drink or who encouraged you to try alcohol. I'm not angry or surprised that you were in such a situation. What angers me is that you chose to be a follower and allow someone to challenge you to do something you knew went against everything you'd been taught—something you knew everyone in your life who loved you and wanted the best for you would disapprove of. Something that had the power to destroy you and those around you who love you!"

Ryan, however, was finished listening. "I don't have to listen to this! You can blab forever about dumping me off at some rehab center, but you can't make me go anywhere!"

Joe nodded his head slowly. "All right then. Would you like to hear the alternative? Because be assured, Ryan, the alternative is not something you're going to like better."

Ryan's eyes narrowed. "What do you mean? You can't make me do anything—"

"Maybe I can't, but the police and the judge in your case can."

"What are you talking about?"

Joe folded his arms. "You seem to forget your visit to the police station this morning, Ryan. And where you were less than twenty-four hours ago. Due to your foolish actions that resulted in a police chase and a car crash, you now have several counts against you. Driving under the influence of alcohol: a gross misdemeanor. Fleeing from a police officer: a felony. And now, you have a court date to appear before a judge. You could also easily be charged with car theft, because you took Dallin's car without his permission. And what about abduction, since you made Rachel go with you against her will? I have no doubt you will be sentenced to some jail time." I watched Ryan put his head down and run his hands through his hair. "If you go to the treatment center, the time spent in the center will be taken off your jail time. Depending on how you act while at the center, you may get even more jail time taken off your sentence. Otherwise, your mother and I have made arrangements for you to wait for your court date in a juvenile detention center. It's up to you: Sunnyside, or the detention center."

"I could wait for my court date at Robert's!"

Robert shook his head firmly. "No, you can't."

Ryan stared first at Robert's determined face and then back at Joe with a mixture of anger, disbelief, and hatred on his face. By the time Joe had firmly finished, matching Ryan stare for stare, Ryan put his head in his hands and wouldn't look at anyone.

"I've been drowning for years and no one cared to throw me a stinking bone—no one! If Dad hadn't died, things would've been different. I wouldn't be this way now—I would've been different. Everything would've been different. He would've helped me!"

Joe shook his head and sighed. "Ryan, I know he would have. But I'm here now, and I want to help you. Your mother and I—everyone here today—want to help you. We all love you too much to let what's happening to you go on even a minute longer. I had to make a choice: to ignore what was going on, or do what I could to help you. Now you have a choice, too." Everyone was still as Ryan rocked back and forth with his head in his hands while Joe quietly continued. "Ryan, I don't know if you remember or not, but the day you broke through your bedroom window, you begged us for help. I promised you at that time that I would help you. You've now heard the help I'm ready to offer to you. If you're ready to accept it, we're ready to take you to the treatment center today."

Ryan glanced up wearily. "I'll think about it."

Robert shook his head at Ryan again. "Think about it now, Ry-Guy!"

Brandon spoke up next. "They're holding a bed for you. You're supposed to check in today."

Ryan glared slowly around the room at all of us. "So that's it, then? You're giving me an ultimatum? All of you?"

Joe shook his head again. "We're not calling it that. We're offering you the best alternative to juvenile detention."

Ryan slumped further back into the recliner. "I guess I'm going to—what's it called again? Sunview?"

"Sunnyside."

Ryan nodded.

Joe smiled and stood up. "Then I guess we're finished. You can go start packing now."

Ryan muttered a few more token protests, but he finally shuffled down the hall to his bedroom and shut the door. Joe directed Brandon and Dallin to stand outside in front of Ryan's window so he couldn't escape via his recently acquired way of entering and leaving the house.

Dallin came running back inside within minutes. "I hate to have to say this, but the window was cracked open a little. Ryan must've snagged someone's cell phone, because he's on the phone with one of his friends. We heard him say he's being shipped off for a month or so but that when he gets back, 'we'll celebrate and party hard.'"

Joe's eyes narrowed dangerously. "If he thinks this is all just a game he has to play in order to get us all off his back, he's seriously mistaken." Then Joe strode angrily down the hall to Ryan's room where he gave the door a brief, sharp knock before opening the door and closing it behind him.

CHAPTER FIFTY-FIVE

When Ryan finally exploded from his room, angrily dragging his blue suitcase with wheels behind him, it was pretty clear that he wasn't happy about the intervention or being sent to Sunnyside. At all. Joe calmly closed Ryan's bedroom door behind him before he followed Ryan down the hall with a firm, unflinching look on his face.

We all stood up to say good-bye to Ryan as he stomped into the living room, gripping the long suitcase handle with one hand. Everyone stood up with encouraging smiles on their faces, ready to give Ryan a big emotional hug-fest sendoff, but Ryan put an end to that the second Robert stepped forward and said his name.

"Get away from me. I hate you. I hate you all! You couldn't make me go at all if I didn't have to pick between it and jail. I guess this is the lesser of two evils. It's better than this hellhole, anyway!"

Mom stepped forward bravely and dared to say she was excited for Ryan. Excited for him to finally be getting the treatment he needed so desperately.

Ryan only narrowed his eyes as he stared at Mom. "You're not excited for me. Don't lie to me!" Ryan was so vicious it was hard to watch. He clearly wasn't himself anymore. It was hard to remember the last time he had been. "You're only doing this because you can't handle me. You're sending me to rehab because you don't know what else to do with me!"

And then Ryan told everyone again how much he hated all of us before breaking down and crying. "Why are you doing this?" he moaned.

Joe reached out and put his arm around Ryan's shaking shoulders. "I'm—*we're*—doing this for you, for all of us, and for your father. I would hope someone would do the same for my son if I weren't there to do it myself."

Ryan shrugged Joe's arm off and turned to stare at Mom. "Why are *you* doing this?"

Tears filled Mom's eyes again as she stared back at him and quietly said, "Because I want my son back."

Ryan continued to stare hollowly at Mom until Robert stepped up quietly and put his arm around him. "Ry-Guy, can we—can we give you a blessing before you go? A priesthood blessing? Would you like that?"

Ryan stared numbly at Robert before mumbling, "I don't know." Brandon pulled one of the chairs from the intervention circle forward, and somehow Robert was able to lead Ryan over to it. After Ryan fell heavily into the chair, Robert quietly asked him again if it would be okay to give him a blessing. Ryan had his head down and didn't answer but gave a short nod. And then Robert, Brandon, and Joe put their hands on Ryan's head and gave him a blessing. A really beautiful blessing.

And then it was time for Joe and Mom to drive Ryan to Sunnyside. I stood in the doorway with everyone else and watched them drive off.

Robert talked about how we'd be able to visit Ryan during family week after three weeks or so of treatment. "They have these great sessions at the center with just the families of the alcoholics meeting together to talk and get support from each other. I think that will be helpful for everyone."

Wendy moved to stand beside Robert and hug him. "I really hope the people at this treatment center can help him."

Robert nodded and hugged her back. "I hope so, too, but in the end, it's going to be up to Ryan now. He's got to decide to help himself. I hope he can do it."

"I'm going to pray that he can."

Brandon shook his head as he continued to stare out the living room window. "You realize this isn't the end, don't you? Recovery from any kind of addiction takes a long time. One intervention doesn't usually solve the problem. This is just the beginning of a long, painful process."

Robert nodded. "Hopefully, it's the beginning of the end of this nightmare with Ryan."

I hoped so, too, but I'd been thumbing through some of the literature on teenage alcohol addiction that Mom and Joe had been reading lately, and I knew that even with all the help Ryan would receive from Sunnyside, he could relapse. And that it was likely to happen.

And then Robert said something that shocked me. "Rachel, would you like a blessing, too?"

I stared in confusion at him. "I—I don't need a blessing!"

Robert smiled kindly at me. Too kindly. "Are you sure? I think you could use a blessing, too."

I was hesitant, but everyone was acting so overly concerned and smiling so encouragingly at me that I finally said, "Okay—sure," and sat down in the chair Ryan had been sitting in only minutes before.

I thought I'd be able to sit through the blessing calmly and basically unemotionally—as if a bishopric member were setting me apart to be the Laurel class secretary—but my lips trembled the second Robert said, "Rachel, it's okay to let go now. It's not up to you to take care of Ryan. Heavenly Father will watch over him, because He loves Ryan, too." Then Robert said Ryan was born of goodly parents, like Nephi, and that he, just like me and everyone else, had been given the gift of agency to use in this life. I was also told that Heavenly Father loved me, too, and wanted me to be happy and move forward with my own life. I really started to tremble hard then, and I couldn't help but cry. And cry.

After the blessing, I wiped my eyes and nodded my thanks to Brandon. Then I turned to Robert, who hugged me tight. "It's going to be okay, Rachel. It is."

After Robert let me go, I sat back down in the chair and realized that everyone was looking at each other uneasily before looking back at me with concern.

"What? What is it?"

Robert looked at me with kind concern again. "Have you heard of Alateen?"

"Alateen?"

"We all think joining an Alateen support group would be good for you."

I didn't say anything. Robert took a deep breath and continued. "We think you could use some help, too, Rachel."

"What—what are you talking about?"

"We love you, Rachel, and you've gone through an incredibly rough time since Dad died and Ryan—"

I couldn't believe what I was hearing. "So you think I need counseling? I need therapy? *I'm* not the alcoholic! I don't need help like that—I don't!" I wasn't about to listen to anything else Robert had to say. Before he or anyone else could say more than "Rachel!" I ran into my bedroom and stayed there for the rest of the day.

CHAPTER FIFTY-SIX

There was no way that anyone could make me visit any therapist or counselor, and I had no desire to go hang out in some weird Alateen group, either. I could make my own decisions, and unlike with Ryan, no one could hold going to jail over my head.

Thankfully, Robert and Wendy and Brandon and Natalie had to leave that night. I faked a bad headache when Mom and Joe finally made it back home and climbed into bed early. I avoided Dallin for the rest of the week, mostly by hanging out at Teresa's, claiming that I needed her help to study for some upcoming big tests. I'd stay there until late, and then I'd head for home just in time to go straight to bed.

I hadn't told Teresa about shipping Ryan off to rehab, and thankfully, she didn't ask. She was kind enough to just be my friend and let me pretend that nothing was going on. By Saturday, though, I needed to talk to someone about everything that had happened lately. Someone who would always listen to me.

It'd snowed a little during the week, and as I crunched through the unbroken snow on the cemetery grounds, I could see my breath in front of my face. I'd sneaked out of the house early before I thought anyone else was up yet, and now that I'd cleared a place to sit in front of Dad's headstone and brushed the snow off the stone as well, ready to talk to Dad, all I wanted to do was cry.

"I should feel better, Dad. Ryan's somewhere safe—with people who can help him. But I don't feel better. I don't! Everything's so messed up—

everything!" I put my hands in front of my face and put my head down and cried. And then, I felt arms around me. Real arms, and when I pulled away, it was Dallin sitting in the snow in front of me, looking sad and concerned. As if he actually cared about me.

"What—what are you doing here?"

"I heard you get up and leave the house this morning. I knew you'd come here."

I looked away and wiped self-consciously at my face. "I—needed to talk to someone."

Dallin looked hurt. "Why didn't you come and talk to me? We're friends, aren't we?"

I shrugged and avoided looking at Dallin's eyes. "I—I don't know."

Dallin still looked hurt. And surprised. "I wish you'd stop avoiding me. You can talk to me, Rachel." I didn't answer, so Dallin quietly continued. "I know you're going through a hard time right now. We all are, you know. If there's one thing I've learned since my mom died, it's that although I can't change everything to be the way I want it to be, I know I can survive whatever comes my way."

I stared dully at Dallin for a moment. "If my dad hadn't died, my life would've been better."

Dallin nodded slowly. Thoughtfully. "Maybe. Maybe not. There's no way to know. I've wondered that since my mom died, too. But I've learned that when I'm going through something hard, if I turn to God for help, He sends me help. Like I told you before, He usually sends me help through other people and in some pretty unexpected and unique ways." Dallin was quiet for a moment until I looked up at him again. "I know He sent your mom to help me. And my dad."

I nodded and sighed. "I still wish my dad was here. I'm sorry, but I'm never going to stop wishing that. But, since he's not here anymore, I can't deny that I've been lucky. Your dad's been a good stepfather. A great one, actually." I looked at Dallin thoughtfully. "I—I think it must've been easier for my dad to move on knowing someone great would come along to be with my mom and the rest of my family."

318

Dallin smiled and nodded. "I think my mom probably feels the same way."

"Do you think—do you think your mom and my dad know each other on the other side now?"

"I'm sure they do. I'll bet they're both happy our families are together. I know my mom will want to thank your mom someday."

"My dad will have a ton to thank your dad for. I don't know what we would've done without him." Dallin was looking at me so intently that I had to look away and nervously draw lines in the snow with my finger.

"I've missed this, Rachel."

I looked back up in surprise. "Missed what?"

Dallin smiled and shrugged. "Being able to talk to someone about stuff like this. About what it's like, losing one of your parents. I've missed talking with you about it."

My mouth dropped open. "With me?"

Dallin nodded. "Of course, with you. You understand. My friends don't. They don't know what this is like, but you do. I read somewhere once that pain is miraculously halved when it's shared, and it's true. I can't believe I've been lucky enough to find you."

I looked down and smiled shyly. "It—it helps me a lot to know that I'm not alone."

"You're not alone, Rachel. You never will be. You know that, don't you?"

"I guess I do."

Dallin sighed loudly and ran his hands through his hair before look-ing at me again. "I have to admit, though, that although it's been good to find someone—you—who knows and understands what I'm going through, it's been hard for me, too. You've definitely made my life more complicated."

My eyes widened at that. "I'm sorry—I know it's been hard living in my home with Ryan and everything—"

"I'm not talking about Ryan. I'm talking about *you*."

I couldn't help frowning in confusion. "What do you mean?"

Dallin smiled ruefully at me, shaking his head. "Rachel, you mean a lot to me. More than you know." Dallin looked down for a long second before looking back up at me intently. "I talked to Brandon—he said that we should try the test of time."

"The test of time?"

"I like you, Rachel. I really do. It would be easy to just go with these feelings, but like I told you on New Year's Eve, since we live in the same house together right now, I don't think it's a good idea."

"I remember," I said.

Dallin sighed and ran his hands through his hair again. "I don't know what's going to happen to me, to you—all I know is that if any of these feelings are real, they won't go away. You'll be a senior when I leave on my mission, and you'll be a sophomore in college when I come back. You'll probably have a serious boyfriend by then anyway."

I shook my head firmly and stared at Dallin. "No, I won't. I know I won't."

Dallin laughed dully for a moment. "I'll guess we'll see, huh?"

"Yes, we will."

Dallin looked at my serious face curiously before he finally smiled. "Well, until then, I meant it when I said I want us to be friends. Will you let me be your friend and not shut me out?"

I nodded my head, and Dallin leaned towards me. He kissed me gently on the forehead and then smiled and pushed a stray lock of hair out of my eyes. "So, friend, how have you been holding up? How are you feeling about the Ryan situation?"

"I'm glad he's someone else's problem now. Is that bad?"

"Of course not."

I sighed. "I'm glad for the distance, too. I'm glad he's not here. You know how he said he hated us all?" Dallin nodded. "Do you think he really meant that?"

Dallin looked at me soberly. "I think he hates everyone right now because he hates himself." I thought about that for a long moment before

WHEN THE BOUGH BREAKS

he spoke again. "You know, I've been looking through those pamphlets, too."

I looked up sharply at Dallin's serious face. "Oh, yeah?"

"That Alateen group—it's not what you're thinking. I mean, I'm sure it *is* a form of therapy for people who go, but it's not you alone on a couch with a head shrink or anything like that. It's a support group for 'younger family members and friends of alcoholics.'" I looked down at my feet and didn't say anything. "I think it's a good idea, Rachel." I still didn't say anything, but what he said next truly surprised me.

"If you'll go, I'll go with you."

CHAPTER FIFTY-SEVEN

By the time Mom, Joe, Dallin, and I arrived at church on Sunday, just about our entire ward knew we'd sent Ryan off to Sunnyside. I sat in the back of the Young Women's room for opening exercises before we all separated into our classrooms. I only looked up from my scriptures when I heard Ryan's name whispered between a couple of girls from my class a few rows in front of me.

"Yeah, I heard they finally sent him off to rehab to dry out. About time!"

"I know. I've felt so sorry for Dallin. He's got to be so glad to be rid of Ryan!"

I bit my lip hard and pretended not to hear anything else. I kept my nose buried in my scriptures during class and tried not to notice any looks from the rest of the Laurels, although I caught Sarah smirking at me once. She'd never gotten over the Skittles fiasco, even though no one had seen the pictures Ryan had taken of her and the rest of the Laurels hunched over the garbage can and kitchen sink.

I almost decided not to go to Sunday School, but when I peeked into the classroom and saw Dallin inside, smiling encouragingly at me, I figured if he was being brave enough to stay for class, then I should be brave, too. I was glad I went to class, because Brother Parker reminded me of something that made me glad I'd stayed.

"In Matthew, chapter 11, verses 28 through 30, Christ issued an amazing invitation that Elder James E. Talmage has called 'one of the grandest outpourings of spiritual emotion known to man': 'Come unto me, all ye that labour and are heavy laden, and I will give you rest. Take my yoke upon you, and learn of me; for I am meek and lowly in heart: and ye shall find rest unto your souls. For my yoke is easy, and my burden is light.'"

I slipped out of Sunday School a few minutes early to save a bench for sacrament meeting. I was thinking about that scripture and a few other things Brother Parker talked about while I watched Dallin help Paul and Brian get the sacrament table ready when I felt a tap on my shoulder and jumped.

"Oh, I'm sorry, Rachel—I didn't mean to scare you!"

It was Sister Jensen, looking horribly frantic, even though she'd pasted a huge smile on her face.

"It's okay. Is something wrong?"

"Well, maybe, maybe not." I could feel my body tense up, wondering what I'd be asked to do, since I was sure I was about to be asked to do something. "You know how we always have someone from Young Women and someone from the Aaronic Priesthood give a short talk in sacrament meeting each week before the main speakers?" I nodded slowly. "It's the Laurel class's turn to provide a youth speaker in sacrament meeting today. Mandy was assigned to speak, and her mother just stopped me in the hall to let me know that Mandy's home sick with the flu today. I was wondering how you'd feel about just bearing your testimony in place of Mandy's talk during sacrament meeting."

"Me?" I gasped.

Sister Jensen smiled. "Yes, you, Rachel. Would you be willing to do that?"

"Can't someone else do it? Wouldn't the bishop be okay with just having one youth speaker instead?"

Sister Jensen nodded slowly. "Yes, the bishop would probably think having just one youth speaker would be all right. And yes, I could ask someone else. But I'm asking *you*, Rachel. I just felt impressed to ask you."

What was I supposed to say to that? I hated getting up in front of people. I detested it. Hadn't the horrifying experience I'd gone through trying out for the school musical proven to me I was no good standing and talking in front of a group of people?

"Okay, I'll do it." I couldn't believe it when the words whispered out of me. Sister Jensen squeezed my shoulders and thanked me before rushing off to inform the bishop.

Before I knew what was happening, Mom had slid onto the bench beside me, I'd whispered to her what had just happened, and ten seconds later, I was sitting up on the stand looking out over our entire ward. My heart pounded hard. We had way more people in our ward than I'd thought. I had no idea what to say and tried to focus on thinking about the main things I'd been taught were important to say in a testimony.

However, after the sacrament had been passed and the bishop smiled and nodded to me after thanking me for pinch-hitting for Mandy, my legs shook and my heart pounded as I trembled my way to the podium and waited for the microphone to be lowered. And then, something inside of me took over, and I knew what I needed to say.

"Today in Sunday School, Brother Parker, my teacher, talked about the scripture in Mark, chapter 2, verse 17, which reads, 'Jesus . . . saith unto them, They that are whole have no need of the physician, but they that are sick: I came not to call the righteous, but sinners to repentance.' Brother Parker quoted Elder Holland, who said that the Church isn't 'a monastery for perfect people,' but that it is 'more like a hospital,' 'provided for those who are ill and want to get well.'

"Everyone is quick to pray and fast for people who are sick. Most of you know my brother Ryan and what our family has been struggling with—with him. My brother Ryan isn't a bad person or a wicked person. He's someone who is sick and needs help. So, I'm asking on behalf of my family, if you would, please remember my brother in your prayers. That the doctors at the treatment center will be able to help him. My brother is a child of God, too, and Heavenly Father loves him as much as He loves everyone else. I know there is still a lot of good in my brother. He was willing to let my stepdad and my brother give him a blessing before he went to the treatment center. I know that will help him. My family will be fasting for him this coming Fast Sunday, and I hope that those of you who will be fasting will remember my brother in your fast.

"I've been praying for my brother for a long time. I've prayed for a miracle—that Heavenly Father would heal him. My stepbrother Dallin told me once that maybe I was praying for the wrong miracle, and he was right. Heavenly Father did hear my prayers, even though for a long time I didn't think He was listening. I was looking for a different answer from the one He gave me. Instead of healing Ryan, like I'd asked Him to for a really long time, He gave me a wonderful stepfather and stepbrother who have helped me and my mom. And Ryan. Ryan wouldn't be getting the treatment he needs now if it wasn't for them.

"Thanks to my Heavenly Father for bringing them into my life, I have something I haven't had in a long time: Hope."

I paused to look over the audience and was shocked—touched, really, at the tears I could see in so many people's eyes. I closed with my testimony of my belief in Christ and in the power of His Atonement and how it can heal anyone of anything if that person will turn to Christ for help, before saying, "in the name of Jesus Christ, amen."

CHAPTER FIFTY-EIGHT

I wasn't surprised to get a huge, tearful hug from my mom and Joe after church or even to have the bishopric and ward members come up and hug me and my family after church. What did surprise me was all the phone calls we received, also from people in the ward, offering their love and support. But what surprised and touched me most of all were the handwritten notes we received from people in our ward letting us know that Ryan and our family were in their prayers and asking for our forgiveness for any unkind remarks, actions, or thoughts concerning Ryan. The bishop even announced a special fast for Ryan, which was more than anyone in our family expected. I'd never thought of my ward as extended family members before, and it felt really wonderful being able to do so now.

When it was time to turn the calendar month to February, things had definitely improved. Even though no one was allowed to see Ryan yet, I was operating under the old adage "no news is good news" and kept praying for Ryan that he would be given strength to do what he needed to do to get well and that he would choose to get well.

I'd been studying with Teresa on Wednesday night, and when I finally arrived home, Dallin was waiting for me in the living room. He stood up when I walked through the front door.

"Where have you been?"

I stepped back against the closed door in surprise. "Studying with Teresa—I told Mom I would be. Why?"

"Your writing teacher called today—"

"My writing teacher?" I repeated stupidly.

"Yeah, your writing teacher—"

"You mean, Mrs. Townsend?"

"Yeah, her—"

"Why would she call me at home?"

Dallin laughed. "Be quiet for a second and I'll tell you!"

Someone rang the doorbell, though, so Dallin was forced to loudly sigh and wait while I turned to open the front door.

"Hi, Rachel!"

My mouth dropped open. My entire Laurel class and Sister Jensen were standing on the front porch, beaming at me. And bearing gifts, no less. I could barely get out a "hi" back to them before Sister Jensen asked if they could come in for a minute, followed by everyone stepping inside, still wearing excited smiles on their faces.

"What's going on? Did I miss activity night?"

Sarah stepped towards me hesitantly. "We—we just wondered if you could deliver these care packages for us."

I stared stupidly back at her. "You want me to mail off missionary packages?"

Sarah smiled and shook her head. "They're not for the missionaries. They're for Ryan."

I had to swallow a great big lump in my throat before I could thank everyone. It was truly kind and truly unexpected. The girls didn't stay long, but they all insisted on giving me a quick hug before they left and asked that we let Ryan know they were thinking of him and pulling for him.

I followed Dallin into the kitchen after I'd waved good-bye and closed the front door behind Sister Jensen. "I think I've been hugged about a million times in the past few weeks!"

Dallin turned from the open fridge to hand me a can of pop. "Me, too. It's not so bad, is it?"

"Nah." I carefully peeled back the tab before looking at Dallin again. "So, Mrs. Townsend called?"

Dallin shut the fridge door and nodded. "She said she just got word that the poems you entered placed in the high school writing contest. She couldn't wait to tell you at school."

I was about to take a swig and froze with the pop can near my lips. I shakily placed the can down on the kitchen counter. "I placed? What place?"

Dallin grinned. "She didn't say. You didn't win, but you came really close. Isn't that cool? You were up against a ton of students all over the state, so I think that's pretty exciting. In fact, I think we should make your mom and my dad take us out to dinner tomorrow night to celebrate!"

I couldn't help laughing. "That's because it's your turn to cook tomorrow night!"

Dallin shrugged and grinned. "Oh—hey—I also got two other cool phone calls."

"Oh, yeah?"

Dallin kept grinning at me. "Yeah. Guess what? Both of our sisters-in-law are expecting babies."

"Really!" I said, clapping my hands together excitedly.

Dallin grinned and motioned for me to pick up my pop again before clinking his pop can against mine. "We're going to be an aunt and an uncle!"

I laughed and took a sip of my pop while Dallin continued to grin at me. Life was definitely always full of twists, turns, and surprises. My life was, at least. And I was glad it was. Really.

CHAPTER FIFTY-NINE

Be Your Own Kind of Beautiful.

I'd been staring at my Mormonad and its single white daisy for too long now. Had I really thought that daisy looked bold before? I squinted harder at it. At this moment, it looked scared to death and more than a little crazy.

I turned my head to look at my calendar instead. Saturday, February 14. Valentine's Day. *The* Day. The Big Reveal. I'd sent the victim of my seminary Valentine's Day assignment a few little rhyming verses on fancy lavender paper in fancy lavender envelopes in the mail for the past four weeks, and now that it was time to face him about it, I was so nervous I could hardly breathe.

> *Roses are red, but daisies are white.*
> *If you want to find out who thinks you're the best,*
> *then meet me on Valentine's Day, all right?*
> *Where: Lotsa Pasta.*
> *When: 1 o'clock.*
> *Happy Valentine's Day!*
> *From your Secret Valentine.*

"Knock, knock. Can I come in?" Mom's voice was unmistakable. I cringed as I took a quick look around my bedroom.

"Uh, sure. Come on in, Mom!" I called back as cheerfully as possible. After all, maybe it wouldn't look as bad to her as it did to me.

"Rachel, honey, that wasn't panic I heard in your voice, was it?" Mom stopped abruptly, her hand still gripping the doorknob, and gave my room one of her shocked-look once-overs. I waded through the ocean of shirts, skirts, and pants to shut the door behind her.

"You're not even close to being ready, and it's almost time for you to leave!" Mom put her hands on her hips and shook her head at me. "I won't even start in on this—disaster—I see everywhere."

"I know, I know. I just can't seem to figure out what to wear. I mean, it's Valentine's Day, and this isn't just any guy. It's—"

Mom cut in quick. "Exactly. He'll think you look fine no matter what you wear."

I wasn't so sure of that, but I didn't protest while Mom rummaged through the mess of clothing all over my room to pick out a sweater and a pair of dressy jeans.

"This outfit will look wonderful." She knew the sweater was one of my favorites, so I didn't argue with her. "Is he going to meet you at the restaurant?"

"Yeah. I know it's kind of a long drive, so thanks for letting me take the car. I promise I'll be careful!" Mom nodded and turned to leave. "Mom?"

"Yes, honey?"

I couldn't stop twisting my fingers together. "He'll be there, won't he? I mean, I told him where to meet me, but he doesn't know it's me, so—"

Mom only laughed. "Rachel, no one could possibly have been more thorough than you, making plans and checking and double-checking everything. I'm sure he'll be there at exactly one o'clock!"

"You're right, Mom. I'm just being silly." Mom smiled and turned to leave again, but I couldn't stop my panicked self from calling out "Wait!" Something in my voice must've sounded pretty pathetic and stressed, because Mom turned back again to look at me with one of those concerned-mother looks on her face.

"Mom, you don't think this is stupid, do you? I mean, me asking him to lunch and having him as my secret valentine? Do you think he'll think I'm really stupid?"

Mom smiled and then walked over to me and hugged me hard. "You're not stupid, and he won't think you're stupid, either. I think this is a wonderful idea. I think he'll be touched you went through all of this trouble for him."

Touched. Well, at least that would be a start.

My heart was pounding as I waited nervously at the table for two I'd reserved at Lotsa Pasta. I'd driven for two hours to get here and had purposely arrived half an hour early in case he happened to arrive first. He hadn't, though, so I'd been anxiously sipping water at our table. He was late. Fifteen minutes late. The restaurant was darkened and filled with romantic candlelight and lots of hand-holding, nose-rubbing kind of couples. *Teresa was right. This was a dumb idea.* I bent down to grab my purse from underneath my chair, my hand shaking—actually shaking. I was stupid—so stupid. He wasn't going to come. He wasn't—

"Your table, sir." Too late. The waiter's voice was above my ear. I sat up, banging my elbow against the table.

"Rachel?"

A good-looking guy with neatly trimmed dark hair wearing nicely pressed pants and a nice shirt and tie was standing by the waiter with a stunned look on his face at the sight of—well, *me*—sitting at the table in front of him. The waiter calmly placed two menus on the table and then turned away to blend in with the rest of the restaurant.

"Are you okay?"

I finally found my voice and tried to laugh. "Of course. That felt great. Just what I needed," I assured him, rubbing awkwardly at my elbow. And then, I couldn't stop staring at him. He looked amazing. So wonderful I hardly recognized him.

"Ryan—you look great—so great!"

Ryan grinned for a second, not taking his eyes off me, before his eyebrows drew together. "You're not—I mean—Are you—"

"Your definitely psycho secret valentine? Yes, I'm afraid that would be me." Ryan was practically scowling at me. I could feel my heart dropping like a lead weight into my stomach. A bad idea. Yes, this was a very bad idea. I was obviously a major disappointment to him.

And then, miracle of miracles, he lifted an eyebrow and then slipped into the chair across from me. He picked up his menu and studied it calmly, but after a second, he shook his head, laughed, and tossed the menu down in front of him.

"So—it was *you*? *You* were the one sending me all the purple notes?"

"That would be lavender, and they weren't notes. They were great, creative expressions of poetry," I sniffed back at him.

Ryan laughed again. "I wondered how anyone at Central could possibly know about everything going on with me. I never thought that it might be you, but now it makes sense. Who else would've known all of that stuff?"

I smiled hesitatingly at him. "So—are you disappointed it was me and not the prom queen?"

Ryan grinned and looked straight into my eyes. "Nah."

With that amazing and honest "nah" from Ryan, our afternoon together continued to improve. Lunch was perfect. Ryan convinced me to try a new sauce on my angel hair pasta, and I refrained from spilling anything on either myself or him.

"So—how's Sunnyside?" I was hesitant to ask, but I wanted to know. I had to know.

Ryan sighed and shook his head, stabbing into his pasta. "It's hard. Really hard. I hated it at first, but it's getting better now. I must be doing better than I think. Otherwise, I wouldn't have gotten permission to come here for lunch with you today."

Ryan smiled a little, and I smiled back. "I'm glad you were able to come."

"Me, too."

"So—what do you do at the center all day?"

Ryan shrugged again. "We're all kept on a strict schedule. And the rules are just like Joe's, believe it or not. I have to keep my room all nice and help cook food. No dating's allowed, so I can't get near any of the girls. But I actually have a job at Sunnyside, if you can believe it!"

I laughed. "I don't know if I can!"

Ryan grinned. "It's all good. I thought I'd be bored, but everyone's kept really busy. Makes it easier not to think about wanting to drink. And I'm taking classes so I can graduate, and I've got volunteer work, too, and of course the alcohol counseling. Group meetings and one-on-one sessions and all that stuff. All the counselors at the center are former addicts themselves. I've been hearing all of their stories." Ryan chuckled and shook his head as he swallowed a bite of pasta and dug in with his fork again. "I thought I'd be able to get around them, but they knew all my tricks. They'd played them themselves. Most of them had played them better than I had."

Ryan's smile faded, and he looked at me soberly across the table. "I've had some pretty intense sessions with my counselor. The thing I've learned—well, that I'm learning—is that the secret to getting better isn't just to stop drinking. The 'ah ha' moment for me happened after I went to a few AA meetings and finally realized and admitted that I couldn't do this alone. First step is to admit you're powerless over alcohol, and then you come to believe that a Power greater than yourself can help you. So I finally broke down and did that. Admitted I have no control over alcohol and that only God can help me now. That I can only get better with His help. Then, I had to be willing to take more steps." Ryan shook his head. "Believe me, none of them are fun. They're hard. Harder than anything I've ever had to do before. I'm not very far down my Twelve Steps list, but I'm trying." Ryan stopped and looked at me thoughtfully. "I'm slowly coming around to the idea of what's taught in our church about true freedom. I thought I was exercising freedom by choosing alcohol, but it was telling *me* what to do. I had no freedom anymore. None at all. The only way I can begin to have freedom again is to stick with total abstinence."

Even though Ryan was completely serious, I couldn't help fighting a to smile. He was talking to me—actually *talking* to me. About something serious and important going on with him. Amazing.

"I tell you, Rachel—that first AA meeting where I realized what I was—an alcoholic—an addict—I actually focused and listened to the other people there. A lot of them had had experiences and feelings like I'd had. I cried like a baby throughout the entire meeting. I was shaking, and I couldn't stop. I couldn't believe this was really me—that I was now in rehab because I was addicted to alcohol. This wasn't supposed to happen. Not to me." Ryan shook his head before he finally smiled a little. "And then, things started to get better. Harder, but better."

I smiled back. "I'm glad treatment is going so well and that the center is helping you, Ryan."

Ryan nodded and looked down and sighed before looking at me again. "The day I left home—that day was strange. I didn't want to go, but at the same time, while everyone was talking to me, part of me was thinking, okay, maybe, maybe I'll be okay. I was excited and terrified at the same time, but I couldn't tell anyone I was actually excited. I'd been hating myself for so long that I felt like finally, maybe, I'd have some relief." Ryan shook his head. "I didn't realize how bad off I was—how long it'd been since I really felt good—until I got the blessing that day. To feel the power of having hands on my head . . . Everything said to me was what I needed."

I nodded quietly, slowly twirling my fork in my pasta.

"The night I totaled Ackerman's car—remember?"

"I doubt I'll forget it."

Ryan laughed briefly, dully. "Well, when I hit my head, the first thing I saw, just for a second, was Dad's face. I don't know—I think I should've been hurt worse, but I wasn't. I think Dad was watching out for me. For both of us, I guess. So then when I got that blessing before I left home, I just knew I wasn't going to be able to do this alone and that if I wanted it, I could get help. But I'd have to want it and put in the work myself." Ryan looked up at me again wistfully. "I saw Dad's face in my mind again, and I knew if I had him pulling for me and God helping me, then if I worked hard myself, I could maybe be okay."

I was quiet for a moment and didn't look up when I asked my question. "Why did you do it, Ryan? If I can ask. How did it start?"

Ryan tried to laugh. "You'd probably like some amazing answer, but my beginning is pretty unoriginal. No one pushed me. Not really. I went to a party my sophomore year of high school, and there was beer all over the place. No one made me drink anything. I'd just always wanted to try it. I don't know why, I just did. And I was sick of always doing everything everyone wanted me to. I was sick of always just being the person that everyone wanted me to be. So I grabbed a beer. I don't remember really anything else about that night. I picked up the beer and it went from there. I started drinking." Ryan shook his head, his eyes thoughtful and sad. "I didn't like the taste of it at first. I had to *make* myself drink it because it was so gross. I grew to like the taste of it, but at the time, it was so bitter I didn't like it at all. Except for how it made me feel. So I was drinking on the weekends at parties at first and then a couple times during the week before it became an everyday thing." Ryan shrugged and took another bite of pasta. "It was easy enough to get. My friends would steal alcohol from their parents, I'd pitch in my seminary bribe money, and I'd steal things from everyone at home to pawn."

"I can't believe you did that. I still can't!"

"I'm not proud I did it, but I didn't feel bad about it at the time."

"If you didn't worry about how wrong it was to take our stuff, how come you didn't at least just feel bad about it?"

Ryan shook his head at me sadly. "I hated everyone. That made it easy. Besides—I needed to drink too much to worry about anything else. It was all about the escape—how it made me feel. The high was worth it. It was worth everything I had to do to get it. At first, anyway. I think with that first drink I was an alcoholic and just didn't know it yet. I started to drink more in order to feel good because my tolerance was getting so high. I needed more and more to get that feeling again, to get to where I needed to be." Ryan stared at me intently. "It's never as good as the first time. It's never as good again. You're always chasing that first high—that first time, but you're never going to get it back. Never."

I didn't say anything. I didn't know what to say, and since Ryan seemed to want to talk—to need to talk—I sat quietly and let him.

"The thing is, it just got to the point where it was out of control. You know that. I could hardly go an hour without something in my system. I knew after a while that I was drinking too much and had to stop. The problem was, I couldn't. I felt worse sober than I did drunk."

Ryan took a quick sip of water and cleared his throat and looked at me seriously again. "When it got that bad, it wasn't like I was thinking all the time, 'I'm so happy to be drinking!' At that point I would've given anything to be able to stop. I knew drinking all the time wasn't what I wanted to do with my life. That's not where I wanted to go, but I couldn't stop." He stopped and took a shaky breath. "Looking back now, I feel like there was a monster inside of me and I couldn't do anything about it. It held me hostage." He shook his head. "It's hard to explain. I still feel it creeping up sometimes now. It scares me—thinking that I'm going to fall back into the habit." He sighed and silently ate a couple more bites of pasta while I waited.

"When Mom and Joe first confronted me about my drinking and wanted me to think about treatment, I told them I'd stop. I was thinking, okay, if this will get them off my back, then okay, I can do this. I thought, sure, yeah, I think I've got a problem. But then, deep down inside of me, even though I said sure, I have a problem, and sure I'll go to treatment, afterwards I kept thinking, I don't want to go. I don't have a problem. I was torn back and forth. One day I'd be thinking, okay, I need help, and then the next day I'd think no, I don't. I'm fine."

Ryan's hand trembled as he took a sip of water and carefully set the glass back down. "Even though I'm getting treatment, I know I'll always be an alcoholic, Rachel. Once I'm out of Sunnyside, I'll need to keep going to AA meetings."

"For how long?"

Ryan looked soberly at me with a sad smile. "Probably for the rest of my life. Even if I never drink again, I know I have the potential to relapse. Maybe some people can drink and not have the same problem as I do—

the same out-of-control cravings, but I'm not like those people. I'm an alcoholic, and I always will be."

"So what can you do about it?"

Ryan shrugged. "Just take it one day at a time. I just commit not to drink on a daily basis. That's what I'm learning at Sunnyside and at my AA meetings. I don't promise to stop drinking for a year, or a month, or even for a week, but just for today. I can only focus on today. I made a choice to change, but I have to keep making that decision every day—to try and keep from going back to my old life."

I nodded and took a sip of water myself. "So how long do you think you'll be at Sunnyside?"

Ryan shrugged again. "I have no idea. When I'm ready, I think I'll move into a halfway house type of place to help me continue drying out. I need all the help I can get. This disease I've got—alcoholism—it can be treated, but it can't be cured. I'll always be a 'recovering alcoholic.'" He looked hard at me, his face a tight knot of sad bitterness. "I've thought a lot about whether or not I'd be like this if Dad had lived. I wonder if he would've been able to handle me better, you know? Or at all. The hardest thing for me to deal with—to live with—is knowing if it wasn't for my drinking, Dad wouldn't have died at all. He'd still be here."

I was stunned. "What are you talking about?"

Ryan stared at me. "You know exactly what I'm talking about! It's *my* fault Dad died."

I stared back in horror. "No, it's not! It's *mine*—my fault. He had to come pick *me* up from Teresa's. If I'd been at home that night, he never would've had to get behind the wheel, and nothing would've happened!"

Ryan stared at me in confusion. "No, Rachel. Listen to me—it was *my* fault. Dad wanted me to go to Teresa's, but I knew I couldn't drive. Mom got after me, telling me to go pick you up, but I put up a fight because I knew I'd had too much to drink, even though Mom and Dad didn't seem to notice. So Dad got sick of listening to Mom and me argue and said, 'Good grief—I'll get Rachel myself to shut the kid up.'" Ryan shook his head again firmly, staring hard at me. "It was *my* fault, Rachel. It should've been me that night. It should've been *me.*"

I tried to protest again, but Ryan waved my words away. "The worst of it is that I never had a chance to say good-bye. Never got a chance to thank him or tell him I loved him." Ryan's voice caught, and at the same time, I felt a lump grow in my throat as he continued. "I remember his funeral. I couldn't cry—I was in too much shock. Just too much for me to deal with. My whole world completely caved in. So all I did was turn to alcohol to hide even more. It became my friend. The only one I had. I already drank too much, and now I had a great excuse to keep on drinking even more."

"I—I didn't know you'd been drinking that night."

Ryan nodded sadly and sighed deeply. "I didn't want anything to do with God after that. I didn't think I deserved to have God in my life anymore anyway. I couldn't imagine He wanted anything to do with me after Dad died."

"But that's what Heavenly Father is there for—for times when you make mistakes!"

Ryan shrugged and wouldn't look at me. "I guess. I still have a hard time believing God loves me or cares about me."

I was shocked. "How can you say that? Of course He loves you!"

"How do you know?"

I reached across the table and dared to put my hand on Ryan's arm. "Because *I* love you, and if your sister can love you—someone who only remembers knowing you not much more than a decade—then Heavenly Father, your own Father who's known you for eons, obviously loves you far more than I ever could. Even more than Mom or Dad ever will." Ryan looked at me briefly before looking away again. I went on. "I can't see all of who you were before, or who you are now, or who you can become, but God can. He knows what you can accomplish, and what you're going to accomplish. You're His son, and He loves you."

I lifted my hand from Ryan's arm and sat back against my chair, staring at Ryan's sad face. I didn't know how I could make Ryan understand that. How do you ever make anyone understand what you know is true?

I knew the answer, though. That word *make* was the problem. I knew there was no way to *make* anyone see or do anything. Ryan would have to learn for himself. Just like he was the only one who could make himself better. With God's help, of course. If he'd continue to turn to Him for help. I could only pray that he would.

"After all I've done to make your life miserable—after I nearly got you killed driving drunk—I can't believe you even care to be here at all."

I shook my head at Ryan again and looked at him seriously, folding my arms. "You know something, Ryan? You don't get it, do you? No matter who comes along in my life, you'll always be my brother. I'm always going to love you and be there for you, and you're just going to have to deal with it because I'm not going away, ever, no matter what. I'm not going to stop caring about you, or worrying about you, or loving you, or praying for you."

Ryan looked up at me and tried to smile. "I'll try to do something nice for you sometime, Rachel. You might think I can't, but you'll be surprised. Someday, you'll be surprised."

The conversation between Ryan and me, although a little painfully stilted at first, slowly had turned until it was relaxed and flowed easily. My face actually hurt from smiling. It was so amazingly wonderful to realize that it was still possible for us to talk and have a good time together.

When the waiter returned to clear away our empty plates, I casually glanced at my watch and then stared bug-eyed at my wrist.

"I can't believe we've been here two whole hours! I'm so sorry—that's it—I know you have to get back to Sunnyside now." I grabbed my purse from under the table, minus smacking my elbow, and looked up at the waiter. "Could you please bring me the check?"

"Hold on just a second!" Both the waiter and I stared at Ryan in surprise. Ryan folded his arms across his chest and practically glared at me. "I still have a little time left before I have to get back. We're not leaving until we've had the most important part of dinner."

The most important part? My mind raced—salad, breadsticks, pasta, root beer—what in the world had been forgotten? I must've had a really confused look on my face, because Ryan burst out with one of his great, loud laughs before shouting, "Dessert!"

———•———

I was sure I was too stuffed for anything else, but Ryan insisted on ordering a piece of strawberry cheesecake for us to share.

"You're mean. That's my favorite dessert!" I moaned. "I can't resist cheesecake, even if my stomach is bloated to three times its normal size, like it is right now!"

Ryan laughed. "That's why I ordered it—because I know it's your favorite."

"I can't believe you remember," I answered, shaking my head while I dug my spoon into the cheesecake.

"You're not the only one who knows how to surprise someone."

I grinned at Ryan for a second before looking down at my spoon as I gently patted the cheesecake with it. "So—Ryan. Tell me the truth. Are you sure you're not disappointed that you have me for your valentine instead of some hot date?" I had to ask again, because the thought had been bugging me like a pebble in my shoe all afternoon long.

Ryan laughed and shook his head. "But now it's your turn to tell *me* the truth."

"Okay," I nodded, taking another bite of cheesecake.

"Why'd you do it? Why'd you pick me as your 'secret valentine'?"

I wasn't sure at first how I wanted to answer that point-blank, but after taking a deep breath, I simply said, "Because—you're important to me. And because I—I really *do* care about you. A lot. And—well—I've missed you. And I just wanted you to know that." I couldn't believe I'd actually said that, but there it all was, and I couldn't take any of it back. But that was okay. I didn't want to take it back, because it was true.

I couldn't help breathing a sigh of relief when Ryan nodded and smiled at me.

———•———

When Ryan and I stepped outside the restaurant, I waited with him until his ride came to pick him up.

"Thanks, Rachel. I mean it. Really. Thank you. And not just for lunch today. Thanks for all of those crazy poems you wrote for me. Would you believe I actually looked forward to getting them in the mail?"

I laughed and shook my head.

Ryan laughed, too. "I couldn't have asked for a better 'secret valentine.' I still can't believe it was you all along. Next time, I'll pay for lunch."

Ryan's words truly surprised me. "You'd like to do this again? Really?"

He laughed and nodded. "Sure. You know—Sunnyside has a family week coming up. I hope you'll come with Mom. And—Joe."

I frowned when Ryan dug his hands into his pockets and looked out across the street with a frown on his face. "You really don't like Joe, do you?"

Ryan shrugged. "I don't think I'd get along with him even if I didn't drink."

I sighed and made Ryan look at me. "I don't think it's wrong to not like that he's taking Dad's place in a way right now, but if that's the only reason you don't like him, then I don't think you're giving him a fair chance."

"I don't like that Dad was taken away from me. I've been short-changed. I didn't want anything to do with bringing a stepfather into our house."

I nodded. "It was hard for me, too, but I also feel lucky to have a chance to have a dad again. I feel like I have two fathers now. I—I think it's okay to have more than one person in your life as a father figure." Ryan didn't answer, so I dared to say something else. "Can he do anything right in your eyes?"

Ryan looked thoughtful before carefully answering. "No matter what, he hasn't stopped trying with me. And caring about me, I guess. That says something about him. He's not all bad."

"No, he's not. Not at all." We were both silent, standing and waiting, until I decided to tell Ryan something else. "By the way, I'm sort of think-ing about going to Alateen, maybe."

Ryan turned to look at me in surprise. "Really? That's great—I think you'll like it. I hope you'll give it a try, Rachel."

"Dallin said he'd go with me."

Ryan nodded. "Ackerman's a good guy. I'm glad you have him around."

I smiled. "Me, too."

———————

When I finally drove up the driveway, it was dark outside. Mom and Joe were still out celebrating Valentine's Day, and Dallin's bedroom door was shut. I wasn't sure if he was home or not as I continued down the hall to flip the light switch on in my bedroom. I stepped inside and tossed my purse on my bed before turning towards my bedroom mirror to see my Mormonad: *Be Your Own Kind of Beautiful*. However, instead of the poster, it was the item below it—strategically, purposely placed on my desk in front of the poster—that caused me to stop and stare before slowly walk-ing over to my desk for a closer look.

Right below the poster's picture of a daisy surrounded by roses was a real glass vase filled with real white daisies. Lots of them. And in the middle of all of those daisies was a single, perfect, just-opened-its-petals, red rose. Lying beside it was our city's newspaper carefully folded back to a page in the middle. I picked up the newspaper and blushed when I saw both of my contest entry poems printed inside and a stickie note beside it in Dallin's handwriting proudly stating, "Look at our famous, published writer!"

A pink envelope was lying beside the vase with my name on it. Inside was a pretty Valentine's Day card with a handwritten note inside:

Dear Rachel,

I hope you had a great time with Ryan. He's lucky to have a sister like you who cares about him so much. I'm lucky to have you in my life, too.

You're amazing, Rachel. You always have been. Don't ever stop being your own incredible kind of beautiful.

Happy Valentine's Day—

Love,

Dallin

I carefully replaced the card in its envelope before leaning down to smell the red rose's pretty scent. Since my life was a forever yo-yo, I knew that although my life would never be the same again, that wasn't necessarily a bad thing. I ran my finger over my name printed in Dallin's handwriting. I could feel a strange rush of emotion working its way from my heart and threatening to spill from my eyes as I gently brushed my fingertips across the daisies. I smiled then as I carefully touched each petal on the single red rose—that newly blossoming, beautiful rose standing tall and graceful in the center of all of those white daisy petals.

ABOUT THE AUTHOR

Kay Lynn Mangum holds a bachelor's degree in English literature from Southern Utah University in Cedar City. She has served in The Church of Jesus Christ of Latter-day Saints as a Gospel Doctrine teacher and in Young Women and Relief Society.

Kay Lynn works as a legal assistant and loves traveling to places where she wants to set her stories.

She is the author of the best-selling novels *The Secret Journal of Brett Colton* and *A Love like Lilly.*